A MINDHUNTERS NOVEL

END GAME

AWARD-WINNING ROMANTIC SUSPENSE

ANNE MARIE BECKER

ALSO BY ANNE MARIE BECKER

END GAME

THE MINDHUNTERS, BOOK 6

ANNE MARIE BECKER

For Lorilee—your love and support mean so much.

And for all my readers who've enjoyed this series.
This one's for you.

PROLOGUE

"Are you going to do it, or should I?" He gestured to the pill in Rocky's hand. He was being generous, giving the man control over his destiny—the final chapter, anyway.

As the boss of an international crime ring, he wore many hats —including one few people knew about: the serial killer known as the Charmer. Each hat he wore had its own specific responsibilities and challenges, but he could handle it all—as long as his hired help did what they were paid to do. Unfortunately, the idiot on his knees in front of him had failed.

Rocky's lip quivered and he pressed his mouth into a thin line, as if he could prevent the inevitable.

The Charmer's nostrils flared. "I've got things to do." He glanced at his watch. "The outcome is the same, no matter what. But if you choose the easy way, it's less mess for me to clean up." Not that he'd actually have to do much. Rocky was kneeling on a plastic tarp in the warehouse on one of Chicago's piers. He'd have the Circle's cleaner collect the garbage and toss him into Lake Michigan. It would give him a chance to try the new guy out. Maybe *he* could manage to complete a simple order.

"The easy way?" Rocky's voice cracked. "I can't commit suicide. I have a wife and two young daughters. The shame would..." His Adam's apple bobbed as hope battled reality.

The Charmer grinned. "I've seen your girls. They're going to be beauties in about ten years."

Panic widened Rocky's eyes. "You stay away from them. You and your...perversions."

"Perversions?" He laughed. "You don't have a clue what I do with my girls. It's not about that at all. I tell you what... I'll keep a close eye on your girls for you." They'd never know their dad was an incompetent ass.

"Don't." Rocky's eyes flicked to the gun as the Charmer raised it.

"You should have thought of them before you fucked up." He hadn't led the biggest, most respected organized crime syndicate in the world for decades by going easy on employees. "All you had to do was take the girl."

"I'll get her next time. I promise, I..." Sweat mingled with snot and tears as Rocky finally saw the writing on the wall. Saw that his boss didn't forgive. Forgiveness was for the weak. The Charmer was far from weak. He was in control, having learned early and often that those in power got what they wanted. That was the way the world worked. But Rocky's fuckup would delay his plans for Damian Manchester and the agents at SSAM.

He pulled the trigger, and the gun, its silencer in place, made a soft *thwump* before Rocky fell on his side. The sequence was so quick that the sound of the plastic crumpling beneath him was louder than Rocky's death moan. *See?* He could be merciful when the occasion allowed.

But not with Damian and his crew. They would see no mercy. And they would acknowledge the Charmer's power—right before he killed them.

CHAPTER 1

A dozen bodies were sprawled on yoga mats, unrolled like little plots of land across the gleaming wood floor. Trying to ignore her wayward thoughts, Abby directed her students through a series of positions. Half Moon, Downward-facing Dog, Tree Pose. While the endless summer heat was driving most Chicagoans crazy, her class had found a cool midmorning oasis at Inner Beauty Dance and Yoga Studio.

Nearly an hour of Zen-inducing stretches later, she rose and surveyed the group. "Remember to stay hydrated out there—and stay centered, too." She'd found peace, even if only for a few precious minutes. But turmoil awaited her just outside the door.

The women rolled up their mats and dispersed to the locker room before hurrying back to offices and homes. Abby slugged water from her bottle, in no hurry to rush back to her life. One of her students approached, waddling gracefully as her third-trimester belly preceded her. Dr. Maggie Levine-Townsend was a radio psychologist and a professor at Chicago Great Lakes University. She was about to add mother to her impressive resume. Her dark red hair was pulled back into a ponytail, but several stray wisps were stuck in the perspiration around her heart-shaped face.

"Great class," Maggie said.

"The modifications have been working for you?" Abby had shown her less strenuous versions of the yoga poses.

"They're fantastic. I don't know what I would have done if I'd had to quit. I need this outlet."

"I know what you mean." Abby was missing her kids. While teaching yoga gave her a second income and something to fill her summers, she looked forward to seeing the smiling faces of a new crop of kindergartners at South Loop Elementary in a few weeks.

If they didn't fire her before then.

Lines creased Maggie's forehead. "Everything okay? You seemed distracted during the session."

"I'm sorry—"

Maggie interrupted her apology with a shake of her head. "No need to apologize. I don't think most people noticed. It's my job to pick up on subtle nonverbal cues. Something's wrong."

"I'll survive." Abby swallowed her anger and fear and summoned a smile. "But thank you for checking on me."

"Anytime you need to talk, give me a call." Maggie fished a business card out of her bag and handed it over.

"Thanks. That means a lot."

"Hell, you've saved my sanity this summer. Unbearable heat *and* eight months pregnant? Not a good combination. Come to think of it, you probably saved my husband's sanity, too."

Abby laughed. "Just a few more weeks. Soon you'll have a little one to cuddle."

"And even more danger to my sanity." But Maggie's laugh indicated she was looking forward to the challenge. After a quick farewell, Maggie left with a friend, laughing over some shared comment. A pang of loneliness hit Abby square in the chest and she set about ignoring it. Feeling maudlin was counterproductive. Keeping busy was the cure.

As the last of the students said their good-byes, Abby moved about the room with a push broom and cleaning wipes. A glint of sun on metal on the floor near one of the windows caught her eye. She moved closer to inspect its source. A charm bracelet. She hurried to the door and poked her head out to look up and down the sidewalk, but saw none of her students. She returned to the bracelet and scooped it up, holding it to the light to study the dozen or so nickel-sized silver medallions dangling from the links, each etched with a different symbol.

Her breath caught as her eyelids closed. The dam broke and images flooded her mind like a series of snapshots.

No. Not now. Not here.

Even as she struggled to slam that mental door shut, her throat squeezed and her exhalation came out as a strangled moan. Her skin grew moist and her mouth went dry. Her pulse pounded in her head.

Too late. The message wanted—*needed*—to come through.

Shelves and shelves of framed photographs of smiling young women, a spotlight highlighting each one. The joy she felt vicariously upon looking at them was incongruous with the black fury that swelled in her chest as her fingers moved along the charms.

And then she *was* each of the young women. Her upper arm burned as if someone had pressed a cigar there. The cloying scent of moist dirt and decaying leaves enveloped her. The breath choked from her throat as a wave of cold water washed over her mouth and nose. Panic clawed at her insides, scrambling for release, but she couldn't move. Couldn't breathe. Couldn't shake off the threat.

Darkness seeped through the edges of the vision, swallowing everything in its path, snuffing out the spotlights on each picture one by one. One, two, three… Eleven in all.

Abby gasped for air as she fought to return to reality. The bracelet clattered to the floor and the yoga studio came into focus as she emerged from the vision, as if breaking the surface of water after running out of breath.

Staring at the bracelet as if it might bite her—or suck her into the terrifying black void again—she dropped it then backed away until her shoulder blades hit the wall. She walked herself through an abdominal breathing exercise and slowly regained control of herself.

It was just a message. It wasn't reality. Not *her* reality, anyway.

She shivered, though sunlight streamed through the window. Outside, people on the sidewalk hustled by, oblivious to her pain and confusion. The air conditioner kicked on and the air from the vent pressed cool kisses along her sweat-drenched skin, raising an army of goose bumps. But the belly cramps and shivers that suddenly racked her body stemmed from an entirely different source.

The girls. They were dead, or soon would be. And somebody, possibly a killer who'd once held those charms, was happy about that. Had she seen something that had already happened or something that *might* happen? Or was what she'd seen simply the dream or imagination of whoever owned the bracelet?

These episodes were never clear.

Abby had smothered her psychometric abilities for so long she'd forgotten what it felt like when they took over. She'd trained herself to control them, insulating herself from both positive and negative messages—unless her defenses were down or the images were particularly powerful. Both were the case today.

Her emotions were raw, making her vulnerable. The impending lawsuit had wrecked her confidence and she was in danger of losing her job. On top of that, her grandfather, whose battle with emphysema was nearing its end, had refused to be admitted to Mercy Hospital last week. He argued that he'd rather die at home. She was torn between being supportive and railing in anger. Of course, the latter wasn't an option. She loved Grandpa.

But watching her last living family member waste away was killing her spirit.

If she'd tuned in to her gift sooner, could she have prevented Grandpa's illness by forcing him to take better care of himself?

If she'd continued to tune it out, would she have avoided trouble at work?

It was all so messed up in her head. A jumble of thoughts, ideas, worries... How could she even trust what she'd just experienced?

But how could she ignore it? Dear God, the girls she'd seen in the images were budding teenagers. How could they be dead or in such danger?

Once the dark joyful and reverential feelings of their killer had passed, the prevailing emotions when she'd touched the bracelet had been of abandonment. Hopelessness. Feelings so close to how Abby had felt lately that she could barely distinguish her own emotions from those connected to the charms.

Abby used the edge of her shirt to keep her fingertips from touching the bracelet as she picked it up again. The charms seemed to pulse with life, calling her to explore. Instead, she dropped it into the lost and found box under the studio's front counter and rushed to the locker room where she struggled, with shaking fingers, to peel off her clothes.

She showered, scrubbing vigorously to rid herself of the remnants of summer heat and exertion, but the images of the dead girls wouldn't be washed down the drain. She sank onto the shower bench and let the water wash over her. The warmth penetrated her hair, turning it into a dark curtain around her.

Had they been real? Or was it the sign of things to come? And what the hell was she supposed to do about it?

The last time she'd let down her guard, she'd picked up a child's toy in the park, intending to hand it back to the child who'd dropped it. She'd gone to the police after receiving a horrifying image. They'd called her crazy and dismissed her. She never did find out if her fears about what had happened to the mother of that child were confirmed.

But this time? *So many.* Girls on the brink of womanhood. She'd sensed their teenage angst and promise. And it had been snuffed out...or would be. Had the murders already occurred? How could she sit by and ignore the possibility that these innocent girls were still alive and could be harmed? The dark images might even be connected to the bracelet's owner, to some previous owner, or some other freaky coincidence. It was even possible that whoever had committed these heinous crimes was already behind bars.

Abby's frustrated tears mingled with the cascade of water. Nobody would see. Nobody would know what she'd seen. Nobody would care.

Nobody, except those girls.

EINSTEIN NEEDED TO SEE HER FACE LIKE HE NEEDED A SHOT OF caffeine. *Desperately.*

The smile of the woman he knew only as Abby—he'd heard the barista call out her name at his favorite place to caffeinate—always radiated a quiet glow of calm and understanding, of optimism and hope. Qualities he was sorely depleted in even though it was only midday on a Monday. His faculties were already taxed by a lack of sleep and an overload of frustration from the dearth of leads on his current case.

Yeah, he could use a dose of Abby's sweet smile today—and the coffee, too.

But the dead girls and their grieving families needed him more, so he stayed at his desk in his darkened office and studied the files for the thousandth time, trying to ignore the headache looming on the horizon.

Family photos of beautiful faces on the cusp of their teen years had become evidentiary photos connected to recovered skeletal remains. Twenty years' worth of murders. Eleven victims who deserved justice, and countless loved ones who yearned for closure. He had to find a new algorithm, a new way to compare the data compiled from the FBI and police departments across the United States. Something, *anything*, that would lead them to the killer known as the Charmer. But his brain had started a steady knocking against his skull.

"Jesus, it's like a cave in here." Max Sawyer's Texas drawl came from the doorway, his words lazy but his gaze astute as he surveyed Einstein's desk, littered with papers, photos and manila folders. "You need to get out. Let's grab lunch."

Max was Einstein's best friend, a fellow ex-SEAL and coworker at SSAM, the Society for the Study of the Aberrant Mind. A private agency, SSAM was dedicated to enlightening the public about safety issues and to hunting violent serial offenders who'd fallen through the cracks of the usual channels of justice. SSAM's founder, Damian Manchester, had started the agency twenty years earlier, after his daughter Samantha had become the first victim of the Charmer.

"Can't take a break," Einstein said. Maybe after his eureka moment, if it ever came.

"Reviewing the files again?"

"I'm missing something. The answer should be there." His analysis of data hadn't failed him in the other cases he'd worked over the past six years. But he'd been over the FBI and police reports, news articles and SSAM interviews with the victims' families so many times he could recite all of them from memory. He could describe the details of each of the eleven victims—pre- and post-murder—enough to satisfy any sketch artist.

A young woman's happy, blond, blue-eyed image had been the last to fill the screen. Fourteen-year-old Tiffany Allsup. Healthy. Happy.

Dead.

Found just a couple months ago in Texas, she'd been the latest victim of the Charmer. SSAM had recently learned that the Charmer was in fact the man also known as the Boss, the head of the Circle crime syndicate. Despite that break in the case, the killer's true identity remained a mystery.

Einstein stood and stretched, then nudged a gap in the blinds with two fingers so he could see the world five stories below. He blinked against the piercing sunlight. The coffee shop occupied the bottom corner of a tall building across the street. Though it was lunchtime, there were few people about. Or maybe the masses were holed up, escaping the heat. The unrelenting triple digits of the past week had prompted the city to institute rolling blackouts to conserve energy, starting this afternoon. He made a mental note to check Chicago's utility site's schedule, back up all of the SSAM computers and ensure they were plugged into the surge protectors. As an added precaution, he'd arranged for a backup generator. A mission could go FUBAR in the blink of an eye if one wasn't prepared for all possible outcomes. *Like Kamdesh.*

One second, he'd been crouched behind the cover of a large rock, checking the infrared chemical lights he'd be using to delineate the pickup point after sunset. The next, a blast had sent him hurtling through space and landing him flat on his back with a gash in his head...

"Yo, Einstein, where'd you go?" Max's eyes narrowed in concern.

To fucking Afghanistan.

They exchanged a look and Max sighed. "Flashbacks are a bitch."

"Not a flashback. A memory." A flashback would have had him breaking out in a cold sweat.

Max's jaw tightened briefly, as he fought memories of his own. They'd been together in Kamdesh, their final battle before injuries had forced them into a new line of business. Memory lane wasn't a leisurely stroll for them so much as a dark alley where they ran for their lives. "How are the headaches?"

Automatically, Einstein's hand brushed over the back of his head. "Better." But not for long. The knocking against his skull was becoming more urgent. He just wished he knew how to answer the damn door and make it stop.

He released the blinds and they snapped back into place. The headaches weren't so bad when he wasn't exposed to too much bright light, too little sleep, or sudden loud noises.

Or silence. That was almost worse.

Give him a room full of softly humming computers and he was happy. His electronic world made sense. There, things were predictable. Safe.

Unfortunately, the rhythmic pounding in his skull indicated some trigger had been squeezed and retreating into his computers wouldn't help.

Max called his bluff. "Bullshit. The lines in your forehead are so deep you could hide a SEAL team in there." He came around Einstein's desk and pushed him into his chair, then rummaged in the corner mini-fridge for a moment. He resurfaced with a canned energy drink. "Caffeine?"

This was the kind of headache that might benefit from the stuff. Einstein nodded only once because it was starting to hurt too much. He caught the can Max tossed him and pressed it to his eyelids for a moment.

"You sure you won't come?" Max's voice radiated gruff concern. "Now that we're not roomies anymore, I don't get to act like your mama and tell you to put your computer devices away and go outside and play."

He snorted. He didn't need a mama. Never had. "As if you could make me do anything I don't want to do."

Max grinned. "Lie to yourself if it makes you feel better. Text me if you want me to bring you back a sandwich."

Once he was alone, Einstein popped the tab on his drink and took a swig. Pretending the throbbing was some sadistic dance beat that could fade into the background, he studied the information on his screen, looking to make sense of the dates, locations, and other characteristics of the murders. So far, no clear picture had emerged other than the commonalities of the victims' ages and gender. It was like looking at a Magic Eye poster and trying to make out the image. There was something there, if only he could see it—some pattern that formed the foundation for the Charmer's crazy world. Just like the fractals that formed microscopic repeating designs throughout nature.

Half an hour later, he leaned back with a sigh. The drumbeat was still pounding away and the words on his screen were jumbling. Perhaps what he needed was something unpredictable to reset his world.

He glanced at the clock. Brave the midday heat for a chance to bump into Abby at her usual break time or soldier through the hunger and ignore his headache?

No contest.

A minute later, he was dodging traffic as he jogged across the street. His sneakers absorbed the heat from the pavement, warming the soles of his feet. Absently, he recalled the melting point of rubber and looked down at his toes, expecting to see them dripping or sticking like a piece of gum to the sidewalk. He wasn't paying attention to his surroundings as he reached the door of the coffeehouse.

"Oh!" A female voice—*her* voice—and the feeling of skin when his brain had been expecting metal brought Einstein back to reality. "Excuse me," she said. *Abby.* His fingers had landed on top of hers on the door handle. She withdrew her hand from beneath his. "Guess we're both distracted today," she said.

Actually, he'd been focused. So damn focused on his inner thoughts that he'd almost let real life slip by unnoticed. His undivided attention was now hers. He pulled the door open for her.

Her lips curved into the smile he'd been looking forward to all day. The dimple that dipped inward on one side of her mouth entranced him. Soft, dark chocolate hair curled against her cheek.

Longer layers hugged her shoulders. But her blue-gray eyes, usually vibrant with life, had a haunted look. Shell-shocked, even. Apparently, she was having a worse day than he was.

They were both standing there, baking in the sun, staring at each other.

With his free hand, he gestured to the open door. "After you."

He followed her as she claimed a place in line. Behind his dark sunglasses, his gaze perused her body, following shapely tan calves upward to a slash of purple in the form of a hip-hugging skirt that matched the splash of amethyst beads in her sandals. The straps of a gray camisole top peeked out from beneath an overshirt.

Einstein had never been one to take notice of fashion, but he was intrigued by her choices. Especially as she moved to the counter and the filminess of her blouse flowed like butterfly wings. She passed under the air conditioning vent and the material pressed to her chest, outlining the curves of her breasts and the dip inward at her waistline.

It had been a while since any female had captured his attention —and his imagination—so thoroughly. Abby had started consuming his thoughts when he'd first seen her a couple months ago. But looking, and daydreaming, was all he would do. Computers, he could understand and deal with—women, not so much. They took work and a level of comprehension that was beyond him.

Still, the fantasies were a nice break from reality. The cases he analyzed were gruesome, and after such dark preoccupations, seeing her somehow made things better.

She cast an unreadable look over her shoulder, then looked away again. He had the ridiculous urge to talk to her, to ask why she seemed so disturbed today. Instead, he retreated to his safe zone—scientific observation. She ordered her usual and gave her name to the barista, flashing her a smile as she slipped her change into the tip jar.

She moved aside and he stepped forward to place his order,

tracking her movements in his peripheral vision and then moving beside her to wait near the pickup counter. It was crowded, and as his shoulder briefly brushed hers, he could have sworn she sucked in a breath and held it.

"I thought your name was Andrew," she said after several moments of silence.

"What?"

"That's what you usually tell the barista." She'd noticed. A warmth spread outward from his chest to his limbs. "Today, you told her you were Einstein. *Two e's, two i's.*"

Shit. His mind was so much into work he'd forgotten who he was to the outside world.

Her lips twitched, but the amusement didn't reach her troubled eyes. "Delusions of grandeur?"

He grinned. "Nickname."

"Ah." She glanced around. "Busy today. They're herding us through like cattle." She shifted an inch away as his arm again touched hers. He frowned. Was she reluctant to touch him?

Wait. What had she said? "Cattle," he repeated.

A tiny furrow formed between her eyes, but he barely registered it. The ideas zinged through his brain as if he'd already consumed his triple-shot of caffeine.

Cattle. He knew how to get to the Charmer.

Did I just touch a killer?

Abby pressed a hand to her churning stomach and tried to avoid touching the man at her side as she waited for the mocha she no longer wanted. Her body warred with her brain, which was par for the course today. She'd been attracted to Andrew—Einstein— in the past. Her body still was. But her brain had questions—such as why had the horrible images hit her again when his hand touched hers?

The pictures of those girls were so similar to the ones she'd seen when she'd touched the bracelet that the experience had stolen her breath. Her pulse was still beating out a staccato rhythm as she struggled to hide her tumultuous thoughts behind friendly conversation.

He was, in a word, *intense*. He was hot in that sexy-nerd, distracted-professor kind of way that had fueled many late-night fantasies since he'd first spoken to her a couple months ago. He'd been wearing some silly T-shirt with a joke about caffeine and they'd shared a laugh. She'd discreetly admired the biceps peeking out from beneath his short sleeves. Her gaze might have dipped briefly to his cargo pants to take in his trim waistline, too. His hard, muscular body indicated he wasn't the complete nerd his wardrobe would suggest.

Most days, a storm of thoughts and emotion seemed to churn beneath the tranquil surface of his hazel eyes and reserved smile. His hair was reminiscent of a military cut that had been allowed to grow out a couple weeks too long—long enough to give him a slightly spiky, tousled look as though he had a tendency to run his hands through it during the day, perhaps in frustration—or absentmindedness, while focused on a problem. Even now, his attention seemed to turn inward after her lame comment about cattle.

Had he used that concentration to kidnap and kill those girls? Had they been a *problem* he'd had to solve? Her brain was playing devil's advocate with her body.

"Abby." The barista called out her name and set her hazelnut mocha on the pickup counter. Abby had hoped sticking to her familiar routine and indulging in her decadent Monday treat would calm her nerves and add a spot of happiness to an otherwise chaotic day. Instead, she was more confused than ever.

She felt his eyes on her as she stepped forward to claim her drink. Her body tightened in response. His gaze, an amalgam of heat and amusement, met hers as she turned around. One side of his mouth quirked upward as he reached beyond her—she was still blocking the counter, she realized with chagrin—to pick up his iced coffee. Should she say something to him? Engage him in conversation and see if he'd reveal the kind of man he was—maniacal murderer or sexy nerd?

Sure, like he's going to simply confess his hobby is killing young women.

Her body and her subconscious were telling her he was the real deal, a trustworthy man who would be worth talking to. Einstein couldn't be a killer.

But, her brain reminded her, she'd been wrong before. If he had nothing to do with the murders, why had touching him caused the same girls to flash through her mind? The images had been slightly different this time and yet somehow the same. Connected.

Or maybe her girls, as she'd come to think of them over the past couple hours, were simply insisting she pay attention, speaking out of turn, and Einstein had nothing to do with them.

He reached past her for a straw. "I missed seeing you Friday."

"I had an appointment." With a lawyer. It was costing a small fortune she didn't have, but she wouldn't have anything if she lost her job due to the lawsuit. Her lawyer had told her she had a good chance at winning the case if it went to trial, but the parent who threatened to sue could ruin her reputation as a good teacher. "Why? Are you stalking me or something?" She forced a smile, not sure whether she was joking or not, but desperately wanting him to reassure her.

His brows came together. "No, of course not. Maybe I should have worn another funny T-shirt."

"What?"

"You know, to break the ice." He glanced down at his attire, plain black tee and well-worn jeans. Which gave her absolutely no idea whether he was caffeinating before going to work out, going back to work, or going out to kill.

He seemed to be struggling for something to say and she got the sense he was disappointed and confused. *Welcome to the club.*

"Consider the ice broken," she said. After all, she'd possibly gotten a glimpse of his deepest secrets. "See you around." Unable to bear the confusion, she gripped her drink and fled, forcing herself to walk like a normal person down the street, though she felt like running.

A few seconds later, she stopped and glanced back over her shoulder, where Einstein expertly dodged traffic to cross to an office building. He probably worked there. Geographically speaking, it was perfectly logical they'd bump into each other so often. Of course he wasn't stalking her.

Her gift had been wrong. A measure of relief loosened her limbs even as an odd tug of disappointment tightened the knot in her chest. She was, once again, in a position of not knowing what or whom she could trust—including herself.

CHAPTER 2

C*attle.*

Abby, his unknowing muse, had provided the eureka moment he'd needed, the idea that could lead to the Charmer's downfall. Rejuvenated, Einstein spent the next hour conjuring up a computer virus. It was good to feel productive again. His headache had even subsided.

After proofreading the host email, he turned to one of his other computers and surfed the malware program's code for glitches. Then, with a few more key taps, he reviewed the list of recipients: over a hundred deserving lowlifes. The sexual deviants who had tried to participate in the Circle's Cattle Call online auction a few months ago—hoping to bid on unwilling sex slaves or watch the carnage via live video feed—would check their inboxes and open a Pandora's box of surprises. Einstein had retained their email addresses after helping bust that particular crime. There was a grim satisfaction in infecting the perverts with this virus—even if it wasn't of the biological variety, it would be a hell of a lot more painful. It would flash a message on the user's screen and steal their personal information and location before sucking their hard drive dry. And it would lead the DEA and FBI right to their doors.

With a grin, he hit *send*. Let chaos ensue.

"You look entirely too happy to have requested an emergency meeting," Nico said from the doorway. The man's dark, secret-filled eyes and tattooed skin reflected his status as a thug working for the Circle. In reality, Nico was a trusted informant, a DEA officer working deep undercover within the organized crime ring for over two years in hopes of reaching the man at the top. To that end, Nico and Einstein had something in common. Separately, they'd come close to achieving that goal, but had yet to discover the Charmer's true identity.

"You received the bat signal," Einstein said.

"It'd better be important." He moved further into the office and crossed his arms.

"Your super-secret multiagency task force is about to crack open the Circle's human trafficking trade. I've sent your team leader an email with the necessary details to track the virus recipients. I expect you guys and your friends to go knocking on some doors within the hour."

Nico arched a brow. "Virus. I'm guessing your methods aren't exactly legal."

"You got a problem with that?"

"Nope. As long as the charges stick."

That was why Einstein was handling the not-so-legal part. "They'll stick."

"If my superiors know the score, why do you need me here?"

"I wanted to be sure you knew this was going down. You're close enough to ground zero within the organization to get burned in the fallout. I didn't do anything that would expose your cover, but I wanted you to be aware."

Nico nodded. "Thanks, man. The Charmer's keeping his distance until he fully trusts me, but I think I'm only a few days away from learning his name and face." His expression darkened.

"Unfortunately, a few days might be too late. A man known as Rocky failed to complete his mission and the Charmer killed him, then called me in to dispose of the body. Rocky's the reason I responded in person to your bat signal."

"What was Rocky's mission?"

"A kidnapping. The Boss—the Charmer—is after another girl."

"SO YOU ALREADY HAVE A DATE TO THIS DINNER?" PRISCILLA ASKED through the phone.

"I don't need a date." Uneasy with his ex-wife's question, Damian longed to end the conversation. After what they'd survived, and the way he'd handled things years ago, he owed her —but not dinner. "Besides, it's not that kind of dinner."

She released an exasperated sigh. "You're the guest of honor. You'll be expected to have someone by your side."

"And I will." Several people. His SSAM agents and their significant others would be there to support him.

"A real date?" Priscilla's tone indicated surprise. "I don't believe you've dated since…"

"Since we split up?" He huffed out a laugh. "A few times over the years, yes." But never for long. And never with anyone who mattered. "I haven't been a monk." And lately, his needs had been growing—for one woman, in particular.

Through his open door, he could see into the office across the hall where Lorena Castro, one of SSAM's mindhunters, worked at her desk. Today, she'd twisted her glossy dark hair away from her face, accentuating the classic lines and high cheekbones of her profile and showing off her smooth caramel skin. It was damn distracting.

He'd hired her fifteen years ago, luring her away from the FBI's Behavioral Analysis Unit where she'd been working on the Charmer's case after the third murder had been discovered. The grief of losing his daughter had still been a fresh, gaping wound, even five years after the event. His marriage had fallen apart and he hadn't had the strength to fight for it. His heart had gone stone cold and numb. Frozen. Somehow, Lorena had seen past all of that and become his friend. Only now was his heart starting to beat at a normal pace again. And now it wanted things it hadn't desired in years, a deeper connection. But opening his heart to another person was a risk he'd been unwilling to take for a long time, and changing such ingrained habits was difficult. He had yet to voice what he wanted.

"I didn't realize you'd be in town for this, Cilla, let alone want to go with me," Damian told his ex.

"I realize we've been divorced longer than we were married, but I thought..." She'd thought he might need the support, especially in front of the political and social elite of Chicago.

He smiled. "Thank you, but I've got it covered."

Lorena would be by his side tonight, but only because all the SSAM employees would be there. That should be enough, but he wanted more. He wanted to make her his, but that could be in direct opposition to what was good for the agency. What if he and Lorena tried dating and couldn't make things work? What if he was no good as a partner in a relationship anymore? He hadn't exactly been good with Priscilla, or with Samantha, for that matter. What kind of man can't protect his daughter from society's monsters and doesn't realize his marriage has crumbled until his wife walks away?

"Well, I'm glad to hear that," Priscilla said, her voice softer now. "I thought I'd offer, since I'm in town. Of course, if I hadn't been staying with an old friend of ours, I never would have known that the mayor of Chicago is giving you a key to the city. That's a huge honor, Damian." Her praise, combined with the sting of guilt, had him pushing up out of his seat so he could pace his office. He didn't deserve the title of Philanthropist of the Year.

"It was nice to talk with you, but I have to get back to work."

"Of course. I'm sure you have plenty to do before tonight. Just be sure to take the time to enjoy the moment, okay? Life is too short to ignore the good parts." They knew that all too well.

"Maybe we can have lunch before you head back to New York?"

"I'd like that," she said.

He hung up and put his phone on the desk. When he turned back around, Einstein was in his doorway.

"Priscilla?" Einstein asked, apparently having heard the mention of New York.

Damian sighed. "Relationships never really end. They just...change."

Einstein didn't respond. The man had lost both parents several years ago and, unfortunately, had experienced few stable, lasting relationships in his lifetime, except for connections he'd made at work. Though he preferred to be a lone wolf, Einstein functioned better as part of a team, first with the SEALs and now with SSAM.

"What can I do for you?" Damian asked.

"You said to do what it takes to get the Charmer."

Adrenaline pumped, hard and fast, into his system as he eyed Einstein's smirk. "You found a way?"

"A virus. Sent via email to the addresses I retrieved from the Cattle Call sting a few months back."

"Not exactly legal." But if it hit the Charmer where it hurt and lured him from hiding, Damian was all for it. "You notified the task force?" They'd need manpower to break apart the Circle's cells.

Einstein nodded. "And I personally informed Nico. I want him prepared for the fallout. The task force is prepared to take down those cells as the virus spreads and returns the data on locations, stolen from the recipients' own computers. They'll get a much-deserved 'F-you' filling their screens, right before it shuts them down."

"Nico's still deep undercover, then?"

"Getting deeper every day."

"Has he met the Charmer in person yet?"

The remnants of Einstein's earlier self-satisfaction evaporated. "No, but apparently he's been promoted. He's cleaning up after the Charmer's messes."

Damian got the sense he wasn't going to like what came next. "He mention any messes in particular?"

"The Charmer killed one of his men, a guy named Rocky, for failing to kidnap a girl."

Damian's heart stopped for a second, then resumed beating, accelerating to triple time. "Who?"

Einstein shook his head. "He doesn't know, except he got the impression that the target is—"

"Like Sam?" Lorena guessed, entering the office. "Barely a teenager?" Her troubled gaze met Damian's. "You know he won't give up on getting the girl." Her profile of the Charmer painted a grim picture—that of a man who would do anything to get what he wanted, was controlling to the point of having a god complex and had evolved to include targeting Damian as his nemesis.

Damian had to work to relax the tightness in his jaw before he could speak. "So, the Charmer's making another move and we've got a ticking clock. Einstein's working on exposing the distant cells of the Circle from the inside, but how do we find the head of the snake before he strikes again?"

"You," Einstein said.

Shocked, he met his steady gaze. "Okay, how do I find him?"

"So we go through everything again," Einstein said.

"We've done that." Many times. So many times it nauseated him to think about their failure to find the monster. If it hadn't worked before... No, that was pessimism talking. He had to hold on to hope that, sooner or later, they'd hit upon something that mattered. He only hoped it would be sooner.

"We do it again, but from a different angle," Einstein continued. "Nico thought this next abduction was a specific attempt to get your attention. When we review the files this time, we consider that he may have held a personal vendetta all along.

What were you doing when Sam disappeared? What roles occupied your life?"

"Father, son, husband. Part-time business professor at CGLU. CEO of Luna Corp."

"I need you to write down as many names as you can from that time of your life. Business colleagues and competitors. Anybody from babysitters to where you took your car to get it washed. Anything you can think of that I can plug into my computer and see if there are commonalities we hadn't considered."

Damian's gaze met Lorena's. "I hate to think that I could be the root of this particular branch of evil."

Her face softened in sympathy. "We don't know that you are yet. And even if the Charmer's obsession is with you, in particular, you couldn't have known that back then, or in the years since. You did nothing wrong. Einstein's being thorough."

But what if she were wrong? What if there was something he could have done, years ago, to prevent these murders? His gut clenched.

Einstein broke into his thoughts. "I'll start it for you. I can generate a list of businessmen who've been in the area for the past twenty-five years and cross-reference it with people Luna Corp did business with. I'll also see if I can dig up the student records for the classes you taught during those years. But that information will be from official records. I need your behind-the-scenes point of view, too."

"Max told me you were reviewing the victims' files again." Damian didn't hold out much hope. He'd been over the damn things himself hundreds of times. But Einstein could sometimes work magic with his computers, finding patterns other people missed.

"Nothing new to add to the algorithms, but I've been thinking about the symbols on the charms left with the victims. They had to mean something to him."

"I've struggled to make sense of those," Lorena said. "I came up with a lot of theories over the years, but nothing certain."

"I'm cross-referencing all possible interpretations of the eleven charms, including the butterfly found on Sam."

Damian felt a twinge of pain. He'd bought her a bracelet, necklace and earring set for her twelfth birthday a year before she disappeared. She'd loved it and worn it every day. Had the Charmer known about that father-daughter bond, or was choosing a butterfly symbol for the charm a coincidence? Or did it have some other meaning?

When her remains had been discovered, and the charm with them, the authorities had thought it was meant to mimic the other jewelry Sam had been wearing. The world hadn't realized a serial killer was among them until the second and third victims had been found, a couple years later, also with charms. Each of the victims had been given a different symbol. A bird, a rainbow, a candle, and so on. All common enough symbols, and probably easy to find on charms, but there had to be a deeper reason the Charmer selected them.

"I'm also trying out a new program on the locations where the victims were found," Einstein added. "As I analyze the businessmen and their travel patterns, I might be able to narrow down possibilities."

The bodies had been found throughout the United States, which indicated the killer could be a transient. But Lorena's profile of an organized killer didn't support that. Sam had been the first, in Chicago. Then Indianapolis, Las Vegas, Los Angeles, Albuquerque... The most recent victim had been found in San Antonio. The charms and method of burying the bodies in remote areas, in addition to the similar ages of the girls and the way each had disappeared from a crowded, public place in broad daylight, had provided enough similarities to profile the killer, but had yet to lead to justice.

"If the Charmer is indeed looking to kill again here, it'll be the first time he's repeated a city," Lorena said. "He's come full circle, perhaps. Maybe he knows he's coming to the end of his reign."

"Maybe he just chose who and what was convenient to get to me faster," Damian suggested. The events in Texas two months ago had indicated a personal vendetta against Damian. Was it because SSAM was closing in on him and interfering with Circle business, or did this go further back? "Any way we can warn the public, especially young teen girls, to be cautious?"

Einstein glanced at his watch. "It's time for school to let out, and that's when the majority of victims were abducted."

"Except that it's the middle of summer," Lorena reminded him, a grin tugging at her lips. Sometimes Einstein lost himself in a case so thoroughly that he forgot the specifics of time and place. Even the heat wave had probably gone unnoticed.

"We can release our suspicions to the press, but it might result in a panic," Einstein said. "And possibly for nothing. But I do recommend notifying the Chicago Police Department so they can be on alert. I'll call Noah." CPD Detective Noah Crandall was a personal friend of SSAM and they'd helped each other on several cases over the years.

Damian ran a hand over his face. "It doesn't feel right, accepting an award for my service to the city when I could be the reason eleven girls died and another might go missing." In fact, it made him sick to his stomach to be acknowledged for taking down monsters when he hadn't found the one monster who mattered the most to him. The Charmer was still at large, and apparently about to hurt another girl, another family. Another set of parents who would grieve if Damian couldn't get to the bastard first.

"ABBY RHODES? THAT'S REALLY YOUR NAME?" THE NURSE WHO performed Grandpa's home visits looked at her with amusement.

Seated in the dining room chair between them, Abby's grandfather grinned. "As you can imagine, her mother was a bit of a Beatles fan. She also had a sense of humor." His raspy voice was muffled by the oxygen mask and he yanked it to the side so that it clung, useless, to his left cheek. At least he'd worn it, even as a brief compromise, to appease Abby and impress the nurse. "I can still picture my Lydia as a teenager, sprawled on her bedroom floor with albums scattered around her and posters all over the walls. She loved music. Said it freed the soul. As if that needed freeing." The twinkle in his eye indicated a fond memory.

"My mother was a free spirit," Abby explained to the nurse as the woman took her grandfather's blood pressure. That was how everyone remembered Lydia Rhodes. And nobody seemed to remember Abby's father—not even his name. Abby had been the product of a one-night stand, so he hadn't contributed anything other than a single, determined sperm. Even the gift—or the curse—of psychometric abilities had been passed down from Lydia, given the stories Grandpa told about her.

Unfortunately, Abby's skills had just begun developing when she hit puberty, and her mother was gone just a few months later, struck by a hit-and-run driver as she was crossing a street. Abby had often wondered if something about the intense grief and loss, intersecting with a time of significant growth and development, had caused a sudden spike in her skills that had made it difficult to interpret the messages correctly. She'd certainly had a heck of a time coping when her entire world changed at once, with only her grandfather for support. The pair had come to lean on each other over the past fifteen years.

Grandpa's face shone with pride. "My Lydia was beyond her years. Though she was young, people from the neighborhood came to her for advice and comfort."

"Ah." The nurse looked up from the chart where she'd been scribbling something. "An old soul." She made another note, shot Abby a sympathetic glance, and collected her things. "Nothing's changed. I'll be back the day after tomorrow unless—"

"I'm not checking myself into the hospital," Grandpa said. "That place is like the Hotel California. You can check in, but you'll never leave." Unfortunately, it wasn't the hospital that would kill Grandpa, it was the emphysema and his own stubbornness.

"Your choice," the nurse said, but she sent a concerned glance toward Abby as she walked her to the door of the two-bedroom apartment. "He needs constant monitoring. He's holding his own at the moment, but he could have a serious setback any moment now."

"I know." Abby nibbled on her bottom lip.

The nurse smiled ruefully. "At least he has a roommate to watch out for him, so the entire burden doesn't fall to you." Abby was sure her back would break if one more straw were placed on it today.

Abby thanked the nurse and let her out, locking the door behind her.

"You're so like her," Grandpa told Abby when she returned to the dining room.

She glanced back at the door. "The nurse?"

"Hah! No. Your mother. An old soul."

She waved off his comparison, but that was how she felt most of the time. Disconnected from current time and place, yet able to link to memories or flashes of insight about past—or sometimes, future—events. Finding her place in the in-between, and knowing how to handle the unwanted messages, especially when they assailed her at the most unexpected times, had always been a struggle.

Like the girls. What the hell was she supposed to do with those horrifying images? During her afternoon yoga class, her mind had wandered and she'd allowed herself to consider the remembered sensation of being tugged backward, which usually indicated an event had already occurred. Which meant there was little she could do for them now. *Or was there?*

She placed Grandpa's oxygen mask over his mouth and ignored

his answering grimace. Instead, she sat beside him and took his hand. The skin stretched over brittle bones and bulging purple veins but it was warm. Her fear of losing him battled with the happy memories of all the meals she and Grandpa had shared at this table, especially the lively ones when her mother and Gran had still been around. Gran had passed just before Lydia. People came into her life, but never stayed. And if she lost her job because of the slander lawsuit a parent had initiated against her for reporting his abuse of one of her kindergartners, she'd lose her students, too.

She pushed the negative thoughts aside and focused on what she had right now, sitting in front of her. "How are you feeling?"

The lines that bracketed his eyes and mouth tightened. "Just peachy."

"Right." She kissed his forehead, careful not to jostle the mask. "Liar," she added softly against his paper-thin skin.

She pulled away and forced a grin she didn't feel. Her nerves were still shaky from the surprises she'd endured today. The victims. Einstein. The call from the principal of her school that she'd let go to voicemail because she just couldn't stomach any more bad news right now.

"I'm better now that you're here."

"Me, too." But how much longer would she have with him? The emphysema, a consequence of decades of smoking and complicated by his drinking, had taken up residence in his lungs. The doctor had advised treatment in the hospital or moving him to a hospice center to care for him in his *final days*. She shuddered.

Grandpa squeezed her hand. With his free hand, he pulled aside his mask again. "Hey, don't get lost in that head of yours. Where'd you go?" The question ended with a wheeze and a series of coughs.

She reached for the mask. He jerked his face to the side, out of reach. "But it helps you."

He held her hand away. "Leave it. We need to talk." The subject of that conversation weighed heavily in his eyes. In the past few days, their visits had turned into the School of Life According to Grandpa. His lectures were his way of saying good-bye, of preparing her for life after he was gone.

Oh God, not now. "Later."

"We might not have later." He only had weeks, maybe less, left. But with the girls' dead bodies still flashing in her mind, she was unsettled and her emotional barriers were down. She wasn't sure she could make it through a good-bye. But when she met his gaze, steely determination stared back at her.

"Okay. What can I do to help you right now?"

He shook his head. "It's not me I'm worried about. It's you."

Her? He had the energy to worry about her? "I'm okay."

"You keep to yourself and your books. You hide away in that tiny apartment of yours."

"I see people. I teach classes. I have my kids." The kindergartners, with their open hearts and minds, were the loves of her life. They reminded her to find the beauty and value in everyday things most adults took for granted.

"You keep all of them at a distance."

Because it was safer that way. No flashes of dead girls, begging for her help.

Grandpa turned his hand over in hers and interlaced their fingers. "Abigail, you deserve to be happy. You deserve to have people accept you for who you are."

"That's why I have you." Besides, the last person she'd trusted, a boyfriend she'd dated for a few months a year ago, had nearly bled her bank account dry before she'd finally seen the light and kicked him out. *Some sixth sense you have there, Abby.*

His face softened. "You won't have me for much longer. And don't pretend you don't know what I mean." *Ouch.* "If you don't accept that part of yourself, nobody else will. It's not healthy to reject who you are."

She snorted. "Easy for you to say. You weren't cursed with this so-called gift." Or the rejection and judgment that came with it.

"Your abilities *are* a gift."

"An unreliable one that can cause more harm than good." When she'd gone to the police about a potential murder years ago, the detective had been unable to hold in his mirth about her wild imaginings. And her boyfriend in high school had looked at her like she was a freak when she'd touched the crucifix hanging at his neck and had an image of his grandmother having a heart attack. Not to mention the parent who was suing her for slander because she'd wrongly accused him of abusing his daughter. She'd been so certain she'd read those messages correctly, and they'd each had disastrous results.

"Is there anything you need?" Abby looked around his meager apartment. It was furnished only with the essentials. "Groceries, maybe?"

He rolled his eyes. "Fine. Ignore the old man trying to spread his wisdom. And no, I don't need anything. Ernie will be back soon. Went out to play Bingo and get food." At least he had a roommate who was a close friend and would do what he could to take care of Grandpa. And Ernie had her number if they needed anything.

"Burgers and fries do not constitute a healthy diet. Next time, I'll cook for you."

"If you want to feel useful, next time you come, bring your mother's touchstone."

Surprised by the request, she shot Grandpa a suspicious glance. "Why do you want her stone?"

"It reminds me of good times." Grandpa, an archaeologist who had once traveled the world before settling in Chicago to teach at Chicago Great Lakes University, had brought it back from a dig in Brazil in the sixties. "Besides, your mother said it had calming properties, and aids in balance and mental organization." While

Abby wasn't convinced the stone had that kind of power, those were indeed qualities Grandpa needed right now.

"I'll bring it next time I come. Anything else?"

"That's all I need." He squeezed her hand. "No hurry, though. Go and be twenty-seven somewhere instead of hanging out with this old fart."

She laughed, dislodging the tears clogging her throat. "You act like you won't see me again."

"You never know. But I'm stubborn and we're not done talking." His gaze narrowed on her. "Your mother would have wanted you to embrace your gift. It's a part of you."

And it could help those girls. She tried to shut out the voice in her head. For goodness' sake, she didn't even know if there *were* any such girls. Her gut told her the girls had been through hell, but when had she ever been able to trust her gut?

"We've got a problem," Nico said.

The Charmer's grip tightened around the cell phone reserved for Circle business. The last word he wanted to hear coming from the other end was *problem.*

From the top-floor office of a downtown skyscraper, the Charmer stood, looking out over the Chicago skyline. Buildings jutted upward like the prongs of a giant crystal, each facet winking in the late afternoon sun. But it all looked blood red to him as he struggled to control the rage bubbling within. "Update."

"The tech you hired traced the source of the virus-tainted email back to the city, but we hit some security measures he couldn't crack."

More incompetence. What the hell did money buy anymore? "SSAM. This is the work of Damian Manchester's guy."

"How do you know?"

He had no doubt the so-called *Einstein* was responsible for the virus spreading throughout his network over the past couple hours. And now a shitstorm had erupted within the Circle network. Damian had initiated a preemptive strike. If only the man had been patient, he'd be entirely wrapped up in the Charmer's plans with no time to order his lackey to wreak havoc.

"What's the status?" the Charmer asked, rather than answer his employee's question.

"Six cells—New York City, Miami, Nashville, Athens, Hong Kong and Paris—have been raided by DEA, FBI and Interpol. Word has spread like wildfire, and customers are pulling out of deals faster than we can control the damage. In a couple locations, rival organizations are attempting takeovers."

"They see a chink in the armor." His armor. *Fuck it all.*

"They see an opportunity," Nico agreed. "Others are demanding someone's head."

He'd love to give them Damian's on a sharp pike.

His fist tightened at his side. His hard-won empire, the reflection of his discipline and success, was crumbling. Though he'd gotten the word out as quickly as possible about the virus, more cells would lie in tatters by morning. It was impossible to reach everyone who could be impacted. His empire was too far flung.

Stick to the plan. The strongest will win.

He let excitement replace the anger that pumped through him as he considered the challenges he'd laid out for Damian. They were designed to break the man. And when the Charmer came out on top, he had several homes throughout the world he could escape to and never be seen again.

"Sir?" Nico asked when the Charmer fell into a thoughtful silence.

"I'll be in touch." He disconnected and tossed his cell phone on the desk.

Needing a reminder of his power and his triumph over Damian, he moved to the six-foot-tall wooden cabinet in the corner behind his desk. Using the key he kept in his pocket, he unlocked it. When the two arched, ornately carved doors swung open, the impression was that of a miniature cathedral. Years ago, when he'd acknowledged the burning need to purge himself in this way, he'd had it constructed to his exact specifications by a master craftsman in Europe.

His girls, the images of innocence and purity, smiled back at him from their frames on the shelves within. The press and an FBI profiler had long ago labeled him the Charmer, both for the jewelry he left at each burial site and his ability to take the girls from public areas without a fight, but it was the girls who had charmed *him*. Carefully selected, each one of them had brought him a satisfaction he didn't achieve from making legitimate billion-dollar deals or via the Circle's illegal endeavors.

For several long moments, he drank them in, running his fingers over his mementos and remembering each experience. Savoring. He was a man of ritual. He did things in a certain way, always to perfection.

His gaze landed on Sam's picture. His first. She would always hold a special place in his heart—for many reasons. Beside the wooden frame was a glass bottle about three inches high. He lifted it, removed the cork, held the bottle under his nose and inhaled the pungent soil. It immediately sent him back twenty-some years, smelling of the day he'd buried her in a couple feet of rain-moistened dirt—just enough to give her a proper burial, but not so much that she wouldn't eventually be found. Because how else was he to torture Damian?

Stroking the container still made his blood fizz with gratification. He replaced the cork and set the bottle beside Sam's picture, ignoring the manila folder that held all the photos, press clippings and police reports he'd been able to get his hands on. Though the reminders of how Damian had suffered would be welcome, there was no time to indulge now. Instead, his fingers moved to a little glass dish that held the token he'd taken from Samantha. From each of the girls, he'd taken some piece of jewelry, something to remind him of them. The bracelet with the butterfly charm lay coiled in the dish, missing its earring partners.

Sam wore one of the earrings when they'd found her body. The other he'd delivered to Damian as a message months ago, telling him that the Charmer was still alive and kicking, walking around free. Taking girls.

Feeling better, he circled his finger around the final spot on the bottom shelf of his cabinet. Empty, but not for long. Rocky had failed to bring him the girl, but the Charmer had other means.

Damian would lose. The Charmer was destined to win this game.

CHAPTER 3

Abby's apartment was a small one, tucked into a building with a hundred others in a South Loop neighborhood. She could walk or take the bus or the "el" to her jobs at the elementary school and the Inner Beauty studio. The two-bedroom space she shared with a fellow teacher, who was currently spending the summer backpacking in Europe, was simple but met her needs. Abby had learned from her single mother how to stretch a dollar.

She'd also learned what was important in life, which was why the primary source of decoration in her space was artwork supplied by her students. Every finger painting and ceramic hand-print was precious.

She shut the door behind her and bolted it, sinking back against it for a moment as if she could block out all of the confusion and horror of the day. The girls. Grandpa's illness. Sexy, stoic Einstein. She'd tried to forget the turmoil during her afternoon yoga class, but failed.

At least there was one request she could fulfill. She dropped her purse and headed for her bedroom. She made a beeline for the carved soapstone jewelry box that decorated her dresser top and found her mother's touchstone surrounded by a few other baubles she'd inherited.

Approximately two inches by one inch, the smooth piece of dark silver, metallic-looking hematite, fit nicely in her palm. Einstein's intense gaze suddenly flashed in her mind. She'd seen similar deep silver flecks in his hazel eyes.

Her fingers wrapped around its cool comfort. Her mother often held the stone while working through problems, insisting it brought clarity, calm and a focus that amplified her gifts. A measure of peace moved over her now, but her lips added a prayer that everything would be okay and she would make the right decisions. And maybe, by some miracle, she'd have more time with Grandpa.

She went to the kitchen to call him. She chewed her lip, trying to keep her blood pressure from rising as the ringing continued on the other end. Finally someone picked up.

"Hello?"

"Ernie?" She blew out a breath. "So you made it back okay."

"With groceries."

"Thank you. Sounds like you have things under control there. Tell him I found what he wanted and I'll stop by with it tomorrow." She clutched the stone tighter.

"Don't you worry, darlin'. I'm holding down the fort."

With one less problem facing her that evening, she eyed the blinking red light of her message machine. No doubt, a similar message awaited her on her cell phone. She pressed the button and forced herself to breathe. As she went about putting ice in a glass she filled with water, her principal's voice filled the kitchen.

"Abby, this is Dan Moore. Wesley Brookes is pushing forward with his lawsuit. I know this isn't the news we were hoping for—"

She lunged for the button and hit save, not wanting to hear the rest. Not today. Besides, he'd already warned her what might happen. There would be an investigation into *her* background now, and the irony was she had tried everything she could to avoid getting mixed up in this type of situation. Unfortunately, when she'd held Laney Brookes' jacket, the signs of abuse had flashed so dark and violent that she couldn't ignore it.

She took her ice water to the living room and turned on the television. She plunked down on the couch, expecting to see the evening news and learn when she could anticipate her turn with the rolling blackouts. But it was the Amber Alert that slid across the bottom of the screen that snagged her attention. Goosebumps rose along the back of her neck as she read the details of the abduction. Fourteen-year-old Mariah Pierce had disappeared from an upscale North Shore shopping mall just an hour ago.

Abby perched on the edge of the couch as if she could reach through the screen and shake the newscaster until she gave more information. A couple minutes later, the story finally became the focus and the feed switched to a reporter on the scene.

"Mariah Pierce was shopping with her mother when she excused herself to go to the restroom. She never returned. Her disappearance is eerily similar to a case twenty years ago, when a young woman named Samantha Manchester was taken by a serial killer. Her remains were found nearly a year later. The killer is blamed for the kidnappings and murders of eleven girls and has come to be known as the Charmer."

Samantha. The Charmer. A chill washed over Abby like an arctic wave, sucking her under. With sudden clarity, she knew that the Charmer was the name of the one responsible for the girls whose images had taken up residence in her head. And that Samantha was one of those girls.

A pang sliced through her heart as she realized what that meant. She had, indeed, seen the past. Those girls were dead. There was no saving them.

And now he had another one.

Was Einstein the Charmer? After smiling at her at the coffee shop, had he gone to take an innocent girl right out from under her family's watchful eyes? Something inside her screamed a negative answer, but maybe that was because she didn't want him to be a killer. Because part of her liked him. A lot.

"The Charmer has been abducting and killing young girls for over two decades," the reporter continued. "If this recent kidnapping is his work, Mariah could become his twelfth victim. Authorities are requesting the public's assistance finding her."

Two decades. That would make Einstein...a teenager when Sam disappeared. Close in age to the victims. Not impossible, but unlikely. *Right?*

Either way, she couldn't let Mariah die. Her gut told her the Charmer had the girl. Abby had to do something.

The memory of the last time she'd tried to help in such a dangerous situation, the image of the detective's sneer as he'd told her she was a crackpot, had her muscles freezing up. She would only talk to someone who would listen, someone she could trust.

As the answer came to her, she rushed to her discarded purse, still lying by the door where she'd dropped it. She sat on the floor and rifled through it. Her fingers found Dr. Maggie Levine's card inside and she stared at it until the numbers and letters swam together.

Could she do this? Telling someone about her gift would risk rejection.

"Please help us find our girl." From the television, a tearful couple faced the camera. "Mariah was looking forward to starting high school next month." The woman choked back tears as the man talked. "She's an honor student. A good girl. She doesn't deserve this."

A good girl. No, Mariah didn't deserve the horrors that awaited her. The other girls hadn't either. Nobody did.

Abby clasped her knees to her chest and focused on her breathing. She gripped Maggie's card in one hand and her mother's touchstone in the other. "What would you do, Mom?"

Lydia Rhodes would have taken whatever risk she had to in order to help someone in need. And so would Abby.

"That Amber Alert was issued pretty damn quick," Einstein said. "Thanks."

Detective Noah Crandall stood in Einstein's office. "Thank you for the heads-up about the Charmer looking for another victim. Time is of the essence in these matters."

Seated beside Einstein's desk, Damian looked up from studying the file Noah had brought with him. His eyes were blank, his face pale. "It's like déjà vu."

Noah shoved a hand through his short blond hair. "Nobody expected him to hit here twice. He's never repeated a location, right?"

"Not until now," Damian said. "We believe he's from Chicago, and may have been following my movements all these years. Einstein's working on gathering info on all of my past acquaintances."

It was a big job that had occupied most of Einstein's afternoon, but he welcomed a task that could occupy his mind. "If you want, I'll skip the dinner and work through the night."

"No, I want you there. I want the whole crew there."

Einstein nodded. Whatever his boss needed. Besides, the algorithms could run on their own once he set them up. He'd retrieve the data after the dinner.

"I'm heading out to talk to Mariah's parents," Noah said. "I'll see if they're willing to talk with you."

"That would be great," Damian said, rising. "I've sent several of my agents into the field to question everyone they can find near the North Shore mall as well as around Mariah's neighborhood. We'll keep each other informed?"

Noah nodded. "Priority one is finding this girl quickly." And alive.

"Lorena thinks the Charmer won't harm Mariah—for a little while, anyway. We're counting on him wanting to use Mariah to get to me."

Einstein prayed that was the case. "That sounds like a logical conclusion. Besides, we still don't know what the killer's gaining from taking these girls. He has a ritual we know little about. Hopefully, the need for the ritual will outweigh the need to kill."

THE CHARMER'S HEART SANG WITH EVERY MUFFLED KICK AND THUMP resounding from the shed. It had been a while since he'd had a girl he could take his time with. He'd had precious little time with Tiffany, with the SSAM agents and police on his heels.

He'd have more time to convert Mariah into one of his girls. This time, he was in control.

Other things were falling into place, as well. The wheels to create Damian's downfall were in motion. The man had a knack for landing on his feet, for schmoozing the public, but soon everyone would know the truth.

Damian Manchester was a fraud. A failure. He cared about nobody but himself.

The game was just beginning. Like the ghostly visits in Dickens' *A Christmas Carol*, Damian would be haunted by his past mistakes, one by one. It was about time he felt the screws turn.

ABBY CROSSED THE NEAR-EMPTY GREAT LAKES UNIVERSITY CAMPUS at the north end of Chicago. Summer school was between sessions and it was nearly five-thirty on a Monday. And damn muggy. People had better things to do than traipse across the city in search of clarity and a killer who might or might not be the enigmatic Einstein.

Using the directory in the parking lot, Abby located the psychology building. Worried she'd be laughed at for her ridiculous notions, she'd decided not to call Maggie first. Or maybe it had been her self-doubt that kept her quiet. This way, Abby could quietly disappear if her courage gave out before she made it to Maggie's office.

And part of her was hoping Maggie wasn't here. What would an eight-month pregnant woman be doing here in the middle of a heat wave without classes to teach? Her question was answered as she entered the building and a blast of cool air sent up goose bumps along her skin. Sweet refuge.

Abby found the office door open. Inside, Maggie was laid out on a couch with her feet elevated on a pillow and a paperback book propped on her protruding stomach. Her choice of reading material wasn't a psychology tome if the muscular male chest on the cover was any indication.

Abby cleared her throat. "Am I interrupting?"

Maggie looked up with surprise, dropped her feet to the floor and motioned to her to come inside. "Not at all. Just stretching out. Temporarily relieves the incessant heartburn and swollen ankles. What brings you to my neck of the woods?"

"You said I could come talk to you...?" Now that Abby was here, it felt wrong. How could she explain her visions to another person? "If you're busy, I—"

Maggie patted the cushion next to her. "There's a reason you're here and I'm betting it's a good one."

Abby didn't have a choice. She needed to trust someone or forget about those girls. This limbo would drive her insane.

Though there was nobody else in the building, Maggie dropped her voice. "I'll keep everything you tell me confidential. When I offered to help, I meant it. This morning, you seemed like a woman with a lot on her mind."

And that was *before* she'd touched the bracelet. "I have had a lot of things come up lately. And after you left, well... I've had a lot of people on my mind."

Maggie's brow knit. "Who?"

Abby sighed and plunged forward. "I don't know, exactly. Please bear with me. I'm not sure how to explain."

"Take your time."

"Sometimes, I have visions, usually after touching an object or a person." She blurted it out quickly, afraid she'd lose her nerve. Several beats of silence followed her declaration. Abby's muscles bunched as if preparing for flight. Any second now, Maggie would point to the door and order her to leave. She might even think her unborn child could be tainted with witchcraft. Abby had heard that one before, too.

But Maggie only looked more interested. "What kind of visions?"

"More like messages or flashes of insight. As if an object is imprinted with a person's emotional and physical experience."

"You mean you have psychometric abilities?"

Surprised, Abby nodded. "Yes. I try to control them by avoiding touching people or their things or blocking things out. Often I'm successful, but today..." Her words trailed off as she replayed the roller coaster she'd been on.

"What happened?"

"At the yoga studio this morning, after everyone left, I found a bracelet someone had left behind. I made the mistake of picking it up."

"It generated an image?"

"And some other sensory impressions. I felt them. Eleven young girls, probably between the ages of twelve and fifteen, all dead now." She shuddered.

"That must have been horrible."

Having steeled herself against the expectation of rejection, Abby was shocked by this woman's warm sympathy. "It was, but not as horrible as what was actually done to them—if what I saw is even real."

"You doubt yourself?"

Abby shrugged. "I haven't used my...gift...in a while. I'm probably rusty."

Maggie's eyes widened. "Wait. *Eleven* girls? Was it a *charm* bracelet you touched?"

"Yes. It has eleven charms, each a small silver disk about the size of a nickel. Each has a symbol on it. Why? Is that your bracelet I picked up at the studio?"

Maggie seemed deep in thought. "No. Unfortunately, it was an educated guess." She went to the bookshelf behind her desk and retrieved a framed photograph.

The spit in Abby's mouth dried as she recognized the smiling image. The girl's blond hair was drawn back in a ponytail, revealing an attractive face and blue eyes. It was nothing like the bruised and dirty image that haunted Abby since touching Einstein, but similar to the photo in the original flash of insight. "That's one of the girls." She looked at Maggie in confusion. "If it wasn't your bracelet, yet I'm picking up messages about your past..."

"Not my past. *Sam's* past. A man known as the Charmer killed my best friend twenty years ago."

"Sam. Samantha?" That had been the name mentioned in the newscast about Mariah. And Maggie was connected to her? It was almost too much to take in.

"Samantha Manchester was his first victim." Maggie frowned. "But that means someone linked to her murder was at the studio." Her hand moved to her belly in a subconsciously protective move.

"The killer?"

Maggie shook her head. "I don't know. Hard to believe any of those women we do yoga with would be capable of murdering eleven girls. Besides, the profilers at the FBI and SSAM are certain the Charmer is male. But what would a man be doing with a charm bracelet?"

"My gift isn't always reliable. It could be simply that the jeweler was somehow linked to the charms used in the murders. Anyone who'd touched the jewelry could have been, for that matter." Abby sighed. "I wish I could tell you more. I just don't know…"

Maggie replaced Sam's picture on the shelf, her fingers lingering on the frame. "I keep this here as a reminder of both the good and the bad in the world, of why I followed this career path. I followed my gut, knowing I could make a difference if I used my gifts." She turned back to Abby. "Trust your instincts. What are they telling you?"

Instead of blocking out her feelings, Abby tuned into them for the first time that day. She'd seemed to be in the killer's point of view for a moment before experiencing the horrors through the girls' senses. "I suspect the girls were wearing those charms when they died. He wanted them to. The fear and pain associated with them was too strong." Abby felt her confidence grow as she considered the messages and saw Maggie wasn't going to throw her out. "But I think the killer held the charms at some point, too. They mean something to him. If they were on a bracelet, he must have given them to someone important to him, right? Or it's part of his insane process. Or he wanted *me* to find them." Fear clawed at her insides, but she didn't let it out of the cage.

"Those all seem like possibilities. Do many people know about your psychometric abilities?"

She breathed a sigh of relief as she realized what Maggie was getting at. "No. I keep it hidden. Most people don't react to the news as well as you have."

Maggie smiled warmly. "I understand. But, in this case, I want you to let it out. Some messages are meant to be passed along. I know it's difficult, but you were the chosen conduit."

She hadn't thought of it that way. "Assuming the killer has no knowledge of my gift, the bracelet showing up at the studio is either an incredible coincidence or he or she knows you're connected to one of the murder victims. You need to hire some protection or something."

Maggie smiled softly. "My husband is an ex-Secret Service agent. He's already overprotective as it is."

"But you'll tell him to take extra precautions? And you won't come here alone anymore? The Charmer isn't done yet."

Maggie's gaze, missing nothing, must have spied the telltale signs of tension in Abby's posture and speech. "There's more that you haven't told me, isn't there?"

Abby nodded. "He has a new girl."

"New girl?" Maggie's focus sharpened.

"It was on the news just a little while ago. Mariah Pierce. An Amber Alert was issued when she disappeared from a shopping area."

"What shopping area?" There was a breathless quality to Maggie's voice and Abby nearly suggested she lie down, but the intensity of the woman's gaze indicated strength.

"Some upscale place on the North Shore."

Maggie grabbed her purse and flew to the door.

Abby stepped in front of her, blocking the exit. It couldn't be healthy for a woman in Maggie's condition to move that fast. "Wait. What's wrong?"

"It's just like Sam." Maggie grabbed Abby's arms and Abby felt the wave of urgency pass between them. "We have to tell Damian. Come with me."

"Who's Damian?"

"Sam's father. He started an agency that hunts serial killers. They've been looking for the Charmer for decades and they'll want to get on this immediately—and they'll want to talk to *you*."

Abby shook her head. "I don't think that's a good idea. Besides, I can't do anything. I just see the images of what's already happened. It's too late."

"Not for Mariah, it's not. Shoot. Wait. It *is* too late." With a flurry of energy, Maggie let go of Abby and moved to the office phone. She rapidly pressed a series of buttons. "Damian's probably left for the dinner tonight but there's someone you need to talk to.

He works at SSAM, and he's been working hard on this case, looking at the old files to draw parallels. His name is Einstein—"

"Einstein?" Her breath froze in her lungs. Einstein worked for Sam's father?

Maggie misunderstood her hesitation. "Well, his real name is Andrew MacKenzie, but he's so smart that—"

Everything and everyone in the world was connected, sometimes in eerie ways. It wasn't really a surprise that Einstein was working on this case, especially if he was the killer. Some murderers liked to keep tabs on the investigations into their crimes. What better way to avoid getting caught than to have an inside track?

Her skin tingled as if she'd touched him again, and she reached into her pocket to grip the touchstone, praying for calm and focus. "No. I don't want to talk to him."

Maggie looked up in surprise. "Why not?"

"He might be involved."

"In the murders? Not a chance."

"I accidentally touched him earlier today."

The crease between Maggie's brows was back. "I don't understand. How…?"

Abby explained the chance encounter at the coffee shop, and how his hand had brushed hers. "The images came through, more of them this time. Stronger."

"That has to be because he's working on the case. It's his job to look at all of the files and analyze the data. I promise you Einstein is one of the good guys. He was a SEAL before he came to work for SSAM."

"That doesn't mean he's not a killer."

"Think about it. What type of images did you see?"

With reluctance, she thought back to the slideshow that had played in her mind. An anxious twisting in her gut became the thrill of relief as she realized… "Skeletons. There were smiling photos of the girls, like before, but there were also crime scene photos of skeletal remains." Which was more in line with someone analyzing an old crime scene. She'd interpreted them wrong, believing the worst of a good guy. While that hurt, she was happy that Einstein wasn't a killer.

Maggie glanced at her watch and dropped the receiver on its cradle. "Guess Einstein's left, too. Everyone's headed to the dinner. I was about to head home to get ready, myself. I tell you what. Come by the Riverfront Hotel tonight. The dinner starts at seven. You can meet Einstein while there's a group of us around."

Anxiety prodded her again. "I don't think that's a good idea. Maybe you could just pass along my comments? If they need me to answer questions, I'll be around, of course."

Maggie's eyes softened. "I understand what it's like to distrust strangers, but I promise you can trust the agents at SSAM. You can trust me."

Abby forced herself to breathe in and out. She'd known telling someone would lead to more complications. She just hadn't been prepared for Einstein to be involved in this way. In the past, he'd brought shivers of awareness to her skin, but he didn't know about her...gift. Enlightening him would mean setting her reservations aside enough to do what Maggie was suggesting and trust the man with the quiet confidence and goofy T-shirts. Was that man Andrew, the sexy caffeine junkie who looked at her with heat in his eyes, or Einstein, ex-SEAL and trusted SSAM employee who examined only hard facts when solving a murder?

Would she have the courage to find out?

CHAPTER 4

The mayor presented Damian with a key to the city while the head of the Better Business Bureau handed him a plaque and shook his hand. Philanthropist of the Year. Feeling like a fraud in his tux and forced smile, Damian accepted his award.

The press captured the moment, their camera lights reflecting off the delicate ornamental butterflies made of white silk and gold glitter that rested among the white rose flower arrangements. The strobe effect almost appeared to lend them flight.

The golden butterfly had become a symbol of Sam Shines, a nonprofit agency Damian had started years ago to help fund crisis counseling and defray other expenses incurred by the victims' loved ones—the survivors who were left behind, frustrated with the lack of justice and overabundance of grief.

Expected to give a speech, Damian moved to the podium as the applause died down.

"Thank you for this generous honor and the kind words. But this night isn't about me, or what I do. My goal to make our world safer has only been achieved with the help of a fantastic team and the support of the community. We've put several monsters away, but evil persists. There's one serial killer in particular who continues to slip through the cracks of our justice system."

Damian paused to let his words sink in and made eye contact with several people, including his SSAM team and friends, seated at the front tables. Ethan and Maggie, Noah and Vanessa, Holt and Sara, Becca and Diego, Max and Catherine. Einstein. Lorena. Even his ex-wife Priscilla had found a way to be here, after all.

"I have good news, though," he continued. "The monsters of this world don't know that they're outnumbered. They don't realize they're doomed to fail. The good far outweighs the evil in this world. If you're intentionally hurting people and think you've outwitted the law, think again. We're coming for you. *I'm* coming for you." The crowd erupted in cheers and more applause as he rejoined his table.

Lorena reached over to squeeze his hand and leaned in close. "Well, if the Charmer's listening, that should rile him up."

"Let's hope so." The more he could deflect the killer's energy and attention from Mariah, the better. Let the monster pop his head out from under whatever rock he was hiding beneath. Damian would be waiting.

THE ALMIGHTY DAMIAN MANCHESTER WAS DOING IT AGAIN, spinning lies so that the crowd was cheering for him. But the tide would turn. The Charmer had made certain a few pertinent details would come to light...enough to lead to Damian's demise.

In the meantime, though, the Charmer quelled his outrage and pretended to add his approval along with the rest of the room's occupants. He'd channel his negative energy into more gratifying pursuits. Thinking of Mariah locked away, waiting for him, made him smile.

As dinner was served, he made conversation with his table-mates, but his attention was on the SSAM group at the other end of the room. They'd pay. Especially the one who'd dared to disrupt his business.

As if sensing he was the Charmer's focus, the man known as Einstein rose and came his way. The Charmer stifled the desire to stand and face the man head on, to announce his presence and demand that Damian reveal the imposter he was. He almost relished the opportunity to come clean and be noticed, and to show Damian as the real monster. The man was a master at pretending he was a pillar of society. If they only knew…

But Einstein continued walking, skirting the Charmer's table and brushing by him on the way to the bar at the rear of the room.

The Charmer was still a nobody to most people. Unrecognized. Underestimated. Soon, that would all change.

"SHE LOVED BUTTERFLIES." PRISCILLA'S STATEMENT JERKED DAMIAN from his distracted mood. She slid into the seat beside him, recently vacated by Einstein.

"Yes, she did." He leaned in to brush a quick kiss across her cheek. "I see you wrangled an invitation. You look lovely, as always." Her white-blond hair was in its usual elegant twist. Sequins glittered on the bodice of her gown.

"These centerpieces are meant to be a reminder of her inno-cence, I suppose." An innocence crushed like a butterfly's wing under a steel-toed boot.

"Or an exploitation of her memory," Damian said, a little too harshly. He cleared his throat. "I'm sorry. I've just got a lot on my plate lately. It's not like the city council has some hidden agenda to torture me." Not like the Charmer did.

Priscilla's sideways glance was part sympathy and part annoy-ance. "Of course not. You seem to be wound awfully tight tonight. Maybe you need a vacation." She knew better than anyone his tendency to throw himself into his work. She looked pointedly at the empty chair on the other side of him. "Where's this date of yours?"

"The ladies' room." But Lorena wasn't exactly a date. Time to redirect the conversation. "It's not like you don't work hard as well."

"But I know my limits. I'm getting plenty of R&R while I'm here." She fell silent, but something else was obviously weighing on her.

"What's wrong?"

"That girl in the news... Is it true? Did the Charmer take her?"

His gut tightened at the thought of another girl going through what Sam and the others had endured. "We don't know for certain, but I've got all of my resources working on it, and our connections with the CPD are keeping us in the loop."

A small smile curved Priscilla's lips. "Noah?"

"Yes." He'd forgotten what a small world they lived in. She knew Noah from a case that had taken them to her world in New York City. "He was here, but left right after dinner."

"Good."

He arched a brow in surprise.

"If the Charmer has Mariah, time is of the essence, right?"

"Absolutely."

Lorena reappeared at his side and, after greeting Priscilla—who was, no doubt, assessing Lorena as his potential *date*—her gaze examined him. "You okay?" He blew out a breath and concern tightened her mouth. "Want to get some air?"

He gave a brisk nod and turned back to Priscilla. "If you'll excuse us..." He felt her attention on them as they rose.

Lorena led him to the banquet room's doors, through the hotel lobby decorated with lush potted palms, pink marble floors and a wide glass front that looked out over Chicago's famous Magnificent Mile and the Chicago River, and out the main entrance. He filled his lungs with warm air and watched the twinkling of city lights and the mirror of the purple twilight reflected in the tall windows.

"You seem tired." Worry weighed heavily in her words.

"I'll be fine. Must be the heat."

"Convenient excuse for all manner of things lately, but I thought we'd gotten beyond the *I'm fine* stage of our relationship." She huffed out a mirthless laugh and his gaze swept over her face. *Relationship?* What had she meant by that?

But she was just as expert at hiding her emotions as he was, and her expression gave nothing away. Though she was in her mid-fifties, her skin was creamy-smooth, the tiny lines around her eyes and mouth evidence of a vibrant woman who embraced her age and her life, both the good and the bad, a woman who was confident in herself. A woman who could have any man she set her sights on.

"Yeah, I hear the heat has been blamed for a riot in South Side and a murder in Archer Heights. Tensions have been running high everywhere, I suppose." He blew out a breath. "And yeah, I'm not fine."

Her brow creased. "Mariah?"

"And the constant reminders." He waved a hand in the general direction of the hotel. "They're highlighting my successes, but I feel like I failed. Mariah must be the victim Rocky was supposed to kidnap for the Charmer. He found another way." Damian released a strangled laugh. "The man is nothing, if not resourceful. And he's waiting for me to fuck up."

"Probably."

Shocked, his gaze met hers again. "Thanks."

"It's not like either of us to sugarcoat things."

That was one of the many things he liked about her. She touched his hand. "But any time you need to talk, I'll be here." Through talking things out, they'd caught dozens of murderers over the years. He felt his burden shift and dislodge, crumbling at his feet.

"I appreciate that." And he'd take her up on it one of these days. Maybe. God knows he needed someone to talk to. Someone who understood. He was feeling as if he could blow his top at any little thing. The heat, indeed. It was the mass of emotion swelling inside him, agitating like a pot of water put on to boil, that threatened to lead to a meltdown.

Her fingertips brushed over his cheekbone and her lips parted as if she would say something. He nearly gave in to the urge to lean down and taste her, but she dropped her hand.

"I'd better get back inside." She hesitated a moment longer, though what she was expecting from him, he couldn't guess. Did she want him to object and offer to take her somewhere else? The city council had some slideshow planned in his honor. He couldn't just leave. But his body screamed at him to do just that. To seize this moment with her.

But duty came first, always. Sam and so many other unfortunate victims were counting on him.

"Whoa. Hitting the hard stuff already? " Max leaned against the bar beside Einstein and smirked at his drink of choice.

He looked up from his virgin Rob Roy to glare at Max. "Funny. I have work to do tonight." First, he'd contact Nico for an update on the task force's progress taking down Circle cells. He'd assess the programs that were analyzing who Damian had done business with twenty-some years ago when he'd been CEO of Luna Corp. Then he'd start working on algorithms to assess the rest of Damian's past connections.

It was shaping up to be an all-nighter. He should have picked up more energy drinks when he'd been out earlier...

A tingle of awareness at the base of his neck had him turning toward the door. *Abby.*

The security guard had stopped her and was checking his clipboard. Was she an invited guest? She was dressed in a simple eggplant-colored knee-length dress that clung to her curves. It lacked the glitz of many of the dresses that populated the banquet room, yet somehow she sparkled more than all the candles, glitter and crystal combined.

"Have you?" Max's question was punctuated with a snort. "You didn't hear a word I said."

"Some of it." His gaze drifted back to Abby. She was flashing her dimple at the guard. Damn, that was *his* dimple. She was *his* fantasy. What was she doing here in the flesh?

Unfortunately, the guard was giving her a hard time and her smile evaporated. As Einstein straightened and prepared to ride to her rescue, he spied Maggie heading toward Abby as if she recognized her.

Max's finger and thumb snapped in front of his face. "Hello, space cadet. Where'd you go?" He followed Einstein's gaze. "Who's she?"

"That's Abby Rhodes," said Catherine Sawyer, Max's fiancé and SSAM's ever-efficient administrative assistant, as she slid an arm around Max's waist. In return, Max tugged her against his side.

How was it that everyone seemed to know *his* fantasy woman better than he did?

Catherine's speculative gaze moved between Abby and Einstein. He was quick to slide his emotional shields into place, afraid she'd start playing matchmaker. He didn't need a match. Dating someone—or worse, falling for them—meant losing focus elsewhere. Love always had a cost. Besides, he enjoyed the fantasy.

But the thought of running his hands over Abby's curves, along the taut length of her thigh to the sweet bend in her knee…

No, reality was never as good as fantasy. There were complications in human relationships. Complications that too often led to pain.

Still, he couldn't resist doing a little reconnaissance. "How do you know Abby?"

"I try to attend her yoga classes at least once a week. The Inner

Beauty studio's only a block away from the SSAM offices, so sometimes I can duck out during a break. Today, I couldn't get away from work." Her eyes narrowed. "How do *you* know Abby?"

He shrugged. "Occasionally, I bump into her at the coffee shop across the street. She likes her mocha with hazelnut and, on Mondays, whipped cream."

Catherine's smile bloomed.

"What?" He was immediately wary. "Hey, don't get any ideas."

"Too late, man," Max said with a laugh. "I know that look."

"You noticed her," Catherine said.

"So?" Einstein couldn't help the defensiveness that crept into his voice. Why did he feel like a skinny high school geek again? He'd been a late bloomer. Hitting puberty, working out and joining the SEALs had helped him take full advantage when his growth spurt had finally come along, but inside he sometimes still felt awkward. Different.

"You noticed her and that makes her special."

"She's just some woman from a coffee shop." Some woman he'd made love to in a dozen different ways in his head.

Catherine looked toward Abby again. "Maybe Maggie invited her." Indeed, Maggie was pulling a reluctant Abby into the banquet room and shooting the stymied guard death glares. They headed directly for Einstein. Anticipating the flash of Abby's dimple sent a fizzy feeling from his abdomen to his head. And that was a biological reaction for which he had no explanation—and apparently, no defense.

WHEN THE GUARD DENIED HER ENTRY, ABBY HAD BEEN PREPARED TO make her escape, but Maggie was a woman on a mission. She currently had a gentle but firm grip on Abby's arm and was propelling them straight toward the bar, where Einstein watched her approach with questions in his eyes. Since she'd basically high-tailed it out of the coffee shop earlier, as if she couldn't get away from him fast enough, she wasn't surprised. He probably thought *she* was stalking *him*. Or playing games. Either way, it wasn't the best way to start this conversation, but Maggie seemed to think Abby could do something to help Mariah.

Abby squared her shoulders as she stopped in front of Einstein and another muscular guy, who was slightly wider than Einstein through the shoulders and a couple inches taller, but somehow less imposing. Just seeing Einstein had the power to make her weak in the knees. And his fierce expression didn't help. All his intensity was focused solely on her, on figuring her out.

She hid a shiver of desire as his gaze swept over her. Where was the quiet, harmless nerd she'd been bumping into for weeks? Hidden inside a heart-stopping tuxedo, that's where. She swallowed hard, knowing that, despite his frown, this image would fuel her fantasies for many weeks to come.

At least the stranger at his side had a welcoming twinkle in his eyes. And Catherine, one of Abby's yoga students, was holding the other man's hand.

"Abby, I'd like you to meet Max and Einstein," Maggie said. "And you know Catherine, of course."

"Hello." Abby smiled at each of them.

Einstein didn't smile back. Instead, his expression was carefully blank. "What are you doing here?"

Good question. She didn't belong. She normally avoided crowds—too much opportunity to bump into someone, to feel what they felt or relive their emotions and memories. "I..." She fumbled for a response that would make sense.

"She has information," Maggie finished when Abby couldn't find her voice.

Some of his hardness softened and he looked at her with curiosity. "About?"

"The girl who disappeared this afternoon. Mariah Pierce."

"How was Abby involved?" He spoke as if she weren't standing right in front of him, her ego exposed and ready for him to stomp on.

"Not involved, really," Abby said. "I'm hoping I can help."

"Hoping?" His hazel eyes were fortified with flecks of gray steel. Soft, and yet hard. Lord help her, her legs went rubbery.

She licked her dry lips. "I don't know anything concrete, but—"

"Have you gone to the police?"

"They won't listen."

"Why not? Is the information unreliable?"

Maggie sighed. "Stop hammering her with questions and give her a chance to talk. They're getting ready for the slideshow. I'm going to go get off my feet." She jabbed a finger into Einstein's chest. "You stay and hear her out." She turned to Abby. "You can trust him." She moved away and Catherine followed her cue, grabbing Max and heading for a table near the podium at the far end of the room.

"Subtle." Einstein rubbed at the spot Maggie had poked. He obviously didn't want to listen to any unverified intel, and she didn't want to be rejected by him. Maybe she should have swallowed her dignity and risked going to the police.

The lights dimmed as a slideshow began, projected onto a large screen hanging off to the side of the podium, where the mayor stood listing statistics on violent crime, the strapped resources of local authorities and SSAM's contributions in assisting with cold cases around the country.

Einstein had been part of that assistance.

He can be trusted.

Now, if only *he* would trust *her*. *Please, just listen.*

But she wouldn't beg for acceptance. She would only hope that, if Einstein disregarded her input, he'd be gentle. She didn't think she could stand him laughing at her.

The nearest occupied table was twenty feet away, so they had a bit of privacy, but Einstein dropped his voice so he wouldn't distract from the show. "So what do you have to tell me about Mariah Pierce?"

She opened her mouth to suggest she simply leave and go to the police as he'd suggested, but a collective gasp, followed by the lights flickering once, twice, and then going out completely, had her thoughts freezing up. Sounds of a commotion came from somewhere across the room, and then a scream pierced the darkness. She felt strong hands on her shoulders—Einstein's hands. But knowing the reality didn't stop panic from rising in her throat. Something soft and warm brushed her ear, provoking shivers, and she realized it was his lips.

"Stick with me." His words temporarily blocked out the panic and the sounds of chaos.

His arm slid around her waist, his hand landing on her hip as if it belonged there. He pressed her against the length of his side as he guided her through the blackness. Somewhere behind them, emergency lights switched on, but on their end of the room, the light was limited to the corner emergency exits, barely penetrating the bar area.

"Stay calm, everyone," someone's voice rang out. Male. Authoritative. "And don't move, or you could get hurt."

But Einstein kept propelling her toward the swinging double-doors that probably led to the kitchen—unfamiliar territory, not to mention plenty of sharp or hot things to run into. Einstein's chest was hard and warm against her arm as he tucked her close, as if, no matter what the threat, he would protect her. At the last second, he pulled her sideways, behind the long oak bar and then down to the floor until they huddled together.

"What are we doing?" she whispered, sensing that he meant for them to hide. But what, or who, were they hiding from? The spike of panic in the room had dissipated as the emergency lighting gave the guests some sense of order. "Wouldn't it be safer out there, where we can head to the door and get to the street? Or, this could just be a rolling blackout."

A puff of breath brushed her temple as he turned to her. "If so, it'll be dark for a while. Those things last about a half hour, if not more." Did he plan to hold her hostage next to him that entire time? Her body shuddered with anticipation.

"Still—"

"Look, it'll all get sorted out soon. Better to wait here, in safety."

"Are we in danger?"

He stilled against her. "I don't know. I'm going to go see if I can help. I want you to stay here."

"Why can't you stay with me?" She hated the fear in her voice, but being with him felt infinitely safer than being alone in the dark, especially if there was danger lurking nearby.

"You'll be fine." His hand squeezed hers in an effort to comfort her.

When the message beckoned, instead of blocking it, she embraced it, opening her mind as if tuning into a channel, hoping it would help her decide she could trust him. But she didn't expect the sharp edge of anger and grief...

A massive building crumbles, releasing a cloud of brown and black dust. Flames. So much destruction. Death. No screams, only silence. Except for the pounding of a heartbeat. His heartbeat.

Abby realized she was seeing the message through Einstein's eyes, on a screen. It was a scene she, along with millions of others, would readily recognize. A television broadcast of 9/11, when the towers went down.

A sob of despair and rage coiled in her chest—things Einstein had been feeling that day, just as most Americans who'd watched in horror had experienced. But this was different. There wasn't the same degree of separation from the emotion. She could almost hear the rush of adrenaline barreling through his body. No, Einstein had been connected to that horror in a personal way.

A flame flickered above their heads. Someone had found candles and was lighting them. Einstein let go of her hand and the horrible images evaporated, but the raw emotion was still there, pulsing through her limbs.

"All clear," someone called. It sounded like Max.

Einstein stood and pulled her to her feet. Wobbly and disoriented from adrenaline as well as the rush from what she'd experienced via Einstein's sensory memories, Abby let him be her rock for a moment. The images were gone. She was both relieved and confused by a stab of disappointment. In those few dark moments, she'd felt so close to him. She'd been presented a sneak peek into his head, and his heart, that she wasn't sure he'd want her to have.

She forced herself to step back. "Was anyone hurt?" Her stomach did somersaults at the thought. She glanced about the room, but all seemed calm. People were distributing the lit candles throughout the room and a warm glow now pierced the darkness at regular intervals.

"I don't think so. Are you okay?" As he examined her, the candlelight amplified the silver in his eyes like tributaries of molten metal. "You look like you're in shock."

"I'm okay." But now she was aware of the deep pain from his past that lay behind his hooded gaze. They had that in common. And then there was the undeniable pull she'd felt, as if an invisible wire bound them together, the zing of electricity arcing between them. Did he feel it too?

"Oh, thank goodness," Maggie said from across the bar. "I wondered where you'd disappeared to. Did you see the slideshow —the last few slides, that is?"

Einstein shook his head. "Missed them."

Maggie looked at Abby. "I didn't see it either," Abby said. "We were about to...talk."

"The Charmer hijacked the show," Maggie said. "He challenged Damian to a game."

"A game?" Einstein's eyebrows came together. "What kind of game?"

But Maggie was distracted as her gaze searched the room for

someone. "I'm sure he'll have his people on it. You and Abby should go talk somewhere quiet."

"She should talk to Noah," he said. "He's a detective with the CPD," he clarified for Abby's sake. "I should help get to the bottom of this sabotaged slideshow."

He was going to pass her off to someone else without even listening to what she had to say? No way. She'd come this far. She followed him out from behind the bar. "Wait. I need to talk to you."

Einstein came to a halt, but not because of her. Another man, one who exuded authority, approached. He was probably in his late fifties or early sixties. The silver at his temples, the crow's feet at his eyes, the sharpness of his cheekbones and jaw, his trim but tall build as well as the cut of his suit, all indicated a man who had the funds to live exorbitantly but the self-control to live in moderation. He also carried an aura of incredible grief that had her taking a second look.

With sudden clarity, she knew. This was Damian Manchester, Sam's father.

"The Charmer won't get away with this, sir," Einstein promised Damian. "Can you have someone on the council email me the slideshow? Better yet, have them send me the entire computer. I'll have it analyzed by morning and see who altered the program."

"Nothing to analyze," Damian said. "The Charmer knew I would be here. He set this up. He wanted to get under my skin." Damian's quiet, tight manner indicated a man in control of his emotions—perhaps too much so. Those types of people tended to snap eventually.

As if noticing her observing him, he introduced himself. "I'm Damian Manchester."

She looked at his outstretched hand. Would she have more visions of Sam if she shook it? Not that she had a choice. Rejecting it would be rude. She braced herself, mentally building walls as she shook his hand. "Abby Rhodes."

His lips twitched. "The Beatles?"

"Mom was a fan." She released a breath as he let go. No unwanted messages had assaulted her.

His gaze moved between her and Einstein. "What brings you here tonight?"

"Abby came to me this afternoon to discuss something she'd seen," Maggie said.

"Seen?" Damian's gaze was sharp as it returned to Abby with renewed curiosity. "About a case?"

"It relates to Sam." Maggie's eyes flashed with eagerness and, worse, *hope*.

"And to Mariah," Abby added. In for a penny, in for a pound. "I saw her parents on the news today. Mariah was taken by the same man who took Sam and the others."

As she spoke, Damian's frowned. "The authorities have been waiting for confirmation on that. What proof do you have?"

"There is no hard proof," Maggie said. "Abby is psychic. She uses psychometry to see events by touching objects associated with them." Maggie put an arm around Abby's shoulders in a show of support—or maybe to keep Abby from fleeing—while, on Abby's other side, Einstein seemed to lean away, distancing himself. She tried to ignore the hard jab of disappointment.

"To *see* events?" Damian asked, his forehead knit in confusion.

"Sometimes it's just a feeling," Abby clarified.

"A *feeling*." Damian's statement was laden with doubt.

Abby's heart sank but she soldiered on. "I didn't know about Sam until today when I touched something related to her murder. When I heard about Mariah's disappearance, I knew they were connected."

Beside her, Einstein's brows now formed a V as he examined Abby, his handsome face hard as stone. "What was the object that generated these feelings?"

"A bracelet I found at the yoga studio where I work."

"A *charm* bracelet," Maggie added.

A spark lit Damian's eyes. "What did you see...or feel?"

"Joy." She bit her lip and shook her head. "Not from the girls, obviously, but I think...I think from the Charmer. And then I had flashes of eleven girls, all in their teens, and the smell of dirt and the feeling I couldn't breathe."

"Did you get an image of the Charmer?"

Regretfully, she shook her head. "The messages aren't usually that clear." If she'd worked on developing her gift instead of hiding it, maybe she'd have that skill by now. Instead, she'd stunted that growth.

Damian was silent for several moments, his expression unreadable. But his stiff stance indicated restrained anger.

"I believe her," Maggie said. "And it's worth a try if we can find Mariah and the leader of the Circle."

"The Circle?" Abby's hand moved to her shoulder, as she remembered the burning sensation she'd felt there earlier. It had intensified as each of the girls' images scrolled through her head.

Einstein followed her movement. "What are you doing?"

She dropped her hand. "Nothing." She didn't understand the feeling, so why would he? He'd already judged her. His dark tone and rigid posture told her as much. Why that hurt more than usual, she couldn't say, except that she'd wanted him to believe her. She'd had a good feeling about him when she'd bumped into him all those times before...until she'd literally *bumped into* him and they'd touched.

His frown deepened. "You came to talk, so talk."

She licked her lips nervously. "I'm not sure..."

Maggie stepped in front of her like a mama bear protecting her cub. "Maybe she would if you'd stop intimidating her." Einstein looked surprised at her observation.

A security guard bustled over and zeroed in on Abby. "You need to come with me." She bristled. It was worse than she'd feared. She'd be publicly humiliated.

"Why?" Damian asked.

The security guard recognized Damian as the VIP of the night and cleared his throat. "I'm sorry to interrupt, sir. I think, given the situation, we should crack down on strangers." His gaze narrowed on her. "She's the only one here who wasn't an invited guest and she arrived just minutes before the slideshow started."

"And she was with me the entire time." It was Einstein's turn to angle himself in front of her protectively. "Besides," he added, turning to sweep a glance up and down her body. "There's nowhere to hide even a thumb drive in that dress."

And she'd only brought her wallet as a clutch. With a limited budget and elegant occasions few and far between, the dress was the best she owned. The heat in Einstein's eyes indicated her appearance met with his approval. Her cheeks warmed.

He turned back to the guard. "I'll vouch for her." His unexpected defense had her heart skipping happily. The guard, however, didn't look appeased.

"I'll leave," Abby offered. "I didn't come to cause problems—or to ruin the special evening," she added, glancing at Damian.

Some of the tightness in Damian's face relaxed. "You didn't. The Charmer did." He glanced at the guard. "She stays." With an abrupt nod, the man returned to his post at the door.

"What was on those slides?" Einstein asked.

"A quantified listing of my failures."

"What?" His incredulous gaze swung from his employer to Maggie and back. "What failures?"

"With Sam, with friends, at work…" Damian's gray eyes flashed with a mixture of dark emotions.

"That's ridiculous. You're not a failure." Einstein huffed out a laugh. "Hell, the mayor just handed you a damn key to the city."

"He's right," Maggie said. "You're surrounded by friends who know the truth."

"It's all a game to him," Damian said. "The last slide said *The game begins now*, was signed *The Charmer* and then a countdown clock flashed on the screen, counting down from seventy-two hours. Then the lights went out."

"Counting down to what?" Einstein asked. "Something to do with Mariah?"

"That's my guess." Damian turned to Abby. "Could the bracelet be part of a game? Maybe Maggie was meant to find it and it was supposed to give her a clue or something. Where is it now?"

"I left it in the lost and found box at the yoga studio," Abby said. "After the images, I didn't want to touch it again." As head of the SSAM agency, the man probably saw images like that all the time. No doubt, he was haunted by images of his own daughter, as well. But for her, it had been a shock.

He looked to Einstein. "Go with Abby and get the bracelet. Then, find out what she has to say. Anything could help, right?"

"Right." But Einstein's scowl indicated his reluctance.

CHAPTER 5

Einstein had never been to a gym that didn't emit the lingering smell of hard-won sweat. The Inner Beauty Dance and Yoga studio, just a few blocks down from the SSAM offices, had gleaming wood floors, neatly stacked yoga mats and hand weights, and the faint scent of pine cleanser and lavender. No respectable gym smelled like a field of flowers. But as his gaze moved over Abby's toned body, he had to admit she was in great shape.

"It's not here." Abby sank her teeth into her plump bottom lip as she fumbled through a shoebox she'd hauled out from beneath the front counter. A lone ballet shoe, a bubblegum-pink gym towel, a few ponytail holders and several miscellaneous forgotten doodads filled the box. Her gaze was troubled as it lifted to his.

"Are you sure?" He tried to disguise his frustration. There were myriad other things he needed to do, like get back to the office and check the programs he'd left running. And call the task force to get an update on the Circle takedown. As much as he liked Abby, this was a useless mission. What could a piece of jewelry tell her that his data crunching couldn't tell him?

She slid the box across the counter toward him and then paced to the other end of the room. She stopped by one of the few chairs that lined one wall and dropped to her knees. Her dress strained against her hips, and he nearly swallowed his tongue.

"What are you doing?" He shoved the box back under the counter. She didn't look up as he moved closer. "Is that where you found it?"

"Yes." She pressed her palms to the floor and her hemline rode up an inch farther along her thighs, exposing just enough smooth, creamy skin to make his mouth water—and yet, not nearly enough to satisfy the need clawing at his insides.

She was like a drug to his system. He'd been addicted for months—to the fantasy of her, at least. But clearly, the woman experienced delusions. Or maybe she was hoping to be noticed. He could have told her she'd gone to a heck of a lot of unnecessary trouble to gain his attention.

In his car on the way here, he'd asked a few questions. She truly believed some innocuous bracelet had somehow transmitted messages to her. And he'd wanted so badly to assuage the anxiety in her blue eyes that he'd almost tossed centuries of modern science aside and told her he believed her.

His defenses were low around Abby, so he armored himself the best way he could—with sarcasm. "It wouldn't just go back to that spot on its own." Not one of the women in his life had appreciated his sense of humor. Not even his mother—especially not her.

"Gee, ya think?" Her words were muffled, but the return volley was loud and clear.

He bit back a grin. "Do you need the bracelet? Didn't you already receive the...messages?"

"I didn't want to hold it very long before. It got too intense and I began to...block it out." Guilt thickened her voice. "But if I tried again, I might get a clearer image of the girls."

"The girls?"

She looked over her shoulder at him with a soft smile. "That's what I call them."

"How many?" Pop quiz time. He'd put her through the paces before he'd trust her, or her so-called gift, to get near Damian again. His employer had been through enough.

"Eleven." Certainty rang clear in her voice. "I think I already mentioned that." Her forehead crinkled before she turned back to whatever answers she was looking for on the floor.

She could have found that information with a little bit of Internet research. Score one for technology—one of many, according to Einstein's ledger. At least with computers, you knew what you were getting, how to control the flow of data, how to make the machine do what you wanted it to do.

Had she simply searched online? After all, he had yet to see physical proof that the item of jewelry existed, let alone held the same charms from the murder scenes. But why would she make up this stuff about the bracelet? Why would she approach Maggie and SSAM? What did she want from them? If she were some crackpot looking to make money off Damian's grief, Einstein would make her pay. God, if he'd been the one to lead a con artist to Damian's doorstep, Einstein would never forgive himself for causing the man additional suffering.

And if he were able to set his cynicism aside and give her the benefit of the doubt, what did that mean? That a killer, or someone associated with one, had been at Abby's studio, within striking distance of her. His gut tightened at the thought.

"So how does this work, exactly?" He couldn't tear his gaze from her as she maneuvered along the floor on all fours.

She looked over her shoulder at him. "The messages?"

"If that's what you call them."

"Sometimes, if I touch an object, it'll give me an image, or a series of images. Sometimes it's just a symbol, or a feeling. Sometimes even a color or a scent. This time, it was like all of my senses were involved. Visually, it was a slideshow of pictures. On a deeper level, the anger and fear associated with them were intense." She shuddered.

"What other sensations did you experience?"

"The smell of fresh dirt. The feeling of not being able to catch my breath."

Since she wasn't rising from the floor, he squatted to take a look at what was so interesting. She was running her hands over the wood and along the baseboard as if she were reading braille, only there were no lumps, bumps or clumps to feel.

"No offense, but those details are vague, yet just specific enough to the cases to sound legit."

She tipped her head and her curtain of dark hair slid to the side. Her angry gaze locked onto his. "Don't you have gut feelings? As a SEAL, didn't you rely on a sixth sense?"

Yeah, he had. And it had saved his butt more than once. "That's different." He'd take numbers and hardcore data over gut feelings any day of the week. His gut certainly hadn't warned him the day his SEAL team had been ambushed and he'd been injured.

"Of course it's different. I'm sure more lives counted on your gut feelings than on my psychometry. But that doesn't make my feelings any less valid." She looked back at the floorboards and sighed. "There's nothing here anymore."

Still crouched at her side, he looked at the empty floor. *Duh.*

"We can go," she said. "There's no residual energy." She sounded disappointed and relieved at the same time. He wondered what it would be like to experience the cumulative negative energy associated with the murders of eleven girls—not that he believed such a thing were possible. But sometimes, after hours of studying the Charmer's victim files, he'd swear he could feel an ache of frustration all the way to his marrow and a pressure on his shoulders as though the girls were there, holding him in his seat until he found their killer.

Abby pushed back on her haunches so suddenly that she lost her balance and tipped sideways into him. Her hands went to his thighs to catch herself. Her mouth formed a cute O and, using him as leverage, she pushed to her feet. The unexpected opposing force pushed him off balance. As the laws of gravity and physics conspired against him, his butt hit the floor. He grunted with the impact.

She gasped. "I'm so sorry." Her fingers pressed against her mouth, but he could have sworn it was less due to surprise and more to hold in laughter.

He accepted her outstretched hand and she tugged him to his feet. The big bad SEAL assisted by a yoga instructor. His pride took a blow. The zing from the contact with her only reinforced that his primary—*primal*—thought at the moment was to pull her against his chest, grip her by the hips and taste her smile.

God, he must need sleep. Even better, sexual release, then sleep. Neither was likely to happen.

HOLY HELL, WARMTH INVADED HER BODY—SOME SPOTS MORE THAN others—at his touch. And this time, it was entirely good vibes she was picking up on.

And the images—dear Lord. Her skin tingled. She could nearly feel him against her, skin-to-skin. Were those his desires she was picking up on or her own?

She wondered what he'd taste like if she leaned up and kissed him. Would she get more insight into his life? That had happened with her first kiss, which had promptly freaked her out. Thank God her mother shared her gift and had been there to explain these things a few months before her death.

In Abby's later relationships, she'd been careful to block stimuli unless she was comfortable receiving it. With Einstein, she was vulnerable. He was the first man to scale her walls in a long time.

He let go of her hand, breaking the connection. "Were you here most of the day? Other than, you know, bumping into me at the coffee shop?"

"No. I only teach a couple classes a day in the summer. The rest of the year I teach a few classes around my work schedule."

"What do you do for a living?"

"I'm a kindergarten teacher." At least for now. She shoved aside her anxiety about the lawsuit. It had no place here, when her goal was to gain Einstein's confidence.

His eyes widened. "Really? And a psychic on the side?" Judgment tainted his words.

She'd heard it all before. And somehow, she expected it from him. He was an intellectual type, and people who lived in their heads rarely understood her gift. Still, his cynicism stung.

She stepped away from him. "Don't worry. I don't force my woo-woo stuff on impressionable young kids."

"I didn't say it was *woo-woo*."

"It's okay. I get it. I'm an anomaly in your world." Which was why she hadn't told her coworkers at the school, or even her roommate, about her psychometric abilities. People either thought you were crazy or wanted to use you to channel dead relatives or predict their futures. It didn't work like that. And she definitely didn't want the parents of her students thinking weird things about her.

She wasn't weird, damn it.

"No, really. I'm trying to understand." His tone was conciliatory but the deeper connection they'd shared was shattered. Her mind was already cycling back to when the police detective had dismissed her and the images she'd had of the missing person. It had taken years to get over that. Hell, she'd never gotten over it, just pushed it down deep along with the rest of her gift. She'd identified with the Greek myth about Cassandra, a woman destined to know the truth, to see the future, but never be believed. Screw that. She wasn't going to suffer the same fate.

She headed for the door of the studio, prepared to lock up, go home and forget today ever happened. Try to forget her grandfather was dying. Try to erase the image of Samantha and the others, God forgive her.

Or maybe she could handle this on her own and find the owner of the bracelet. It had to be someone who'd taken a class at the studio within the past few days. He or she must have shown up again to get it out of the lost and found box. Abby could ask the studio owner and the other teachers if they'd seen anyone with it.

"Wait, where are you going?" he asked.

"I obviously came to the wrong person. I made a mistake."

He darted in front of her and angled his muscular frame in front of the door. She stopped just inches away.

"Give me another chance." He raised his hands slightly, but then dropped them back to his sides. Was he afraid to touch her? "Come by the office tomorrow morning. I want to hear what you have to say. And bring a list of your yoga students. Maybe we can track down the owner of the bracelet." His thoughts had run the same path as hers.

She looked away, avoiding his intense hazel gaze. An unmovable boulder, he stood, waiting patiently for her to acquiesce before he would budge.

Anger reared up, clutching at her throat. Did he believe her or didn't he? People were so quick to dismiss her—until they needed something. "I'll think about it."

"Abby, I'm sorry."

She met his gaze. "For what?" For hurting her feelings? For not trusting her? For avoiding touching her? She understood the first two, though he could have given her the benefit of the doubt. As for the last question... She didn't want to contemplate why that one hurt so much.

"For not listening." He grimaced. "Sometimes, I'm not so good at human conversation. At least with females. Hell, you've seen me several times over the past few months and I was only able to talk to you after you initiated it."

She was so surprised, she laughed. "You're doing okay now."

His shoulders relaxed. "I am?"

He was an interesting combination of hot body and sexy brains, yet he didn't seem to realize his appeal. That he exuded strength and confidence as well as insecurity and vulnerability was something that tugged at her heart.

She sighed. "I'll stop by tomorrow, but you have to promise to listen with an open mind." She nudged her way past him before either of them could reconsider.

WHEN EINSTEIN DROPPED ABBY OFF AT HER APARTMENT BUILDING, she darted from his car before he could insist on walking her to her door. The moment he got to SSAM, he did some digging and found her phone number. A quick conversation assured him she'd locked herself in her apartment for the night and that she still planned to see him in the morning.

An hour later, he was still finding it hard to focus. He'd sent out the bat signal, but Nico had yet to respond. Einstein hoped the undercover agent was okay, even as he secretly enjoyed thoughts of the Charmer losing control because of the long-reaching effects of the virus. A call to the head of the task force revealed that several Circle cells had fallen worldwide.

Satisfied that things were going well in the outside world, Einstein settled into his cave to get some computer work done. But thoughts of Abby continued to intrude.

As one computer ran a program to cull keywords and names from a Better Business Bureau catalog that listed Chicago businesses that existed twenty-five years ago, he turned to another to search for an entirely different type of information. He typed *psychometry* into the search box and lost himself for a half hour, reading articles, blog posts and board discussions, until Max showed up.

"Damian had me wait at the mayor's office until the city

council released this to me." Max handed him a laptop. "He said you wanted the whole thing, not just the slideshow."

He'd see if he could dig up a user name. Or, at the very least, he could see when and how the file had been altered. "Damian went home?"

Max nodded. "He wanted to be here but Lorena put her foot down."

"Good. There's nothing he can do tonight. Better that he gets some rest." Tomorrow, Einstein would have some difficult questions for him. He needed to do some probing if he was going to fill in all the gaps—the nuances of personal relationships and possibly hidden information his computer searches couldn't provide.

Einstein opened the laptop and loaded the slideshow he'd missed. Watching it now, anger jabbed at him like a white-hot poker as the decreased crime statistics quoted by the mayor morphed into a series of slides listing Damian's supposed failures as if they were damaging facts.

One failed friendship, one failed marriage, one dead daughter, one disemboweled company. Hundreds of people disappointed and hurt. Countless promises broken. Three days to rectify them.

In the final slide, a cartoon of a ticking time bomb appeared, and then a countdown, set at seventy-two hours, began in the center of the screen.

It's time to even the score. The game begins now.

Max watched over his shoulder. "Jesus, it reads like a demented to-do list. What does it mean?"

"I think you're right—it is a kind of to-do list. He intends to make Damian pay for every one of these perceived mistakes." But Einstein would make sure that never happened. His employer had been nothing but kind and generous to everyone he knew, even when they didn't deserve it.

Einstein set his wristwatch's timer to sixty-nine hours and thirty-eight minutes, which was what they had left, by his calculations. He glanced up as a shift in lighting from the hall caught his attention. Like a shadow, Nico had moved soundlessly to darken his doorway.

Beside him, Max straightened. "Well, look what the cat dragged in."

"Twice in one day." Nico looked unhappy that he'd been summoned, yet again. "Are you crying wolf or is this important?"

Einstein bristled at the man's implication that he didn't have anything of significance going on. "First, I wanted to make sure you survived the carnage."

Nico spread his arms wide. "I did."

"And the Charmer?"

"Alive and kicking."

"So we noticed," Max drawled. He gestured to the laptop. "Did you have any idea he was going to manipulate the slideshow and try to make Damian look like a fool?"

Nico's entire body went rigid.

Einstein's instincts dialed to high alert. "You did this job for him."

"I told you I was moving up in the ranks. I have to show he can trust me to get things done." Defensiveness was thick in Nico's voice.

"And just how far will you go?" Would he kill someone? Nico had been on the other side of things for two years now. Had he sacrificed his moral compass in his drive to meet the end goal?

"To take down the most ruthless criminal I've seen in my lifetime?" Given Nico's history with the DEA and working deep undercover, that was saying a lot. "I'll do what it takes." He shrugged. "Switching computer programs and rigging a power outage at just the right moment is child's play." His dark gaze met Einstein's. "Besides, I'm quite sure your boss survived a little over-dramatic name-calling."

"And the implication of this game?" Einstein pressed. "A ticking time bomb with a countdown clock? What the hell, man? Is he planning to kill Damian?"

"What do you think?"

"And you'll sit back and let that happen?"

"Of course not. If anything, seeing this slideshow should help you guys figure out what's going through this asshole's head. And cooperating with his little pet project might actually help me get to him before he succeeds. The Charmer wants Damian to rectify these wrongs."

"Perceived wrongs," Einstein corrected.

"Whatever. We all have secrets in our past. Figure out your boss's and you'll figure out why the Charmer's obsessed with Damian Manchester."

CHAPTER 6

T he inside of All Saints Church was warm and dark, the rolling blackouts hitting the Kenilworth neighborhood fifteen miles north of Chicago even at nine on a Tuesday morning. But the sunlight filtered through the stained glass, casting slices of color about the pews and across the walls. Damian often came here when he needed to regroup.

He rose from the kneeler after reciting the same series of prayers he'd said for decades. Maybe one of these days God would hear him and deliver the Charmer into his hands—preferably within the next two days.

What the hell had the killer meant by *the game has begun?* Begun, how? With Mariah's abduction? But the clock hadn't started counting down until the slideshow was over. What the hell was supposed to happen in the next—he glanced at his watch—fifty-nine hours?

He exited the church and crossed the street to the cemetery, a journey he'd made so many times he could walk it blindfolded. In the far left corner, a towering oak stretched a long, thick branch over Samantha's grave like a protective arm. Not a leaf moved in the still air. It seemed the heat was going to build to an inferno again today, without the benefit of even a slight breeze.

He rounded a tall headstone and a wave of shock hit him as his brain struggled to realize what it was seeing. In the middle of summer, Sam's grave was blanketed in white. He hurried forward, his throat tightening and his heart speeding up with each step. He dropped to his knees and scooped up two handfuls of pristine white rose petals. Ripped from the flowers that had fostered them and pungent with perfume, they covered her entire grave.

He stilled when he saw the butterflies. They were real—or they had been. Eleven of them, pinned among the flowers with hatpin-like skewers. *Dear God.* The symbolic desecration of such innocent creatures twisted his stomach.

There was only one person he could think of who would do this—the Charmer.

His fist closed. His nostrils flared as he breathed deeply and slowly, trying to temper the explosion building within. He clamped his teeth together tightly to subdue the roar that ached for release. The ache had been building for over twenty years, and soon it would find relief.

In a little over fifty-eight hours, he'd face down the Charmer and this would end, no matter what.

THE SSAM OFFICES WEREN'T WHAT ABBY WOULD HAVE EXPECTED from the tiny downstairs lobby. The elevator doors opened at the fifth floor, revealing glass doors etched with the agency's name. Beyond them, warm leather chairs and cold marble floors presented an impression of calm confidence.

Catherine finished a phone call and looked up from behind the receptionist counter to greet her with a warm smile. "Good to see you. Einstein told me to expect you. I also heard about..."

"About the psychometry?"

"Yes."

Abby wondered if Einstein would also be glad she'd come, or if, after he'd had a night to think things over, she'd be given the same cold brush-off she'd had from authorities before. It would be even more disappointing coming from him. And what would the others think? Maggie had been understanding, but Catherine had just learned of Abby's abilities.

"I heard you might be able to use your gift to help Mariah," Catherine said.

Gift. Abby wasn't so sure she'd label it as something beneficial. Not yet, anyway. "I hope so. But sometimes I'm wrong." She steeled her backbone, surprised when Catherine came around the counter and embraced her. Most people avoided touching after they knew the truth about her.

"I think it's fabulous," Catherine said as she pulled away. "Can I get you anything? I have tea and coffee brewing in the back."

"I'll take some tea." She wasn't thirsty, but Catherine's departure would give Abby a chance to collect her thoughts. Catherine's touch had evoked a strong sense of security and being right with the world. Of happiness. It had also elicited a breath of scent, a sweet newborn baby smell. Did Catherine even know yet that she was pregnant?

"Have a seat. I'll be right back." The tall, slender, not yet obviously pregnant woman hurried away.

Abby sank into a chair, closed her eyes and did some deep breathing to relax, pressing her hands to her abdomen to feel her belly rise and fall.

"Are you getting a message?"

Her eyes shot open. Einstein stood at SSAM's front door, holding two coffee cups from the shop across the street, looking bemused.

"What?" she asked. He moved closer and the aroma of coffee and—*holy cow, he'd remembered*—hazelnut mocha warmed her senses.

He handed her a cup. "I'm honestly curious. I'm not trying to be a smartass."

"This time," she mumbled. He grinned and she couldn't help smiling back. She pushed to her feet, uncomfortable with him towering over her. "I was just taking a moment to gather my thoughts."

Catherine returned with her tea and eyed the cup in Abby's hand as well as the one Einstein carried. She smiled. "I see you've got her covered. How thoughtful."

"Let's go on back," Einstein said hastily, his ears turning red as he strode ahead of her.

"Damian called to say he'll be here in twenty," Catherine called after him.

Abby followed Einstein as he pressed his palm to a security panel beside a door, just to the left of the reception area. "You have a meeting?" she asked.

He pushed the door open and held it for her, then led her down the hall past a series of closed doors. "To work on figuring out the meaning of the slideshow, discuss whether the Charmer took Mariah—"

"He did—"

"And, if so, where he took her," he continued without missing a beat. "Among other things." He stopped and turned back to her, brows arched. "Which door shall we go through?"

"A test?" She resisted the urge to turn on her heel and leave. "Or maybe you don't understand psychometry and clairsentience. It doesn't work that way."

"Enlighten me." Again, she sensed more honest curiosity from him than judgment. Maybe he really didn't understand. Maybe he really wanted to.

"It's hard to explain, especially using statistics you'd respect." She walked past him and into the office on the left. Spying his stunned expression, she rolled her eyes. "I didn't sense this was your office. The *I heart caffeine* sticker on the door is a dead giveaway."

He grunted. "Max put that there."

His office was small, dominated by a television and two computer screens. There wasn't a personal item in sight. Apparently, Einstein was all business when he was at work. Was his home life any different? She'd seen glimpses of humor and personality over the past few weeks, but maybe computers really were his life. Judging by the scattered energy drink carcasses littering his desk, maybe he didn't have a home.

He set his cup on the desk and, following her gaze, knocked the three cans into the trash with one sweep of his arm. "Long night."

"Did you even go home?" she asked, eyeing him. He'd changed into a new T-shirt and a different pair of jeans. She was sad to see the tux go, not that it really mattered. He still looked delicious.

"I showered and changed," he said evasively. He gestured to her to take a seat near the desk. He turned on the three computer screens that filled his desk and a side table. Each varied in size and content. One was set to a news channel. Another appeared to be...*holy hell, was that a live satellite image?* The third was the slideshow from the dinner last night.

Einstein tapped a button on the keyboard and two fluffy gray cats with long white whiskers replaced all three images. She wouldn't have pegged him as a cat person. Then again, he was sleek and quietly dangerous, and she sometimes felt like a mouse under his probing gaze.

"My neighbor moved and left his cats behind," he explained, quickly pressing more buttons to get rid of the screensaver. "Everyone in the building feeds Em and CeeCee."

"E equals MC squared. Einstein's famous mass-energy equation?" She laughed and he glanced at her in surprise.

He grinned. "Guess I'm not as innovative as I thought."

"I thought they were your neighbor's cats."

"His castoffs. Not fair to let them wander nameless and homeless. They didn't deserve that." His vehemence took her aback. Then he shrugged. "I give them the occasional table scrap."

"Uh-huh. And you just decided to take their picture and make them your screensaver."

"Back to you. What could you tell about me?" The suspicion was clear in his gaze.

I can tell you care about outcasts who need a home. Did he feel like an outsider? "By looking at you and your office?"

"By touching me."

Her skin flushed warm. "Not much."

"But something?"

Unable to hold up against the intensity in his eyes, she looked away. Somehow, she didn't think he'd appreciate the images she'd picked up when he'd touched her at the coffee shop, or the ones while they'd waited for the lights to come back on last night. Intense grief was a private affair.

"If you touched me right now, could you read me?"

Her gaze shot back to him and his body went still, as if anticipating exactly that. If she leaned forward in her chair, she could reach him. Her fingertips twitched, wanting to consciously give her gift a try for the first time in years, but she resisted, tucking her hands together in front of her.

She shrugged as if it were no big deal. "I might get flashes of what you're thinking or feeling."

Or dead women you'd been thinking about or had murdered.

"I don't always get messages," she explained. "And when I do they can be difficult to interpret. It's hard to explain, but certain objects might call to me, or I get the sense they have a story. If I touch them, I might get one or two sensory impulses. A sound, a sight. Maybe a smell. It's often like a puzzle. I'll get pieces that may not even look like they fit with the overall picture, but somehow, they do."

"And you got pieces of insight from the bracelet," he said.

"Several of them. Very strong messages, in fact. There was a lot

of emotion tied to that bracelet. These girls were abducted, frightened and brutally murdered while wearing those charms." Her
upper arm hurt again and she rubbed it. His eyes followed the
motion.

"What's wrong?"

"When I think of them, I get a burning sensation on my arm."

"Describe it."

"It feels like a cigar burn, or a ring seared into my skin. Right
here." She tipped her head toward her arm.

His mouth tightened.

"What?"

"The Circle—the organization we believe responsible for
taking these girls and others to sell via the human flesh trade—
brands all of its victims with their symbol. Most of the Charmer's
victims are only skeletal remains by the time we recover them, but
the Charmer's most recent victim was found just hours after her
death and she bore the brand."

"The Circle? An *organization* is responsible for the deaths of
these girls?" That didn't feel right. She'd definitely had the sense of
one man perpetrating all the murders.

"The identity of the man in charge of the Circle remains a
mystery, but there he's known as Boss. He uses his organization as
a cover for his serial killing and other illegal activities. The authorities labeled him the Charmer years ago, for the charms he leaves
with each body, though the press believes it's because of the way
he lures the girls. They don't know about his connection to the
Circle, either."

"What was the branded image like?" She'd pictured a circle, hot
and orange. "Is it a flaming circle?"

His eyes widened, and then narrowed. "Anyone with a connection to law enforcement could have researched that information."
So, they were back to distrusting her abilities. She scowled and he
quickly backpedaled. "I'm sorry. It's in my nature to play devil's
advocate."

"Happens all the time." And it hurt a little every time.

"From what I read, psychometry can be developed, like any other skill."

He'd done some research? That pulled a reluctant smile from her. "It can be. And I had been working on honing it, until college."

"But you stopped?"

"I was…discouraged."

He frowned. "By someone in particular? Did you get a lot of that?"

Uncomfortable with her past failures, she looked to change the subject. "How about you? Were you always a mindhunter?" She'd done her own research on SSAM after he'd left her at her apartment last night.

"Actually, the mindhunting is for those better trained in the psychology of the human brain. I do the statistical analysis, information gathering and cyber-hunting to fill in the gaps for the mindhunters as they profile the killers."

Abby wondered if she'd get a peek at the Charmer's profile today—and how close it would come to her impressions of the man.

"And no, I didn't always do this," he added. "I was in the Navy. A SEAL." That explained how his body had the look and posture of a seasoned warrior.

"Maggie told me."

His gaze clouded for a moment. "When I left the SEALs, I called Damian. I'd heard of SSAM. I liked their mission."

"And accepted it as your own."

He smiled. "They do good work. I'm proud to put killers behind bars." How could she ever have thought this man could be a killer himself? He was so obviously on the right side of the law. But he was also rigid in his devotion to the gods of data and technology.

She reached into her purse and pulled out the thumb drive that held the information he'd requested. "I talked to the director of the studio and she cleared me to share the student roster with you to find the bracelet's owner—as long as we don't antagonize her students or mention how we got the information. She didn't recall seeing anyone with the bracelet yesterday, and nobody asked about the lost and found box, but all of the students know it's there."

"That's okay. With the rosters, I should be able to track down the bracelet owner by—"

Damian stopped in the doorway, his expression grim. "My office. Abby, too." He disappeared down the hallway.

Abby tucked the thumb drive back into her purse. "Is he always that intense?"

Einstein was gazing intently at the empty doorway. "I'm guessing there's been a development." He stood and grabbed his laptop.

She followed him to a door at the end of the hall. Inside, Damian sat behind his desk, and a dark-haired woman with exotic features and the legs of a supermodel rose from a chair to greet them.

"I'm Lorena Castro."

Cool confidence was the impression Abby got as she shook her hand. "Pleased to meet you."

They all took seats as an agitated Damian spoke. "The Charmer covered Sam's grave with rose petals. White ones."

Confused, Abby looked to Einstein for an explanation. "Damian brings white roses to his daughter's grave every weekend." He glanced at Damian. "But today is Tuesday."

"Not my normal routine, but after the dinner last night I wanted to regain some sense of peace. The Charmer must have guessed I'd go there." He passed his cell phone to Einstein. It was cued up to a picture.

Beside her, Einstein stiffened. "This is more than a few roses. And are those butterflies?"

"Eleven of them."

Einstein cursed. "Why didn't you ask one of us to go with you?"

"I needed the space." And he probably hadn't expected someone to violate his daughter's grave. Abby's heart ached for the man. "Noah's got his people scouring the area for clues."

"It had to have been done recently," Einstein said. "These look fresh and it's hot as hell out there."

Damian nodded. "There wasn't anyone around, that I saw."

"And when he returned to the parking lot, this was on Damian's car." Lorena passed them a Ziploc that contained what looked like a thank-you note opened and laid out flat so the inside was visible. "It was originally in an envelope, which the police are already processing. We'll pass this along to our own forensics team."

The first reckoning comes today. Your life will be ending as Mariah's is just beginning. She'll be the next butterfly to emerge and be set free, wholesome and out of your reach.

"So what part of this is the game?" Einstein asked, passing the note back to Lorena. "What does he expect you to do?"

Damian frowned. "I'm about to pay a visit to the Pierces and see if they can shed any light on how Mariah's life might be just beginning. That's the only move I can think of." He looked weary but pushed away from the desk and rose.

"See if they'll let me look at Mariah's computer," Einstein said, standing.

"You can ask them yourself." Damian's gaze shifted to Abby. "I want you both to come."

"Why Abby?"

"It's worth a try," Damian said. "I don't care how we find a lead, as long as we find Mariah alive. We're not going to lose another girl to the Charmer."

WHEN SHE REALIZED THE SSAM TEAM TRULY THOUGHT SHE COULD be of help to Mariah, Abby agreed to cancel her yoga classes for the day and focus her energy on the case—on one condition. She'd asked Einstein if they could go by the North Shore mall on the way to the Pierce home.

His fingers went to her elbow to guide her around a group of teens who came toward them without shifting to the side. He barely touched her, immediately dropping his hand and returning his attention to surveying their surroundings. She pretended not to notice, but wondered if he was afraid of what she'd *read* from him.

"Guess they're looking for a place to cool off," she said.

He glanced back at the teens. "And burn off restless energy. At that age, I would have done anything to get out of the house."

"Too chaotic?"

"Too quiet." The tersely spoken words seemed to hide a world of hurt. He guided her to a courtyard with a cluster of tables surrounding a large fountain. "This was the last place Mrs. Pierce saw Mariah."

"No surveillance in the parking lot?"

"None that showed Mariah leaving. Noah went over it with a fine-toothed comb. There is one exit near the rear of the mall that isn't monitored. We're guessing the Charmer lured her out that way."

She surveyed their surroundings. "It's a central location. I would think she'd be noticed if she screamed or fought someone off. Guess he's charming in more ways than one, if he could get her to come with him without a struggle."

"That's how he got his name, actually. The public doesn't know about the various charms. Which makes it all the more fascinating that you say you found a charm bracelet. We suspect his victims knew him."

"How?"

"Working on that."

"Those algorithms?" A smile tickled her lips. Einstein and his magnificent techie skills.

He gave her an answering grin. "Something like that. Unfortunately, I'm not sure what you can do here, but there might be something *I* can do at Mariah's house."

"Sometimes an object kind of...calls to me, but I'm not picking up anything at the moment. Do you know where Sam disappeared from?"

"Just that it was this same mall. No video surveillance back then, and the stores were different."

"Then let's move on to Mariah's house."

A few minutes later, they were parked in front of a well-manicured upper class home with Spanish arches. The walls were gleaming white, nearly blinding them as they reflected the midday sun.

Lorena met them at the door. She and Damian had arrived a half hour earlier. "There have been no calls to the tip line," she said. "Damian's been consoling them."

Einstein stepped over the threshold. "Is he getting anything they wouldn't tell the police?"

"They admit Mariah's behavior had changed recently and she'd become more secretive and combative, especially toward her father. She was active on social media but they can't get past her passwords."

"If they're willing to let me have a crack at her computer, I think I can find additional information."

Lorena led them to the living room and introduced Phillip and Rowena Pierce.

"You're the psychic?" Rowena's eyes glowed with excitement as they locked on to Abby. "Damian mentioned he might have a secret weapon the police didn't have."

"I'll do what I can—" Abby began. Her words fell away as the woman grabbed her up in a fierce hug. Her throat had constricted, choking off what she'd planned to say. With Rowena's embrace, intense desperation warred with hope and threatened to suck the breath from her lungs.

"I'm Andrew MacKenzie." Einstein must have sensed Abby's

distress because he stepped forward, forcing the woman to break the embrace so she could politely shake his hand.

But Rowena's hope wouldn't be denied and she quickly turned back to Abby. "Damian said *you* contacted *them* after the news about Mariah." Rowena's voice broke on her daughter's name. "You must know something. Please, can you tell us where our daughter is?"

"She'll try her best." Einstein spoke for her, rescuing her again. "If you wouldn't mind letting us look around your daughter's room and search her computer, we'll see what we can find."

PHILLIP PIERCE LED THEM TO MARIAH'S ROOM. EINSTEIN immediately moved to the typical teenage girl's desk, complete with photo board on the wall displaying a myriad of friends and social activities, and opened a laptop with a pink leopard-print case and stickers proclaiming Wildcats Cheer.

"You tried calling her cell phone, I assume," Einstein said as Phillip watched over his shoulder. It might be better if the man weren't here to see what secrets his daughter might be hiding, but how could he ask the distressed father to leave?

"They tried tracking it." Phillip's eyes were haunted with grief. "She never went anywhere without the damn thing, but it didn't matter. The police found it in a dumpster behind the mall."

Einstein perused the posters on the wall and the corkboard full of pictures and turned to Abby. "Any vibes about her password?"

"Can't you just do what you do and hack in?"

He arched a brow at her belligerent tone. "Probably, but it would take longer."

She picked up a few items from a bookshelf, then examined Mariah's pictures as he had and listed off activities she'd been involved in. Einstein shook his head. "Too common. I'd say the name of her best friend. Or a boyfriend."

"No boyfriends," Phillip said. "We had a rule about no dating before sixteen."

Einstein bit his tongue against his reply. Just because she couldn't publicly go out with a boy didn't mean Mariah had avoided involvement with the opposite sex. "If not a boy's name, then something else meaningful?"

He followed Abby's gaze to a photo of Mariah with her friends at what appeared to be a summer cheer camp. The smiling girls were gathered around a carved wooden signpost. "Camp Spirit."

"Spirit?" He typed and hit enter. Mariah's social accounts were now active on the screen. He clicked on the private message history. "You get that insight from touching something?"

"Just instinct and powers of deduction. Like you," she added.

"That's amazing," Phillip said. "Why didn't I think of that?"

"It's sometimes hard for parents to see things from their kids' perspectives," Einstein said without looking up from the screen. "Some parents don't have a clue what's important to their children."

Beside him, Abby went still. "And sometimes parents are too close to their kids to see beyond the little girl she once was," she said in a soft voice.

Shit. He realized too late how harsh his words must have sounded. He'd let his inner cynic out of the box.

Phillip nodded solemnly and turned to leave. "Let me know if you find anything."

Once alone, Abby flicked her pointer finger against Einstein's ear, surprising him. "Ow!" He ducked away and sent her a glare. "What was that for?"

"You're so wrapped up in yourself that you have no clue what your words do to other people, do you?"

"I'm trying to find his daughter."

She cocked her head at him as if trying to figure him out. And damn, was that sympathy in her eyes? "Do you blame him for what happened to Mariah?"

He returned his attention to his work. "Not if he's the type of father who's there for his kid."

"Does this have something to do with your own parents?"

"Drop it, Abby. Stick to what you know and don't try to analyze me."

"What did they do to you?" Her voice had taken on a soft quality that was as effective as a punch in the chest. Damn. He'd dealt with his past long ago. There was no need to dredge it up now.

"Nothing." Which was, in effect, true. He gestured to the screen, dispelling the intensity of the moment and distracting her from probing further. "Looks like someone set up a meeting with Mariah at the mall for yesterday afternoon."

She bent closer to read the series of emails. "The Charmer."

"He even used *Prince Charming* in his email address. But his profile is nearly empty. Generic pic of flames. No description." He scrolled upward. "But he's been contacting Mariah via private messages for weeks." He read bits and pieces. "*If you were mine, I'd show you every day how important you are, how a family should be. It's the little things that matter. Everyone deserves a new start.* A bit on the cheesy side, but effective."

"He was acting like her boyfriend?"

"Or her father. He probably cyber-stalked her until he figured out what she thought she needed in her life."

"And then he became that. Diabolical. Can you figure out who or where he is?"

Einstein spent a few minutes clicking away at the keyboard, before leaning back in his chair. He muttered an expletive.

"That doesn't sound good."

"He knows how to cover his tracks. Lucky for us, I know how to keep digging, but I'll need to get back to the office." He closed the computer and stood.

The sound of a commotion from outside lured them to Mariah's window. The Pierces were on the front lawn with Damian and

Lorena, facing off with a reporter. Einstein hurried from the room with Abby on his heels. He stepped out onto the front porch as a cameraman joined the reporter and aimed his camera at the house. Operating on reflex, he reached to push Abby behind his back, but it was too late.

"Is this her? Is this the psychic?" The reporter hurried forward and thrust a microphone toward them.

"She's going to help us find Mariah," Rowena Pierce said. "Abby Rhodes is our secret weapon."

"How are you going to do this, Miss Rhodes?" the reporter asked.

Abby's eyes widened. Damn, he wished they hadn't released her name. His muscles tightened with the need to scoop her up and run, to take her somewhere safe.

Damian stepped forward and spoke up, drawing the attention to himself. "We're not sure she'll be able to help, but we're trying everything." He looked straight into the camera. "I want the Charmer to know we're coming after him, and this isn't a game to us. He *will* pay for what he's done."

As the reporter began shooting rapid-fire questions at them, a dark sedan parked at the curb. Two men in suits emerged and wove their way between the cameraman and reporter. Sensing a potential threat, Lorena and Einstein closed ranks, shifting closer to Damian. Einstein gripped Abby's hand, tugging her along with him.

"Mr. Damian Manchester?" the dark-haired one said. His gaze moved over the assembled group, uncaring that a camera and microphone were now pointed their way.

Damian nodded. "That's me."

The man flashed a badge. "FBI. You need to come with us."

CHAPTER 7

"Any word from them?" Abby asked as she caught Einstein covertly checking his cell phone for text messages while they waited at a red light.

"No." He gripped the steering wheel so tightly she thought it might bend.

"I'm sure the FBI just wants to talk to him."

"They could have picked a better time to haul him off. Jesus. The cameras were rolling. He'll be all over the news."

"Lorena will let you know if there's anything we can do, right?" Lorena had followed the FBI agents in the car she and Damian had driven to the Pierce home. The look of anger and concern in her eyes told Abby she'd do what it took to protect her employer. Just as Einstein had tried to protect Abby when the reporters had focused on her. Her heart warmed at the memory.

"Yes, she'll contact me if they need me." Clearly, though, it didn't sit well with Einstein to be out of the loop.

"What would Damian want you to do in the meantime?"

"Stay the course. He told me to get into Mariah's laptop and track down the Charmer." A grin tugged at his lips as he cast her a sideways glance. "Are you applying some yoga techniques on me or something? Relaxation via reasonable thinking?"

She snorted. "Hardly. I'm using the methods I'd use with my kindergartners—follow the directions unless the teacher tells you otherwise."

His laughter filled the car, warming her heart. He cast her another quick look. "I bet your students are crazy about you."

Her heart slid a little further down that slippery slope. She sighed. "It won't matter once my boss and my kids' parents see the news. They'll be demanding my resignation by morning."

"It'll be okay." Einstein's words rang hollow, but she clung to them. At least he'd gotten her out of there before any more damage could be done. "People can't help but see that you're a good person. You mean well, and I'm sure you're great with the kids."

She loved being a teacher. She only hoped this lawsuit wouldn't rip the rug out from under her feet, leaving her floundering.

Einstein's phone rang and he put it on speaker. "Hey, Noah."

"Damian asked that I make it possible for you and somebody named Abby to see—or rather, feel—the evidence from Sam's crime scene. Said she had some kind of sixth sense he wanted to try."

"He did?" Einstein frowned. "He must not have had the chance to tell me."

"I can make that happen if you can make it to the station within the next twenty minutes."

Einstein glanced at Abby. She wasn't sure she wanted the opportunity to dig further into this case. But Mariah needed her. She nodded.

"We're headed there now," Einstein said.

Ten minutes later, Abby brushed her clammy palms along the seams of her skirt and licked her dry lips. Being at the police station brought back bad memories.

Einstein took the seat next to her in the depressingly outdated waiting area. "Noah's a good guy and a damn good detective. He's open-minded enough to give this a try."

Unlike you? She bit the inside of her cheek to keep from questioning Einstein's faith in her. Though he'd occasionally reached out and touched her in gestures of comfort, they were always brief, and when he wasn't caught up in events, he went out of his way to avoid contact. She sensed an inner conflict raged.

He had a right to his reservations—just as she had a right to be skeptical that he could protect her from the media, the Charmer, or from her own fear and self-doubt, no matter how much he wanted to. Touching some stranger's bracelet was one thing. Touching objects that were known to be associated with the death of a young, vibrant girl? The emotions connected to anything from the scene could be a thousand times more intense.

As they waited for Detective Crandall to emerge from somewhere within the police station and escort them to the evidence locker, Abby was careful not to touch the surface of the chair, aware that any number of horrific stories could be waiting at the brush of a fingertip.

Even as her stomach rumbled with a reminder that she'd skipped lunch, she was glad she'd said no to Einstein's offer to pick something up on the way. She wanted to get this over with. Einstein was quietly studying her, his hazel eyes filled with unspoken questions.

"Are you mentally dissecting me?" She was unable to keep the defensive note from her voice.

"What?"

"The best way to understand something is to take it apart and study each piece. Isn't that what you scientist types believe?"

One corner of his mouth kicked upward. "*Scientist types?*"

"Your name *is* Einstein, right? I'm guessing it's not because of your hairstyle." No, his hair was thick and brown, not crazy-messed-up, scraggly gray like the images she remembered of Albert Einstein.

Nor did she remember Albert having the kind of sculpted biceps currently peeking out from beneath Einstein's *beam me up* T-shirt.

Einstein pinned her with a look. "I believe what I can see, hear, smell, feel or taste." She hid a shiver as her body ignored the argument behind his statement—the argument *against* her gift. "I make no apology for that," he said. "And I don't want to call you a liar."

"But you believe I might be."

"I'm usually pretty good at reading people, and I think you're a good person and that *you* believe you can help."

"Gee, thanks. That's a resounding endorsement if ever I heard one."

He ignored her sarcasm. "Why did you react so strangely to me when we ran into each other at the coffeehouse yesterday?"

She froze. "I wasn't aware you'd noticed that."

"I did." He probably noticed a lot more of his surroundings than people gave him credit for.

"You might be more intuitive than you realize."

"Or maybe I'm more in tune to *you*."

What was she supposed to make of *that* statement? But before she could go down that path with her questions, he prodded her to answer his original one. "What did you sense when my hand brushed yours? It had to be something. The look in your eyes was...shock."

She swallowed hard at the memory. "I saw the girls. The murder victims." She had to stop thinking of them as *her* girls. If she didn't find some distance, this case would crush her. "When I touched you, they flashed through my mind. All of them, one at a time. Just like when I touched the bracelet. I thought, maybe, you were linked to their deaths."

He huffed out a humorless laugh. "That just goes to show that my scientific methods are more reliable, because I'm *not* the Charmer."

"I know that. *Now*," she muttered. "You wouldn't kill anyone."

His gaze slid to hers. "I never said I hadn't killed anyone."

Shocked, her jaw dropped just as someone called out to him.

"Einstein." A tall man with sandy-blond hair and a boy-next-door smile hurried over to them and shook her hand as Einstein introduced her. Detective Noah Crandall. His suit jacket was missing and his tie was askew as if he'd already put in several hours.

"How's the investigation going?" Einstein asked as Noah led them onto an elevator and pushed B.

"We've interviewed Mariah's family and closest friends. Rolling blackouts hit us this morning for about an hour before the chief cracked some skulls and reminded the power company that certain facilities are not to be tampered with. Can you imagine what could happen in the city if word got out that emergency services couldn't perform business as usual?"

"Chaos," Einstein said.

Would her grandfather be okay in his apartment without electricity? The blackout schedule had indicated his neighborhood would be powerless later that afternoon. Frustration gnawed at her. If only he'd let her move him to a hospital or even to one of the temporary shelters set up around town, she wouldn't have to worry.

"Dungeon's this way." Noah led them off the elevator and down a darkened hallway. He glanced over his shoulder. "That's what we call the evidence locker in this building. At least it's cooler down here."

"Don't worry," Einstein leaned down and said in her ear, outside of Noah's hearing. "I only killed those who deserved it, and only while serving my country." When she looked up at him in confusion, he frowned. "You seemed preoccupied. I thought it was related to what I said before Noah appeared."

"Actually, I'm worried about my grandfather. The blackouts might hit him hard." The heat had already been blamed for a few deaths among the sick and elderly. Grandpa was both.

"We can check on him if it'll make you feel better."

Something inside her shifted and fell away. Maybe having his support would lighten her load, even if for only a short while.

Ahead of them, Noah pushed through a windowless door and they entered a room with an ancient gunmetal-gray table and chairs. "You guys wait here." After he left, Abby blew out a breath and slid into a chair.

Einstein sat across from her, leaning forward with his elbows on the table as his eyes searched hers. "Is it hard on you?"

"What?" Her foot swung from side to side, unable to contain all the nervous energy coursing through her system. Soon, she'd have to let her barricades down and let in the darkness of murder.

"Is it difficult, emotionally or physically, to receive the messages?"

"It depends." Part of her was already preparing for what was in store. Opening up to the messages without losing a part of herself would take focus and willpower—things she wasn't sure she had a grasp on right now. Remembering something she *could* grasp, she slid one hand into her purse and removed the hematite touch-stone. She gripped it under the table.

"Psychometry is just another way of being connected to the world. However, those connections lead to things most people don't see or feel on a daily basis. The things I experienced after touching the bracelet were supercharged. Those girls went through so much." She stopped, her chest suddenly tight with remembered pain.

Einstein reached across the table to take her free hand and brushed his thumb across her knuckles. He let go as the door opened.

"Look who I found." Noah entered the room with a box and set it on the table. Behind him, Damian and Lorena entered and joined them around the table.

"Everything okay?" Einstein asked, his gaze assessing as it swept over the pair.

Damian nodded but avoided eye contact. "The FBI had questions. I wasn't going to give them answers without a lawyer. They didn't have anything to hold me on." It was a condensed version, and Einstein's mouth tightened with frustration but he didn't press for more. "What did you two find?"

"Mariah's social accounts show someone set up a meeting with her at the mall."

"The Charmer?"

"Yes, but I'll need to get back to SSAM to search her computer for more information."

"Abby?" Damian's gaze swung to her.

She shook her head. "I didn't pick up on anything other than a normal teenager with typical teenage issues, but I didn't have much time."

"Because we were interrupted." Damian's gaze became hooded again. His skin was tight and pale with exhaustion and worry. *What had happened with the FBI?* Suddenly, he straightened and gestured to the box. "Let's make up for lost time, shall we?"

Noah cleared his throat. "Right. Here's what we have from the scene where Sam's remains were recovered." He cast a concerned gaze toward Damian, whose gaze was glued to the box, his mouth set in a hard line. "Of course, there were ten other victims."

"This is a good start," Lorena said. "We just want to see if Abby can get any additional information."

As everyone's attention swung back to her, Abby gripped the stone tighter under the table, hoping her mother's spirit or God or whoever was listening would help her generate something useful. She dropped the stone back into her purse and reached for Sam's box. She lifted the lid and examined the contents. Everything was in plastic or paper bags. One held several scraps of faded pink with dirt smudges. The remnants of a shirt, she realized. She studiously avoided looking at Damian, but her thoughts were on him and the wall of pain surrounding him. She continued sifting through, spying a baggie with an earring in the shape of a butterfly made of gemstones—opals for the wings and a tiny pink stone for the body. Her hand stilled as she spied the bag with a charm. It was a perfect match to the one on the bracelet, the one with a butterfly stamped on it.

"Are these common?" she asked, picking it up.

Einstein glanced at the bag. "We haven't found anything exactly like them and there's no stamp on the back identifying the jeweler."

"This looks exactly like one of the charms on the bracelet." The object seemed to warm, even through the thin plastic shield. "May I?" she asked Noah.

He nodded. "All of this has been processed thoroughly over the years. You may touch it as long as it stays in my sight."

After a fortifying breath, she opened the bag and dumped the charm into her palm. The size and color of a nickel, the surface was etched with the image of a butterfly elegantly perched on a branch above the cocoon from which it had emerged. She closed her palm around the piece and shut her eyes to focus, shutting out everyone else.

Behind her eyelids, she let the picture emerge. A trio of butterflies fluttered, their wings beating the air. She could feel it tickling her face. Their cocoons glowed golden. Her shoulder burned hot and she let out a soft moan as her eyes flicked open. She dropped the charm and it clattered against the tabletop.

"Are you okay?" Einstein was perfectly still, as if he hadn't moved the whole time.

"You can breathe. It won't disrupt the vision."

"So...it worked? You saw something?"

She nodded. "Three. The Charmer had three charms of each imprint made. He has the girls wear all three until he kills them and then he distributes the charms. One to leave on the girls, one to put on that charm bracelet—"

"And one for himself," Damian guessed. "Son of a bitch. He *does* like to keep trophies."

Lorena's wheels seemed to be turning as well. "If we can find where he stashes them..."

"Shelves," Abby said. "At least, that's how I saw the girls' pictures for the first time."

She reached for the Ziploc with the lone earring and slid the piece of jewelry onto her palm. Despair hit her like a battering ram, pulverizing the last of her barriers. Instead of the warmth she expected from the metal as she squeezed it, the cold deepened. Bone-deep frigid. And it flooded over her skin, from the waist upward like a wave washing over her. She gasped as her head was plunged backward and the cold reached her lips. Her lungs seized for a moment before she disconnected from the message. She blinked Damian's image into focus. "Did Sam drown?"

Einstein's gaze went to Noah, Damian, and then Lorena. Some unspoken communication passed among them.

"What?" she asked, irritated when the silence stretched on. "I get the sensation of suffocating in water...cold water."

"We're not sure," Damian finally said. "The coroner found water in the latest victim's lungs, though her body was dumped miles from any significant water source. None of the other bodies were found near water."

"The water's important," Abby said with certainty. "It's part of the need that drives him."

"Can you figure out how it's part of his ritual?" Lorena asked, leaning forward.

"I'll try." She closed her hand around the earring, knowing she needed to go deeper. To get every drop of information she could share with Einstein and the SSAM team. *Talk to me, Sam.* Her eyes slid closed. "No fear at first. A black car with a driver. She climbs inside without a qualm, even after the man flashes gold teeth at her."

As if from a distance, Abby heard Einstein whisper to the others. "Gold teeth? Could be Tony Moreno."

"She went with him willingly?" Damian's voice was shocked.

Squeezing out the real world, she continued to dive inward. "Familiar surroundings. Safe, cherished. A man hands her a necklace with three identical charms on it, reaches around her to secure it. He's asking her to trust him. It's only after...after they leave and pass her home that she feels alarmed. Betrayed. He sticks a needle in her neck and then everything goes dark." Abby shook her head to move past that blackness. "When she wakes up, she's in a cell. It smells like a basement. My shoulder hurts, burns."

"*You're* Sam now?" Einstein's question came from far away, as if an invisible wall separated them. Or a cell made of stone on three sides and a large iron door with one tiny, horizontal slit for a window. Abby didn't respond, didn't want to break the connection. Sam deserved to tell her story, even if Abby had to surrender herself to be the conduit.

"This isn't what I wanted," she said. "I can't be what he wants. Now I'm on a shore. A lake. No, smaller. A pond. The grit and mud presses into my knees. I'm shivering so badly my teeth are chattering and it's dark except for the moonlight. He presses his palm to the charms on the necklace, so hard it hurts my chest. I hate it. Hate the charms, hate him. I want to go home."

"Can you hear what he's saying?" Einstein asked.

"He's behind me, chanting. I don't like it. I'm scared and so cold. I trusted him. The sick bastard is going to kill me. He's pulling me toward the water, but I can't resist. Can't lift my arms."

A scream filled the room, but that wasn't right. The drugs made Sam's muscles weak and kept her from reacting. Some part of Abby knew it had come from her own throat.

Another scream. She couldn't stop. One after the other, they pierced the silence.

Two arms came around her like steel bands and a familiar voice spoke beside her ear.

"Come out of it, Abby. Come back to me. Shhh." *Einstein.*

Abby gasped for air as she returned to herself. Her nostrils flared and she inhaled deeply of Einstein, his unique masculine

scent with a hint of musky sweat. His warmth replaced the sensation of cold. It was intoxicating and reorienting at the same time.
She took a minute to steady herself, focusing on the long, smooth
strokes of Einstein's hand, up and down her spine.

Across from them, Lorena sent Damian a concerned gaze. The
man looked even more miserable. She looked up in surprise when
Noah entered the room with a can of soda and handed it to her.
She hadn't even heard him leave.

"Is it always like that?" Lorena asked.

"No." She took a deep swallow of the fizzy soda and, regret-
tably, Einstein shifted away. "It depends on the connection
between the victim and the object. Sam must have gone through
hell while she wore this." She fingered the earring, shuddering at
the remembered fear, and then sent an apologetic glance to the
group. "I'm sorry. I know you all have a vested interest in this case.
Did any of what I said make sense?"

"That was...incredible, actually." Einstein shook his head as if
trying to resettle his thoughts.

Noah voiced his agreement. "What you said is consistent with
details that weren't released to the press. The puncture mark in
Tiffany's neck, the water in her lungs. It makes sense that Sam and
the others were killed in a similar way."

"No." Damian's icy interjection had Abby freezing. "Very little
of this makes sense. Sam went willingly with Tony? No," he said
again, fiercely. "He was a street thug for the Circle."

Abby looked to Einstein for an explanation. He cleared his
throat and, after a hesitant look at his angry employer, answered
her silent request. "Before he was killed, a man named Tony
Moreno admitted he'd been hired by the Boss at the Circle to take
Samantha. We hadn't considered that she actually planned to meet
with him, though."

"Because that can't be possible." Damian's eyes were twin flecks
of steel, and pain was etched in every line of his face. "I can't
believe she'd do that. She wouldn't have left us by choice." He

pushed away from the table and strode out of the room. Lorena quickly followed.

"Maybe I should..." Noah's suggestion trailed off awkwardly. He sighed. "You done with this?" At Einstein's nod, Abby handed over the earring and Noah replaced the contents of the box. "I'll return this and check on Damian." When he looked at Abby, his gaze was sympathetic. "Take your time here."

Soon it was just Abby and Einstein and the unbearable quiet. Was he judging her? Was he thinking about Sam or Damian? Was he angry?

"I'm sorry," Abby murmured. "I made things worse." Stomach twisting, she rose on shaky legs. It was best if she went back to her world, where she hid this part of herself. Where she couldn't hurt anybody.

EINSTEIN SNAGGED ABBY'S WRIST BEFORE SHE COULD RUN OFF. SHE had the look of an injured animal seeking a place to hide so she could lick her wounds. And she was much too pale.

He tugged her back into her chair and thrust the soda at her again, then scooted his chair close to look into her eyes, because he sensed she needed him to anchor her in the present. "Hey, you didn't make things worse. We asked you to do this, remember?"

She sucked in a shaky breath. "I didn't mean to upset him."

Incredulous, he tipped up her chin until she met his gaze. "You're worried about Damian?"

"Well, yeah..."

He huffed out a mirthless laugh. Hell, he was worried about his boss, too, but Damian had been through this pain before. The man was in shock, but he'd digest what she'd said and eventually apply it to finding the Charmer. "I'm worried about *you*," Einstein said. "You're the one who had to relive the fear and panic Sam felt." *Christ.*

Abby shook her head. "I'm certain Damian feels that same pain on a daily basis. Why else do you think he created and runs SSAM?"

"True, but you didn't ask to be a part of this. You volunteered your help. I hate to see you hurt." And there was a compulsion deep within him to soothe her. Giving in to impulse, he pressed a kiss to her temple, lingering a moment to breathe deeply of her hair. She wasn't the only one who was feeling shaky. Her screams still echoed in his head. He'd never forget the anguish that had twisted her features. And she'd put herself through that for him. For Sam.

"It's not me who was hurt. It was Sam. And there's a feeling I can't shake... Something that makes what happened to her even worse."

How could it be worse? "What's that?"

Her troubled gaze met his. "Sam knew the guy who took her—not the Tony guy who drove the car but the Charmer. She trusted him."

"So he lured her like he lured the others. We suspected as much."

She shook her head. "No, she really *knew* him. Damian was right—she wouldn't have gone with a man like Tony. The Charmer had known her a long time. He was a family friend."

THE CHARMER GRINNED AS HE WATCHED THE NEWSCAST FOR THE hundredth time, then paused it on his favorite shot—Damian's stoic face as the FBI man flashed his badge.

The careful walls Damian had built would come crumbling down. The man was shocked on the inside. Damian never had been able to tolerate anything but perfection. It was one thing that had made it so easy to lure Sam away.

Being accused of insider trading from his days at Luna Corp would knock the vain man down a few pegs. The FBI would soon be trolling all of his financial records for any hint of impropriety—

everything from the past as well as his precious SSAM agency. Even the Sam Shines nonprofit organization. That would hurt him. It didn't matter that there was no basis for the accusation. The public would turn on Damian as the stigma attached itself to him. The seeds of suspicion and doubt had been cast and his reputation would be in tatters.

The Charmer frowned as he shifted his focus to the two faces behind Damian in the frozen camera shot. He recognized the man as Einstein, the lackey who'd likely sent the virus. He would pay for that. The other face, a woman, was unfamiliar. Her blue-gray eyes were wide. Earlier in the story, the reporter had called her Abby Rhodes and said she was a psychic working with the Pierce family to find Mariah. That could be a problem. He wouldn't have figured Damian the type to trust in the metaphysical. Then again, maybe the man had become desperate. The Charmer would have one of his men look into Abby Rhodes' weaknesses, just in case.

He looked up at a knock on his office door. Only his secretary would interrupt him now, and only for urgent matters. "Come in. What is it?" He didn't hide his irritation as the woman poked her head inside.

"I thought you'd want to know someone stopped by to see you. I sent her away, but she insists you'll want to see her. She said she'll return in a few hours and you'd better be willing to talk."

He arched a brow at the demand. "Who was it?"

"She said she's your daughter."

CHAPTER 8

By the time Abby's color had returned to normal and Einstein escorted her from the evidence room, Damian was long gone. He figured he'd meet up with Damian and Lorena back at SSAM, and a text from Max confirmed it.

Damian's here. What happened? Never seen him so pissed off.

"I'm not sure I should be here." Abby looked miserable as they walked through the parking garage beneath the SSAM building. "I don't think Damian will want to see me. Besides, I don't have anything more to add."

"We still have to find the owner of the bracelet. I'd like you to sketch out a diagram of yesterday's class, just before you found the bracelet. Who was there, where they were located in the studio... and who was the instructor before your class. I'll need to know who was on that roster, as well. I assume their contact info is on that thumb drive?"

"Is that all?" she muttered.

"No, actually." He stopped and spun to face her. He hadn't wanted to alarm her earlier, but she had to understand what kind of danger she was in. "We don't know how much of that reporter's story aired, or who saw it."

Her eyes widened. "The Charmer. You think he could come after me?"

"It's a possibility." A strong one, if the man saw her as a problem. He had a habit of dealing swiftly and violently with people who became threats. If he thought Abby could help them find him... "I want to keep you close by until we figure out how to deal with him. Is that a problem?"

"No. But I need to check on my grandfather first."

"Of course."

She took out her cell phone and dialed. He watched, transfixed, as her face lit up when someone answered. Her brief conversation was warm as only that between two people who shared a loving, lifelong relationship could be. An unexpected stab of jealousy hit him right behind the breastbone.

"I'll be by as soon as I can, but that might be tomorrow," Abby said as the conversation wound down. "Are you sure you're okay until then?" Her brow crinkled. He could almost feel the waves of worry coming off of her. "Please consider going to the shelter during the blackout period. Ernie has been instructed to take you there the moment you give the word." She listened for a moment, and then sighed. "Eat something. I'll be by tonight, tomorrow at the latest."

His heart squeezed at her concern for her family. Her grandfather obviously needed her. But so did SSAM.

She hung up and turned to him. "Where were we?"

"Everything okay?"

"Sure." Apparently, she wasn't going to share anything about her family with him. Which was fair, considering he hadn't exactly been an open book.

"Still ready to do this?"

"Yes." A spark of determination lit her eyes, chasing away the last remnants of worry and fear. "The Charmer won't scare me away from helping you."

He resisted the urge to lean down and kiss her. She'd stirred up emotions that were foreign and confusing to him. He wasn't sure where this unwelcome vulnerability came from but he had to push it aside. "Then let's get back to finding the Charmer."

"Wait, don't we want the elevator?" she asked as he led her past the doors.

"We need to make a stop in the training area first." He opened the entry to the stairwell and gestured to her to precede him. "Basement level."

"Again?" The sound of muted gunfire brought Abby to a halt. Einstein nearly ran her over. "It's okay. We have a shooting range down here to keep our skills sharp."

"Wow. Damian knows how to keep you on your game." Her eyes flew to his. "You brought me here to talk to him, didn't you?"

He repressed a pang of guilt. "Hopefully, he'll be thinking clearer by now."

"He was really angry and now he'll have a gun in his hands." She aimed an accusing glare at Einstein.

"I've never known him to shoot anyone." They walked into a room separated from the shooting range by a thick concrete wall and soundproof windows.

Max was watching Damian from one of the windows. "He's almost out of ammo. His aim's improved and he seems really focused. Maybe because he's imagining killing someone?" The paper target with the silhouette of a man's head and torso was punctured with bullet holes. Sure enough, the majority of holes were clustered in the head and chest areas. Max slid a glance toward them. "What happened today? Before she went upstairs, Lorena told me the FBI wanted to talk to him, and then you all met up at the CPD."

"Damian wouldn't say what the FBI wanted. As for the CPD..." Einstein cast a quick glance at Abby. She was standing so rigid he thought she might break in half. "Let's just say the day was an escalation in frustration."

"And a painful reminder he really didn't deserve," Abby added.

"I figured as much," Max said. "But pain can be cathartic."

As if sensing they were talking about him, Damian looked their way and lowered his gun. A moment later, he handed his pistol and protective earmuffs to Max. "My office in ten," he told Einstein gruffly. "Both you and Abby."

"Not exactly a warm reception," Abby said under her breath.

"It'll be fine." Einstein took her up to his office. "Want something to drink?" He opened his mini-fridge and withdrew two cans of soda and a couple individual packets of string cheese. They'd skipped lunch and she had to be starving, though she hadn't complained. Abby absently consumed the snack, worry etched in every line of her face.

"Where's that thumb drive?" He hoped to distract her by looking over the student roster. She reached into her purse and handed the drive over. In return, he slid her a blank piece of paper and a pencil. "Sketch the layout of your class for me."

A few minutes later, they'd narrowed down the roster to women who'd been in Abby's midmorning yoga class or one of the two classes earlier that morning, taught by a different instructor. Einstein printed the information to take to Damian. He also started running a program to cross-match the name to any criminal records or to the list of people from Damian's past.

In Damian's office, Lorena was already seated in one of the chairs. Einstein gestured to Abby to take the other one while he held up the wall near the door.

Damian's expression was carefully blank. "Tell me more about my daughter and this arranged meeting with the Charmer."

Abby looked confused. "I'm not sure there is more."

"Then tell me the same, but again. My...emotions...were raw last time. I'm ready to listen now."

. . .

WHERE TO BEGIN? SHE'D ALREADY RIPPED OUT THE MAN'S GUTS AND, while he seemed to have shoved them back in, she didn't want to torture him again.

"Please," Damian said. "We need to figure out this puzzle. Another girl is missing. I need to know who the Charmer is."

Abby licked her dry lips and took a deep breath before plunging back into those murky waters. "It wasn't Tony she was planning to meet, but she knew the Charmer had arranged it. Sam was hopeful of achieving something, but I'm not sure what. Her excitement turned to fear." Her gaze met Damian's, but he was an excellent poker player.

"Go on," he said.

"The man she trusted turned out to be a monster. She couldn't be what he wanted her to be, so he killed her. She would have fought him but he'd drugged her."

Damian's eyes darkened with restrained emotion. "The part I don't get is why she trusted this older man. He was the ringleader of an international crime syndicate. What did he have to offer her? How did he get to her and gain her trust?"

"With Mariah, he appears to have used her social media accounts to connect with her," Einstein offered. "I'm guessing it was a similar scenario with Tiffany and other recent victims. Before that, before the Internet and social media were prolific, he must have had alternate methods of preying on young women. He made himself into whatever the girls were searching for."

"As for why Sam trusted him, I think this man was a close friend or colleague of your family's," Abby said. Her gaze was on Damian, which was how she saw the flash of pain before he hid it.

Damian raked his hands down his face. "I still don't understand why he's obsessed with me. Or why Sam felt the need to go to him. He must have a hell of a lot of patience if he wanted to get to me all this time."

Abby couldn't stand the intense pain in Damian's eyes. "Your fight didn't have anything to do with her leaving that day." A shocked silence fell over the room.

"What did you say?" Damian asked.

"Your argument. One of the messages I sensed from her was that she was sorry you two had fought before she left that day. That wasn't why she met with this guy. She'd already planned the meeting days in advance, had looked forward to it."

Damian swallowed hard and his eyes misted. "Nobody, not even Priscilla, knows about that fight."

Lorena went to Damian and touched his shoulder in comfort. "The Charmer knows what he's doing, knows how to manipulate and take advantage of weaknesses for his own sick rituals." She looked at Abby. "Did you have any additional sense of the importance of the water?"

"It's definitely part of his process," Abby said. "What were the symbols on the other charms again?" She'd only had a quick look at them when she'd held the bracelet.

Einstein began listing them. "A rosebud, sunrise, dove, rainbow, candle, a water drop..."

"Baptism," she said as more pieces of the puzzle slid into place. "He's renewing his victims in the water, promising them a new life."

"You're sure?" Einstein asked. There was no judgment, only wonder. "That was one of Lorena's many theories, but we had no way of confirming it."

"He wants to make them reborn, in a way, to mark them as his. But they're never pure enough to satisfy him...until they're dead." That was the joy she'd felt through the bracelet. When he gazed upon their photos, he believed he'd achieved his goal, at least until the next time he felt the urge to purify.

"That he targets females in their early teens has to be significant," Lorena added. "He wants to purify them at an age when they're becoming sexualized, turning into women. Yet, the killings haven't been about sex." Her brow knit. "That's where it gets confusing."

She'd kept her hand on his shoulder, and now Damian looked up at her. "In the note on my car this morning, he mentioned wanting to keep them from my reach. As if I would taint them. How could anyone think I'd corrupt my own daughter—or anyone else, for that matter?"

"Serial killers don't always think rationally."

Einstein gestured to Damian. "Any of this raising any red flags from your past? Anything about a thirteen-year-old girl?"

Damian sighed. "No. But your advice yesterday is spot-on. We need to examine my past more thoroughly. Use your programs and algorithms on me. Lorena's psychological profiling skills. Figure out if something I did brought this guy into my orbit twenty years ago, and why he wanted to *purify* my daughter. Why he wanted to baptize her and make her his own."

Einstein pushed away from the wall. "Are you sure?"

"You're the best team member for the job. You have the ability to distance yourself. To be impartial."

Einstein's jaw clenched as if holding back things he wanted to say.

"I was a different person back then." Damian's tone was softer and he looked ashamed by his admission. "I was a slave to the dollar, eager to build my businesses. I worked damn hard and relished my financial accomplishments. I took a lot for granted." His gaze found Einstein. "The answers are inside of me, in my past. Think of this as an order, soldier. Tear me apart."

AFTER DAMIAN ORDERED HIM TO RIP APART HIS PAST, EINSTEIN disappeared with Abby to his office to gather the equipment he'd need. Lorena shut the door to Damian's office with a soft click. Her lips were pressed together in quiet anger.

"Are you sure you want to do this?" she finally asked.

Damian took a seat opposite her and swallowed past the tightness in his throat. "I've relived so many pieces of the past over the years, trying to figure out what I'd done wrong. Why God punished me. One more time won't hurt. Besides, I trust you to be gentle."

"You obviously haven't been on the receiving end of my interrogation techniques."

He was surprised to find himself smiling. "True." He sighed. "What if it's been too many years to remember anything of significance?"

"I don't think that'll be the problem."

He arched a brow. "But you do think there will be *a* problem."

"Perception tends to become…colored…by media, memories, emotions."

"Which is why I'll have Einstein running the more technical analyses. Maybe his computer will pick up a pattern we missed." It had happened in many previous cases. He glanced at his watch. Less than fifty-three hours left on the clock. "Your contact was able to buy me some time?"

Lorena nodded. "The FBI started digging into your financial history, but they won't detain you for questioning unless they find something."

"I did nothing wrong, so they shouldn't find anything, but who knows if the Charmer planted something? And we have no clue what he has planned for the next step in his game."

"Don't borrow trouble. Let's focus on the things we *can* control. Why don't you lie down?" Lorena gestured to the couch.

He sat. "Are you going to hypnotize me?"

"Making you my puppet would have some benefits, I suppose." She gently pushed against his shoulders until he lay back. Her knees bumped his as she moved farther down to lift his feet. "Let your mind drift." A cool hand smoothed his brow, encouraging him to relax into the cool leather. A lock of her long, straight hair fell over her shoulder like a curtain before she efficiently tucked it behind her ear.

"My mind doesn't drift." Unless he was fantasizing about her.

"You asked for this," she reminded him.

"That's some bedside manner you have, Dr. Castro."

She paused, her lips parted as if she would say something in response. Instead, she straightened and moved to sit in a chair near his feet as Einstein and Abby returned. They quietly took seats near his desk, out of his line of sight. But he could hear Einstein's fingers tapping gently away on his laptop.

"Try to relax," Lorena said. Listening to the soothing cadence of her voice made it easier. "Tell me about the day Samantha disappeared. Don't leave out any details, no matter how insignificant they may seem."

His daughter's image, as she was at age thirteen, filled his mind. "She was going shopping for the school's fall dance. She didn't want me or Priscilla coming with her. I dropped her off at the mall, where she was supposed to meet up with a friend. I watched Sam go inside a store." His throat tightened at the memory of the last time he'd seen Sam alive.

"And the friend?"

"Maggie Levine. She was also thirteen at the time. She was sick and couldn't make it, but apparently Sam didn't get the message. Or she never told us." He twisted his neck to look at Abby. "I never told anyone, but she and I had fought earlier that day over the boy she wanted to go to the dance with. I didn't think she was old enough to go alone with a date. It's possible... Maybe she had other plans at the mall that day. Plans that she hid from me."

"Go on," Lorena said softly and he realized he'd stopped talking for several long seconds. "When you're ready."

He was ready. Beyond ready. Sam needed to be put to rest. She deserved peace. God, he hoped he deserved it, too. He needed to move on.

"Sam wasn't where she was supposed to be at the time we'd

arranged for pick-up. I searched for her for hours, lapping the mall and all the stores within a several-block radius. Nobody remembered seeing her, not even the store clerk right by the door where I'd seen her disappear. It was as if she'd vanished without a trace.

"I got the call from the police nearly a year later. A year of pure hell, hoping, fearing..." And now somebody was determined to put him through it again.

A knock at the door interrupted.

Damian swung his feet to the floor. "Come in."

With an apologetic glance at the group in his office, Catherine entered carrying a cardboard box that looked to be five inches on each side. "Sorry to interrupt but there was a delivery for you. Sandy sent it over." Sandy was the SSAM crime scene technician he'd sent to process and analyze the petals and butterflies left at Sam's grave. "Said you'd want to see it right away."

Damian stood and took the cube from her hands. He felt a thrill of excitement. He'd been waiting for the Charmer to make his next move. Time was running out. And every moment the Charmer was occupied with Damian and the game was a moment he wasn't focused on hurting Mariah.

Einstein handed him a pair of latex gloves and he donned them before reaching inside to remove a blue velvet box with a familiar logo. He recognized the jeweler's box. He opened it, knowing what he'd find inside—and exactly the message the Charmer had wanted to send. Cufflinks branded with the Luna Corp logo—a wolf that symbolized cunning and strength—winked at him with sapphire eyes.

Lorena leaned forward to look over his shoulder. Could she hear his heart beating? It was so loud, a constant *thwump, thwump, thwump* in his ears, like the beating of helicopter blades.

He looked up to see four expectant faces watching him. He expelled a breath, ruffling the edge of a folded square of printer paper tucked beside the lid. He removed it and handed it to Einstein, who'd also put on gloves.

"'The strength of the pack is the wolf and the strength of the wolf is the pack.'" Einstein quoted from the note, and continued with the Charmer's own words. Damian's gut twisted with every word. *"I'm not the only one who gives charms to my victims. Sam. The general public. Ron. Who else did you make promises to and then fail?"* Einstein tossed the note onto Damian's desk.

"Do the words mean anything to you?" Lorena asked.

Damian nodded. "The first part is a quote from Kipling, one I often used in my pre-SSAM days to inspire my executive team at Luna Corp." It had been a different world, a different lifetime. "Success in business was everything when I was CEO of my own corporation. The moon was our company logo, but among my inner circle, I used the wolf as a symbol of cunning and intellect and I stressed loyalty to the pack."

Over his shoulder, Lorena studied the cufflinks. "I find it interesting that Luna Corp's symbol was the moon. The Circle's symbol is a sun. That can't be just a coincidence. Maybe the Charmer wanted to distinguish himself from you…to be your opposite. But at the same time he wants to be you. And he hates that." The room grew quiet for a long moment as the team processed that. "Who is Ron?"

Damian released a harsh laugh. "The Charmer's right about one thing. I failed Ron—in business and as a friend. These cufflinks were a gift to him when I left Luna Corp in his hands so I could found SSAM and put all my energies toward finding Sam's killer. Ron Little took the helm at Luna Corp. He was a good friend." His throat squeezed.

"Was?" Lorena asked gently.

"He committed suicide a few months after becoming CEO of my company. In the aftermath, there were accusations of corporate espionage, and we think Ron believed he was going to get caught. Some say the pressure of filling my shoes was too much."

"Was Ron guilty?"

He sighed. "I don't know. After his death, I sold the company to the person who'd threatened to sue, as a gesture of good faith, and I moved on. I didn't care anymore. My focus, every ounce of energy I had, went toward SSAM. When I lost my daughter, I lost myself. Building SSAM was the only way I was going to get it back."

THE CHARMER COULDN'T BELIEVE HIS DAUGHTER WAS SITTING IN HIS office. After his divorce, her mother had done everything she could to keep him away from their daughter. He'd missed out on so much. Now in her thirties, Hannah would always be fourteen in his eyes.

Hannah licked her lips nervously. "I need help."

"What kind of help?"

She blew out a breath. "I don't know how to ask you for anything. It's not like you've been there for me."

He gripped his hands together as he fought a wave of anger. He hadn't been there for her because his ex-wife hadn't allowed it. "You and your mother have been well taken care of. She had her hefty divorce settlement. You have your trust fund for the rest."

He'd rarely heard from Hannah, but even less frequently since her trust fund had become active when she'd turned twenty-five, which led him to conclude her minimal attempts at keeping in touch before then had been a ploy to keep tabs on her money. *His* money. Money he'd worked damn hard for. Outwardly, he remained calm, but his blood ran hot like magma through his body.

She smiled sadly. "I'll admit, I backed away from you over the past few years."

"Generous of you to accept a portion of the blame," he said. "It takes two to make a relationship work."

"Exactly. And I never knew *you* well enough to figure *us* out. It was like you became a different person right before Mom divorced you. It was…scary." With shaky hands, Hannah lifted the glass of water his secretary had supplied. Was she frightened?

"What's wrong? Does talking to me scare you?" He huffed out a laugh. "Awkward, yes. Intimidating? Maybe. But scared…" He rose and took a few steps toward her. Her body tensed and he stopped his forward progress. "Only if you're here to take advantage of me. Then you should be concerned."

Hannah squared her shoulders. "I'm not scared. I came because Mother wouldn't. She's sick, Dad. She needs medical help and insurance won't cover it."

Sick? Bullshit. "*She* left *me*. She gave up her rights to my money, my protection, years ago." Especially when she'd taken their daughter far away from his reach, determined he wouldn't taint her.

"I knew coming here was a mistake." She spun away, grabbing her purse. The charm bracelet jangled against her wrist, sending a wave of emotion through him like chimes generating a cascade of musical notes. Each delicate disc represented a girl, a young woman much like his daughter at the age she'd left him. And like another Hannah from a lifetime ago.

"Then why did you?" *Say you love me. Say you've missed me. That you wouldn't leave me again if given the choice.*

Her bow-shaped lips, so much like her mother's, pressed together beneath the aquiline nose and brown-and-green tortoise-shell eyes she'd inherited from his side of the family. "I didn't have any other place to go. But I won't beg."

Now, *that* trait was all him. He wondered how far these similarities went. Would she do anything to get what she wanted? Would she understand the things he'd done to fill the gaps, to satisfy the needs, in his life?

"I told you, your mother made her choice long ago. And you've been an adult long enough to make your own choices." Which hadn't included her father unless it got her something in return. At one time, he would have killed—in fact, he *had* killed, he thought, glancing at her bracelet—to have her notice him. He'd sent her the charms, made her an unknowing keeper of his mementos, as a way to feel connected to her. He'd made a mistake.

He didn't want her anymore. Not like this, not on a begging mission for her mother—if that was even what this was. The Hannah he'd named his daughter after—the beautiful young woman with a soft heart—would never have sunk to this level, never have let greed become more important than love, never have taken advantage of him like this. But that Hannah was gone, too.

He released a tired sigh. "Don't come around here anymore."

She froze. "What?"

"We're done. If all you want is money—"

Anger flashed in her eyes. "Maybe I wanted more. Maybe I want to *understand*." She lifted her wrist and wriggled it, sending the charms tinkling against each other. "I know what these are."

A jab of panic socked him in the gut, but he maintained an outward calm. She couldn't know the whole truth. "What are they?"

Hannah's nose flared and she was silent for several long seconds. "Attempts to buy me. Little reminders you're still lurking in the background of my life."

She wasn't entirely wrong. The charms had been worn by his girls for the few days he'd had each of them. Sending her the mementos had been a way of including Hannah in his life, of asking for her acceptance.

She whirled toward the door as if she couldn't wait to be out of his life again, but paused with her hand on the knob. "Unless you help me, there's no future for us." And then she was through the door, snapping it shut with a sharp click that reverberated through his office.

He reached for the water glass Hannah had left on the table and threw it against the wall. The noise was briefly satisfying.

His secretary appeared in the doorway, looking flustered. "Sir?"

Her gaze moved to the wall. "Oh! I'll clean that up." She quickly disappeared, efficient and respectful as ever.

If only his daughter had those qualities. Then again, his ex-wife had raised her.

He moved around his desk and tapped away at his keyboard, barely paying attention to his secretary as she returned with a broom and dustpan and went to work on the mess.

He'd tried with the other girls…tried to be a father, a mentor, a god to them. None of it had worked. He'd never succeeded in recreating the original Hannah—his sweet Hannah Rose—or in saving her. Still, he'd have another chance again soon, with Mariah. She was already proving to be a fast learner.

"Will that be all, sir?"

He'd forgotten his secretary was even there. "Yes. And please make sure my daughter doesn't show up again. She's not welcome here." Shock registered on his secretary's face before she remembered her role and, with a nod, left.

It was time for the next step in the game. Only a little over fifty-two hours remained until the showdown.

CHAPTER 9

"Damian didn't recognize any of the names on our list," Einstein said as they returned to his office. "But I'm going to forward the students' driver's license photos to him to see if he recognizes any of the faces. And I'll forward the list of names to Maggie, see if any of them rings a bell." They were working on the theory that, in order for a bracelet connected to the Charmer to end up at the Inner Beauty studio, the bracelet owner must have been following Maggie. Otherwise, it was too much of a coincidence that a bracelet linked to the murders showed up just a few blocks from the SSAM offices.

Abby's surprised gaze met his. "How'd you get those photos?"

"You don't need to worry about that." He reached for the paper coming out of his printer and handed it to her. "I've arranged the list of female students, sorted by those who might have attended one of yesterday's classes and then ordered them in the most convenient travel route." He'd also emailed it to himself so he had it on his phone. The clock was ticking and he was determined to find the bracelet's owner—and the bracelet— today. Not that he wanted to subject Abby to any more images.

The *messages* she received seemed more like painful experiences. After watching her put herself through that, even the scientist in him couldn't deny she was picking up *something* from those objects.

"When did you have time to hack into the DMV computer?"

"I set things up before we went into Damian's office, so the information would be ready when we came back."

Abby grinned. "You're really efficient."

Efficient. Not the adjective he wanted to hear from a beautiful woman.

She laughed. "Stop scowling. It was a compliment. Believe me, I've been around enough inefficient people. Organization is a quality I admire."

Was it just his imagination, or had her voice gone soft? And who were all these inefficient people who'd disappointed her? Men? Who had created the shadows of doubt in her eyes? Jealousy and protectiveness warred within him.

He spent a couple minutes making some adjustments to his other programs and inputting more parameters before turning to her. "Ready to head out into the heat?"

She groaned. They'd agreed a door-to-door approach would be best, in case the bracelet's owner was involved in the murders and wouldn't be honest in a phone conversation. Besides, Abby's skill set supposedly worked best when she could touch things or people. So they were going to be field agents today, in temps that again reached the triple digits.

"I'll feed you along the way." His bribe did the trick and she immediately stood. He pulled a chilled drink from the fridge. One of her sleek brown eyebrows rose. "Is there a problem?"

"Not for me. *You,* however, have a serious addiction." She gestured to the energy drink in his hand. "It's like you need an infusion every couple hours to survive."

"Something has to fuel this fine-tuned machine." He patted his abdomen and her eyes followed the movement. Her cheeks heated and she licked her lips. As his body began to respond to her, he jerked his gaze away and headed for the door. "Let's go."

They spent the next hour driving from one destination on his list to the next, hoping the brief respites of air conditioning would keep them cool. Rolling blackouts had continued, but only the last of the addresses, the farthest from the yoga studio, was without power when they arrived. They had to hike up six floors via stairs, but Abby didn't complain. Neither did Einstein, who enjoyed the view as she preceded him up the stairwell.

She was wearing a long, soft skirt that swished around her ankles, caressing her legs. Further up, the fabric molded to the fine curves of her ass. The sway of her hips was mesmerizing. Then again, it had been a long time since his last sexual encounter and his body was wound tight after so much time spent in Abby's company. Unlike some of his SEAL buddies who capitalized on their elite status when the opportunity arose, he liked to know his sexual partners. And since he rarely took the time to get to know anyone—

"Who is it we're looking for?" Abby asked, interrupting his thoughts as she reached the landing.

"Hannah Smith."

"Don't recognize the name. Sounds generic."

He couldn't disagree. "Doesn't mean she's using an alias. It's a popular name." But it didn't mean she wasn't hiding her true identity, either. "According to the studio records, she was in the class just before yours yesterday."

At the apartment door, he stepped past her to knock. A light sheen of sweat glistened on her forehead from their exertions. Her plump lower lip was rosy.

Nobody answered.

"Damn." Abby chewed her lip and Einstein nearly reached out to smooth a thumb over the surface. It had to be sacrilege to damage such prime real estate. "What now? There's no phone number next to her name." She was perusing the printout Einstein had given her. The other women had either been home or had a phone number on the roster. If they hadn't been able to talk to them face-to-face, he'd had Abby leave a phone message requesting they call her ASAP.

"We'll leave a note, asking her to call you. Like the others, she'll probably be more comfortable talking with someone from the studio."

She reached into her purse and took out a business card, scribbling a hasty message on the back before slipping it under the door.

She straightened. "Well, I guess this is where we say good-bye."

"What?" He hadn't been prepared for that.

She shrugged. "I helped as much as I can for the moment. If you guys get another lead on Mariah and think of a way I can help, let me know."

"Right." Her announcement left him hollow inside. How could he, a loner by choice, have gotten used to having her around in such a short amount of time?

"What, you don't think I can help further?" Outrage laced her words, and she pushed past him to the stairwell. She'd misunderstood his silence for doubt. "I thought I'd done enough to prove myself today."

Uncertain what he'd done to give her the wrong impression, he scrambled to follow her down the stairs. Damn, she could move fast for someone in danger of tangling in her long skirt. "Slow down, Abby." She was going to break her damn neck. "I do think you've helped. You've been great."

"But you still don't believe in my gift." She muttered some things beneath her breath, things he was certain he didn't want to hear.

"I do believe. It took some convincing, but I believe."

She paused at the next landing to face him, hands on hips. "But you think I'm weird."

He cursed. How had he gone from desiring her to not wanting

her to leave him to having to explain himself? How could she believe he thought she was weird? With sudden insight, he realized it wasn't him she was reacting to—it was her own insecurities.

He stepped closer. "You're outside my area of expertise, but that doesn't mean I don't want to get to know you better."

She huffed out a humorless laugh. "You won't even touch me." She spun on her heel and continued her hair-raising descent.

"What?" He hurried to follow, wondering at the change of subject.

"And you like things wrapped up nice and neat in a box," she tossed back over her shoulder.

"Hey, I think outside of the box if I need to. I actually do quite a bit of it. I try, anyway."

"I suppose I should appreciate your honesty. A lot of people would either cloak their opinions in sarcasm or simply fall off the face of the earth."

"As in, stop talking to you?"

She'd reached the bottom floor and stopped abruptly. The stairwell went so quiet that her panting echoed. He was having trouble catching his breath as well, but it wasn't due to their pace. He reached out and spun her to face him. "What do you mean I won't touch you?" It was all he could do to keep his hands off her. Was she was telling him she *wanted* him to touch her?

She shrugged. "Several times, you've almost reached for me and then pulled away instead." Her accusation didn't come across as offhand as she'd probably intended. Hurt lay beneath the words.

"Abby..."

She held up her hand to stop his rebuttal. "No, it's okay. I get it. People are afraid of what I might see. Or they think I'm tainted."

The breath stilled in his lungs. Had people told her she was damaged goods? She sure as hell didn't deserve that kind of treatment from anyone. She was tender and good-hearted, open and hopeful about life despite the things she'd experienced. And so damn beautiful it made him... Hell, it made him want things. She embodied everything he'd hoped for from life but had been denied.

He reached out and pulled her to him. Her eyes widened, heat and hope reflected in their blue depths as she looked up into his face. "I'm not scared of you, Abby Rhodes, and I sure as hell don't mind touching you." Knowing she needed this as much as he did, he proved it to her, bending his head and capturing her mouth with his.

She moaned and wrapped her arms around his neck, pressing her chest against his as she clung to him like a lifeline. She slanted her head and opened to him, letting his tongue sweep into her mouth. She tasted even better than he'd imagined. So damn sweet. He drank from her, but pulled away when, somewhere on an above floor, a door opened. She was making him crave more, needs she couldn't satisfy in the stairwell of a busy apartment building. He took a step back and her arms fell away.

She continued to gaze up at him in wonder. "You didn't have to prove anything to me." She grinned. "But I'm glad you did."

"I believe in you, Abby. There's scientific evidence that the power of belief can move mountains," he said. "Well, maybe not mountains, literally, but you get the idea. The human brain has the capacity for so much more than we use it for. How can I not be intrigued by the possibility you could be tapping into things science doesn't even understand yet? It's not weird at all. It's exciting, actually." He leaned in conspiratorially. "And there's always the possibility you're one of the X-Men. That intrigues the hell out of me."

She laughed out loud and his entire body tightened with pleasure. She sent him a look from under her lashes. "Never underestimate my power."

"I don't." She had a power over his body that he wasn't entirely comfortable with. He wanted to kiss her again, with laughter lighting her eyes and erasing the worry from her face. But the sound of approaching voices indicated people were nearby.

He followed her out to the sidewalk and fell into step beside her. "I want you to come home with me."

Shocked, she stopped and turned to him, ignoring the oven-like heat that reddened their skin. "What?"

"I'll feel better if you're safe, outside of the Charmer's reach." She'd apparently forgotten the danger she could be in.

Her face fell. "Oh, that. I'll stay on Grandpa's couch."

He didn't like that answer. He couldn't watch over her there. And he sure as hell couldn't steal another taste of her. "I'll at least see you home to get your stuff."

She looked as if she might object, but then let him escort her to his car, where they hurried to climb inside and turn on the air. Her soft scent, a feminine creaminess overlaid with sunscreen, filled the air between them.

A few minutes later, they pulled up in front of her building. Thankfully, the blackouts weren't yet in effect there and they could use the elevator. She let him into her apartment and tossed her purse onto a side table.

"Mind if I have a quick drink before I head back out there?" he asked, looking for an excuse to stay a bit longer and appease his curiosity.

"Sure." But she shot him a suspicious look before she headed to the kitchen.

"You live here alone?" Einstein stood in front of an oscillating fan as his gaze traveled the living room. Potted plants, family pictures, and a myriad of books filled every corner and shelf, and a corkboard dedicated to kids' art projects hung on one wall. The furniture was functional and comfortable. Homey. There were no signs of a male on the premises—at least, not a live-in one. Not that he'd thought Abby would kiss him if she were involved with another man. Still, a surprising sense of satisfaction came over him.

In the kitchen, she pressed a button to receive her messages, then put it on speaker so she could move about while listening.

She filled two glasses with ice. There was nothing from Hannah Smith yet. Instead, the soft tremble of a little girl's voice filled the silence.

"Miss Abby? I wanted to talk to you. I miss you. Please call me." The girl sounded as if she might cry, or had been crying. Abby clicked a button on the phone to switch the call to private and picked up the receiver, listening at her ear. She rapped her fingers against the kitchen counter as the furrow in her forehead deepened, then hung up without saying a word.

Einstein knew he shouldn't butt in, but she was worrying her lip with her teeth again, deep in thought... Thoughts she wasn't willingly sharing.

She moved about the kitchen with renewed energy. "I don't have anything caffeinated. How about water?"

"Sure."

"Ice cream. I have that if you're hungry. Might as well eat it in case the power goes out." She yanked open the freezer.

He moved to stand behind her. "Who was that girl?"

She jumped, apparently not having heard his approach. "A student."

"She's calling you at home during the summer?" Did kindergartners even know how to dial a phone? He had zero experience with kids. But thinking back, he'd embraced any kind of technology he could get his hands on at that age.

She grabbed a carton of butter pecan ice cream and closed the freezer. If she turned around, she'd be in his arms, but she didn't. In fact, she seemed to be closing in on herself in an attempt *not* to touch him. He moved away and she visibly relaxed. With effort, he smoothed out his scowl before she looked at him.

"It's nothing you need to worry about." She grabbed two spoons and headed for the couch. Apparently, they were going to eat straight from the carton—a solid plan he could get behind. He sat next to her and snagged a spoon. They ate in silence for a few minutes, letting the ice cream and fan cool them inside and out.

The girl's message replayed in his head. "You going to call her back?"

She huffed out a breath. "You're not going to let it go, are you?" But her frown told him she'd been thinking about the girl, too.

He scooped a healthy dollop of ice cream. "If I can help…"

"That's just it." She looked miserable. "I'm not sure what anyone can do that wouldn't make her situation worse. My radar is…*off*… with her."

Confused, he examined her. Unfortunately, she chose that moment to suck a helping of ice cream off her spoon. He strangled a groan as her tongue darted out to lick off the last bit. He'd had a taste of that tongue and his body craved more. But she was deep in thought and he snapped back to the subject at hand. "Tell me more."

He took her long pause as a refusal. And why should she tell him anything? He hadn't exactly been a paragon of openness and trust.

Then she spoke. "Laney was in my class this last year. I got the sense things were…difficult…at home." She sighed. "I thought being a kindergarten teacher would be the safe path. If I happened to touch an item that belonged to a kid that young, I figured it would be mostly happy and light thoughts that infiltrated my barriers. Unfortunately, kids deal with dark stuff, too."

"Abuse?" His fingers tightened around his spoon. *Fuck.* Parents beating on their kids, whether physically or emotionally—or both —was beyond his tolerance level.

She shot him a quick glance, evidently sensing the emotion he held back with that single word. "When I touched her jacket one day, holding it out for her, I saw things." She frowned. "I got an overwhelming sense of desperation, and loneliness and misery no child should experience. When she told me some things that confirmed my suspicions, I filed a report."

"That's the law, right? If you have evidence of abuse, you're required to report it."

She sighed. "Apparently, I was wrong. The investigator from Children and Family Services interviewed Laney extensively and Laney denied anything happened."

"Doesn't mean it didn't happen."

She looked at him with surprise.

His eyes widened. "What? You think you were wrong?" She did, he realized. It was part of the same cycle of doubt she'd been struggling with over the past day and a half. How many times had she struggled with that before?

She shook her head. "I'd been wrong before."

"And you've been right all day today. It's more likely Laney's father convinced her to recant her story."

"He's suing me for slander."

Einstein froze, disbelief and anger hitting him with a double whammy. "You're kidding."

She shook her head. "I wish I was. I may lose my job over this." She looked toward the kitchen, where the phone sat on the counter. "What am I supposed to do?"

"Your gut, and your gift, are telling you Laney is still in danger. After hearing her, my gut's telling me the same and I don't even know the girl."

She frowned. "She didn't sound like she was in immediate danger on the message, but after you leave, I'll probably go check on her."

She'd go alone? Like hell. "I'm coming with you."

She sent him a surprised look. "Feeling chivalrous?"

"More like murderous."

"Which is why having you there wouldn't be a good thing. Laney's father might be a bully with a lawyer to back him, but he wouldn't dare hurt me. Humiliating me will be enough for him. I'll be fine. It's Laney I'm worried about." Her frown deepened. "Her caseworker promised me she would keep close tabs on her." But the system could be overloaded. And with the heat raising tempers and lowering thresholds, the police were busy. It looked like it was up to them to make sure Laney was safe.

"You'll feel better if you check on her. I'll feel better if I come with you."

Her expression immediately brightened. "Okay. Thanks."

He got the impression she'd had to face a lot of difficulties in life alone. Maybe they had more in common than he thought.

"THIS IS THE PLACE." ABBY SHADED HER EYES AS SHE LOOKED UP AT the old apartment building. Einstein had found the address within minutes by doing a computer search. The post-it-note-sized yard consisted of a few square feet of bare dirt with a tipped-over, rusting bike and a few broken toys.

"Do a lot of your students come from this area?" Einstein's face was set in grim lines.

"The school's only a few blocks away. But my students are the same happy kids that populate the rest of the world. Some of them need a little extra TLC or a meal here or there."

"A *meal*." He slid his sunglasses down his nose to meet her gaze head on.

She shrugged. "I try to have granola bars and dried fruit on hand for those who didn't have breakfast. Having food in their bellies helps them concentrate. It's a win-win."

"On your salary, that must be tough." His gaze softened and her heart expanded in her chest, pressing against her breastbone. "And those are physical needs. I'm sure the emotional ones can be even harder to meet." A series of quick, complicated emotions flashed in his eyes before he slid his glasses back into place.

She led the way into the building and scanned the mailboxes in the foyer to find the name and corresponding apartment. The wallpaper was peeling, which was just as well. It had to be from the seventies and should have been stripped and replaced decades ago.

Its orange and gold had turned brown and drab. Dirt had congealed in the corners and along the baseboards.

"Jesus," Einstein muttered.

A trio of young men came down the stairs, their laughter and curse words echoing in the small lobby area. They gave Abby a thorough once-over as they passed. Einstein's hand went to the small of her back in a gesture of support and they hurried along, Einstein's presence deterring them from voicing the inappropriate comments she'd read in their eyes.

"I won't let anything happen to you," Einstein whispered against her ear.

Trying to ignore the rapid hammering of her heart, Abby led the way up a couple flights of stairs. Even if the elevator were working, with the six-story building in this ramshackle shape, she wouldn't have risked it. Abby knocked on the door marked 3B.

"Who is it?" a small voice asked.

"Laney, it's me, Miss Rhodes."

The door opened, revealing a six-year-old girl with dark brown hair and a shabby sundress that had to be a hand-me-down. The vibrant pink still evident on the straps had faded to a Pepto-Bismol-pink in the more worn places such as the front panel. Her cheeks were red from the stifling warmth emanating from within the apartment. "You came! I knew you would." She launched herself into Abby, who caught her up in a hug.

Trying to smile as if her heart wasn't cracking open, Abby put one hand on her shoulder and stroked the other down her sweaty head of tangled brown curls. "Is your dad home, honey?"

Abby walked Laney, who hadn't let go of her waist, backward into the apartment. Behind her, Einstein did a visual sweep but there were no signs of a parent. Or anyone, for that matter. In fact, the only sense that registered was smell. Decaying, spoiled food. She spied the takeout containers on the counter. The apartment was overly warm, encouraging the growth of bacteria. The lack of cleanliness in other areas certainly didn't help.

Laney finally pulled back. "I haven't seen him."

"Since when?" Einstein asked. Laney narrowed her gaze at him.

"It's okay," Abby told her. "He's a friend."

She seemed to weigh this a moment, then shrugged. "It's been a few days."

Days? Einstein muttered a curse under his breath, low enough for only Abby to hear.

"You've been alone that long?" Abby asked. "No adult supervision at all?"

Laney moved to the fridge where she studied a magnetic mini-calendar with some mechanic's ad on it. Abby's hand flew to her mouth to stifle a gasp at the same time Einstein went stone still. They'd both caught the mark on the girl's back, a bruise between the shoulder blades, in the shape of a man's palm. In the back of her mind, the realization that her gift hadn't led her astray—that she'd been right about the abuse in Laney's life—and that physical abuse was minor compared to the despair Abby felt that nobody had been able to save the girl from this situation. Anger swarmed her body like a disturbed hive of bees, prickling her skin and ready to sting. She wanted to scoop Laney up and get her out of there before Wesley Brookes returned. Apparently, Einstein had similar thoughts. As he took a step forward, Abby stopped him and shook her head.

"Let me," she said, her eyes pleading with him. *Let the calmer person, the one Laney was familiar with, handle this.* Because though she was certain Einstein would never hurt a kid, it would be a struggle to keep the anger at Laney's father from his voice and body language, and Laney would misunderstand it. Einstein backed down, but frustration darkened his eyes. She knew the feeling well.

Laney spun back to them after examining the calendar, which showed the entire year at a glance. "Four days."

Sure enough, there were pencil markings through the past four days on the calendar. The few days before that were untouched, but Abby's anger intensified as she spied many more slashmarks in the previous month, and the month before that. No doubt, Einstein was putting two and two together, as well.

Abby knelt to put herself at Laney's level. "Honey, does your daddy disappear a lot?"

Laney's face scrunched up. "Sometimes, yeah. He always leaves me some food, though."

"Some food?"

Tears flooded Laney's eyes. "I was really hungry, so it's all gone already. I'm not supposed to call anyone, but…"

Abby's gaze moved to the cartons on the counter. Had the poor girl even known she should store them in the fridge? Then again, the dim interior and utter silence of the apartment indicated the electricity was out. Or cut off. Since the rest of the building had seemed to have power, she was betting on the latter. She would strangle Wesley Brookes with her bare hands.

"I'm sorry I lied before," Laney said, her lip quivering. "Don't be mad." It seemed Laney had picked up on the undercurrent, after all. "Dad told me the police would take me away if I said he hit me."

Abby hugged her, careful of the bruise on Laney's back. "I'm not mad. Not at you."

"I didn't know what to do. Before, when you helped, things were better for a little while. Usually, Mrs. Humphrey down the hall will give me something, but she hasn't been home either. And then the lights went out. I…" The girl swallowed. "I was scared. Luckily, the phone came back on long enough to call you but then it went out again." Probably due to an unpaid bill.

"What about your mother?" Einstein asked. Abby sent him a subtle shake of her head, but Laney seemed to take his question in stride.

"She's in heaven," Laney said. "She died because she had me. That's what Dad says, anyway."

Still kneeling, Abby looked the girl in the eyes. "You're going to come with me and we'll get you something to eat. Einstein and I are going to find the help you need." Without looking at him, Abby reached her hand back to take Einstein's in a show of solidarity.

"I'm not supposed to go with strangers." Laney bit her lip. "Dad will be mad."

Einstein followed Abby's lead when she tugged his hand gently. He knelt beside her and, in a gesture that had Abby biting back a smile, used a finger to make a cross over his heart. "I promise I'm not a bad stranger. And I know you're not supposed to believe that, but you know Abby—Miss Rhodes—and she'll vouch for me."

"He's one of the good guys," Abby said with a fierce nod.

Not like Wesley. How could he hurt his daughter? How could he leave the sweet girl alone? And where the hell had he gone?

"Go find some shoes," Abby encouraged her, and the girl padded into a bedroom. Without rising, she turned toward Einstein and he opened his arms to her. She buried her face in his shoulder. "Tell me she'll be all right."

His arms came around her and held her tight. "She'll be all right. We'll make sure of it."

A sigh shuddered out of her and she pulled away and got to her feet as Laney came bounding back into the room. She'd donned a little light that fit around her forehead like a headband.

Abby grinned. "Looks like you're prepared for anything." Her smile faded as she realized the headlamp might have been the girl's only source of light after the sun went down.

"I'm ready!" Laney skidded to a stop by the door. "I should leave Dad a note."

Abby found a pencil and paper in a drawer and hastily scribbled her name and number. "He can reach me if he comes home while we're gone."

As they left, Einstein brought up the rear. From the corner of her eye, Abby caught him swiping the paper off the counter and tucking it into his pocket.

"What the hell?" She hung back to ask, out of Laney's hearing.

He didn't apologize. "If the slimeball comes back, I sure as hell don't want the guy to have your personal number. I don't want him near you, or the kid, for that matter. The cops will locate him and he can figure it out that way. Your lawyers can sort out the rest." He was being sweetly protective of them both.

"Thank you."

"You guys coming?" Laney said, appearing in the doorway again.

"Coming," Einstein said. Laney slipped one hand in Abby's and looked tentatively up at Einstein before her tiny fingers slid into his in a gesture of trust. "Ready for an adventure?" He gave Laney a charming smile.

The fist around Abby's heart squeezed tighter.

CHAPTER 10

An hour later, Abby's heart was cracking in two. "I can't just leave Laney here. I tried that last time and look what happened." Exactly zero improvement in Laney's situation. But Wesley had legal custody and, though he couldn't pay his electric or phone bill, he could apparently afford a damn good lawyer. Her lawyer had advised her to walk away. That was the one thing she couldn't do. Even if it were only providing a quick meal before bringing Laney here for outside help, Abby would do what she could.

"You're making me dizzy." Einstein glanced up from his laptop, his gaze following her as she paced the waiting area—the same dingy place with the gray plastic chairs and the dented vending machine, inside the same CPD station she'd been in earlier that day—the one with the remains of Sam's burial site in the basement —while Laney visited with a child protective services representative from the Illinois Department of Children and Family Services.

Einstein set his laptop aside, rose and stopped her, placing his hands on her shoulders and waiting until she looked him in the eye. "You've done what you can. Fed her, comforted her. It's in the caseworker's hands now."

She snorted. "Given how that worked out last time, forgive me if I'm not exactly reassured."

He was infuriatingly calm. His body was set in a stiff line, his muscles tight as if awaiting an order. A dangerous vibe ran beneath the surface. He was just as frustrated and angry as she was, she realized, which was somehow comforting.

The front door opened and a tall, gangly man with dark eyes stepped through. Laney's father, Wesley Brookes. The man spied her and made a distinct detour to head her way, his face red with fury. Einstein pulled her against his side as the other man stalked toward her.

"You. Did you call the cops on me again?" Wesley's clothing was rumpled, his hair uncombed. "Who are you to decide I can't care for my own?"

Adrenaline mixed with anger like a potent cocktail. "Who am I? Apparently, I'm all your little girl has. Where've you been for the past four days?"

Einstein maneuvered his body so that he was a shield, taking the brunt of Wesley's glare. "This isn't about Abby. I suggest you back off." Einstein's voice was cool and controlled but vibrated with warning.

But Wesley either didn't hear it or chose to ignore it. "What the hell business is it of yours? Who the fuck are you?"

"A friend of Laney's."

"A pervert, then. You get off on saving little girls, huh?" Wesley's sneer turned to Abby. "Or big girls."

A muscle jumped in Einstein's clenched jaw. "I find it interesting that you haven't even bothered to ask if Laney is okay. We are, after all, in a police station and you haven't seen your daughter for days."

"You can't believe what a six-year-old says."

"You should have stayed gone. We all would have been better

off."

Abby stepped in front of Einstein again, nudging his hard body back a step. His heat scorched her back. "Laney's with the case-worker. Her future is in the hands of the authorities, now." But Abby would keep close tabs on how things developed. She could only hope they made the right decision this time.

"The guy was right. You're nothing but a nosy bitch." Wesley jabbed a finger in Abby's face. "Watch yourself." She was glad he didn't touch her, as she was certain she'd experience waves of intense negativity and even rage.

"What guy?" Einstein asked.

Wesley's smug grin widened. "Wouldn't you like to know?" Before they could question him further, the caseworker appeared and called him back.

"Do you know who he was talking about?" Einstein asked her.

She sank into a chair and put her face in her hands. "Could have been a few people who aren't happy with how I handled things." His hand traced a pattern between her shoulder blades. She peeked through her fingers but he wasn't looking at her.

His gaze was on the hallway where Wesley had disappeared. "Could have been the Charmer."

She shuddered. "I doubt it. First of all, how would he know he could get to me this way? Second of all, I'm small potatoes in this game." She hoped. "Wesley was probably referring to his lawyer."

"The Charmer's the head of a crime ring. He can get any bit of information on anyone." His gaze met hers head-on, the concern in his hazel eyes warming her from the inside. "I'm sorry you had to get mixed up in this. And now, possibly Laney, too."

She sighed. "I would do anything for that girl, but how did the Charmer know that?"

"The lawsuit, and probably the report you filed."

"How did he get Laney to call me?"

"Maybe she really did need your help. Or maybe he slipped her your number to encourage her along." Einstein stood. "I'm going to ask her. She might even have seen the Charmer in person."

"What? No." Abby was on her feet in an instant. "We're not putting her through anything else. The caseworker has been asking her questions for almost an hour. Now her dad's here. The kid's got to be exhausted and confused."

But the decision was taken out of her hands as the new caseworker, an older woman named Mrs. Benson, approached. "I'd like to speak with you, Miss Rhodes."

"Certainly." She followed Mrs. Benson, sensing Einstein was right behind her, though he hadn't technically been invited. Still, she felt better knowing he had her back.

She was surprised when the caseworker led them to an empty room. She didn't ask them to sit, just shut the door and turned to them. "I'm going to be blunt, Miss Rhodes."

"Please, call me Abby."

The woman nodded. "It's getting late and Laney needs a place to go tonight. Given the case history and the new evidence of potential abuse and neglect, I'm not comfortable releasing her to her father." Neither was Abby. "But our resources are strapped, especially with the shelters overtaxed in this heat wave, and we don't have a foster home to place her in at the moment."

"There's something else you should consider," Einstein said.

Mrs. Benson's stern gaze landed on him. "Enlighten me."

"My name is Einstein. Andrew MacKenzie. I work for an organization called SSAM that works to protect the community. I believe someone we're searching for has decided to use Laney to his own purposes, to get to Abby. I want her to be safe."

A ghost of a smile played about the caseworker's lips. "Laney speaks highly of you. Says you helped Miss Rhodes *save* her. And I've heard of SSAM. The fact remains that Laney needs a safe environment to stay in tonight." The woman looked thoughtful as she held Einstein's gaze.

"I'd guarantee her safety," Einstein said solemnly. "In a location that neither her father nor the man we think he's working for knows about."

Abby's heartbeat slowed, then sped up again. Was Einstein offering to protect her and Laney? Would Mrs. Benson even consider that option?

"I think Laney would feel safest with you," Mrs. Benson agreed. "I'm confident I can find an alternative solution by tomorrow afternoon. Besides, I called her aunt, Laney's mother's sister who lives out of state. She isn't willing to take on the child, but she gave me permission to release her to Abby. Said Wesley wasn't a viable option anymore."

Abby blew out a breath as the weight on her chest lifted.

"Where's Wesley now?" Einstein asked.

"He was angry when I told him our decision to take this to court." Mrs. Benson's eyes grew hard. "But there was no denying that handprint on Laney's back. I left him in a room by himself to cool off."

"And Laney?"

Mrs. Benson smiled. "She's having a cookie in the officer's lounge." Her gaze landed on Abby. "You were the only person she could name when I asked if she had any family she would like to visit while we sort this out."

Abby's throat tightened. "I'll take good care of her."

"*We'll* take good care of her," Einstein amended.

A few minutes later, Einstein had one arm around Laney and one around Abby as he led them out into the parking lot. At least the heat was slowly abating as the sun slipped beneath the horizon. Glancing back, she saw Wesley exiting.

"Hey!" Wesley shouted.

But Einstein had them in his car and the doors closed and locked before Wesley caught up. Standing beside the car, Einstein met him head-on. There was an exchange of words that Abby couldn't hear, though the vibe was intense. In the backseat, crinkles of concern had formed across Laney's forehead.

"You'll be safe with us, honey," Abby assured her. "You know that, right?"

Wide blue eyes met Abby's. "Yeah. I just don't want Dad to hurt him."

Abby bit back a smile. "You don't have to worry about Einstein. He knows how to take care of himself, and us." She almost wished Wesley would throw a punch and Einstein could lay him out—but not in front of Laney. She expelled a sigh of relief when Wesley walked away without so much as a backward look and Einstein slid into the driver's seat. "Everything okay?"

"I think we've reached a temporary understanding." Einstein backed out of the parking space. "And I told him if he's working with the Circle or the Boss in any manner, he'd better report it immediately or face the consequences. He didn't seem startled by any of my accusations."

"What consequences?"

Einstein simply arched a brow and returned his attention to his driving. She had no doubt Einstein could fight—physically, mentally, or with technology—and win.

Abby sank back into her seat and willed her muscles to relax now that the threat was over. In the side view mirror, she spied Laney who was losing the battle with exhaustion as her eyelids drooped uncontrollably. Abby wasn't the only one who felt safe. It was hard to believe that just yesterday she'd doubted Einstein's integrity.

"Thank you," she said, rolling her head against the headrest to face Einstein.

He shot her a quick glance. "For what?"

"Being there. For me. For her."

He glanced at Laney in the rearview and smiled. "She's a sweet girl. She doesn't deserve a parent who doesn't give a damn."

"Nobody does."

His mouth tightened. Whenever she brought up parent-child relationships, it seemed to hit a sore spot.

"Thanks for the ride, too," she said. "Where are we going?"

He kept his eyes on the road. "You two are staying with me tonight. I'm not letting you out of my sight."

Surprised, she sat up straight. "You don't have to do that."

"That man had murder in his eyes. And I have a feeling the Charmer's involved in this."

She shuddered. "We can find somewhere else to go. I can afford a night or two at a motel."

"You have somewhere to go. My place." He slanted her a look. "Don't bother arguing. I was number one in my debate class."

"I don't doubt it." She sighed and tipped her head back against the seat again. Besides, she didn't want to fight him on this. The truth was, she *wanted* to go home with Einstein.

"RON'S WIDOW DOESN'T REMEMBER ANYONE COMING AROUND, asking for his cufflinks or bringing up the past," Damian told Lorena. "She doesn't remember when the cufflinks disappeared. Could have been years ago."

Lorena brought their plates over and sat in the chair across from him at his dining room table. He was still struggling to embrace the fact that she was here, in his home. Rarely did he invite SSAM employees into his house. From the beginning, he'd instituted the invisible barrier as a way of remembering he had to remain separate. Though his employees had become like family members, he was still their leader.

But those lines had been blurring of late. In recent years, his employees had become more like family. And when Lorena had suggested she bring over dinner from his favorite Italian restaurant so they could go over more of his past—and, he suspected, so she could keep an eye on him in case the Charmer contacted him with the next step in this game of his—it had seemed perfectly innocuous.

His body knew differently. It responded to her as if it were made of iron and she were a magnet. No, more like lightning drawn to a metal rod.

Her wide lips wrapped around her pasta-filled fork and tugged. He felt an answering tug in his abdomen. He hadn't been a monk since divorcing Priscilla but he hadn't been so keenly *aware* of another woman since then, either. He'd dated, even slept with, a few women he knew, but that had been more about getting bodily needs out of the way so he could re-focus on his life's sole purpose —finding Sam's killer.

Lorena was different. Her looks were dark and exotic, but her mind was even more beautiful. As a mindhunter, profiling killers, she was among the elite in her field. He was still surprised she'd remained with him at SSAM after all these years. He'd wooed her from the FBI with promises of setting her own hours, schedule, and caseload, but if anything, she'd worked harder than she would have worked with the Feds.

He tried to focus on his meal, but ended up pushing his plate away.

"Not hungry?" she asked.

"I keep thinking about the seconds ticking by. Only about forty-eight hours left. Any moment, he could unleash the next step in his game." The waiting was the hardest part.

She sighed. "We do seem to be at his mercy."

"That's not good enough." Hurt flashed in her eyes before she disguised it. He reached out to take her hand, which went immediately still under his fingertips. "I didn't mean that the way it sounded." He waited until her dark gaze rose to his. "That anger was directed at me, not you. I'm frustrated."

"I am, too." A flash of fire turned into something like sympathy. He much preferred the fire. "I wish I could do more."

"You're already doing what you can. Hey, you brought me dinner. Plus," he added, smiling for her benefit, "you're distracting me from the bad stuff." And she hadn't removed her hand from beneath his.

She gestured with her free hand to her case notes, which littered the rest of his dining room table. "I'm doing a damn poor job of it."

"I appreciate you trying, but what I need now is focus, not distraction."

"Abby seems to be bringing a new energy to the investigation." She studied him as she said the words.

He huffed out a laugh. "It's okay to come out and ask. Have you ever known me to be fragile?"

"Okay. How do you feel about what she said today?"

"I was in shock at first," he admitted. "She was right on the money about the fight." Ashamed, he looked away.

"You didn't want your thirteen-year-old going out on a date with an older boy. Sounds like a normal father-daughter argument to me. Rules are necessary, especially at her age."

"Except this time, it made her vulnerable to the promises of a predator."

"And if you hadn't had the rule, she could have been just as vulnerable to other dangers. Besides, the predator had already been lurking, looking for a weak spot," Lorena pointed out. "You couldn't have known that. You were only doing your job as a dad." She shoved her plate aside. "Are you ready to dig more?" Though she clearly didn't like his *tear me apart* request, she'd taken it to heart. "How about we move this to the living room?"

It was odd to see her graceful body, lean and slim as a dancer's, her long legs shown to simple perfection in her pencil-line black skirt, gliding about his house, but he found his gaze glued to her as she set about fluffing pillows, muting cell phones, and making sure they were comfortable and wouldn't be interrupted.

He sat on the couch and she sat next to him, giving him some space but close enough that he could reach out and touch her. "Where do you want me to start?" he asked.

"Tell me about your childhood."

That surprised him. "What does that have to do with anything?"

She arched a thin, dark brow. "Humor me. You might be surprised."

"Okay, Dr. Freud," he joked. Her lips curved, but her expression was serious. He lay down, figuring he'd immerse himself in this psychoanalysis for better or worse. Once settled back into the couch cushions, he stared at the ceiling—her body was too damned distracting—and thought back to a time he rarely revisited. "What do you want to know?"

"Just start talking. Anything that comes to mind."

He didn't lift his head but cracked open one eye to see her. His bent knees had left room for her to sit at the other end of the couch. She'd kicked off her heels and curled her legs under her. To an outsider, they might have looked like two longtime friends having a relaxed chat. Except that he had volunteered to gut himself and put his innards on display.

She saw him peeking at her and the arm that rested on the back of the couch reached out to him, her fingertips lightly brushing his knee. "It's just me. I can handle anything you tell me."

I want you.

The words were on his lips but he bit them back. Instead, he closed his eyes and focused on the task. The Charmer was after him, loathed him and wanted revenge on him for some dark purpose. As if taking Samantha's life hadn't been enough, the fucker. He tensed.

Immediately, Lorena was there. He hadn't heard her move to sit on the floor beside his head. Her fingers soothed him with long strokes up and down his arm, from shoulder to elbow to wrist.

"I had a normal childhood here in Chicago," he said. "Parents who loved me. More money than we needed, with all the perks of being members of high society." He released a mirthless laugh. "I didn't appreciate what I had. Went away to an Ivy League college, emerged with business contacts that would ensure anyone success —" Here, Lorena interrupted with a grunt of disapproval and he cocked open an eye. "What?"

"Why do you berate yourself and belittle your background?"

He blinked slowly. Was that what he'd done? "I didn't realize—"

"Coming from wealth is nothing to be ashamed of. Coming from privilege and throwing it in people's faces would be horrible, but you don't do that. You did the complete opposite. You made something. Something that matters. Something that makes a damn difference in our society. Does that sound like something you should be ashamed of?" Conviction rang in her voice, building with each word, vibrating through his chest cavity and shaking the hard layer surrounding his heart until it shattered.

Their gazes met and held. Damn, she was beautiful, a raven-haired Valkyrie willing to fight for what was right. "So...maybe I was wrong?"

"It happens."

He closed his eyes again. "I had friends, mostly from the same circles as me. Ron was one of those."

"Any who would wish you harm? Someone who wanted what you had?"

"Not that I can think of. Jesus. I hate to think a *friend* could kill my daughter." Yet he had no choice but to consider the possibility. After all, he'd seen all manner of evil over the years.

"Monsters come in all shapes and sizes. Sometimes they lurk quietly and you don't even know they're there."

When he'd interviewed Lorena for her position at SSAM, he'd been stunned by her vehement dedication to taking down the worst monsters in society. She'd seen the worst when her parents had been killed by a man on a crime spree when she'd been only seven. She'd witnessed it, having hidden in a cupboard with her sister, where her mother had stuffed them when the man had burst through their door. Lorena had lost half her family that day and had then been taken in by an aunt. That kind of experience scarred a person deeply. Even worse, probably, because Lorena had been at a young, impressionable age.

He closed his eyes again, trying to go back to a time when his future had seemed bright and secure. That had been another Damian Manchester, a lifetime ago.

"At Yale, the competition became more fierce," he said. "But nothing unusual."

"Did you hurt anyone specifically, maybe during your climb to success? Any devious deeds, no matter how small?"

"Not that I'm aware of. But business isn't always about making —or keeping—friends."

"Tell me about Ron."

"I met him in boarding school. He was part of our group of high school friends. Most of them went on to become successful businessmen, but Ron always seemed to want to stay out of the limelight. He was more comfortable behind the scenes. I think I thrust him out of his comfort zone when Sam was murdered and he had to take over for me. The stress broke him. He'd tried to reach out to me in that time, but I wasn't answering calls."

Damian had disappeared from life for a while, ignoring any attempts by friends and colleagues to draw him back into the real world—a world without Sam. And his business was better off in the hands of people who could function normally when all he could think about at the time was revenge.

Sympathy was heavy in her eyes and she reached out to take his hand. "I want you to remember that you aren't responsible for Ron's actions. Or for Sam's death."

He released a sigh. "Hard to do that."

"You're a good man. You can believe that." Her hand let go of his to lift to his cheek.

In the space of a breath, they were kissing. Damian wasn't sure if she'd moved to bridge the gap or he had—probably, they both had. What mattered was the heat that flooded him, the soft, pliant woman in his arms. Her fingernails scraped lightly against his scalp, sending delicious shivers that were both hot and cold at once. *God, yes.* He'd wanted to kiss her so many times over the years, but she was his employee. She was also his confidant, his rock, his friend... *His.*

Their mouths tangled in a hot, passionate merging that had him groaning when she pulled back. She was breathless as her passion-glazed eyes searched his.

"Why did we wait so long to do that?" he asked.

Her lips curved. "Because you weren't ready."

Vixen. She thought she knew everything. He lifted his head to kiss that curve of triumph, and her lips awakened again beneath his. His hands were shaking as he reached for her, pulling her on top of him on the couch. His fingers roved from her waist, traveling up her back and slipping beneath the dark curtain of silky hair to hold her head to his.

Slow down. The angel on one shoulder wanted to savor this.

The devil on the other shoulder told him to speed up. Life was short.

But both were in complete agreement. This was right. This woman belonged in his arms.

CHAPTER 11

The rolling blackouts had hit his building by the time Einstein drove Abby and a sleeping Laney into the community garage. Luckily, someone had left the gate open in anticipation of the loss of power. Still, it was dark and he used his headlights to search the corners until he shut the car off. He reached across Abby's lap to the glove box and removed a flashlight, then handed it to her.

"You got her?" Abby asked as he pulled the slight girl out of the backseat and into his arms.

"Yeah." Little puffs of breath tickled his cheek as Laney settled her arms around his neck and murmured in her sleep. She smelled sweetly of sweat and the strawberry lollipop the caseworker had given her.

"Poor thing's exhausted. We might as well tuck her in and I'll make sure she takes a bath in the morning." Abby grabbed a couple grocery bags and a jug of milk from the trunk. They'd made a quick stop so she could run into a store and purchase some necessities. Einstein had spent the time watching Laney sleep in the backseat, her cheeks rosy and her expression relaxed. How had he, a man dedicated to avoiding complicated relationships, succumbed to the wiles of a little girl and a woman from a coffee shop?

"It's going to be a bit of a hike," he told Abby as they bypassed the dead elevator and hit the stairs. He shifted Laney in his arms but she didn't awaken. His top-floor apartment, while not the most expensive place in Chicago, had cost a pretty penny when he bought it six years ago. Despite rooming with Max, the place was his personal retreat, and was worth every cent. After Afghanistan, he'd become possessive of his space, wanting a place where nobody could see him struggle with headaches or flashbacks. Max understood and kept out of Einstein's business—most of the time —but Abby had no idea how huge a step it was for him to invite her here.

"Unfortunate timing for a blackout," Abby said. A dark strand of hair clung to her forehead, perspiration holding it captive.

He admired her stamina. She'd kept up with him the entire day as he'd hauled her all over the city, picking her brain and her emotions. He'd dragged her through hell.

Insistent meows met him as he approached the door. *Crap.* He'd forgotten the cats. They must not have been fed today. By casual agreement, he and his neighbors had shared the chore of caring for them, letting them roam the building and rooftop most of the time.

Abby's amused gaze landed on him as the pair of white-and-gray cats scurried up to him, pushing past them as he opened the door. "They sound happy to see you."

Moonlight streamed through the large windows that filled one wall of his penthouse apartment, giving them some light to navigate by.

"They're not mine. They just think they are." One of the buggers twined about his legs, nearly tripping him as he carried Laney to the spare bedroom.

"Maybe because you take care of them?" Tossing him a grin

over her shoulder, Abby jumped in front of him to turn down the sheets on the bed that used to be Max's. She dropped her shopping bag near the door. He gently laid Laney down and Abby removed the girl's shoes before tucking her in. Gazing down at Laney, Abby smoothed the hair back from the child's face.

Einstein's throat tightened at the tender gesture. He was glad he could help Laney, even if only for one peaceful night.

Abby moved past him and out of the room. With a last look at the sleeping girl, he closed the door quietly and followed Abby to the kitchen. As he went through the motions of feeding Em and CeeCee and refilling their water bowl, the cats purred in bliss.

Abby's laugh was warm as she watched the felines jockey for position. "Not sure getting them their own bowls is the proper way to tell them they don't belong. They know you care and now they're yours." She turned her smile on him and his breath caught.

What if, when Einstein opened the door to his apartment, that smile, that dimple and those curves, were there to welcome him? What would it be like to have her to come home to?

He shook his head at his ridiculous imaginings. Relationships were more trouble than they were worth. His parents had proven that years ago and he'd never seen evidence to the contrary. In fact, in his experience, love was a death sentence.

Still, after the events of the day, he wanted to devour her like the Big Bad Wolf. The memory of their kiss had invaded his thoughts all evening.

Needing to occupy himself so he wouldn't reach for her and indulge in another taste, he found candles and matches in the cupboard and went about setting them out in the living room, giving the place a cozy glow that only served to increase his tension.

He eyed the bag of takeout she'd carried up. He didn't have a table, as he'd given it to Max and Catherine when they moved into their own place. It wasn't like he and Max had used it much, anyway, and it had been a thrift-store reject. "Living room okay?" A picnic amid the romantic glow of the candles was intimate, but it would have to suffice.

"Sure." Carrying the sodas, she followed and sat next to him on the couch, kicked off her sandals, and curled her legs under her. She set her cell phone on the table and frowned at it.

"Everything okay?" He took out the pita wraps and laid hers in front of her.

"I should have checked on Grandpa again."

"Go ahead and call. Might ease your mind to know he's okay."

Instead, she reached for her wrap. "It's late. I'm sure his room-mate would have called if anything were wrong. I can wait until tomorrow. I just wish he'd gone to the temporary shelter."

"He wouldn't?"

She sighed. "He's stubborn. Heck, I can barely get him to the hospital for a checkup. Not sure why I thought he'd listen to me about this."

Her concern was obvious and Einstein felt a twinge of jealousy. And a stab of anger at *Grandpa* for ignoring her. With chagrin, he realized a part of that anger should be directed at himself for monopolizing her time today. It was obvious, Abby so easily gave to others—to the point they took advantage of her and her feelings. He didn't want to be that kind of person.

She shook her head at herself. "I'm sure he's fine or I would have heard something."

As they ate, Einstein checked his phone.

"Expecting a call?" Abby asked.

"No. Checking emails. With the blackout, the Internet is out here, but I set up the computers at SSAM to send me periodic updates on the programs I'm running."

"Any news?"

"Maggie says nobody with a bracelet has approached her, and her husband is keeping a close eye out for anyone following them, but hasn't seen anything suspicious. Oh, and Damian didn't recognize any of the women from the photos I gave him." It seemed they were striking out when it came to finding the bracelet owner.

"I'm sorry there's nothing new. Maybe by morning…" She balled up her trash and put it in the bag, then sat back with a contented sigh. The warm day had curled the ends of her hair around her neck and collarbone. "And I'm sorry about earlier."

"Earlier?"

"In the stairwell of Hannah Smith's building."

He froze. Was she talking about their kiss? There was no way in hell he wanted to erase that moment.

She grimaced. "I was needy and I think you felt the need to comfort me."

"I sure as hell hope you don't think that's all that kiss was about. If you did, I was doing it wrong."

Her cheeks turned bright pink. "No. You did it exactly right." When she raised her gaze to his, her eyes were dark with need. "Most people who know about my gift are creeped out or want me to use it to their advantage, so I've learned to hold that part of me back."

"That must be hard."

She shrugged. "It can be lonely. Like any human, I like to touch, and be touched."

It took him a second to clear the image of him touching her. "Must be hard to block out life's bad stuff, at the cost of the good. It took guts to talk to me after what flashed in your mind at the coffee shop." He grinned. "I'm glad you no longer believe I'm a murderer."

"I had my doubts." She smiled back. Whatever she'd thought, she was no longer threatened by him.

"That just goes to prove that your methods can be unreliable."

Instead of the objection to his criticism he expected, she nodded. "They aren't always reliable because I have to interpret the messages. And they're not usually clear. But that doesn't mean your method is foolproof or best." A spark of challenge entered her gaze and he found he liked it. He couldn't remember the last time someone had taken him to task—or the last time he'd enjoyed it.

"I have science on my side."

"And scientists are never wrong?" She sat back and crossed her arms over her chest. His gaze went to her breasts when her movements pushed them upward. She had a beautiful body. His own body awakened as it remembered how she'd felt pressed against him.

Oblivious to the direction of his thoughts, she cocked her head at him. "Must be hard having to be right all the time. Then again, trusting only what you can see *is* the safe path."

Ouch. A direct blow. But her comments hit close to home. "In the real world, there are certain rules that are understood. Outcomes can be predicted, even expected." He turned so he was facing her, his arm draped along the back of the couch, his fingertips toying with the ends of her hair. "But there are things that are unpredictable, too."

"Yeah? Like what?" Her words had a breathy quality that told him he was affecting her.

"There's nothing safe about you." She was his complete opposite. Where he was hard, she was soft. Her emotions were the kryptonite to his stoic realism. And yet, he craved more. The silence stretched on as their eyes communicated.

"I believe in some science," she finally said. She scooted closer to him, her knee lightly bumping his. Her eyes held an invitation he was all too ready to accept.

"Yeah? Like what?" He threw her own words back at her. It was a wonder anybody could hear his words over the pounding of his heart.

"Like sexual chemistry." She leaned forward another couple inches. "Pheromones. There's a lot of science to support animal attraction."

His fingers, draped along the back of the couch near her shoulder, moved from the tips of her hair to her neck. He leaned closer until her mouth was only an inch from his. Time hung suspended for a long moment as his eyes searched hers. She released a little sigh of surrender, her eyelids flickered shut, and she pressed her lips to his, once again proving his point—reality could be so much better than fantasy.

For as long as she'd known him, everything about Einstein had indicated focus and a sense of purpose, so it was no surprise that his method of seduction was the same. Every scrape of his teeth or tangle of his tongue was skillful. She'd almost think it was calculated to make her melt. And yet, she sensed the same fire burned within him, a passion waiting to be unleashed. *By me.* The knowledge of that power made her bolder.

She submersed herself in Einstein, his scent, his taste and, oh God, his *feel.* Their first kiss had been a wonderful surprise. This was even better. There was no doubt he wanted her, or that he enjoyed touching her. In fact, his hands were drifting toward parts that hadn't been stroked in way too long. She arched into him and swallowed his moan along with her own.

She scooted closer, encouraging him to take the kiss deeper, to let his hands roam, to feed her greed. God, it had been so long since she'd let a man go this far. Hell, his hands were nearly touching her most sensitive parts, his thumbs resting on her ribcage just under her breasts. If she were a less proud woman, she might have begged him to inch upward just a tad.

He groaned. The evidence of his arousal was hard against her hip.

Well, hell, maybe she could beg, just this once.

But he pulled away suddenly, jerking his head back and staring at her with glazed eyes. She wanted to scream at the tightness coiled inside, aching to be let loose. But doubt and hesitation were in his gaze. She took small comfort in the way his chest heaved for breaths as if they'd climbed another ten flights of stairs.

"Maybe we should go to bed." His voice was thick, as if he'd just woken from a deep sleep. But his expression was a grimace of pain, not at all inviting. "Think you can share with Laney? It's a queen."

With a feline dexterity that had probably served him well in his years as a SEAL, he sprang to his feet and away from her. Did they train SEALs to have that kind of grace or did it come naturally?

It took her a moment for her engine to go from ninety miles per hour to zero. *He was shutting this down?* She tried—and failed—to look like she wasn't embarrassed. She pushed to her feet. "Of course. Thanks again for putting up with us for the night." Of course, none of this line-crossing would have happened if he'd just left her alone. She'd be in her own bed, or at a motel, as she'd originally suggested.

And you'd have missed another kiss.

"Abby."

"What?" As she spun back to him, control warred with the need in his eyes. "I want you but…"

"But you're weirded out by me, after all?"

"No. Absolutely not." He muttered a curse and shoved his hand through his hair. "I don't do things like this."

She arched a brow. "Sleep with women? Are you trying to say you're gay?"

His gaze went to her lips, curved with wry humor. Damn, he wanted to taste them again. Wanted to feel their soft heat and hear her low moans of encouragement.

But if he gave in to that one temptation, the floodgates would open. He wouldn't be able to resist taking this further, claiming her, marking her as his in other, much more primitive and satisfying ways. *Sexual chemistry and pheromones, indeed.* He couldn't get enough of her.

And that was dangerous. She was so open and giving and he... wasn't. He couldn't destroy her. And he'd never had a relationship that had stuck, which obviously said something about him.

He scowled. "No. I enjoy women." Especially the one standing in front of him.

"*Women,* but not me?" Her eyebrows rose higher. "I got a very different impression." Her gaze flicked over his body and damn if certain parts of him didn't respond in wholehearted agreement.

"We can't do this. Not tonight." His voice rasped with need, but he sent a glance toward the closed bedroom door. Feeling like a coward, he'd use Laney as an excuse to regroup. Abby had thrown his entire game off.

She followed his gaze and shook her head. But her eyes were understanding as she turned back to him. "Okay. But when you're ready to do *this,* I'll be here. I'm not going anywhere." She walked to him and slid her hands up his chest, shoulders and neck, until they were against his scalp. Leaning into him, she melded her lips to his. The kiss was softer this time, but the passion was no less intense. Just as he was starting to doubt his control and cave to impulse, she pulled away. "Let me know when you're ready to do some more *chemistry* experiments."

He nearly groaned as all kinds of great ideas for experiments came to him. But the ultimate outcome would be her leaving him.

He cleared his throat. "The bathroom is the other door off the hallway. There are extra towels on the rack."

She clasped her hands together in front of her as if resisting the urge to reach for him. He appreciated the effort, as he wasn't sure he could rein in his impulses again. "I'll probably take a quick shower."

"If you need anything, I'll be right across the hall." Where he'd lay in bed, staring at the ceiling, trying to forget the taste of her on his tongue and the feel of the curves his hands had recently traversed. He'd need an ice bath to get the images of what he wanted to do to her out of his head. But that wasn't to be, either. He gulped as, a minute later, he heard her turning the shower on. With it came a wave of new ideas for experiments.

CHAPTER 12

When Abby woke early the next morning, she found three pairs of curious eyes aimed at her. They belonged to two cats and Laney.

Laney, who was back to wearing her headlamp, grinned, exposing a gap in the middle where a tooth had been just last night. She proudly held the expunged tooth up for her inspection. "I wiggled it and it popped out. Einstein helped."

"He did?" She half expected to see the man in the bedroom. Maybe *hoped* was a better word. "Where is he?"

"Living room. He made me cereal and milk."

Abby bit back a grin. "Sounds like a real chef. I guess you've met Em and CeeCee."

Laney stroked the nearest kitty, who released a torrent of contented purrs. "They're sweet. Dad never let me have a pet. Can I have one here?"

Abby's breath caught in her throat. "Honey, I'm not sure yet how everything's going to end up. But I do know I won't rest until you're in the best place you can be—the home you want."

"I want to stay with you and Einstein."

The girl had latched on to Einstein quickly. *So did you.* She still remembered the taste of him, as well as the haunted look in his eyes as he told her they couldn't be together. He'd used Laney's presence as the reason for backing away, but her gut told her the conflict was much deeper—and she was listening to her gut more often these days.

"We'll see." As much as Abby would lavish her love and attention on the girl, Laney might have extended family somewhere. "I was wondering… How did you get my number and know to call me?"

Laney's nose scrunched up. "I thought you put it under my door. The note had your name on it."

Abby's breath caught in her throat. So, the Charmer *had* stooped to involving a child from her past in this mess. And he'd come close enough to the girl that he could have hurt her. She swallowed her fear and smiled for Laney's sake. "You did right, calling me, honey."

With all the worldly confidence of a six-year-old, Laney nodded. "I know."

"Did you save any breakfast for me?"

Abby followed Laney out of the bedroom and found Einstein sitting on the couch, typing away on a laptop. He looked up and the same hot gaze from the night before swept over her, as if she were breakfast and he were a starving man. She was more determined than ever to discover the root of Einstein's reasons for pulling away.

"Good morning," he said. His jaw was rough from hours without a razor. It was the sexiest thing she'd woken up to in… ever. "Help yourself to coffee. We've got electricity."

"That's good news." Though she hadn't exactly minded the candles.

"There's cereal, too, if you like."

"It's the good kind of cereal," Laney said, grabbing Abby's hand and pulling her toward the kitchen. "With marshmallows," she added in a hushed voice that wasn't so hushed.

Over her shoulder, Abby caught Einstein's guilty grimace. "You just happened to have that on hand, huh?"

He shot her a grin that made her heart stop. "Just because you get older doesn't mean you have to grow up." Despite the smile, the haunted look was in his eyes again. She had the impression he'd had to grow up early. Which was what made this playful side of him all the more endearing.

Before she could find a way to sample that smile, Abby let Laney finish tugging her to the kitchen, where a pot of coffee released a delicious aroma that made her mouth water and her brain kick into gear. "I thought the rolling blackouts are designed to only last a couple hours," she called to Einstein when she spied the carton of spoiled milk in the sink. Good thing they'd stopped for a fresh carton last night.

He appeared in the doorway, and the small space shrank to closet-size. "It wasn't the blackouts that made it go bad. More like tuning out. I've been too busy to shop. Forgot, actually." He frowned toward Laney. "But I can run out if we need more for growing bones. Someone here was drinking the new stuff like it was going out of style." He ruffled a hand over Laney's tangled mass of brown curls and the kid giggled. Over Laney's head, his troubled gaze met Abby's. They both knew Laney probably wasn't receiving the best nutrition at home.

"How long were you guys up together?" Abby asked, stunned at the easy bond the two had made since last night.

"About an hour," Einstein said.

"He likes to get up early," Laney announced.

"You get to see more cartoons that way." He winked. Abby wondered if any of his programs had yielded new information.

"He likes the roadrunner, too," Laney said. "And the marsh-mallow cereal."

Abby grinned at the image of them bonding over colorful marshmallows and Road Runner and Wile E. Coyote antics. "Apparently, you two have a lot in common."

Einstein leaned toward Abby conspiratorially. "I showed her my iPad. Lots of apps out there for kids. Who knew?"

His playfulness made her smile—until his gaze lowered to her mouth. Her smile froze as a different kind of pleasure flooded her. His attention shifted as his cell phone rang from his pocket. She could tell from his tone as he answered that the call was work related. She sighed. Reality was about to intrude on their peaceful morning.

"Let's get you in the bathtub," she told Laney and made herself busy for several minutes getting her settled and washing her hair. "I got you some clean clothes, too. I'll lay them out on the bed for you, okay?"

"'Kay."

"I'll be back in a second. I'm leaving the door cracked so you can call if you need anything."

Leaving Laney to splash in the bubbles from the soap she'd thought to buy at the store, Abby went to the bedroom to get dressed. When she returned to the living room, Einstein had disappeared, presumably into his bedroom, where the door was closed. Laney was still happily playing in the bubble bath, so Abby decided to give her a few more minutes before they faced the real world. There were so many unknowns for Laney, for Mariah. Abby hoped they'd all find happy resolutions by the end of the day.

She'd visit Grandpa first. Seeing Laney might even be good for him. She'd find someone to cover today's yoga classes. Then she'd talk to Laney's caseworker. Whatever Einstein needed, regarding finding Mariah, she'd be at his beck and call. The Charmer's clock was still counting down.

A photograph on the window ledge called to her. The frame was rustic pine and the glass was gone, but the photo inside showed a smiling family—father, mother and a younger, scrawnier teenage Einstein in the foreground. The high school graduation cap and gown indicated the occasion, and the group was smiling, but somehow, his parents seemed apart, standing in the background.

On impulse, she picked up the frame and was shocked by the jolt of grief that hit her. The photo depicted a celebratory occasion, but some intensely painful memory was associated with it. *Einstein's* remembered pain. Feeling as if she were intruding, she set the frame back on the ledge with shaky hands.

"That was taken a few years before they died." Einstein's voice had her spinning to face him. He stood only a few feet away in a plain black tee and jeans. His hair was damp and his skin had that just-scrubbed look.

"I'm sorry for your loss."

"Don't be." The muscles in his jaw tightened and his arms crossed over his chest in a typical defensive posture.

Her eyes were drawn to his right hand. It seemed to radiate warmth and light, calling her to touch it. She'd learned to ignore these notions unless she wanted to receive a message. She gauged the hard look on Einstein's face and resisted. Besides, when they found Mariah alive and well and nailed the Charmer to the wall, Einstein would likely be out of her life. He'd happily go back to his computers and maybe they'd bump into each other on occasion in the coffee shop. The thought of going back to casual-acquaintance status depressed her.

"Noah called," he said. "There haven't been any new leads regarding Mariah. I also checked in with Laney's caseworker. She's still looking for a placement for Laney. In the meantime, Catherine can keep an eye on her at SSAM while we run an errand for Damian."

"What errand?"

He wouldn't meet her gaze.

"Is something wrong?"

"It's a favor for Damian," he finally said.

"And it's not something you want to agree to?"

"It's *you* who has to agree." Now that his earlier good humor was gone, tired lines had formed around his eyes and mouth. She wanted to kiss the creases and smooth them out, to bring back the playful man she now knew was hidden inside.

"Me? What can I do?"

"There's someone who might know how to find the Charmer."

She stepped closer. "Still not seeing how that involves me." She gave into the urge to smooth a fingertip over the crease in his forehead. At her light touch, he sucked in a breath but didn't move. "You're so worried it's scaring me."

"That person wasn't a nice guy."

"Past tense?"

"He's dead now."

"So you want me to touch something a not-so-nice dead guy once owned?" She hid a shudder and dropped her hand. While going through a dead person's stuff to seek out information regarding a murder wasn't on her list of enjoyable activities, she was invested in this case now and would see it through to the end. "I'll do it."

His gaze, unreadable, landed on her and he nodded. "Thank you. I hate to put you through that—"

"I'll do it, on one condition."

His brows drew together. "What?"

"We make a quick stop on the way. I'll feel better if I can check on my grandfather." And give him the touchstone that was still in her purse.

Einstein's lips turned up on one side. "Sure."

"I'll get Laney ready."

His hand seemed to glow again as it reached for his laptop and put it into its case. She looked closer at the scar that ran along the base of his thumb and around his wrist in a jagged line. It called to her, but she resisted.

Until he willingly opened up to her, Einstein's life, and his secrets, were his own.

"Grandpa, this is Laney." Abby placed a hand on Laney's shoulder. "And this is Einstein." She gestured to the man at her other side.

Laney beamed. "I lost a tooth. Think the Tooth Fairy can find me at Einstein's?"

"I'm absolutely certain of it," Grandpa said. His eyes sparkled within his wrinkled face. He'd even donned his oxygen mask without much argument once he let them into his living room.

Abby didn't point out that Laney might not be staying at Einstein's tonight. Hell, Abby might not be with Einstein tonight. Anything could happen in the next twelve hours, including finding the Charmer.

"What's that?" Laney asked, pointing to the plastic mask over Grandpa's mouth. As he explained, Abby moved to the kitchen, intending to scramble some eggs, but Grandpa called her back.

"Ernie fed me before he left. I'm good. Besides, I don't get many visitors. I'd rather spend my time getting to know my guests." His gaze moved from Einstein to Abby as she sat in a chair across from the couch, where Grandpa and Einstein sat at opposite ends. Laney drifted off to a nearby table where a couple photo albums were stacked and started flipping through. "Did you really stay at this man's house last night?"

"Yes," Abby said.

"Want to clue me in as to how you suddenly have a readymade family?"

"No." She reached into her purse and pulled out the hematite stone. "I brought Mom's touchstone, like you asked."

Grandpa took it, held it a moment with closed eyes, then handed it back to her. "Good."

"That's it?" She took the stone back and looked at it.

"I think it's better off with you. You need the help more than I do." He winked.

"Gee, thanks." But she couldn't deny the truth in his words, or the wave of comfort she felt as she held the stone again.

"What does it do?" Einstein asked. He'd quietly watched their exchange, but curiosity had him leaning forward to inspect the stone.

Abby handed it to him. "It's hematite. It's supposed to sharpen focus and encourage a sense of calm."

He inspected it and handed it back to her. "Does it work for you?"

She thought about the intensity of the images and her increased connection to them. "I'm not sure, but I've definitely been more focused on my gift."

"Saw you on the news last night," Grandpa said.

She froze. "At the Pierces'? I forgot to watch."

"I didn't," Einstein said. "They mentioned your name." His scowl indicated he wasn't happy about that. He looked at Grandpa. "That's why I took her home with me."

"So you are helping with this investigation?" Grandpa asked her.

"I'm trying to," she said.

He grinned. "You took my advice."

Uncomfortable with the way Einstein was watching her, she shrugged. "If I can help, I will."

Grandpa looked back to Einstein. "I'm glad you were there to protect her. Abby takes after her mama. Lydia was one of the good ones. Loving, generous, smart. But her heart often landed her in trouble."

"Sounds like Abby inherited a lot from her." Einstein's warm gaze drifted over her.

"Now it's just me and her. Soon, it'll be just her." Grandpa's eyes narrowed and he pulled his mask aside so that his words were no longer muffled. "I'd like her to have more than that."

"Grandpa," Abby growled. "I didn't bring them here for an interview. I was just checking on you."

"I'm fine."

"And to see if we can take you to a shelter today…?"

"I'm fine," he repeated. "Ernie will be back soon."

She stood. "Good. We'd better be on our way."

"The investigation?" His question was for Einstein.

"We can really use her help. I promise I'll keep her safe."

"That's what I like to hear. A man who appreciates my grand-daughter." He sent a significant look her way before turning to Laney. "Hope I'll see you again soon, sweetie."

Laney bounced to her feet. "Me too. I like your pictures." She hugged Grandpa and his eyes misted. He suddenly looked a decade older and Abby's heart squeezed. Grandpa didn't have long. Laney would be leaving soon, hopefully for a better, stable family. Einstein would return to his work and be done with her.

Soon, Abby would have her life back and it would be so much emptier than ever before.

ABBY AND EINSTEIN WENT TO THE SSAM OFFICES TO CHECK IN with the team before heading out to whatever errand Damian had suggested—to touch some dead guy's stuff.

"We're going to have so much fun." Catherine took Laney's hand and led her behind the front desk. "I've made up a little area for you to color and draw."

"I'll make a picture for the Tooth Fairy," Laney said. Abby made a mental note to leave a dollar and Laney's tooth with the caseworker.

"Thanks for keeping an eye on her," Abby told Catherine as Laney settled in the lobby with her art supplies.

"My pleasure. Besides, I'll need the practice." Catherine's face glowed as her smile widened. "I'm pregnant!"

Einstein's stunned expression was quickly masked as he stepped forward to hug her. "Congratulations. Does Max know?"

Catherine rolled her eyes. "I told him first, of course. He was shocked but he's already planning how to be the best daddy ever." Her hand went to her stomach as her gaze moved to Abby, who'd been quietly taking it all in. "Oh my God. You already knew, didn't you?"

"What?" Abby said. Her cheeks flushed guiltily.

"You did. How? What did you see?" Rather than being upset, Catherine seemed genuinely curious.

Einstein's gaze narrowed on Abby. "Is that true? You knew?"

Cornered, Abby considered lying, but she'd always been bad at that. Still, in her experience, this was the type of huge, important news that people didn't want her to know until they revealed it. "I thought she and Max should be the first ones to find out. I wouldn't want to rob them of that excitement."

"How did you know?" Catherine asked again.

"When you touched my shoulder yesterday morning, when you were welcoming me and offering coffee."

"I knew it. That's amazing."

"What did you see?" Einstein asked.

"It was more of a smell, actually," Abby said. "You know, that newborn baby smell? And the feel of downy curls against my fingertips. Strawberry blond." She smiled at Catherine. "She's going to be beautiful."

"She!" Catherine clapped her hands. "I can't wait."

Einstein frowned. "Maybe you should move up that wedding, then."

"Oh, we will. Max already called his parents to see if they can join us in Vegas in a month." Her eyes narrowed on him. "As best man, you'll be expected to be there, too."

"I'll put it on my calendar," Einstein said with a forced smile. Catherine didn't seem to notice his discomfort.

Abby decided to change the subject for him. "We'll let you get to work. Laney, behave for Miss Catherine and I'll see you in about an hour." The girl nodded without looking up from her drawing.

Einstein escorted Abby down the secure hallway to the back offices. He immediately switched on his screens. "So you can see the future, too?"

Startled by the subject, Abby was momentarily taken aback. "Sometimes. When it's something from the past, I'll feel this tug backward or to the left. If I feel pulled forward or to the right, it usually indicates something that might happen. I don't often see future things."

"Did you see anything with us?" His eyes met hers and held.

Her breath caught. Was he hinting he could see them in a relationship? "No. Not yet, anyway."

He went back to fiddling with his computers. "We'll leave in a few minutes. I just want to see how the data is coming along. I've hired a hacker to look into the social media account of the person who set up a meeting with Mariah."

"You can't do that yourself?"

"I've been a little busy."

She bristled. "With me."

He sighed. "With you, but your contribution is important." She read between the lines. Her *contribution*. But not *her*.

"I'll be out of your hair tonight. I think I'll go wait in the lobby with Laney."

"Abby, wait." He was out from behind his desk and had snagged her wrist before she could retreat to the hallway. "I'm sorry. I'm frustrated, but that doesn't give me permission to take it out on you."

"About what?"

"Huh?"

"You said you were frustrated. We have a lead with this dead guy you mentioned, the caseworker is looking for a placement for Laney, I'm cooperating… How are you frustrated?"

He huffed out a humorless laugh, ruffling the strand of hair that lay against her cheek. "Take your pick. Socially, job-wise, sexually—"

Whoa, wait. "Sexually?" She'd practically offered herself up on a silver platter and he'd said no thanks.

His eyes heated. "*That's* the one you picked?" He laughed and his gaze went to her lips. "I know how to take care of that one."

"So do I." Her words were a whisper. She glanced at the open door. "But maybe not here or now?"

He took a step back. "See? Frustrated."

"You're not the only one," she muttered.

His gaze shot up to meet hers. "Really?"

"Hello. You're a super-intelligent, mega-talented guy with a great sense of humor. And you're not hard to look at."

"And yet, somehow I'm easy to leave. Let's go." Einstein walked by her, intent on leading her out, but she snagged his wrist as he had done to her. He swung back to her as she stepped into him and landed a kiss on his mouth. Stunned, he didn't move for a full second.

She swept her tongue across his lips and he opened to her with a hungry growl. The kiss turned hotter as he practically devoured her. She wanted this, wanted him to want her with a burning need, just as she wanted him.

With a groan, he pulled back. Heat and desire that matched her own were reflected in his eyes. His attention lowered to her mouth, and regret tightened his features. "We need to get going."

"And we will. But I'd like to point out that it's *you* who keeps walking away. If you're doing that to protect yourself—from me—there's no need. I'm not going to leave unless you want me to."

A low growling sound came from deep in his throat. "What I want, I can't have. What I need…" He shook his head. "Right now, I need you to go with me to solve this case."

"And then?"

"I can't think about that right now." Despite the indecision that gripped him, he stroked a finger down her cheek and looked thoughtful. With another growl, he dropped his hand and spun on his heel.

"Frustrated." She muttered the word to his back as he walked away. She'd have to see what she could do about that.

CHAPTER 13

Hannah strode into his office as if she owned the place.

The Charmer looked up and scowled. "I thought I told you not to come back."

She used her pouts the same way her mother did—as a weapon. "I was going to leave town, maybe take a long cruise, but with this godforsaken heat wave, flights are booked with people looking for a way out. And I thought you might have had a change of heart." She strode around his office casually, but with a hidden agenda.

Annoyance flared. He didn't have time for her antics. "What do you want?"

"I brought the total of Mom's medical bills." Hannah took a folded paper from her pocket and slid it across the desk, like in the movies. *Amateur.* He nearly laughed. After Hannah's last visit, he'd discreetly checked into her story and confirmed his suspicions. His ex-wife wasn't sick.

Which meant Hannah was manipulating him. Rage, like roaring rapids, bucked and flowed beneath his skin but he concealed it.

Hannah sighed. "She doesn't know I've contacted you to enlist your aid. I don't want her to know." She glanced at her nails as if deciding whether it was time for a manicure.

Jesus, at least look at me if you're going to attempt to scalp me.

"Such a loving, doting daughter I have—when it's for your mother."

Hannah rolled her eyes and brushed at her bangs, setting off a chorus of soft tinkling at her wrist as the charms jostled. He'd done so much for her, and she had no respect for him. "I only came to you because it's so damn expensive. The payments from my trust fund don't cover it all and it's cutting into my lifestyle." Maybe she *was* more like him than like her mother.

"She's not sick."

Slowly, Hannah turned to look him in the eye. "You *will* pay me."

Curious how far she would take this charade, he cocked his head. "Why would I do that?"

"Because I know things. Things you don't want others to know." As she spoke, she continued her walkabout, pausing every few words in front of his bookshelves, his coffee table, and various other points to look with feigned interest at his trinkets and decorations. "You think you've been so careful, but I've been doing my research and you've been up to no good for years." She stopped in front of his cabinet and he held his breath. "I know your secrets..."

Did she know? No, she couldn't.

"Secrets that could land you in jail." Triumph glittered in her eyes as she finally met his gaze. "I'm not asking for much. Consider it a bonus for keeping quiet."

He considered her for a long moment but she didn't flinch, didn't blink. She seriously thought she had something on him—something worth several million dollars, according to the slip of paper. He needed time to deal with this little blip in his game. "I'll get you a check by tomorrow night. Come by my house."

"That new place in the country?" She pursed her lips.

"It's not exactly country, but yes." It was a sacred haven for him about an hour northwest of the city. "Be there at seven-thirty."

"Here would be so much easier."

But it wouldn't fit in with his plans. "You'll meet me there, or you'll get nothing."

She seemed to think it over for a moment. "Sure. I could use a drive in the country. But make it cash. No checks." Her grin was predatory. "Good talk, Daddy."

He watched her walk out his door and wanted to throw something at the wall near her head, just to get a fucking reaction out of her. Something other than disinterest or greed. No, she was nothing like his Hannah. *His* Hannah would never have treated him this way. She'd been the only one to love him.

He'd have something for her by tomorrow evening, but it wouldn't be what she'd expect.

He picked up his cell phone to make the arrangements and saw he'd missed a call from the same man he was trying to reach. Perfect synchronicity. Perhaps the man could be trusted to move up into his right-hand-man position.

"Yeah," Nico said in answer.

At the gruff greeting, the Charmer grinned. Everything was going to be okay. He'd initiate the final stages of his game and take care of this problem in one fell swoop.

"I have another job for you."

"So, who's the dead guy whose stuff I'm supposed to be *reading?*" Abby asked as they drove toward the southern fringes of the city.

Einstein slid her a look from the driver's seat. "Tony Moreno."

"The guy who worked for the Circle?" The one who'd been ordered by the Charmer to take Samantha.

"Personally, I wouldn't want to touch the stuff from his storage room with a sterilized ten-foot pole." He glanced her way. "But Damian was excited about the idea."

"Tony kept his mementos in this storage room?"

"Yes. Max spent some time with Tony a few months back and, last night, remembered the possible existence of this storage room. Max got the keys from Tony's mother, who never visited the unit. Tony had threatened her life if she *touched his stuff.*"

And now Abby was supposed to touch it.

Hard to believe the man with the gold tooth from her vision, capable of so many horrible acts against humanity—including young women like Sam—had a mother.

Einstein drove into the parking lot of a storage facility. Max climbed out of the truck that pulled up next to them. They greeted each other and Max held up a key. His gaze moved to Abby. "You sure about this?" Max asked, but it was Einstein who answered.

"She wants to help Damian." Einstein's tone indicated he wasn't happy about this.

The trio advanced through a gate, where hundreds of orange metal doors extended in neat rows for what seemed like infinity.

Max led them, taking a couple turns before coming to a unit near the back corner. Despite the heat that beat down on her head and shoulders, Abby shivered. They were in the right place. She could feel the evil crawling along her skin, eager to get inside her head. Einstein made quick work of the lock and slid the orange door up. It disappeared into the ceiling and they stepped inside.

Shocked, Abby met Einstein's gaze. "Cool air?" It hit her cheeks and arms with blessed relief. A portable air conditioning unit was plugged into the corner.

"The storage facility records I found indicated Tony had paid in advance for the next ten years," Einstein said. "He must have arranged for the temperature control, too."

Max snorted and wiped the sweat on his brow. "I'm not about to look a gift horse in the mouth." He gestured to Abby to precede them.

Einstein pulled a dangling cord to turn the single light bulb on, then pulled the door down to keep the cool air in, closing them into the eight-by-ten room together. There were several towers of boxes—everything from shoeboxes to regular cardboard packing boxes—along each wall.

"Where do you want me to start?" she asked.

"Are there vibes leading you to any particular box?"

She gestured to a box at the top of a stack in the back corner, right next to a folding lawn chair. "If you had a stash of treasures, things so important you decided to pay to keep them air-conditioned, what would you do with it?"

Einstein's lips curved in a humorless smile as he followed her meaning. "Take it out every once in a while and look at it."

"Exactly. And that chair, that box…"

As she spoke, Einstein was already sliding on a pair of latex gloves and squeezing past her to get to the box. His body brushed hers, its caged tension making him seem even edgier than usual. He pulled the box down and set it in the chair, opened the lid, and peered inside. He reached into his jeans pocket for his keychain and used the portable flashlight there for extra light. He lifted a pair of panties with tiny yellow flowers from the box. Little girls' panties. Not women's.

Abby's stomach flipped over. "Is that what I think it is?"

Einstein met her gaze. "There're more."

"How many?" But she was already looking over his shoulder. Dozens. And not just young girls', but women's too. "He didn't discriminate."

"Tony Moreno wasn't a nice man," Max said from behind her.

Abby's gaze flew to Einstein's. "These are trophies."

"Yes." Expression set to grim, Einstein sorted through the box, then felt along the inside edges and corners. He paused, then withdrew his hand. It held a business card.

"Pinnacle Holdings?" She turned her questioning gaze to him.

"Haven't heard of it, but the address is in downtown Chicago."

He turned it over, then sent a glance to Max and handed the card to him.

"Ten twenty-five." Max pressed his lips together tightly.

"Could be coincidence, or something else." The line in Einstein's forehead said he suspected there was nothing coincidental about it.

"It means something to you?" she prompted.

"It's the date Sam disappeared." Einstein eyed her. "Up to giving it a try?" He held the card out to her and she took it and pressed it between her palms.

She closed her eyes and concentrated. She opened her eyes a moment later, exhaling with relief. "Nothing."

"Maybe something else from the box," Max suggested.

"No." Einstein slid the lid back on the box. "Let's pursue the card. We'll have Damian send a SSAM team to go through the rest." He squeezed past her again and slid the orange door open.

Abby blew out a shaky breath. If she'd had to touch any of those other things…

Max nodded. "I'll let Noah know about this unit. He'll have the crime scene techs go over the rest. I'm sure if they find anything else that could lead to the Charmer, they'll let us know ASAP."

Abby focused on slowing her rapid heartbeat as they reached Einstein's car. He looked over at her. "You okay?"

She nodded. "I didn't help at all."

He lifted the business card. "We still got what we needed."

"How can you be sure?"

"Remember how you're not the only one with gut feelings?" He grinned. "I have one about Pinnacle Holdings."

"I HOPE THIS IS A GOOD IDEA." DAMIAN SPOKE IN LORENA'S EAR AS they entered the bustling restaurant. Park Grill was a popular gathering spot for business lunches and people touring Millennium Park or Shedd Aquarium. It was crowded, filled with the buzz of conversation.

"Priscilla was a major part of your life when Sam disappeared," Lorena said. "She might remember something or someone that could be important." It had been Lorena's idea to arrange this lunch, and Damian was glad Priscilla was still in town. "Besides, I know it won't be easy to tell her you're the target of the Charmer's obsession."

"Or to tell her about us," he said.

Lorena smiled up at him and he got lost in memories of the way those lips had moved across his skin last night. His body tightened with a fresh wave of need, but something in his peripheral vision caught his attention. Priscilla was waving them over to a table.

"Hello, darling." Priscilla rose and presented her cheek to Damian. He bent to kiss it. Still smooth as ever. He couldn't help but compare hers to Lorena's soft, nearly makeup-free skin. They were both beautiful women. Similar, but different in many ways. And while Priscilla had thrown her energy into the ethereal world of art and beauty, Lorena, like him, was grounded in a gritty, dark reality. Lorena had the same mission he did—catching monsters.

He assisted Lorena and Priscilla in taking their seats opposite each other, on either side of him at the square table.

"I didn't realize you were in town more than a couple days," Damian said.

"I'm staying with a friend who has a lovely downtown loft near several local galleries."

Lorena smiled. "That must be nice for you."

Priscilla had poured her heart and soul into the New York City art philanthropic efforts after she'd relocated there—after Sam's body was discovered and they'd divorced. She'd made a good life for herself.

They chatted about Priscilla's life in New York until they'd consumed half their meal.

Priscilla looked at him over her glass of iced tea. "I confess, I'd hoped the two of you were here to give me good news."

Damian paused and set down his fork. "You'll be the first to know when we catch the Charmer, but there is something we want to talk to you about regarding the investigation."

Priscilla leaned forward and dropped her voice. "I knew it. There is something new. Is it about the slideshow? Did it lead you to the Charmer?"

Damian sighed. "Not yet, but we're getting close. We're learning things every day."

"Such as?"

"Sam was very likely drugged before she was killed." Which was a comfort, at least.

Her eyes filled with tears. "I've prayed it was a merciful, quick death. How do you know after all this time?"

"Tiffany Allsup, the recent victim in Texas, was killed in that manner." He caught Lorena's look of encouragement. "And a woman with psychometric abilities suggested Samantha's death was similar."

"Psychometric abilities?"

"She receives messages and feelings from objects she touches," Lorena explained. "We were doubtful at first, of course, but she's relayed some things that only the victims or law enforcement who've been privy to the confidential details would know, such as the possibility she was drowned."

"Drowned?" Priscilla's eyebrows drew together. "She was found buried in an abandoned field."

Damian could see the place now. The crime scene haunted his nightmares. The fallow land had smelled rich, having recently been pummeled by a fall storm. He'd insisted on visiting the site the minute they'd discovered it, though law enforcement had warned him to stay away.

"We're still trying to figure out the killer's ritual," Lorena said. "And why he would kill in that manner, but Abby seems to think it's a type of baptism or renewal. Does that mean anything to you?"

"Abby's the psychic?" Priscilla's eyes shot to Damian. "Wait, why are you asking me about baptisms? And would she be able to tell us more? Maybe if she visited the crime scene..."

Damian sighed, knowing he'd have to douse that hope once more. "It's been too long. She touched some of the things we recovered from Sam's burial site, and that's how she was able to tell us about the drowning theory. I promise to keep you posted." He hoped that would tide her over for a while...or at least a few days, until this game with the Charmer came to a head. "In the meantime, we believe the Charmer is someone from my past. Someone who was close to our family."

"Baptisms and someone we knew back then?" Priscilla shook her head. "I can't think of anyone who would want to harm us, or had some kind of religious bent. It's too much to take in."

"I know it's a lot." He reached out to cover Priscilla's hand on the table. "But we're so much closer. In fact, we think we may find the Charmer within the next couple days." It was that or become a victim of his game.

"Before that ridiculous countdown is over, you mean? Can you imagine a world in which Sam's killer is behind bars?"

He nodded and swallowed the lump in his throat. "Yes, I can. Finally. We're so close. Think about whoever was in our lives back then, or even earlier. Can you remember anyone who would have wished me harm?"

"You? Shouldn't this be about Sam?" She pulled her fingers from beneath his. "When I saw that slideshow, I thought this was about your work with SSAM."

"We've come to believe the Charmer has an...obsession that dates back many years. An obsession with me."

"Anything you can add could help," Lorena added.

Priscilla shook her head. "Friends? Colleagues? Women from the PTA? What are we talking about here, Damian?" Her incredulous gaze met his. "I can't fathom anyone from our lives being involved. It's just... It's too much. Excuse me." She pushed away from the table and stood. "I'll call you later if I think of anything—or anyone."

"Cilla, wait—" Damian sighed as his ex-wife hurried toward the main doors, upset. Once again, he'd failed her.

CHAPTER 14

"It makes sense," Einstein said. "Before he died, Tony mentioned that we weren't looking *high enough* for the Charmer. We didn't know then whether he meant that literally or was referring to him having the highest position."

Abby tipped her head back to take in the entirety of the skyscraper that housed many businesses, including Pinnacle Holdings. "I'd say both."

In the lobby of the building, Einstein stopped and pulled her around to face him. "You're sure you won't stay behind?"

"It's an office building in the middle of a work day. I'll be perfectly safe with you."

He studied her for a long moment and she did her best to look confident and determined. "Stay right beside me at all times." He stalked toward the bank of elevators and she hurried to keep up.

"Floor thirty-five, right?" Abby scanned the list of numbers and company names. "There's no thirty-five." Beside the name Pinnacle Holdings was a note to see the guard.

"It's a private elevator." He whirled and strode toward the security station just off the lobby.

A guard looked up from his sandwich with disinterest. "Can I help you?"

"Floor thirty-five, please," Abby said when Einstein simply scowled.

"You'll need to sign in." The guard slid a clipboard across the marble countertop and then handed them a plastic card. "Just swipe it over there. That elevator will take you straight up."

Einstein took the card and pulled Abby aside. "He's expecting us."

"We don't know that," she said. "Besides, the Charmer can't do anything to us without raising suspicions. He'd have employees as witnesses and the guard knows we're here."

"It doesn't feel right."

"Nothing about the past few days feels right." Except being with Einstein.

His gaze went to his ankle, where, he'd showed her earlier, his pistol was in a holster beneath his jeans. Inside the elevator, he swiped the card through its slot and the doors slid closed. They began the ascent.

She swallowed a sudden sense of panic. Maybe he'd been right to be suspicious. Still, thirty-five floors would have been a long hike, uphill the entire way. And what could the Charmer do to them in an elev—

Her breath lodged in her throat as the elevator jerked to a sudden stop. She lost her balance, but Einstein was there, his hand at her waist to steady her, his feet apart to brace himself. The lights went off and she held onto him. Emergency lights switched on. How many floors had they gone up? Ten? Twenty? Oh God, were they suspended hundreds of feet with only a cable to support them?

She glanced at Einstein in the bluish-white light. "Rolling blackout?"

He shook his head. "The guard would have said something. Besides, it shouldn't hit this area until tonight, after work hours."

He eyed the tiny video camera in the corner. "Someone stopped us on purpose." The red light was blinking on the camera. If the power were out, would it still do that?

"The Charmer?" she whispered, then realized how ridiculous that was. Either he could hear everything they said or he couldn't hear at all.

"Probably."

How could he be so calm? Of course, he'd been through much worse things and survived. The thought calmed her. "You think he's watching us now?"

"My gut says he's using his escape plan, probably jogging down thirty-five flights of stairs about now. Or walking a few floors down and then taking the main elevators, which may not have been impacted." Einstein pushed the emergency button and informed the guard they were stranded. They were promised help was on the way.

Abby hugged her arms to herself. "What do you think he has in mind?"

"We're not sitting here, waiting to find out." Einstein tried to pry apart the elevator doors and managed to get them open a few inches. Just enough to see that they were between floors and the concrete slab at eye level was marked *28*. Though the elevator was an express one, it appeared that it could stop at the other floors if someone rigged it that way. His back muscles flexed between his shoulder blades with the effort to push the doors apart. He glanced back at her. "Think you could squeeze through?"

She eyed the options. "I can slip through to the floor below and drop. But what about you?"

"You could go for help, or find something to prop the doors open."

She was stepping forward when, with a whir of sound and blinking of the main lights, the elevator suddenly jerked and started moving up again. Einstein released the doors and stepped back, pinning her against the corner as if to shield her. He raised his gun and aimed it at the doors, but when they opened at the thirty-fifth floor, there was only a darkened lobby to welcome them.

A large sign behind an empty reception area proclaimed *Pinnacle Holdings* in elegant gold script, each letter nearly a foot tall. Behind the letters was the symbol of a mountain with a sun gleaming at the peak.

"Is that...?" She pointed to the sun in the symbol. While hidden within the rest of the company's logo, the sun's shape and image were nearly identical to the Circle's symbol.

"It sure as hell resembles the Circle's logo," Einstein said.

"Where is everyone?" Abby whispered. A lamp was on behind the desk, indicating that power was indeed still flowing to the office. But there were no other sounds. When she heard her breathing had become tight little puffs, she forced herself to do some deep-breathing techniques.

Einstein grunted. "Maybe they get Wednesdays off. More likely, this is a front for illegal activities, so they only have staff when necessary. Stay here." He pointed to a spot just outside the elevator. She hurried to claim that spot, not wanting to be trapped within again, and certainly not without Einstein.

"Yell if anybody comes, got it?" Einstein's expression was dialed to fierce. Gun raised, he disappeared down a hallway to the left, presumably to see if the Charmer was, indeed, gone. Abby got the feeling he was. After all, why would he stick around for a confrontation with a big, bad, armed ex-SEAL?

An eternity later, Einstein returned to her side.

She blew out the most recent of her deep breaths. "Anybody?"

"A dead body in the corner office."

"What? Who?"

"Don't know, but he hasn't been dead long. A computer screen is lit up. It shows the camera feed from the elevators."

"The Charmer can't have gone far, then."

He eyed the elevator. "I'm going to take the stairwell. It'd be safer if—"

"I'm not staying here alone." And certainly not with a dead body. "The killer might come back, expecting to find us here."

He looked as if he might argue with her, but must have seen the determination in her eyes and the reasoning behind her argument. "Stay a floor behind me, okay? He could be lying in wait for us."

"Hard to imagine a board member of a major corporation waiting in a hot stairwell to shoot us."

"Always be prepared for anything."

"Sounds like the Boy Scouts."

"I'm no Boy Scout." He winked, uncoiling some of the tension in her stomach. "Ready?" He searched her eyes for any signs of fear or weakness and she gazed right back, projecting calm steel. "Let's go."

Thirty-five floors. Walking as quietly as possible, they took each flight, watching for danger at every curve. *Thirty-four, thirty-three.*

She counted each floor to center and calm herself, reminding herself she had to make it out of there to take care of Grandpa and to find Mariah. And to make sure Laney found a stable home. People were counting on her. She couldn't let them down.

Twenty-nine, twenty-eight...

Sweat trickled between her breasts and her breath came faster now. At least she was physically fit. Apparently, the building designers hadn't deemed it necessary to air-condition the stairwell. Einstein remained a flight ahead of her. She saw him as he rounded each curve. He wasn't even winded.

Sixteen, fifteen, fourteen...

Now, beads of sweat dotted his forehead and his snug black tee was gripping him in places she'd imagined gripping him with her hands, her thighs... She swallowed and watched her feet.

A minute later, they came out a side door into a narrow alley.

Sunlight pierced her skull. She blinked rapidly, shading her eyes, even as Einstein shoved her behind him and aimed his gun at something she couldn't see. Tension radiated through his back muscles.

"Whoa, it's just me," an unfamiliar male voice said.

Einstein relaxed and lowered his weapon. "Fuck, man. You don't sneak up on someone like that. Did you see anyone come this way?"

As her eyes adjusted, she saw a man who looked to be similar in age to Einstein. He was also muscular, but slightly larger. Tattoos covered one arm.

Einstein whipped out his sunglasses from where they'd been hooked on the neckline of his tee and handed them to her. She shook her head and fumbled in her purse for a second, coming up with her own so that he could keep his. After all, he was her first layer of defense and should be appropriately prepared. She noticed he hadn't holstered his gun.

The stranger's head turned to her. "Going to tell me who she is?"

She bristled at his tone but Einstein didn't seem to mind. "Nico, this is Abby Rhodes."

The man named Nico arched a brow until it peeked over the edge of his sunglasses. "The psychic from the news. The Charmer's curious about you."

"Don't worry. He's an undercover agent."

"Way to protect my cover," Nico said with a shake of his head.

"She needed to know you aren't a danger to us. Unless you are?" Through their sunglasses, the men seemed to stare each other down for several tense moments.

Nico caved first, the corners of his mouth tipping upward. "Didn't see the Charmer, if that's what you're asking. He keeps dodging me."

"Then why are you here?" Einstein asked.

"A job."

"So this *is* about the Charmer. That job didn't include messing with an elevator, by any chance?"

Nico's narrowed gaze shifted to the stairwell exit behind them. "No. What happened?"

"Let's just say he tried to stall us. If not that, then what kind of job are you here for?" When Nico didn't respond, Einstein swore. "You're here about the body."

"Kind of the point of my new position."

"Position?" Abby asked.

"He's been promoted to the Charmer's cleaner," Einstein explained.

Abby's jaw dropped. "As in cleaning up after his *messes?*"

Nico ignored her. "I'm assuming you found a body upstairs?"

"You assume right," Einstein said. "Didn't recognize him. And I'd guess the computer's already been wiped clean." He stepped closer to Nico. "What I don't understand is how the Charmer knew we were coming."

Tension thickened the air. "Anything for the mission, right? Next time you use the bat signal, you might not want to bring me to your office. Gives me all kinds of access to things..." His gaze moved to Einstein's pocket, where his phone rested.

"Fuck. You're tracking my phone?" Einstein stepped up into Nico's personal space. "Why?"

"Guess you'll have to see how this plays out." Nico pushed past Einstein and disappeared inside the building.

Despite the heat, a shiver moved across her skin. "*Plays out?* Is that another game reference? Is he kidding?"

Einstein's gaze was narrowed on the door. "Unfortunately, I don't think so."

EINSTEIN DIDN'T WANT ABBY TO RETURN LANEY TO MRS. BENSON alone, so he insisted on accompanying them to lunch and then the police station. He sat in the same CPD waiting room, searching on his laptop for anything related to Pinnacle Holdings or the CEO who'd been found dead on the thirty-fifth floor. He'd had Noah and the CPD there before Nico could do any *cleaning*, but the dead man was only a figurehead for the company, which appeared to be a legal-looking façade for the Circle's illegal dealings, from what Einstein had dug up online. He had no doubt the Charmer was the real one pulling the strings. Pinnacle's legitimate worldwide shipping networks had been used to transport guns, drugs, even human cargo. The multiagency task force charged with taking the Circle down had already moved in to confiscate all of the computers. On which side of that did Nico stand?

Nico had texted him when his cleaning job had been mucked up by Einstein calling the cops. *Stop fucking this up.*

Einstein hadn't responded. He wasn't sure he could trust the man any longer. Whatever he was up to couldn't be good if he wasn't sharing with Einstein and the SSAM team. Damian hadn't recognized the name or photo of the dead CEO, or the name Pinnacle Holdings, but nobody doubted that the Charmer had claimed another victim. Einstein was betting Pinnacle's CEO-slash-puppet was the only one who might have been able to lead them to the Charmer. Probably knew what the man looked like, since they worked so closely together.

One more loose end tied up for a killer, and one less potential lead for SSAM. And only twenty-nine hours left on the clock.

He stood and stretched, his gaze moving toward the hallway where Abby and an anxious but brave Laney had left him. He missed them. Laney's sweet grin and Abby's warm smile and positive energy had kept him going the past couple days. He chalked up his softness to the fact he'd been spending way too many hours with Abby. Withdrawals were natural after such a fierce addiction was fed.

A ping on his phone indicated one of his algorithms had discovered a pattern. He read the update and grinned. They were getting closer. Pinnacle's IP address matched one of the Cattle Call emails he'd sent out the day before. The virus hadn't been activated, or he'd have found the Pinnacle connection yesterday. *Damn.*

That IP was also connected to the social media account that had been used to contact Mariah. *Bingo.* All he had to do was hack into the original account, even if he didn't have the Charmer's computer, and he'd find the messages. It seemed they were right on the Charmer's tail. The irony of hacking from within a police station was not lost on him, and he was grinning as he found the message history and hurriedly scanned the information before emailing it to the SSAM team.

"I hope that grin means you have good news," Abby said.

Surprised he hadn't heard her approach, he looked up to find her standing over him. He could tell by the look on her face that something had gone wrong.

"Laney?" he asked, glancing behind her.

She shook her head and bit her lip to stop its trembling. *Fuck.* Had they given her back to her asshole of a father? Where was the justice in this world?

She kept walking and he hurriedly scooped up his laptop and other belongings. He found her standing in the parking lot, looking lost. He put his things in the trunk and walked up to her, opening his arms in invitation. She walked into them, wrapped her arms around his waist and tucked her face into his chest. Her muscles quivered as she shuddered beneath his hands.

But a moment later, she pulled away and gave him a brave smile. "Sorry. It was just so difficult to leave without her. I didn't expect it to hit me so hard, I guess."

He brushed her hair back from her face. "What happened?"

"Wesley's lawyer used yesterday's newscast against me, making it out like I was some con artist psychic preying on the Pierces."

"First of all, you weren't preying on them."

She pulled a face. "No, but it could be twisted that way."

"Second of all," he continued, "Wesley has Laney?" His heart pounded harder at the thought.

"No, Mrs. Benson has a place for her in temporary foster care until she can interview me more formally and determine the best course of action. At least Laney's not with *him*."

"Interview? For the case against Wesley?" If so, the man could be gunning for Abby. His protective instincts reared up again.

Abby sent him a hesitant glance. "It's a different type of interview. I put myself up as an option for a home...maybe even a permanent one...for Laney. She doesn't have anywhere else to go. Nobody seems to want her. Am I crazy for trying?"

His heart squeezed at the doubt and hope in this beautiful woman's eyes. She could easily have turned her back on Laney. But that wasn't Abby's way. She fought for the underdog because she cared. Self-sacrifice was nothing to her because she gave her heart freely to those who needed it. "No. You're giving and generous." And so damn sweet. "Laney would be lucky to be with you." And so would he. Could Abby deem *him* worthy of her love? The air was sucked from his lungs just thinking of what it would be like to be loved by her.

"I hate leaving her with strangers."

"Was she okay?" If Laney wasn't happy, or if she was placed with yet another family who would neglect her, he'd personally swoop in and rescue her. No kid should face that—certainly not when there were better options like Abby ready and willing to take her in.

"She took it well." Probably because Abby had been strong for her. She was strong for everyone around her, taking care of them, always putting her own needs last. "I never should have let myself get caught on camera as being associated with that case. That was stupid. And now it might hurt Laney."

Einstein hooked a finger beneath her chin and lifted her gaze to his. "That news crew caught both of us off guard. I'm as much to blame as you are. Besides, the Pierces needed you. Mariah needs you. I need you."

She nodded, shaking free of his finger. "To find the bracelet's owner." She blew out a breath. "That's next, right?"

"No." Her surprised gaze met his. "When I said I needed you, I didn't mean for that. I need you for me."

This time, he wouldn't let her shake free. He clasped her sun-warmed face in his hands, and tipped her mouth up to his. Their tongues did a slow dance as they remembered the feel of each other. The taste of her was intoxicating, heating his blood, making his head spin. Her hands slid around his waist, pulling him closer until he could feel her breath hitch in her chest. She was just as affected by him as he was by her, which only drove him crazy for more—more of her.

Reluctantly, he pulled away. The dazed look in her eyes had one corner of his mouth lifting in masculine satisfaction. But he couldn't finish the job here and now. He wanted Abby in his bed for several hours so he could show her exactly how much he treasured her generous heart.

She smiled. "Did that help?"

"Absolutely." But it wasn't nearly enough. He traced a finger along her cheek. "I do have to get back to work. And you're right. Finding the bracelet's owner is next on the agenda."

"So the current theory is that someone special to the Charmer owns the bracelet? Maybe a daughter?" And that maybe it was the missing Hannah Smith.

Beside her, as they walked the same sidewalk, retracing their steps from just yesterday to visit the few addresses where the women from the roster hadn't replied to their messages, Einstein nodded. "We think he played to the victims' anger with their parents, using that to lure them away."

"And, what…? When they didn't measure up, didn't want him to be their daddy, he killed them?" She shuddered, but what he said fit with what she'd felt from the charms. Trust turning to betrayal.

Shock. They had to have expected one thing from the Charmer and he turned the tables on them.

"I guess so." Einstein held the door for her as they arrived at Hannah's building.

"But what are the chances that this bracelet would show up at *my* yoga studio, so close to the SSAM offices?"

"I wish I knew. It would help if there were some record of the woman's parents. It's like she started a new life with a new name and erased her connections to her past."

"Maybe Hannah suspects what her father's done."

Einstein stopped in the empty stairwell and faced her. "How do you figure?"

"Think about it. If you had suspicions, where would you start exploring them? Would you go to your father and accuse him of murder?"

"Doesn't sound safe."

"Exactly, especially if she did change her name to distance herself from him. So maybe she'd go to the victims' families."

His brows arched. "Maggie?"

"Maggie was Sam's best friend. The bracelet's owner might have been searching for answers, or at least a sense of where to begin." At Hannah's apartment, the corner of Abby's previous note still stuck out from beneath the door. Nobody answered her knock. "I don't think she's been home. Think that's a sign she's in danger?"

"If she knows what her father did and tried to confront him..." Einstein shook his head as if to rid them both of the most horrible possibilities. "I'm hoping the Charmer's been too busy with this game to hurt his daughter. Or Mariah."

Einstein followed Abby down the stairs. On the sidewalk, the sun, while low in the sky, continued to bake their bodies. At least the weather forecaster had predicted thunderstorms tomorrow. Hopefully, it would provide much-needed relief.

"It's so frustrating not getting anywhere," Abby said. "How do you deal with it?"

"I have faith that one day I'll catch a break. I'm hoping digging into Damian's past again will reveal more information."

"But how can one ever be prepared to revisit the most painful parts of their past? I don't know how Damian does it, living with his pain every day."

"He doesn't have a choice. Every weekend, he lays white roses on Sam's grave after church. It's a wonder he still attends faithfully after all this time."

"What do you mean?" She looked at him from across the roof of his car.

"His daughter is taken from him, murdered, and the killer gets away with it for twenty years? Goes on to commit many more heinous crimes? Yeah, that would seriously challenge my faith." He climbed into the driver's seat and she got in the passenger side.

But she was still intrigued by his views on faith. Einstein had seen the worst—in combat with the SEALs, in humanity through his cases at SSAM. What gave him the strength to crawl out of bed each day? "I take it you don't go to church?"

He shook his head. "Not since…"

"Your dad. Not since September, 2001?"

Shocked, he swung his gaze from the road to her. "How'd you know?"

She reached over to squeeze his shoulder in comfort and he went totally still.

"You read that in one of your messages?" His gaze reflected horror.

Rejection, strong and swift, hit her square in the chest.

CHAPTER 15

He got the impression he'd hurt her, which made him an idiot. But her insight had shocked him, and there were some things he didn't want her to see. And the fact that she'd seen *that*... It had been one of his lowest moments. She'd seen his vulnerability.

"Did you read that in my thoughts?"

She bit her lip and looked away, focusing on something beyond her window. "More like from your emotions. But I've gotten vibes before that you've lost your father." Her voice softened during the last part.

He gritted his teeth against a wave of pain and regret. And guilt. He should have made more of an effort while he'd had the chance, while his parents had been alive. But nothing he'd tried in the past had seemed to break through. And the way he'd lost them had shaped his whole adult life.

Luckily, they'd arrived at his apartment building, sparing him from further contemplation.

"Am I supposed to walk home?" Her teasing tone didn't hide

the uncertainty in her expression. He'd blown their tentative trust to pieces.

"Stay with me." Einstein met her gaze, willing her to accept, not that he'd made it a question.

"Okay." She mirrored his expression by raising her eyebrows. "I'm being toyed with by a murderer, and an abusive father is angry with me for squealing to the cops. I know when to accept help. Thank you for offering—again."

SHE'D SURPRISED HIM BY SAYING SHE WANTED TO STAY. BUT HER entire body thrummed with a potent emotional cocktail—a mix of frustration and anticipation.

The rejection still stung, but she knew his secrets ran deep. He didn't trust easily, and she was lucky he was letting her in as far as he was. He was all brawn on the outside and brains on the inside. Buried even deeper was his heart, but it was there. A thick protective coating had formed over the years, but she'd seen his heart in the way he took care of her and Laney. In the way he fought for the victims and their families to find the justice they deserved. It was a risk to expose her own heart, but she was ready to take a leap of faith and trust he'd eventually lay down his shield and let her get close.

"Do you need anything from your place?" he asked as he unlocked his door. It appeared they had electricity for the moment. Em and CeeCee showed up to meow at them. Einstein went to feed them and she followed him to the kitchen.

"No." She still had the toiletries she'd purchased yesterday. "I think I'll take a quick shower. I'll feel better."

Fifteen minutes later, when she returned in yoga pants and a fresh tank top, he'd cleaned up, too. The ends of his dark hair, still damp, curled against his neck. She'd heard the shower from his master suite, on the other side of the wall, when she'd turned her own off. The relentless stab of need she'd brought to heel while in the shower hit her again and she struggled to ignore it.

"Hungry?" He padded barefoot across the kitchen to his refrigerator. She'd never thought a man's feet could be sexy, but Einstein's were. She swallowed hard.

"More tired than hungry. But wired, too." She was exhausted, but so much had happened over the past forty-eight hours that she wasn't sure she could rest. And thoughts of Laney settling in with her new, temporary family continued to hound her. *Was she doing okay?* He raised a beer in question and she nodded. "Would you mind if we sat and...talked? Or watched TV? Anything to turn my brain off."

His brows shot up. "Most women want me to turn *my* brain off."

"Really? Why?" Those women must be insane. Or self-absorbed. Or after one thing...

Her gaze traveled over his physique, clad in athletic shorts and a dark T-shirt that illustrated the molecular structure of caffeine. Deceptively casual, but underneath lay washboard abs and a lean, toned body. His biceps flexed as he tipped his beer to his lips and her mouth watered like one of Pavlov's dogs expecting a reward.

Yeah, she could see where some women might only want *that* part of Einstein. She quashed a hot spark of irrational jealousy.

He shrugged. "Damned if I know what a woman wants. But their eyes tend to glaze over when I talk neural connections and stuff."

"Try me." Deciding she needed something to do with her hands, and somewhere else to direct her gaze, she reached past him to open the refrigerator again. She should eat something, and Einstein had to be starving.

Gathering eggs, butter, cheese and anything else that looked like it could be thrown into an omelet, she set to work as Einstein leaned against the counter and talked. She liked the low and unhurried cadence of his voice and the confidence with which he spoke of things she might never fully understand.

"My undergraduate degree is in electrical engineering, but I have a fascination for all things biological as well."

Her skin heated as she imagined his focused concentration on her body. "But you ended up in the SEALs, then at SSAM, fighting crime."

His expression darkened. "Sometimes things don't work out how you expect."

"Like?"

He turned to the cabinet to remove two plates. The silence stretched on as she served up the omelets and followed him to the living room where they settled on the couch.

"Like losing the only family you have—as emotionally unavailable as they were—over the span of a year," he said suddenly in answer to her question. "It put things in perspective."

"You lost your mother and your father? And no siblings?"

He nodded to both questions. "Little orphan Andrew." His joke fell flat but she bit back her sympathy, sensing he wouldn't welcome it right now. She was well aware that she was treading on dangerously sensitive territory—things he'd kept stuffed down for years.

"Losing loved ones can make it hard to trust other people." She should know. Grandpa was the only family member who'd stuck around and now he was on his way out of her life, too. "Makes forming new relationships tough, doesn't it?"

He swallowed a bite of food and narrowed his eyes at her. "Are you trying to psychoanalyze me?"

"Just trying to understand." As she finished her own meal, she pushed the plate away. "And trying to figure out if you're afraid to let me touch you again."

His gaze made a slow caress up her body that had her skin heating. "I like touching you."

Sitting sideways on the couch, she tucked her feet under her. She held her hand up, palm out. "Hold my hand."

He didn't take it, but looked at her warily. "Why?"

She huffed out a laugh. "Hmmm…let me think. Maybe because you're smart and sexy and sweet." He winced at that last adjective. "And I want to hold your hand. People who like each other do that. I liked when you touched me before. But after I…read…you, you backed away—mentally, at least. I thought things were going well between us. Did I say something wrong?"

"No, it was…it was too right. It hit too close to home. It had nothing to do with you, and everything to do with me, and how I feel about that time in my life."

"And now?"

"I haven't had much time to process it." He rubbed at the stubble lining his jaw, reminding her it was late. But she didn't want to go to bed alone. Besides, she loved talking to him. "I wasn't ready for you to be that close."

"And now?"

"Now I'll take as much as you'll give."

Tentatively, she reached for his hand, her fingertip tracing the jagged scar on his wrist that had called to her earlier. The images that hit her slammed through her body like a pinball in a machine.

Dust billowing as the tower collapsed. Horror as the reality hit home. "Dad!" Crumpling to a chair at a small desk. A small room. Books lining the walls. Science trophies and ribbons. With a roar, he swept his hand across it all, tumbling things to the floor with a loud crash. Glass shattered and a sharp pain shot up his arm.

Her gaze moved to the windowsill behind him, where the glassless frame held his graduation picture. His wrist had been sliced that day by the shards. She brushed her finger over the scar again, shivering at the depth of emotion it conveyed.

She couldn't stop herself from voicing the question. "Did your dad die in the 9/11 attacks?"

Einstein went still except for the pulse thumping in his neck.

"Dad was a broker at a firm in Tower One. He died that day." The statement was so simple, spoken without emotion, but there was a depth of feeling in his eyes when he finally swung his gaze to hers that stole her breath. "Is that what you wanted to hear?"

"No, of course not." But that was what she'd witnessed.

As if sensing her thoughts, his eyes narrowed and he pulled his hand away. "Is that what you saw when you touched my scar? Dad dying?"

"No. I saw *you.* Felt your pain and helplessness as you watched it on TV."

His mouth opened, then closed.

"It was as if I was in your shoes. I saw the towers collapse. Knew the cost of life—and the personal cost." She wanted to reach out to him, to touch him again, but hesitated. "You lost so much that day. Mainly, the chance to know your father, to earn his respect."

He wouldn't meet her gaze. His hand fisted and relaxed in a repetitive motion.

She brushed her fingertips over his and the motion stilled. "Those are your thoughts, of course, not his. You hurt yourself on some broken glass, glass from that frame on the sill behind you." Her fingers burned to touch the scar again. She resisted. Anything else she wanted to know would come from his own words.

His Adam's apple bobbed as he swallowed. She must have crossed some boundary into unbearable territory. *Damn.*

Back when she'd used her gift, before she understood the ramifications, she'd often done that. Her best friend in tenth grade hadn't appreciated when Abby had warned her the boy she was going steady with was going to dump her. Instead, Abby had been the one dumped. By her friend. And even after her friend had, indeed, been left behind by the boy, they'd never been friends again.

Her throat felt raw and achy. She didn't want to lose this bond with Einstein. Whatever they'd shared over the months, those shy smiles and warm looks, would be gone. As would any chance at the deeper bond they'd been forging.

"I'm sure your father was proud of you."

"You don't know that." He blew out a breath. "*I* don't know that. And then Mom…"

"What?" she prodded gently when he seemed to lose himself in memories.

"After Dad died—that way—I finished my final year of college and signed up for the military. I wanted to make a difference. Fight back."

"A noble mission."

He shook his head with a gruff laugh. "But my mom…she was diagnosed with cancer while I was in Afghanistan, just a year after Dad died. She didn't even fight it. I think she was still grieving for Dad. They'd always had a special bond I couldn't even begin to intrude upon. The cancer was aggressive but she didn't even try. Since Dad's death, it was like she'd stopped living, anyway." His gaze met hers and the misery she saw there stole her breath. "I wasn't enough for her. Her only son wasn't enough to make her fight."

His mother had probably had other reasons for not choosing treatment, but to the man in front of her, to the boy he'd once been, she'd rejected him once again in favor of her own one great love. His mother hadn't seen that her son, though grown, needed her.

Suddenly, Einstein looked at her. "You saw all of that, *felt* all of that through me?" Emotion darkened his eyes and roughened his voice.

"Glimpses, yeah."

"From just a touch?"

"Yes. But the connection I've sensed between us could heighten it." Her cheeks heated.

"Jesus, that must have been rough." He shoved a hand through his hair and then reached for her, taking her hand and pressing it against his, palm to palm. "What am I thinking now?" His mouth was only inches away.

"Sometimes it doesn't take superpowers to tell what someone's thinking." Her voice was husky with need. He wanted her. His expression and body language were enough to tell her what he wanted. And it didn't take a psychology degree to understand that he also wanted relief from the pain of remembering.

"Can you turn it off?" His inner scientist took over as he shook off the melancholy of his past.

"To some degree." She paused a moment, not sure how much to say. But with him, she found she didn't want to hold back any longer. He'd think what he wanted to of her, anyway. "With you, I find I want to know more. I don't *want* to block you out. But I will, if you want me to."

He pressed closer, releasing a shaky breath that ruffled her hair. "I'm tired of blocking you out."

The need pulsed through her limbs, so hard and sweet it made her ache. The feeling of being held, of being wanted, was like a drug, clouding some senses and enhancing others. She squeezed her eyes shut to memorize this moment, to immerse herself in his musky scent, his uneven breathing, the zing of his skin touching hers.

"Einstein?" She wasn't sure what he was feeling. God, she had to know if he was going to pull away again. She couldn't open herself up to rejection.

"Yes?" He pulled back to look into her eyes. The soft orange of the setting sun slanted across the living room, creating a warm glow and highlighting the green and gray flecks in his eyes.

"Is this really what you want? This isn't just some way to keep from talking about your past?"

"You're so much more than a distraction." His hands journeyed from her back to her waist, his thumbs brushing the underside of her breasts. He lifted her and pulled her into his lap until she was straddling him. Her eyes widened as she felt just how interested he was. He released a strangled laugh. "I thought you could tell what I was thinking."

"You sort of, um, short-circuited that ability."

He cocked a brow at her. A slow grin spread across his face. "I can do that to you?"

"Oh, yeah."

Slowly, his hands meandered until his thumbs were touching across her belly, his fingers gripping her hips. "I like that I can do that to you."

He dipped his thumbs down to stroke her core. Heat pooled between her legs. If he kept doing *that*, she'd let him do anything he wanted.

She sucked in a breath as he placed little nips along her neck and jawbone. "Men always want to be in control." She stifled a moan of surrender.

He must have felt her hard swallow against his lips because he pulled back from her neck and sent her a wicked grin. "I'll let you be in control if you want." He ground his pelvis against the apex of her thighs and this time she couldn't stop the moan of pleasure— and frustration, since clothing remained between them.

She rocked against him. "Again, *letting* me be in control implies *you're* in control." She rocked again and enjoyed his sharp inhalation.

Suddenly, he stood, tilting her world. But he quickly righted it again, holding her against him, his hands cupping her ass and encouraging her to wrap her legs around him.

He stilled and looked her full in the face. "Say you're okay with this, with going to bed with me."

"I am totally okay with that." She rained kisses across his face, punctuating each word.

"Thank you, God." He was already carrying her to his bedroom, one hand's questing fingers reaching around to find her through her clothing. His fingers brushed her in gentle circles. Her thighs tightened on his waist. This was so much better than she'd dreamed it would be and they hadn't even gotten to the good stuff yet.

He dropped her gently on his mattress. She wanted to take the time to look around, to explore his inner sanctum, but the need in her was too great. She reached for him but stopped when he gripped the edges of his shirt with crossed arms. The image of his bulging biceps was replaced with a spectacular view of his tight abs and—*hallelujah*—his pecs as his shirt slid up and over his head. The material was gone in an instant.

He arched a brow as she sat there admiring. "I think you're falling behind."

She stood and was about to toss off all of her clothing, but caught the flare of his nostrils and decided to draw out the delicious anticipation and make him as hot for her as she was for him. The moves she'd picked up when the studio had hosted a burlesque class last summer would be put to the test.

SWEET JESUS. HE'D THOUGHT HE WAS HARD BEFORE BUT HIS GROIN tightened further when he caught the glint in Abby's eyes and realized her intent. Her fingers tugged at the straps of her tank top, sliding them down her shoulders and giving him a glimpse of the creamy skin underneath.

He wanted to put his mouth on that skin. He wanted to taste it all, to do comparative testing on every inch. Especially when he caught the pebbled peaks of her nipples pressing against the thin cotton of her top. Her bra must be whisper-thin. He'd start there and investigate for himself.

But damn, this self-denial was almost better—if her striptease didn't kill him first. His anticipation of pleasure almost bordered on pain.

He must have released a groan because she shot him a wicked grin and tugged the straps back into place. This game of peek-a-boo might be the death of him. The crafty woman shifted to her lower half, her thumbs dipping beneath the waistline of her yoga pants. Her hips cocked upward on one side so that she could slowly slide the elastic down, revealing lighter, even creamier skin there. Then she raised the other side up so she could echo the movement.

Einstein's gaze was riveted to every curve, every inch of exposed flesh as the garment hit the floor. He was certain she would taste as sweet as her mouth did. She kicked the pants away, a wisp of fabric gliding across his bedroom floor—exactly where it belonged.

"You're so damn beautiful." His words were ragged with need. He reached for her, certain he could find some way to make her burn hot for him, hot enough to strip naked and end his torment. But she surprised him by lightly slapping his hand away.

Her white teeth flashed. She circled him, trailing a fingertip along his collarbone. His head swiveled to follow until she disappeared behind him. Her teeth raked lightly across his ear until he hissed out a breath. She continued her circuit, returning with a scrap of fabric—the tie he'd left on top of his dresser. She ran the smooth material over her nipples, still hard beneath her tank top and bra, then let go with one hand and trickled the fabric between her breasts. Suddenly, he was enlightened to the advantages of wearing a suit and tie to the office.

"Abby," he growled. He had to touch her. Not able to stand the mounting pressure another moment, he stepped forward. The tie froze. Over it, her eyes met his in silent challenge—which he gladly accepted. His fists gripped the bottom edge of her tank top and he peeled it off until it joined the pants on the floor, exposing her bra. Thin, indeed. It barely hid her breasts or her arousal from him. It was another layer of tease, since it was skin-colored but not actually Abby's skin. He wanted all of her bare to him. Just for him. All to himself.

His gaze locked with hers as his head bent to lick the flesh right above the bra line. With a breathy sound, she arched toward him.

When her hand came to the back of his head, holding him to her chest for more, he grinned with victory. Her other hand reached around her back to unclasp her bra, freeing her breasts to his gaze. And to his mouth.

He dipped his head to suck on a nipple and she cried out, her fingers clutching at the back of his head. She was so damn responsive, primed for him. How long had it been for her? How many men had she let do this to her? Foreign feelings—jealousy and possessiveness—rose up within him. But this gift he'd just unwrapped was all his.

Besides, he suspected she wasn't the type to take many men to bed. She didn't give trust easily. And a woman with a heart like Abby's would have to trust before she'd give herself to a man. It made this gift all the sweeter.

He kissed his way downward, his hands sliding down her sides to her hips as he dropped to his knees before her. His head was level with her belly. He could smell her arousal and the faint scent of her soap—could already imagine taking her in the shower next. His blood pumped harder at the thought. When his hands slid up the insides of her thighs, her muscles quaked with need. He pressed gently outward, grinning as she immediately complied, spreading her legs for him. He dipped down, inhaling her. Heaven.

It had been months, maybe even a year, since he'd invited a woman into his bed. He was a man who took pride in controlling his appetites. But his control had never been challenged by the likes of Abby. Her warm smile and sparkling eyes rendered him powerless.

His own muscles were shaking with the effort of restraint, but she deserved a slow build and an intense orgasm.

She shook her head as if answering a question. "Don't stop." As if he were about to argue, she stifled any response from him by tugging him to his feet, pressing her chest to his, aligning their hips so that she cradled his arousal. "Don't you dare hold back now." Grabbing his shoulders as if to keep him from retreating, she pressed her lips to his, opened her mouth and hoisted herself up to wrap her legs around his waist—an exquisite benefit of sleeping with a yoga instructor.

If she wanted it hard and fast, he'd give it to her. He gripped her ass and reached around to swipe a finger across her clit. She cried out and he tipped her back onto the bed. He took a second to admire the sight of her, splayed out against his sheets. Exactly where he'd imagined her hundreds of times. Soft waves of mahogany hair spread across the charcoal-colored sheets. Creamy limbs reached for him.

She sat up so her hands could explore, delving into his shorts and underwear, helping him shuck them and freeing his hard shaft. Then her hands were there, too, smooth against his length. They wrapped around him and he bit back a groan.

Hard and fast was sounding better and better. He could take her slow later.

"Protection?" Her voice had taken on the husky breathiness of a vixen.

"Side drawer," he managed, hoping it hadn't sounded like a croak. But damn, all of his blood flow was directed into a different region—a very happy region that jutted toward her like a divining rod as she took a condom from the drawer and opened it. He watched her slide the sheath over him.

"Fuck." He hissed out the expletive as his restraint nearly broke. "Feels so good."

She scooted backward across his bed, perpendicular to the normal way he slept. Which was perfect because this woman tilted his world by at least ninety degrees. He was about to show her what that experience was like.

HE PUT A KNEE ON THE BED, FRAMED HER HIPS WITH HIS HANDS, AND then crawled his way, slowly—oh, so slowly—up her body, kissing and licking as he went until she thought she might spontaneously combust. His mouth blazed a trail of heat across her abdomen and between her breasts. Her nipples hardened and ached and she arched into him, adding a little mewl of demand to encourage him. His huff of laughter made her skin erupt in goose bumps. Then he licked and wrapped his lips around one nipple and she nearly came undone. Her hands fisted in his hair and her legs wrapped around his flanks. He took his time, bringing both nipples to tight peaks that had her tummy tightening and quivering with need.

He levered himself up with his elbows on either side of her head and looked down into her eyes. Her breath caught at the strength of purpose in his gaze, at the reverence she saw there. His eyes gleamed, dark with desire and a need she wanted to fulfill. She wanted to take him in and comfort him. To be his everything.

"Abby." Her name on his lips, on an exhalation of breath, was hotter than anything he'd done to her.

And then he entered and filled her, touching parts of her she'd kept hidden away for far too long. She rocked her hips against him, trying to ignore the depths of her feelings or how far she was falling for this man. But as he surged into her again and again, her arms wrapping around him and her skin tingling as his hot breath mingled with hers, she knew this wasn't just physical. Her heart and soul were all in.

CHAPTER 16

The jarring sound of absolutely nothing woke Einstein. No gentle hum of electric devices. No light from the bedside clock. No dusty, howling wind outside a forsaken desert cave.

Beside him, something stirred and a rush of adrenaline hit him before he remembered and released a steadying breath. *Abby.* A smile curved his lips, but it took awhile to slow his pulse rate. Sometimes even subtle changes in his environment could lead to reactions like that. *Fucking Afghanistan.*

Soft, questing fingers crept across his chest as Abby rolled into him, tucking herself against his side. "What's wrong?"

"Power's out."

Her pillow shifted. Her hair tickled his shoulder as she lifted her head. "It's dark," she mumbled.

"Sleep." He whispered the command but his body still held the tension of his initial awakening and she must have sensed it.

"There's something else. What is it?" She placed a kiss on his shoulder.

Her gentleness was nearly his undoing. He longed to flip her onto her back and drive into her, to restrict their relationship to satisfying physical needs. The other needs she was awakening in him were pathetic. God, her soft touches would break him more efficiently than any terrorist's methods could. Then again, the SEALs hadn't trained him for defense against knowing blue eyes and a siren's smile. He could see those features despite the darkness. They were emblazoned on his brain, since she'd been his *happy place* for months. Now that he'd felt and tasted that paradise, how would he be able to let her go?

"Einstein?" She was still waiting for his answer.

He couldn't face the memories, didn't want to taint what they'd shared that night. But he couldn't help the tension that flowed through every nerve and muscle. He rolled away, dislodging her. The room went quiet again, but this time he could almost hear her thoughts.

"Fine, shut me out." But she tucked herself up against his backside, her breasts pressed into his shoulder blades. Skin to skin, no barriers. She traced a finger along a spot behind his ear and he froze. Another scar. Another reminder.

He groaned. "Don't, Abby."

"Afghanistan?"

"Don't," he repeated, forcing the word out between gritted teeth. He didn't want to go there. Her sweetness and light didn't belong in that hellhole.

"It's why you were afraid when you woke up, right?"

He huffed out a mirthless laugh. "You're not going to let this drop, are you?"

She stayed silent, waiting him out.

Fuck. Part of him wanted her to understand. Another part wanted to frighten her away. Talking about that day would do both. And what better place to speak than in the dark, facing away from her and her guileless eyes?

The breath he exhaled was a little shaky. "Right before the

rebels found our SEAL team, everything in the nearby village went quiet."

"Like it is now." Her statement was barely a whisper.

One reason he enjoyed the hum and whir of a room full of computers was that it was nothing like that place and time.

"It was dusk," he continued. "They attacked from the shadows between the shacks that made up the village, using women and children as barriers while they opened fire on us. They killed a couple of men from our team before we retreated to the hills. We'd been there long enough to know where to hide. Lucky for us, the insurgents were from a different village. After they'd used human shields, none of the locals helped them find us. Several of us were wounded."

"You?" Her fingertips traced the scar beneath his hairline again. He'd grown his hair longer to cover it. Not long enough, apparently.

"Head injury. Sliced the scalp and rattled my brain, but I was one of the more mobile injured." He didn't mention the psychological shit that he'd processed in therapy when he got stateside. Or the headaches that plagued him at times. He'd seen too much mucked-up stuff come out of the war, and didn't want to be one of those ex-military who were pitied and jumped at every sound. Instead, he jumped when it was too quiet.

Her touch was soothing, and her hand slipped under his arm and pressed against his heart. He could feel her heartbeat as well, strong and steady, against his back. He could feel other things, too, like how her thighs formed to the back of his and her stomach was against his ass.

And how being so close to her brought all of his walls crashing down. She was dangerous.

He rolled over, facing her, and smoothed a strand of hair away from her cheek. She shivered at the contact and sighed. Yeah, he knew how to flip her world. "You didn't see any of that by touching me? I don't want you to have those images in your head."

She lifted her head to place a gentle kiss on his lips. "I didn't see anything."

He breathed a sigh of relief. His hand drifted from her shoulder to elbow to wrist, lifting her hand from his chest—from his heart—to his neck. But he'd overestimated his powers of distraction.

She leaned forward to press her lips where her hand had been. His heart. He felt the light pressure from the surface all the way to the organ that lay buried deep in his chest. There was a new tenderness, a shift in chemistry between them that had his thoughts scattering and his pulse thumping. Hers was the smile he remembered when he wanted to lose the rest of the world. He wasn't supposed to lose *himself* in her, or to go, with her, to those dark places deep inside.

He needed to remind her, and himself, that this was just sex. He didn't like this downhill slide, this spiraling vortex feeling. Seeking to reassert control over himself and the situation, he made a fist in her silky hair and gently tugged her head back. The darkness made it easier to pretend she wasn't breaking through his walls with every tender look, gentle stroke or soft sigh.

He crushed his mouth to hers and shifted, rolling her under him. He paid homage to each and every square inch of her, making her squirm and moan. But in the end it was he who was aching to claim her. And it was his heart that cracked open, silently calling out her name, as he came inside her.

EINSTEIN WAS STILL HOLDING HER CLOSE, STILL TRYING TO ANALYZE what had emotionally gone down between them through all the hours of the night—because there *had* been a paradigm shift some-where—when Abby's phone rang from the living room. The elec-tricity had returned at some point in the past hour.

Abby stirred. "I need to get that. Could be Grandpa needing something."

He pushed himself to his elbows to admire the silhouette of her sweet heart-shaped ass, highlighted by the light he'd left on in the bathroom. She scooped up his discarded T-shirt from the floor and slipped it over her head. It hung to mid-thigh. Lucky for him, he was blessed with an excellent memory and her naked image was imprinted on his brain. His body wanted another round with her. His heart knew he might not survive.

Instead, he forced himself to get up and pull on some clothes, and then headed to the kitchen. Her long legs were bare as she paced between the kitchen and living room. He tried not to be so attuned to her as he loaded the morning brew in the coffeemaker, but failed as he noted the broken conversation and the sizzle of tension in the air. Her forehead creased as she listened intently to whatever someone had to say.

"I'm telling you, I have no idea where she is," she said into the phone.

He heard yelling coming from the other end of the line. "You're lying. I'm going to kill you, bitch!" Male voice. Obviously worked up to the point of disrespectfulness. And it sounded like he was just getting started.

In two steps, Einstein was standing in front of Abby. He took the phone from her hand. She gasped as he put the device to his ear.

Wesley. He'd recognize the fucker's voice anywhere, especially raised in anger toward Einstein's woman. His brain did a double-take at the last part of the thought, but his adrenaline was spiking, ready to protect, so he focused on that.

"Enough," he ground out. The man stopped his tirade. "Laney's missing?"

"If you know where she is, tell the cops and get them off my ass or I'll come looking for your girlfriend." Wesley hung up.

Einstein immediately called Mrs. Benson, who confirmed the news. After the quick call, in which he assured her they'd contact the authorities if Laney came to them, he filled Abby in. "Laney ran away from the foster home during the night. Guess the cop on the scene didn't think to notify us." Or Abby was further down on the list of suspects who might have taken the girl.

Her face was lined with misery. "Where would she go?" Forgetting she was nearly naked, she hurried to the door and swung it open, but there was no little girl waiting in the hall.

Einstein tugged her back inside and nudged her onto the couch, then poured her a cup of coffee.

Abby took a fortifying swallow, her eyes large as she met his gaze. "We can't just wait for the authorities to find her. And I definitely don't want Wesley to find her." She nibbled at her bottom lip. "Why would he suddenly care, anyway?" Her jaw dropped. "Oh, God. Did the Charmer take her? Because of me, because I got involved in the investigation?"

He sat next to her and pulled her against him. "Let's not jump to conclusions. The foster home probably felt strange to her and she made a statement by walking out. She couldn't have gone far." His words aimed to comfort, but his throat burned with unspoken concerns. Left on her own, where would a six-year-old go, if not to her home? And what if the Charmer really did have a hand in this? Hopefully, the man was too busy being on the run after the events at Pinnacle yesterday. Unless those events had served to stir the hornet's nest and he was striking back.

Abby pulled away. Mussed hair framed pale cheeks and wide eyes. "What am I supposed to do for her?" Again, she was trying to save the day for someone she loved. This time, he could help.

"Get dressed." He stood and tugged her to her feet. "Think of places Laney might go, while you're at it." In the meantime, he'd try to contact Nico, see if the man had any idea if Laney was with the Charmer. Despite the weird vibe he'd picked up from Nico yesterday, the man was their closest connection to the monster they hunted.

"Why didn't you call me right away?" Abby could spit nails.

But the anger was better than the panicky feeling that had settled in her stomach when they'd first heard the news that Laney was missing—from Wesley, no less. Guilt stabbed at her. She'd had too much time on their way from Einstein's apartment to the police station to reconsider how she'd handled Laney's situation. She should have kept the girl at her side. Should have fought harder against the system so she wouldn't lose another person who was precious to her.

"Nobody noticed she was gone until this morning." Mrs. Benson looked pissed, too, which helped a little.

"The foster home is a reputable one," Noah told them. Einstein had called him as she'd been dressing and arranged for his backup. The detective had agreed that, because of the Charmer's possible connection to Laney's disappearance, he should be in on this conversation. "I checked it out after you called. There were no signs of foul play, and they're not sure when she snuck out, but a backpack and a few items—a blanket, her headlamp-type flashlight, a compass and a cell phone—were missing. I've got a crime scene analyst there now, looking for anything that could lead us to her or tell us if someone took her."

Einstein had stepped outside to call Nico again, but now returned to the interview room where Noah had taken Mrs. Benson and Abby to talk. He shook his head once, indicating he still hadn't been able to reach his contact. Abby clung to the hope that the Charmer preferred slightly older girls.

"You can't beat yourself, or anyone else, up." Einstein stroked a hand down her arm and she took comfort from his quiet confidence. "We all thought she was safe. We'll find her."

"After what you told me, I sent a uniform to Wesley Brookes' apartment," Noah said. "I wanted to know if the Charmer contacted him in some way. But Wesley wasn't there." He directed his attention to Abby. "I've read the file on Wesley, and I'd like to add your input as to Laney's personality and state of mind. You were her kindergarten teacher this past year? You were close to her?"

Abby thought back over the past few months. "At school she stuck to me like glue, even after she recanted her story about abuse. But until the other day, I hadn't seen or spoken to her since the last day of school, over a month ago." And Laney had sat alone on that day, looking sad when other kids were excited to begin their summers. Closing her eyes against images of Laney sitting in reading circle, long curls flowing wild or in a haphazard ponytail, always raising her hand to contribute, Abby swallowed to regain her composure. Laney was a self-reliant child, but Chicago would swallow her up. And the Charmer... She didn't even want to think what he'd do to the girl. All because Abby had gotten involved in this case.

Einstein seemed to sense her distress and put a hand on her shoulder in support.

"Laney called Abby's home phone," Noah said. "Would she have gone by her apartment?"

"I don't think she knows where I live. Besides, it sounds like, with a blanket and her headlamp, she was preparing to leave for good." Abby looked up suddenly. "Wait, did you say a cell phone went missing?"

The caseworker nodded. "The foster parents confirmed that Laney took her cell phone with her when she disappeared."

"What cell phone?"

"The one you left for her before you left yesterday."

"I never left a phone for her," Abby said. "Just a dollar for the Tooth Fairy to bring her." Her gaze flew to Einstein's. "Do you think the Charmer found a way to get a phone to Laney? Maybe through Wesley? Maybe this is one of the Charmer's ways of luring girls away from their homes."

Einstein's answer, simply a tightening around his mouth, confirmed her worst fears.

Noah stuck his small pad of notes into his pocket. "I'll file the missing persons report and release an Amber Alert. I'm also sending out a BOLO on Wesley. He might simply be out canvassing the neighborhood for her." His gaze met Einstein's.

"Or he might be doing something for the Charmer," Einstein finished.

"Or for himself. The man's been suspected of dealing drugs."

Abby gasped. "What?"

"No concrete evidence, but when I asked around, I learned he's been under surveillance a time or two."

"Then he could have a connection to the Circle that way," Einstein said. "Or the Charmer exploited that in order to get to him, and to Laney."

"And thus, to me," Abby said. "What can I do?"

"Revisit where Laney might have gone. Contact her classmates and friends. Keep me in the loop."

"We'll do that," Einstein shook Noah's hand. "Thanks."

Noah smiled. "I can see she means a lot to you."

"They both do," Einstein said, low enough that he probably hadn't intended Abby to hear, but she had.

Back in the parking lot, needing Einstein's comfort for just a minute, Abby folded herself against him and breathed him in. His shoulder shifted beneath her cheek as his arms lifted to wrap around her. His hand lightly rubbed her back. Had he meant what he'd told Noah? Had she come to mean something to Einstein?

"I'm lucky to have you with me at a time like this," she said. Beneath her cheek, he stiffened and she pulled back to look into his face, wondering what she'd said that he'd reacted to. But his eyes were shielded and she didn't try to read any messages from him. She wanted him to *want* to open up and share what he was thinking.

He smoothed her hair away from her face. "Let's go find Laney."

"What about Damian? Won't he want you looking for Mariah?"

"I think the Charmer could be involved in Laney's disappearance as well."

The blue sky had begun to sprout clouds that were more white than gray, but the weather forecast had indicated a strong possibility of thunderstorms as the day went on. The city seemed to tremble with anticipation that a break in the heat was imminent. Abby felt only dread. She sent up a quick prayer that Laney was somewhere safe, out of the heat and the potential storm.

Einstein started the car and swung out of the parking lot.

"Where are we going?" Abby asked.

"If Laney doesn't know where you live, or if she does know but you weren't there, where else might she go to feel connected to you? What else was part of her normal routine, a place she'd feel normal and safe?"

Her gaze flew to his. "The school."

A short while later, they pulled up to the elementary school. In the middle of summer, the place took on a sense of desolation that reminded her of a ghost town.

"Do you have a key?" Einstein asked as he followed her across the grass toward her classroom.

"No, but one of the windows in my classroom is always unlocked." At his reproachful look she shrugged. "The lock is broken. I've never had a problem."

"I'll fix it for you when this is over."

She nearly stumbled. Was he implying they had a future beyond this case? Her heart fluttered at the thought and she ruthlessly squelched the spark of hope. Laney's immediate safety was what was important.

"Would Laney know about the broken window?" Einstein asked.

"Maybe." She led him straight to it and tried to slide it upward. It resisted. With the changes in temperature and season, the old wood frame was swollen. Her heart sank. "I doubt she came in this way."

Einstein reached out to help her. "It might have slid open easier last night, before the change in humidity."

"Or maybe she remembered the break in the fence near the playground and found another way into the building."

Einstein shot her an incredulous glance. "Does nobody care about your safety?" As if to illustrate his point, he gave one more shove and the window gave way, sliding upward.

She crawled through the open window and into her darkened classroom. Like stirring up ghosts of the past, it was an odd feeling to be in her classroom while it was empty, with no hope of filling it for several weeks yet—if she was able to settle this nonsensical lawsuit with Wesley in time. She tried the light switch, but nothing happened. Still, the sunlight through the windows was enough to make her way around the familiar terrain.

"Laney?" she called softly. She searched, watching for any sign that Laney was there, or might have been earlier. Throw pillows— the kind she kept available for the students' daily reading time— were arranged in a rectangle, like a bed, in the reading nook. Granola bar wrappers from the stash of snacks she kept in her bottom desk drawer were scattered nearby.

"She's been here," she said as Einstein came up behind her. "Laney!" she called again, more loudly.

"Are you picking up on any of those...vibes?"

She knelt by the makeshift bed. It was only a few feet long. Laney was so young, so small. *Please let her be safe.* She lay down and put her head on the pillow that had a small indentation, as if that was where Laney had lain, and let her mind drift.

Sticky and sweaty. It's so hot. Should have brought a toothbrush. Daddy will be so mad if I get another cavity. I wonder if the Tooth Fairy will find me here. Where is she? Miss Rhodes should be here by now. What if Daddy finds me first? A noise... Heavy feet. Not Miss Rhodes. So scared. Why isn't she here?

A touch on her arm made her jump. "Abby? Did you hear me?"

Einstein's face came into focus. Concern wrinkled his forehead and shadowed his eyes. "You seemed to go somewhere else."

"She was here." She shook off the cloudiness in her brain but couldn't get rid of the uneasiness that the final part of the message had left with her. Hope, and then fear. Laney had been waiting for her, counting on her. So, who had finally come for her? And where the hell was Laney now? "I think the Charmer took her."

"Any idea where they went?"

Frustration twisted her insides. "I have no clue. I only know she's scared, because of me."

His gaze was full of compassion. "You would never purposely put her in harm's path."

"It doesn't matter. She was waiting here, for me. And he got to her…because of me." She glanced around but didn't see what she was looking for. "The cell phone. He must have gotten to her that way, told her I'd be here to meet her."

If anything happened to that sweet girl, Abby would never forgive herself.

CHAPTER 17

The Charmer looked at the girl in the rearview mirror. She huddled in the backseat, her knobby knees drawn to her chest as she stared, unblinking, out the window. She was a tiny thing. He could break her in two if he had the notion.

"You've done well this far," he told her.

This time, Laney met his gaze. "You promised me Miss Rhodes would be there. You said we'd be a family, me, her and Einstein."

He could have told her families were illusions. That proclamations of love were false and used only to manipulate. But he needed the girl's cooperation for a little longer.

"Think of this like a game of hide-and-seek," he said. "If Miss Rhodes and Einstein come for you, if they solve the riddle and follow the clues, you'll know they're worthy of you. You'll know you all were meant to be a family." Too bad they'd all be dead.

"What if they don't come?" The question was softly spoken, as if saying her fears aloud might make it come true.

"Then you belong with me." He smiled but she was back to gazing forlornly out the window.

He maneuvered his car into his private parking place. He'd

have to coax the girl to come with him without arousing suspicions of the people they might bump into, but that was only a matter of finding the proper motivation. And Wesley had been forthcoming about what would motivate his daughter. Because the Charmer had a knack for reading people, for knowing how to get what he wanted by using what they wanted. And Wesley had been easy to read. Money and drugs were his motivations.

"I have Miss Rhodes' phone number, but I need you to come with me to call her. After all, she'd rather talk to you than me." He sighed as if he'd thought of a problem. "They don't allow little girls like you in this building. I'll need to sneak you in and then hide you in the special place where you'll meet Miss Rhodes and Einstein."

The girl shuddered and hugged her knees tighter. "I don't like small spaces."

"It won't be for long." And she didn't have a choice. Whether he used the drugged water bottle waiting in the cup holder to get her to willingly come with him, or whether he lured her with flattery and promises, it didn't matter to him. Either way, she was a pawn in this game.

EINSTEIN LISTENED IN FRUSTRATION AS YET ANOTHER CALL WENT TO Nico's voicemail. "Call me ASAP. I need to know if the Charmer is responsible for Laney's disappearance." Nico was a phantom—Einstein didn't even know his last name—so if he wasn't answering, there was no other way to dig up information on him. And that didn't sit well. He couldn't even trace the man's cell phone because Nico used a separate answering service. It had seemed a smart idea in the past, since it would keep their communication from harming Nico's undercover identity. Now, Einstein was starting to wonder if Nico had other reasons for being so secretive. Was he playing both sides?

Beside him in the passenger seat, Abby looked out the window and scanned every alley they passed. They'd notified Noah of their belief the Charmer had Laney. Damian had been informed of the latest development. There was nothing to do but keep Abby's spirits up while he did some online digging. She held herself together until they made it to his office and shut the door.

She slumped in a chair and put her face in her hands. "Where would he take her? She's just an innocent girl."

Einstein dropped to one knee in front of her and pulled her hands away from her face so he could look her in the eyes, hoping she could see his conviction and, hopefully, draw strength from it. "We'll find him. I promise he won't hurt her." If it was the last thing he did, he'd return Laney to Abby safely.

She scanned his face as if absorbing his confidence. Beneath his fingers wrapped around her wrists, her pulse settled into a more relaxed pace. She believed him. She trusted his abilities. Silently, he vowed that he would prove her trust was well placed.

Her phone rang. Their gazes held.

"Let me get that," he said.

She blew out a breath. "You think it's him."

"Might be." He tried not to sound as angry as he felt. This woman had been put through the wringer, and all because she'd tried to help. She didn't deserve this and he wanted to protect her with every ounce of his being.

She nodded and handed him her phone without looking at the screen.

The caller ID said only *unknown caller,* but Einstein knew. "Hello."

"Give her the phone," the monster said. Einstein memorized the sound and cadence of the man's voice, hoping he'd hear it in person soon—right before he wrapped his hands around the man's neck and squeezed the last breath from him.

A chill prickled the nape of his neck and radiated outward. "This doesn't involve her."

The low chuckle grated. "Of course it does. You're not dragging some no-name psychic across Chicago and back in the ungodly heat for no reason. I'm not stupid." His tone had turned unyielding. Apparently, the Charmer didn't like to be underestimated. Lorena had been right about the man's ego. Unfortunately, the monster was entirely too smart for the good of society.

"Although," the Charmer continued, thoughtfully, "I can see how she might have *other* uses." Einstein stiffened. "Put Abby on. I need to talk to her alone. No cheating and putting me on speaker."

Abby's eyes, locked on him, went wide as he handed her the phone.

ABBY'S VOICE CRACKED AS SHE SAID HELLO.

"This is the Charmer," he said.

She wasn't sure what she'd expected, but it wasn't the normal-sounding deep voice on the other end of the line. "What do you want? Where are Laney and Mariah?"

"We'll get to the second question…if you help me with the first. That man in front of you is using you."

"I volunteered my services to SSAM and the Pierces."

"And they put you on television to mock you in front of the world. Where have your so-called gifts gotten you? You certainly haven't found Mariah." He chuckled and the hair on her neck rose.

"And yet you're hurting an innocent girl."

"You're deluding yourself. *You* dragged Laney into this. You're scared. Scared you won't get little Laney back safely. Scared you'll fail Mariah or that computer geek boyfriend of yours. Scared nobody will listen to you in time."

She gritted her teeth against each accusation. Anger ran, lava-hot, through her body. "What do you want?"

"Are you alone with Einstein?"

"Yes, we're alone." In fact, Einstein was regarding her intently, trying to hear the other half of the conversation.

"And he's not listening?"

"No."

"I have only one request, and I'll release whichever girl you choose."

Choose? "Is this part of your game?"

He chuckled and it grated in her ear like sandpaper. "No, that's for Damian. But sure, if you want to consider this your contribution, I'm happy to oblige." What the Charmer said next sent ice water through her veins, dousing the anger. "Take Einstein's gun and shoot him."

"What?" At her exclamation and expression of alarm, Einstein made a low growling noise and stepped forward, reaching for the phone. She jerked back and put out her free hand, indicating he should hold back another moment. "I can't do that."

"Sure you can. Mariah and Laney are depending on you."

"But why him?" Her gaze was held prisoner by Einstein's, locked on target. He seemed to be trying to read her thoughts.

"That's not important, other than he's part of SSAM." *Bullshit.* The Charmer was worried about Einstein, and about her. Certainly, between the two of them, they covered the technical and metaphysical ways of hunting him down. He *was* worried. The thought made her grin. Einstein's eyebrows went up.

"Don't be confused by your feelings for him," the Charmer continued. "He knows how to manipulate."

"One could say the same of you."

Another chuckle. "You're feisty. I like that. Next time I take someone…"

Her blood ran cold. "Where are the girls?"

"Both alive, for the moment."

"They'd better stay that way." There was a brief silence. Maybe she'd surprised him.

"You have twenty minutes to complete the request."

"No deal. If you want us, you'll have to come and get us. Better yet, just stay where you are. We'll be there soon. And if anything happens to another person, I'll personally make you pay."

"I'd like to see you try," the man bit out. "In fact, I'd like that very much. I'll be waiting for you, Abby. But I'll give you twenty minutes to change your mind. If you don't…someone else will pay." The line went dead.

"I GUESS I SHOULDN'T HAVE PRESSED HIM." SHE SIGHED AS SHE handed the phone back to Einstein.

"Actually, I enjoyed that very much." Einstein smiled at her shocked expression. "You're a fighter. It's an admirable quality."

"But it didn't do any good."

He hated the self-doubt he saw in her eyes. "You would rather kill me?"

Her jaw dropped. "You heard that?"

"I heard enough to understand what he was telling you. And I saw the way your eyes darted to my ankle, where my gun is holstered. Thanks for not agreeing to the deal, by the way."

"The day is young."

He grinned. He couldn't remember a time a woman had kept him on his toes like this. Or the last time he'd had a partner he'd come to trust so quickly. He realized her value in that moment. She was someone who could make him laugh during the darkest hour or lift a burden from his shoulders just by being there. Though he didn't understand her skills or how they worked, he trusted her and liked having her on his team.

The humor dissipated, leaving them with the heaviness of reality.

"Twenty minutes?" She released a strangled groan. "If I don't produce your corpse, who's he going after next?"

ACCORDING TO EINSTEIN'S WATCH, HE HAD SEVENTEEN MINUTES TO show up dead, which gave them no time to spare.

He found Damian in his office with his head in his hands,

elbows on the desk, fingers shoved into his salt-and-pepper hair. Einstein rapped his knuckles against the open door. "Sir?"

Damian's head shot up and it took him a moment to focus. "Come in."

Abby followed him inside and they took chairs side by side, facing Damian. "I take it there's been no news about Mariah or Laney," Einstein said.

"Noah just called. They can't find Wesley, either. Apparently, I'm just supposed to continue waiting for *game* instructions while the Charmer claims victim after victim and highlights my failures." He looked miserable. But as he focused on them, he must have sensed their tension. "What is it?"

"The Charmer just called Abby."

"Did you get a trace?"

Einstein shook his head. "No time. But he'll be contacting us in some way." He checked his watch. "In fifteen minutes." And there were only about eight hours left before the deadline he'd given Damian. Shouldn't that be keeping the Charmer busy?

"He claims he'll abduct another victim if she doesn't kill me within the time limit." Einstein reached out and took her hand. "She generously told him no." But they were all worried about who that next victim could be.

"You realize he's already taken someone else," Damian said. "This is just another ploy to keep anxiety running high."

Abby gasped. "What?"

But Einstein had already suspected as much, as well. "He's toying with us. Like a magic trick, he's trying to keep us busy watching this direction while he's committing other acts somewhere else."

"But who?"

"I've been trying to reach Priscilla. She's the only one left on that list of people I've supposedly wronged." He dialed his phone. "And she's still not answering. I gave her some space after I saw her yesterday. I was asking her questions about our past, trying to see if she'd remember anything I couldn't."

"Either way, I think we're about to find out." He glanced at his watch again. "In about eleven minutes."

EXACTLY ELEVEN MINUTES LATER, ABBY RECEIVED A TEXT. "*I assume you didn't go through with it. Check Mariah's email account,*" she read aloud to the assembled group.

Einstein had set up his laptop in the conference room and she, Damian and Lorena had gathered around to brainstorm and strategize. He brought up Mariah's account and projected it on the conference room's larger screen. "An email with a link to a picture." An image had been divided into quadrants.

"This looks like Mariah," Damian said, pointing to the upper left corner where a blond girl lay in the fetal position in what appeared to be a cage.

"And the next is Laney," Einstein said. It sounded as if his heart were as heavy as Abby's. The girl's slight form was huddled, knees to her chin, in the corner of another cell, though this one appeared to be more of a padded room than a barred cage.

"She must be so scared," Abby whispered. Rage and fear warred within her.

Suddenly, Einstein shifted to block the left half of the screen. "You've seen enough." He was about to click on something to make the picture disappear when she realized what the image in the lower left corner was. She released a strangled groan. "Grandpa."

Einstein's gaze brimmed with commiseration and under-standing but it wasn't misery she was feeling. It was fury.

"He *did* take someone else I care about." Each word felt like chewed glass as it passed her lips. "A sick old man with only a few weeks left to live? Why the hell would he bother?"

"Because he enjoys the game," Damian said. The Charmer was a megalomaniac. "And manipulating people."

"Who's the fourth?" Abby asked.

Lorena studied the screen and spun to Damian, a look of alarm on her face. "Is that...?"

A muscle ticked in Damian's jaw. "Priscilla." His gaze met Lorena's and they exchanged some wordless communication but empathy was clear. Damian swung toward the rest of the group. "Any ideas on where they're being held? Clues from the backgrounds?"

"Mariah's cage looks to be metal," Einstein offered. "And old. There's rust on the wall behind her, while Laney's looks to be newer construction, and probably indoors. No sign of exposure to the elements." He zoomed in on Laney's image. All Abby saw was the fear written on her face. Worse, there was an emptiness to her gaze that indicated hopelessness. *Hang on, girl. Don't give up yet.*

"Do you recognize the location where your Grandpa's being held?" Einstein asked her.

Abby walked closer to the screen while Einstein zoomed in on that picture. Unlike the others, probably because he was weak, he wasn't in a small room. His head was bowed, his back hunched as he slumped on a hard wooden bench.

She shook her head. "Doesn't look like his apartment, or anywhere I know."

Einstein clicked on Priscilla's picture to get a closer look.

"I don't recognize the location," Damian said.

A ping from Einstein's computer had them all turning to him. "A new email just came through Mariah's account," he announced. He replaced the projection of the images of the Charmer's latest abductees with the email.

Damian read the message aloud. *"I've killed many, and yet SSAM has failed to find me. Damian's ultimate failure. This is your last chance. These four will be my last before I disappear, forever beyond your reach. Which one will you save? Can you save them all in the time that's left? It had better be by sunset, or I claim them as mine. You'll only get one at a time. Follow the clues or you lose. And I win."*

A weighty silence filled the conference room.

Abby waved a hand toward the screen. "How can he claim four people, presumably in different places around the city, at the same time?"

"He's always had connections," Damian said. "That's what's made it so hard to get close to him. He's rich and has power. But the point is to defeat me." Again, the man exchanged a significant look with Lorena. "He wants me to fail."

"It's a Kobayashi maru." Einstein shoved his hands through his hair and faced them all with a shake of his head. "From *Star Trek*. A no-win scenario. If he wants you to fail, he should make you do it fair and square."

"He can't beat me on a level playing field," Damian said, lifting his chin. "And it's not just me fighting to save these people. *We're* going to save them. Together." He glanced at his watch. "It's almost noon now and sunset should be around..."

"Eight twenty-seven. The countdown clock ends shortly before that." Einstein suddenly sat forward, looking at his computer. "He just sent the first clue. *An eternal vow on the horizon. The perfect spot to begin a new life. Too bad it was an empty promise.*"

Damian reread the email when it appeared on the big screen. "It's a riddle."

Lorena stepped up to his side. "Any idea where this would be? Maybe the church where you got married? Of the four who are missing, I'm guessing the *eternal vow* reference must denote your wedding vows and Priscilla."

"It's about the promise, and the word *horizon*." He glanced at the assembled group. "I know where this is. Lorena and Max will come with me. Einstein, call Noah and fill him in. It'll be outside his jurisdiction, but he'll want to be in on this. And see if he can have the local police and the FBI meet us there. I want you to stay here with Abby in case we get more clues. The other victims could be spread out around town and where I'm going is a couple of hours north."

Einstein's forehead knit in confusion. "Outside of Noah's juris-diction? Where should I send the cavalry?"

"The place where I proposed to Priscilla. On *Bright Horizon*, a boat. I made a vow there, a promise that I broke when I divorced her. We're going to the place where that failed journey began. Winthrop Harbor."

MAX DROVE WHILE LORENA AND DAMIAN OCCUPIED THE BACKSEAT of the SUV.

Lorena slid him a look. "You're thinking so hard, I can hear the gears grinding."

"You saying I'm not a well-oiled machine?" Damian frowned. The Charmer wouldn't make every clue this easy, of that he was certain. There had to be an underlying layer, some hidden message. Something the Charmer could use to mock Damian, and say he wasn't smart enough to solve the subtext.

"Of course not. But maybe if you spoke your thoughts out loud, we could figure this out together. That is what you pay me for, right?"

"My thoughts..." Well, she'd asked. Maybe there was no time like the present to address his concerns. Besides, they might not have much longer together, if the Charmer had his way. Damian was certain death was the end game, the Charmer's ultimate hope for Damian. "I was thinking that maybe you'd stick around after all of this is over."

Her elegant brows rose high over dark-chocolate eyes. "That's what you're worrying over?"

It had been one of the things on his mind. They hadn't had time to talk alone since the intimacy they'd shared, and he wasn't sure where she thought things were going.

"I work for you," she said. "Where else would I go?"

"I'd like you to stick around for other reasons. Hell, Lorena, I want you to choose *me*."

She interlaced her fingers with his on the seat between them. "I'll always choose you."

"It's about time," Max drawled from the driver's seat. His smiling eyes met Damian's in the rearview mirror before he returned his attention to midday traffic.

Damian's heart swelled and pressed in sweet pain against his ribcage. He cleared his throat. "Good. Well, now that that's settled, and at the risk of talking about my ex, I've been thinking about the significance of the Charmer knowing about the place I proposed to Priscilla."

"Was it a secret?"

"It's not like nobody knew, but only a few close friends were aware of the details."

"Then that should tell us something right there."

Someone who'd known him and Ron since boyhood, had met Priscilla around the same time he had, someone who'd known Samantha for her entire life… Someone he trusted and counted as a friend had done the unthinkable. He swallowed the bile that rose in his throat and struggled to control his rage. His heart pounded so hard he thought it might leap out onto the floor of the car.

"Who is it?" Lorena asked. "I can see you have a suspect in mind."

"I won't say until we find Priscilla. I need to talk to her. I don't want to start a witch hunt until I'm sure." And then he'd cut the monster down himself. It was his duty. It was his right.

CHAPTER 18

An excruciating hour and a half later, when the sun was still high in the sky but had definitely dipped over the zenith, Damian's heart raced again as he spied the place where he'd proposed to Priscilla.

"Winthrop Harbor," Lorena read from the sign as Max parked. "It's beautiful. I can see where it would be romantic." She shielded her eyes with a hand as she scanned the rocky shore. "But where would he hide Priscilla?"

"My dad's boat," Damian said.

Max paused in his own perusal of their surroundings. "I thought your parents had passed."

"He left *Bright Horizon* to me a long time ago." Damian pointed toward the harbor. "I pay someone for the upkeep but rarely take it out."

"And that's where you proposed to Priscilla?" Lorena asked.

"I'd planned a day of sailing, a picnic lunch and a proposal," Damian said, smiling wryly at the innocent dreams he'd had back then. "How ignorant I was of the world."

"You were untouched by evil." Lorena put a hand on his arm in understanding. She'd been *touched* at such an early age. What kind of woman would she have become if she hadn't lost the ones she loved? What kind of man would he have been? They'd each taken their experiences and created strength and a sense of purpose from them.

An unmarked car parked nearby and Noah climbed out. "Thanks for waiting."

Damian grunted. "Thanks for hurrying. If you had been another minute, we'd have been out to the boat already." He started toward the dock.

"Wait," Noah said. "You can't just walk out there."

"Watch me. Besides, he's not here. This is just the beginning. He's waiting for me at the finish line." Damian was sure of it.

The elegant thirty-foot sailboat was docked beside similar vessels. Damian paused as Noah and Max boarded the silent craft. "Wait here," he told Lorena. "Watch our backs."

She nodded and he leapt aboard, memories hitting him as it rocked lightly with his weight and the gentle waves of Lake Michigan. Saturday sails with his father, summer jaunts with college friends and carefree weekends with Priscilla, and then with Samantha. *Bright Horizon* indeed—for a time.

He ducked his head to go through the doorway and down the few steps into the cabin. "Cilla," he breathed and rushed forward as he spied her tied up on the floor.

Max had knelt and was taking her pulse. "She's alive and her pulse is steady."

"Oh, thank God." Damian moved to her side.

Noah and Max searched the rest of the small cabin, called for an ambulance and then went upstairs to give him some privacy.

He bent to his ex-wife's ear. "Cilla, come back to me, honey. I need to ask you a question." He gritted his teeth, not wanting to utter the words. Not wanting to make it a reality.

Had one of their closest friends, whom Damian had known since boarding school, stolen their daughter from them? It was unthinkable. Unimaginable. Hell, he'd seen this man at events over the years. They'd been friendly competitors at school and in the business world. He'd even tried to date Priscilla in college before Damian had asked her out.

Thinking back, he remembered the quiet rage and rejection he'd seen in John Thorpe's eyes before John had been able to disguise it. Damian had come to believe he'd imagined the jealous spark over the years, because John had been a good friend. Before their divorce, John and Vicky had come to parties at their house, they'd brought their daughter Hannah over to play with Sam and had shared the occasional Thanksgiving or other holiday celebration. They were trusted friends.

Priscilla's eyes fluttered open and she moaned.

"Was it John?" he asked.

Fear and anger flared in her baby blues, fighting the fog of drugs. She jerked her head once in the affirmative.

He'd be taking down one of his oldest friends by sunset.

EINSTEIN ANSWERED HIS EMPLOYER'S CALL ON THE FIRST RING. "DID you find Priscilla?"

As Abby leaned on his desk, he put the phone on speaker so that they could both hear. They'd been waiting nearly two hours for an update. Meanwhile, he was searching his data for anything that could lead to where the other three victims might be. Abby had nearly chewed her bottom lip to a pulp.

"Yes, and she's going to be okay, physically at least." But Damian didn't sound relieved. He sounded like a man bearing the weight of the world.

"But not emotionally?" Abby asked.

"We've had a...shock. But we've confirmed the identity of the Charmer. His name is John Thorpe. He lured Priscilla here, fed her drugged food and wine and then tied her up for us to find."

"But why...how? How did she trust him? You warned her he might try to contact her, right?"

"He was a family friend, and she thought I'd invited her to come out here to talk. So when she saw John at his boat just a few down from mine, she wasn't suspicious. It all seemed like a chance meeting."

"Jesus." Einstein blew out a breath, but it didn't calm the buzzing in his head—it was quickly galloping toward a headache. They finally had a name. John Thorpe. "Why do I know that name?"

"You might have read it over the years. He's a big name in business in Chicago and has been for years. Hell, he was a contributor at SSAM fundraisers."

"And he's the Circle's Boss. And a killer." God, what Damian must be going through. Abby seemed to be experiencing the same riot of emotions. Her gaze was clouded with them. Einstein rubbed at a temple to ease the pounding.

"The CPD and the FBI are both searching for John now. Priscilla tried calling Vicky, his ex-wife, but hasn't been able to reach her."

"Does he have a daughter? Someone who might own a bracelet? Or maybe it was Vicky's?"

Damian released a mirthless chuckle. "You know, with the events of the past hour, I hadn't even thought about the bracelet. Yes, he has a daughter. Hannah was Sam's age. She'd be in her thirties now, though I haven't seen her for years."

"Hannah," Abby whispered. "Hannah Smith." The woman they hadn't been able to track down from the studio.

"In the meantime, he has to know we're onto him," Damian said. "But he left a clue anyway. Two, in fact. They were stuck to the backside of the boat cabin's door. Max is texting a picture to you now."

"What do you want us to do?" Einstein asked, itching to get into the game. He reached into his mini-fridge for caffeine. Maybe it would dislodge the headache. He'd need the boost for what was to come.

"Go to his company's downtown office. I think that's where this clue points. I think maybe Laney could be somewhere in that vicinity, since her cell seemed to be indoors." Damian rattled off the name of the company John Thorpe owned. "We're almost two hours north of town, with traffic, so keep us posted. Noah's got a call to the judge. He's rushing the warrant."

"Won't need it," Einstein said. "It's the middle of a workday and we'll sweet-talk the receptionist if we have to." Anything to get to Laney as soon as possible.

"Abby?" Damian asked.

"Yes," she responded. She'd stood and was coming around the desk. "What can I do? I'm at your disposal." She was offering herself up to them again. Einstein's heart swelled with gratitude and admiration even as he nearly moaned with relief as her hands worked at the knots in his shoulders and neck.

"I want you to go with Einstein. I don't think the Charmer—John—will be there, but maybe you can pick up a message from something in his office."

"I'll do my best." Her fingers moved upward, sifting through his hair to massage his scalp. The pounding lessened.

"I know you will. And thank you. Without you…we might not have gotten this far. Certainly not this fast." He paused and cleared his throat as if emotions had lodged there. "I know we'll find Laney and your grandfather soon. And Mariah, too. Have faith."

Soon. He hoped so. They had five hours, by Einstein's measure.

"I will," Abby said. "And the same to you."

As Einstein hung up, he caught her hands in his. "How did you know about the headache?"

"I could see the pain in your face. Give me your wrist." She applied a gentle but firm pressure at a few points. "This is supposed to help with headaches."

"Some kind of yoga technique?"

"Something like that. Does it help?"

"Having your hands on me helps." To his surprise, it had. Before the pain could grow worse, the pounding had subsided to a dull ache that was manageable.

With a chuckle, she went back to massaging his scalp and temples as he found Max's text. He sent the image to his computer so he could enlarge it.

Abby read over his shoulder. Her hair tickled his ear as she leaned forward. Her light, sweet scent filled his nostrils and the remembered taste of her made his mouth water. She'd invaded his world, imprinted herself upon him, and thoroughly taken over his thoughts. He'd been powerless against the takeover. Worse, he willingly surrendered. He only wondered if he'd survive when she withdrew from his life as his parents had. She'd feared rejection, but was unaware his fears ran parallel to hers.

Abby's breath brushed his cheek as she read the latest clue aloud. *"To reach your next destination, tear down the façade. That's where innocence lies. The real me is waiting where your world, and your heart, cracked open. You were never the same because you failed to protect those you claim to love."*

"Façade." Einstein nodded. "Makes sense why Damian would want me to visit John's office. It's how the world knew him, but hid the monster within."

Abby turned her face to his. "And innocence. That has to be Laney."

ABBY REACHED FOR THE DOOR OF THE OFFICE BUILDING AT THE SAME time Einstein did and their hands brushed. This time, she didn't jump back. She relished the strength and confidence she sensed in him. She desperately needed both now. Would her gift be enough to find Laney? Would Grandpa be next?

Over her shoulder, she sent Einstein a smile.

"I love that dimple," he said, surprising her. He absently stroked a finger over it before seeming to snap back to reality and ushering her through the doorway. By the time they entered the elevator, he had slipped back into ex-SEAL protective mode. "Damian doesn't think the Charmer is here, but don't let down your guard."

"I kind of have to if I'm going to pick up vibes."

"When it's time for that, I'll be your guard."

She smiled. "I like the sound of that." But as the elevator climbed toward the floor occupied by a bona fide venture capitalist company called Thorpe Enterprises, she wondered how a legitimate businessman could hide the pure evil burning within him for so many years. Could John Thorpe, someone so close to Damian's family, have done such despicable things as kidnap and kill nearly a dozen girls—and head up the Circle, an international crime ring, as well?

She didn't realize she'd spoken the questions aloud until Einstein sent her a grim look. "I've seen any number of horrors over the years, in the 9/11 attacks, as a SEAL and as a SSAM agent. Behaviors I never would have believed a human capable of committing." His eyes darkened for a moment with memories, and she was glad she wasn't touching him. At the same time, she wished she could soothe away the old hurts and replace those memories with good ones.

If he decided he could see a future with her, maybe she'd have the chance. Einstein had never even hinted that he wanted anything beyond this strange bubble they'd created together to fit the odd circumstances. Their affair was entirely situational. Except it didn't feel situational. It felt like the real deal. It felt like she'd known him forever, and like he'd always be there. Could this go beyond the coffee shop flirtation and their current craziness to survive the real world? Did he want it to?

"We don't know what we'll be walking into," he warned as they stepped off the elevator. His face flashed concern before he carefully dialed his expression back to stoic soldier. She wanted to reach out and take his hand, to reassure him that she had no doubts she'd be safe in his care, but she sensed he was pulling invisible armor on in preparation for battle.

They checked in with the receptionist, who immediately stood and led them down a long hallway to another receptionist, John's personal assistant, who stood guard at a large oak door. She gestured that they should go inside.

Abby sent her a quizzical look. "Is he here?"

The polished woman sent her a withering look. "No, but he said to admit you or anyone else from SSAM the moment you arrived. I wasn't to let anybody else inside." Her brows knit together. "And he said to tell you congratulations on achieving step two. I assume you understand what that means."

Abby shivered. She didn't like that they were expected. It was as if he were in control of the trail of breadcrumbs. Needing reinforcement, she reached into her purse for the touchstone. Its cool weight gave her confidence as she stepped over the threshold, into the lion's den.

Everything in John's office screamed successful businessman. From the floor-to-ceiling windows overlooking the river to the shelves lined with what looked like precious artifacts from tribes and peoples across the world. A collector.

A couch and winged-back chairs formed a sort of conversation area at one end of his large office, near the windows. A wardrobe-style cabinet dominated the corner of the room near an enormous desk. The ornately carved doors seemed to pulse with a cold glow that lured Abby, enticing her to explore it. It wasn't the only thing that longed to be touched. Many items on the shelves seemed to call to her with varying degrees. And yet, something within her—perhaps a primitive survival instinct—begged her not to progress farther into the room.

But the cabinet... There was something about it. It held answers.

"See anything that could be helpful in finding..." Einstein's words trailed off as she walked past him and around the desk.

A curious glow was there, evident only to her. The cabinet seemed to pulse with life. She ran a hand over the wood and shivered, chilled by what should have been a warm material. John's cold heart and egomaniacal sense of pride had tainted it. Whatever was inside would be the key to everything. But it could take everything out of her, too.

Einstein came up behind her, seeming to know he shouldn't speak. Instead, he moved to the desk to search for a key to the cupboard. Coming up empty, he reached into his pocket and pulled out a small pouch of tools. He went to work using them to pick the lock. A moment later, Abby gasped as the doors swung open to reveal the secret inner contents. They both froze.

"A shrine." Just like in her initial vision, several rows of shelves held the pictures and mementos of the eleven Charmer victims. Tentatively, Abby reached out.

Einstein grabbed her hand. "Let me take pictures first and get the police here. This evidence will be enough to put John away for the rest of his miserable life."

Abby pulled her hand back, partly relieved and partly frustrated, since she knew the objects held more messages for her and the families of the victims. Struggling for patience, she hugged herself as she moved about the rest of the room, listening as Einstein phoned Noah and then left yet another message for Nico.

"Damian's not answering either," he said, hanging up with a frustrated shake of his head.

"The team will protect him," she murmured absently. Her fingers twitched as her attention was drawn to a shelf at about eye level across the room. It was part of a bookcase that encompassed a large portion of the wall.

"Noah is still at the marina, but the CPD will send officers—" His sentence broke off as he realized she was barely listening. "What is it?"

"Can I touch the books?"

"I don't see why not. They aren't evidence."

Her forefinger and thumb rubbed together an instant before Abby let herself trace the spine of one of the books and tip it toward her.

EINSTEIN GRABBED ABBY WITH ONE HAND AND REACHED FOR HIS GUN with the other as the bookshelf swung outward on hinges.

"A hidden room?" Abby peered around him.

"Maybe a panic room," Einstein suggested, inching forward with caution. "Some high-up corporate types have them, I've heard."

He recognized the padded room from the Charmer's emailed picture at the same time she spied the small figure huddled in the dark corner.

"Laney!" Abby pushed around him and crouched beside the girl, who raised her head at the sound of her voice.

"Miss Rhodes?"

Abby sat next to the girl and opened her arms. "We're here, Einstein and me. You're safe now. The police are on their way. Are you hurt?"

With a sob, Laney launched herself at Abby and tucked her head against her chest. Einstein's own chest squeezed and he backed out into the main office to wait for the police, unable to hear the cries that were so like the villagers who'd been injured or had lost loved ones—all-too-often children—to bombs.

"Einstein?" Abby called softly. He couldn't go in there. As much as he wanted to comfort Laney and be there for Abby, it would just be more difficult when this all came to an end and they were no longer part of his life. He needed to start rebuilding the walls Abby and Laney had so skillfully knocked flat.

The enormity of what could have happened if they hadn't found Laney hidden in the walls, if they'd given John even a few more hours to decide it was time to come back and make good on his threats… He felt sick to his stomach and rubbed a hand across the knot that had lodged behind his sternum.

But if Laney was hurt, he had to act. "Does she need an ambulance?" he asked. "A hospital?"

Abby's eyes were full of questions at the way he stood apart from them, but she shook her head. "She doesn't appear to be hurt."

A uniformed police officer arrived and Einstein explained the situation, as well as the importance of the cabinet. "Contact Detective Noah Crandall if you have any questions about how to proceed, but the items in this office are critical to a case."

"Will they let me explore?" Abby asked. One arm was still looped around Laney, who had her arm wrapped tightly around Abby's waist as if afraid her rescuer would disappear. He was shocked when Laney pulled away from Abby to embrace him.

"I knew you'd come. I kept praying and you came."

Uncertain what to do, Einstein simply clasped a palm to Laney's head and held her to him. His gaze met Abby's in a silent plea for help.

Mrs. Benson's voice came from the doorway. "What a sweet reunion." She smiled warmly at Laney, who'd tightened her grip on him at the caseworker's approach. "I need you to come with me for a bit, honey."

He crouched to the little girl's level. "I'm so glad you're okay. I'll never let anything happen to you again." And he meant it. His throat tightened and he had to clear it a couple times before he could speak again. "But we have to help Abby's grandfather and catch the man who took you, so I need you to go with Mrs. Benson for a little while."

Laney's face pressed into the side of his hip. "She'll send me back to that house."

"Could you take her to a friend of ours for the night?" Abby asked. "Dr. Maggie Levine. She's a psychiatrist and she told me to contact her if we need anything. I think she'd like to help, especially under the circumstances." Abby and Einstein were hunting the man who'd killed Maggie's childhood friend and would soon have answers about the woman with the bracelet, and whether she'd planned to harm Maggie.

"I think that's a great idea." Einstein smoothed a wayward curl from Laney's cheek and smiled. "You'll like Maggie. I've worked with her before. And she and her husband Ethan are about to have a baby of their own. Ethan's really good at keeping people safe."

"I want to stay with you." Laney's lower lip stuck out so far, there was a risk she'd trip over it.

"I promise I'll come find you when this is over." The future was so uncertain, but the faith reflected in Laney's big brown eyes— faith in him—was unwavering.

Abby put a hand on Laney's shoulder. "I promise, too."

"But what about the Tooth Fairy?" Laney asked. "I left the other house before morning, so she didn't find me. And I left my tooth at the house." Her eyes shimmered with fat tears.

Einstein thought fast, intent on avoiding a flood. "I'll text the Tooth Fairy and tell her where you'll be. I'll explain what happened. She'll understand." Abby bit her cheek to keep from smiling, but approval shone in her eyes.

Laney's eyes grew wide. "You can do that?"

"I've come to believe Einstein can accomplish anything," Abby said, sending him a warm look that was full of...love, he realized. The shock rooted him to the spot and he cleared his throat against a wave of conflicting emotion. Anticipation and fear. Excitement and frustration. Hope.

Laney threw her arms around his neck and kissed his cheek. "Thank you." As she turned to do the same to Abby, he took a moment to compose himself.

The child's belief in the unseen, her faith in the unknown... It was a wonder to behold. As was Abby's faith in him. His parents might not have been there for him emotionally, obsessed with their own relationship and careers and uncertain how to handle a precocious child, but that didn't mean he couldn't choose a different path.

Mrs. Benson led Laney from the premises, under the escort of a CPD officer who would see to it that they got to Maggie and Ethan's house safely. He watched until Laney was gone.

"You still too scared to trust in love?" Abby asked from behind him. "I think your heart would be safe in her hands."

Einstein turned to her. The depth of understanding and compassion in her eyes was almost overwhelming. She looked like she might reach out to touch him so he stepped away. The emotions were too much. Too fast and furious. Too new and uncertain.

"Let's focus on getting your grandpa and Mariah home safe."

"And then we'll talk. Your heart is safe with me, too, Einstein. I'm going to prove it to you."

ABBY THREW ALL OF HER MENTAL ENERGY TOWARD FINDING THE next clue. Though Laney and Priscilla were safe, two more potential victims were counting on them and there were only four hours left before the Charmer's deadline. The thought of her sick grandfather and a young woman in the hands of a killer sent shivers down her spine and twisted her stomach. She channeled her fears and desire for focus, rubbing her mother's touchstone until it was warm. Two victims had been saved. They could save two more. *You can do this.*

"Can I touch?" she asked, gesturing to the cabinet that loomed in the corner.

Einstein's expression was grim. "I think we'll need you to. Can you handle it?"

"With you here, I can." Maybe she shouldn't wear her emotions on her sleeve, but he needed to hear it, needed to understand that she was as vulnerable to him as he was to her.

The police were more interested in the room where Laney had

been held, and in managing and questioning the crowd of employees who'd begun to gather outside the door, curious as to what was going on in their boss's office.

But Abby tuned it all out. She stood in front of the open cabinet doors and put herself in his shoes. Here, the Charmer had likely taken out his trinkets, fondled the mementos and…what? Relived some perceived glory? What would a killer get from those memories? A high of some sort, maybe. What need had it satisfied?

She scanned the shelves. On the bottom, where there was a space, presumably for Mariah's mementos, there was a folded scrap of paper. "Einstein." She drew his attention to the item.

He used his gloved hands to retrieve and unfold it. "It's the next clue. *Did you find Laney in time? Ashes, ashes, we all fall down. Ashes to ashes, dust to dust. There's a lot more at stake than you think.*"

"Can you make anything of that?" Einstein asked, his brow furrowed.

Abby studied the words again. "He repeats *ashes* so many times. Sam wasn't cremated, but maybe he's referencing the cemetery where she was buried? Could Mariah be there?"

Einstein's phone rang and his mouth pressed into a grim line. "It's Nico. Finally." She read the suspicion thick in his words. "About time you called me back," he said into the phone. "The shit's been hitting the fan here but we know now that the Charmer is John Thorpe. Now we just have to find him. Any idea what he's up to?" He listened for a few minutes and Abby could only study his face, which displayed a rainbow of emotions as he went from doubt to surprise to concern in the space of a few heartbeats. "We'll be right there." He hung up and grinned. "Looks like Nico saved us some time. He knows where your grandfather is."

"He does? How?"

"The Charmer ordered Nico to take him."

MARIAH'S WHIMPERING STOPPED AS THE DRUGGED WATER TOOK

effect again. As thunder rumbled outside, John smeared the sweet-smelling chrism on her forehead in the sign of the cross, and her glazed eyes stared up at him from her pallet. He repeated the action, tracing the cross with the oil on her chest, just above her heart, praying this time it would purify her mind and her heart.

"It won't be long now." He bent his head to her tear-streaked face so she could look him in the eye. She'd worn mascara for their meeting at the mall, probably to impress him, but it looked messy and unkempt now. As was her hair. He picked up a brush from the plastic tub of supplies he'd brought with him. He didn't like his girls looking untamed. They were neat, pretty and proper. It was part of their transformation.

He glanced at his watch, noting that his daughter would be there in two hours.

"I have some preparations to make, but I'll be back soon. We'll finish this." Anger burned in Mariah's eyes for a moment before the drugs extinguished it. It both impressed and saddened him.

Samantha had fought and clawed until her fingernails were broken and the skin of her fingertips worn off. At that time, he'd had to use one of the Circle's human trafficking cages in an empty warehouse to keep her. Since then, he'd learned a few things, refining his process.

But Sam had been a fighter until the end. He still had a slight scar on his neck to prove it. He grew melancholy with regret whenever he saw it staring back at him in the mirror. Not regret that he'd killed her, but that she hadn't fulfilled his every expectation. She hadn't measured up to his Hannah—the original Hannah Rose, not his daughter.

His daughter was a disappointment. Why did people continually fail him? Including Damian. He only asked for discipline and loyalty. Still, though he had tried a dozen times, none of his girls had measured up.

The need to test Mariah burned within, but he would wait. He wanted Damian to witness this one. And he needed the others to be distracted. The game was working out well in that aspect. But that was only the beginning. He had more surprises in store— more ways to destroy Damian Manchester.

He reached out and released the catch on the necklace he'd placed around Mariah's neck, and removed the final charm.

CHAPTER 19

Abby tried to feel relieved at the news, but until she saw Grandpa with her own eyes, her chest remained tight with anxiety.

"Looks like your ashes-to-ashes assumption was correct," Einstein said as they sped across town. "Nico says the Charmer ordered him to take your grandfather and tie him up at the church." The church Damian attended weekly, the one with Sam's grave across the street. The image the Charmer had sent, of her grandfather sitting on a bench, had actually been taken on an old pew in the basement of the church.

"Grandpa's okay?"

"It sounds like it. Confused and exhausted, though."

She blew out a breath, trying to loosen the heaviness in her chest. It didn't budge. "Thank God, Nico called. It could have been hours before we figured the clue out."

He slid her an incredulous look. "I can't believe you're not furious with the man."

"He did call to tell us where Grandpa is. And it sounds like he stayed with him to make sure he's okay. Why? You still don't think we can trust him?"

Einstein shook his head. "Nico ended by saying the weirdest thing. He said that at least he didn't blow us all to hell."

"What?" Abby twisted to face him. "You're serious?"

He shrugged. "That's what he said. He also said he *handled* everything." He pulled into the parking lot of All Saints Church. Abby was out of the car before he could remove the key from the ignition. She took the front steps two at a time and yanked open the tall church doors.

By the time she'd located the basement stairs, Einstein was beside her, gun in hand. "Stay behind me," he ordered, nudging past her. She let him step in front of her, trying not to hurry him along on his descent as he proceeded with excruciating caution.

But the moment they reached the basement level and she spied her grandfather lying on a hard wooden pew along the wall, she pushed past Einstein. She heard his growl of disapproval but didn't give a damn. Grandpa was her only surviving family and she wouldn't have him much longer. Besides, she didn't sense any malicious presence nearby. After all, she wasn't the Charmer's end game. But if the Charmer's actions had taken even an hour off of Grandpa's life, she would kill the murderer with her bare hands.

She fell to her knees beside her unconscious grandfather, her gaze scanning his body for injury, but seeing none. His head rested on a makeshift pillow that appeared to have been created from a rolled-up vestment.

"I tried to make him comfortable," Nico said, drawing her attention to where he sat in a shadowed corner. Einstein had already spied the man and holstered his gun.

Einstein grunted. "You could have made him comfortable by leaving him in his apartment. Or calling us a heck of a lot earlier."

"Then the Charmer—John Thorpe—wouldn't have trusted me." Nico's eyes burned with unnamed emotions. If Abby had to guess, guilt, impatience, frustration, and a desire to mete out justice were competing with his duty to stay and guard her grandfather until help arrived. As if realizing he was now free to pursue his own needs, he stood and strode toward the stairs.

Einstein stepped in front of him, blocking his way. "Where are you going?"

"Things to do."

"You know where he is, don't you?" Nico didn't move. Einstein's gaze narrowed. "Mind sharing the intel?"

"Actually, I do. The task force will locate John Thorpe, and then I'll handle him. I'll take care of my responsibilities." Nico's gaze shifted to Abby and her grandfather. "You take care of yours."

"What did you mean about not blowing us all to hell?" she asked before he could mount the stairs.

A rare grin curved Nico's lips. "I was offered an exorbitant amount of money and a higher position in the Circle to blow up the SSAM building. Lucky for you, that's not necessary to completing my ultimate mission. I have a friend who's a reporter. She's going to make up a story to make it look like I followed through. She'll make it credible."

"Meanwhile, you'll be hunting John," Einstein said, clearly unhappy Nico wasn't going to keep him in the loop. "I'll see you at the finish line."

With a nod of acknowledgment, Nico bounded up the steps and disappeared.

Abby turned her attention to her grandfather as he groaned. His breath turned irregular and raspy as he tried to wake up. "Call an ambulance," she told Einstein.

But he was already dialing when she cast a look over her shoulder. He was at her side an instant later. "On their way." He took her grandfather's pulse. "Can you hear us?"

"Grandpa?" At that, there was a murmur of an answer, but he didn't open his eyes. "Drugged?" she asked Einstein.

"Not sure, but we'll get him help. His pulse is erratic, but strong."

Everything was a blur as Abby whispered words of prayer and the paramedics arrived and took over. Einstein was a constant presence at her side, wrapping an arm around her as they followed the team outside and watched as the pair got Grandpa into their van and sped off in the direction of Mercy Hospital.

"I'll take you there," Einstein said.

"But what about Mariah?" Now that Grandpa was safe, there was one more victim to recover before the deadline. And only a couple hours to go, if the sun's low position in the sky was any indication.

Einstein's gaze swept over her and he reached up to cup her cheek. "Already worried about the next person."

"Never stopped. Mariah's the whole reason I came to you, remember?"

"And we'll find her." He dropped his hand and strode quickly to his car. She followed. "There were no clues in the basement." He'd done a quick search of the premises as the paramedics had treated her grandfather.

"Maybe Grandpa knows something?" She hoped they could get the clue before it was too late.

THE STAFF AT MERCY HOSPITAL WERE BRISK AND EFFICIENT AS THEY hurried Grandpa to the back. Einstein gently wrapped an arm around her shoulders and led her to the waiting area.

"He'll be okay, right?" Her voice was croaky with fear. She couldn't lose him. Not yet. Not this way. She sat, elbows on knees, and sank her head into her hands. "He was afraid if he checked into the hospital, he'd never leave."

"He's fighting hard to stay with you." Einstein's low, calm tone was a comfort. A moment later, he put a plastic cup in her hands.

She sipped at the cool water. "Thank you." The image of her big bad SEAL as a caregiver brought a pained smile to her lips. "I appreciate you being here." He took the seat next to her and stretched out his legs and patted his shoulder, inviting her to rest her head there. She rolled her head to look at him, but he was scrolling through the screen of his cell phone. "What about the SSAM team? Any word?"

His thumb swiped the screen. "Just got a text from Max. Apparently, SSAM went down in flames a few minutes ago." She sat up and gaped at him and he shook his head. "Catherine confirmed that it was, as Nico promised, a mock newscast." His lips twitched. "Eve Reynolds is a legit reporter who has some fantastic connections—including access to file footage of buildings demolished by explosions and fire."

"John Thorpe wants to destroy Damian and all of you in every way, doesn't he? It's a good thing Nico gained John's trust but works on your side. Whoever else John might have hired could actually have gone through with it." And then Einstein and the other agents at SSAM could be dead or wounded. She shuddered. "No word on Mariah?"

He pulled his laptop from a bag beneath his chair. "Noah reported in. The CPD finished searching all known Circle warehouses but didn't find anything. I'm sure John would have expected that."

"Good idea. It's like Mariah just dropped off the face of the planet. Where does he keep these girls? A high-functioning businessman like that has to have a social life and people who would notice that kind of weirdness."

"It seems he's rich enough to have a hiding place to stash them somewhere—with equal parts meaningful and practical." He accessed what looked like a data report.

"What's that?"

"A search on everything I can find related to Pinnacle Holdings, Thorpe Enterprises, or John Thorpe, especially deeds to buildings, though I'm certain there are things that aren't on here.

I suspect he had other bogus companies to hide behind. It'll take more digging to unearth those." Digging they didn't have time for.

She sighed. "We need that next clue."

"If there was one."

As a doctor approached, she quickly rose. "Are you here about Jim Rhodes?" the doctor asked.

"Yes, I'm his granddaughter. How is he?"

"When he was brought in, he was under the influence of a light sedative, dehydrated and in need of medication. But he's stable now."

"Oh, thank God." Her knees went wobbly but Einstein's hand was immediately at her back to support her. "Can I see him?"

"Yes, but just for a few minutes. Rest is what's best. We'll want to keep him here a couple days, especially given his condition. I believe you are aware that he doesn't have long?"

"Yes, I know." But the reminder still hurt. She parted ways with the doctor and headed toward her grandfather's room.

Einstein dogged her steps. "Are you okay?"

She stuck her chin in the air. Now wasn't the time to break down. There was too much to do. "Maybe now, at least, he'll admit he needs round-the-clock care." She wanted Einstein to fold her against him and tell her everything would be okay, but soon they might go back to seeing each other only in the coffee shop, maybe exchanging the occasional smile and comment about his T-shirts. Her heart cracked a little bit further, expanding the ache in her chest as if a crowbar pried it open.

Sleep had ironed the lines from her grandfather's face but his eyes opened to slits when he heard the door.

"Hi, Grandpa." She went to his side. "How do you feel?"

His lips curved slightly. "Hit by a truck."

"Sorry about that."

He reached for her hand and squeezed. At his touch, a blanket of warmth and unconditional love enveloped her. *This* was what she needed. It was what she deserved. Grandpa was right. She couldn't settle for less.

His eyes narrowed. "No worries, girlie. I'm in great hands. Thank you for coming for me." His gaze shifted behind her, to Einstein, to include him in his gratitude.

"Of course," she said. "It was all my fault, anyway."

Einstein's hands came down on her shoulders. "Don't listen to her. It's not her fault at all."

"It is," she insisted. "I got involved in chasing a killer."

Grandpa squeezed her hand again, this time in admonishment. "No. You're doing what's right, what God wanted you to do. Finding that girl."

"We haven't found her." Her heart sank to her feet.

But she only saw encouragement in his rheumy eyes. "You will. I have faith in you. You have help." He winked at Einstein and some of the anxiety in Abby's chest lifted.

"That's right," Einstein confirmed. She tried not to feel a rush of pleasure as his hands rubbed her shoulders, but she was shocked to sense the same warmth and love she'd felt from Grandpa. Did Einstein have deeper feelings for her than she realized—or maybe deeper than he even realized?

"But we do have a question for you," Einstein said. "Did Nico leave any kind of clue with you?"

Grandpa's eyes grew wide. "That must be what this was." He patted at his chest until he remembered he was in a hospital gown. He gestured toward the corner. "In my shirt pocket."

Abby retrieved the shirt from the tiny closet and found a folded piece of paper. She opened her mouth to read it, but shut her mouth again, then raised a questioning glance to Einstein. "It's just a bunch of numbers."

SEVEN DIGITS, A FORWARD SLASH AND SEVEN MORE DIGITS. DAMIAN

stared at the numbers on his phone's screen and then put it back to his ear. "What do you think the numbers mean?"

"Not sure yet," Einstein said. "But I'll figure it out. I'll text them to the rest of the team and see if anyone has input. But if Nico knows where John Thorpe is, the task force might be taking him down as we speak."

Damian couldn't let that happen. "Keep me posted." *If you can reach me.*

Damian was about to go off the grid. Not because that was the next logical step in John's plan for their reunion, but because Damian wanted the man all to himself. He deserved a face-to-face confrontation and *answers*, damn it.

Since the last message about *ashes to ashes*, Damian had an idea where John was hiding out, probably with Mariah, but these numbers confirmed it. Now, he knew exactly what the Charmer was trying to tell him.

He hung up and looked toward the doorway of his office, where he met Lorena's considering gaze.

"Oh, my God," she said slowly. "You know where the killer is."

He schooled his features into surprise as he came around his desk to face her. "If I knew that, would I have driven you all the way back to SSAM?" He and Lorena had made it back a short while ago, and as Einstein had reported, Nico had arranged to make the world believe SSAM had been blown up so he could send the footage to John, who would think his game was going according to plan. That Damian's agents were dead. It wasn't enough that John had taken his daughter and so many others, the man was determined to take more and more until everything in Damian's world was gone.

Rage pumped through his body, slow and hot. He wanted to wring the man's neck, slowly—after John explained why he'd taken so much from Damian and after he made sure Mariah was safe. Where had this obsession with Damian's failures and successes begun?

"Tell me." Color bloomed in Lorena's cheeks and her eyes sparkled with the excitement of the hunt. Damian had always enjoyed that about her. She had a love for life, justice, everything that had been important to him.

But now, he couldn't let her follow him into the bowels of hell where he had to go.

"This is a map of Chicago," she said, holding out a paper. "Point to a spot and we'll leave right now." When he didn't reach for it, she shoved it at him. Temper sparked in her dark eyes. "You're not going to leave me out of this."

He put the paper on his desk and turned back to her. "Go home and get some rest. I can take it from here."

Her nostrils flared. "Like hell."

"Then wait here for me."

"Wait for John to kill you, you mean? Or for you to go to prison for his murder?" Angry tears filled her eyes. "How long, exactly, am I supposed to wait? I've been waiting for fifteen years for you to love me."

Stunned, he couldn't suck in a breath to save his life. Finally, he forced air in and out. "Excuse me?"

She crossed her arms over her chest. "You heard me. Last I checked, murder is illegal in the state of Illinois, no matter what the justification."

Somehow, he didn't care. There was no excuse for letting the monster who'd killed his daughter continue to walk the earth.

But Lorena wasn't done with her lecture. She had the appearance of a warrior going into battle as she stepped up close to him. "You don't get to have a final, heroic showdown all by yourself. I've been hunting this asshole almost as long as you have." Her finger jabbed into his chest. "And there's no way you're allowed to put yourself in danger with no backup. In fact, you have a team of people who will be insulted if you don't let them help. Each of us has had a stake in this manhunt since the day you hired us. They're currently scattered to various quadrants of the city, awaiting your orders, and you're just going to ignore them, disrespect their loyalty and their feelings for you. They care about you almost as much as I do. We're a family."

He hardened his heart against her words. As much as he loved his team, there was no room for them in what he had to do next. "I said I can take it from here." He'd make his team understand his decisions later.

She wrapped her fingers in the lapels of his suit jacket, yanking him closer. "No way. You may think you can best him because he's your friend and you know him—"

"*Was* my friend." Admitting even that much brought the taste of bile to his mouth.

"But you clearly don't know him."

He would have taken a step backward at that one, as it hit him where it hurt.

Her vise grip on his lapels loosened and her fingers slid up to cup his face. "I won't allow it. You need help with this. Please..." The last word was a whisper. "*Please* let SSAM help you. Let *me* help you. Let me in—all the way in."

He couldn't say a word or he'd give in. He couldn't be weak and accept help. John would know. He would kill Mariah.

No. Damian was what John wanted. Damian was all he would get.

He tried pleading with Lorena with his gaze, letting her see his love for her. Lightning flashed against the window and in her eyes. A second later, thunder rattled the building, breaking the spell.

Damian shook his head once. "I can't let you close to him, don't you understand? I can't lose you, too."

With a strangled groan, she pulled his face to hers and kissed him with a passion that burned him from the outside in. Desire kindled and he wanted to wrap himself around her. Or wrap her around him and form a protective layer from the world. He was tired, so tired of all the fighting. But he had one last fight in him.

The taste of her salty tears on his lips was like a kick to the chest, but he steeled himself.

One visit to John and it will all be over.

When Lorena pulled away, she was heaving for breath. She swiped angrily at her spiky lashes. "I love you." It was a fierce declaration, a fact stated with resolution and in a manner that sounded like a command, or a veiled plea to not let her down.

His heart stuttered. Stopped. Started again slowly and built until it was galloping madly. "I love you, too." But he had a duty to fulfill, a mission twenty years in the making.

She smiled at his declaration, but upon scanning his hard features, her lips turned downward. "But you're not going to let me help."

"No."

"Will you let anyone help?"

"No."

"You know where he is, don't you?" That question, he didn't answer, only held her gaze. "I'll take that as a yes." She snorted. "Here I thought professing my love might change things. *Idiota.*"

He stiffened as she cursed herself, and then reached out for her before she could turn to leave. He pulled her close, wrapped her tightly in his arms, and buried his face in the silky curtain of her hair. "You're the best part of my life. You're my future. But I have to take care of this on my own. I can't lose you."

"And I can't lose you." She released a shuddering breath against his shoulder before jerking back to shoot him an angry look. "Don't you dare die, or get maimed, or...or end up in prison for life."

He gave her a half smile and stroked a soothing hand across her cheek, his thumb swiping away another tear. "I promise I'll do what I have to in order to finish this, to close the lid on my old life and move on to a new one. I hope that'll be with you."

At the question underlying his last statement, she muttered something under her breath that he couldn't understand. More

Spanish curse words, probably. He bit back a smile, knowing that she only swore when she was passionate about something.

"You can go," she said, as if it were her decision. "But don't expect me not to follow."

He'd expected nothing less from his team. But he needed a few minutes alone with John first. "Fair enough. But don't expect me to make it easy."

CHAPTER 20

The rain broke free from the heavy clouds just as Einstein and Abby emerged from the hospital. Steam billowed from the pavement as the cool shower released the heat that had been hoarded there for days.

Einstein grabbed Abby's hand and they made a dash across the parking lot for the shelter of his car. Where they would go, he didn't yet know, but Abby's grandfather was resting and Einstein just had to get out of there, had to clear his head and think. There was one more person left to save and Mariah was counting on them.

Think, damn it. What could those numbers mean?

The parking lot was full of cars but absent of people. Apparently, they were the only pair to brave the rain. By the time they got to the car, his shoulders and the edges of his jeans were soaked, as was Abby's clothing. He hurried to slide his laptop case into the spot on the floorboards behind the passenger seat.

But when he straightened and closed the door, he was surprised to find Abby hadn't found refuge in the passenger seat. Instead, she'd tipped her head back and was laughing at the sky, clearly exhilarated by the break in the relentless weather and celebrating that two of her loved ones were safe.

She was beautiful. At the expression of pure delight on her face, he couldn't resist pulling her in for a kiss. But the innocent peck he'd been planning turned hot and greedy at the familiar taste of her. Soon, he was backing her against the car, pressing her up against the door, heedless of the storm around them.

She seemed just as caught up in the moment as him. Her arms went around his waist and her fingers fisted in the T-shirt that clung to his skin. Raindrops were deliciously cool against the patch of lower back her hands had bared. Her mouth moved across his jaw and down his neck, and she licked the spot where his pulse was jumping. Would he ever get enough of this woman?

The answer was astoundingly clear. *No.* He wanted her. Forever.

"Abby." A groan of surrender crossed his lips as need clawed at his insides, driving him crazy. He pulled away and spun her around so he could survive her questing mouth. With her back pressed to his front, and her front against the car, he trapped her wrists so he could lean in and speak in her ear. But the words wouldn't come.

Oh, he finally *had* the words. The name for the emotion that had scared him for so long. *Love.* He loved this woman. But his tongue wouldn't form the sounds. His brain wouldn't string them into sentences. His breath hitched, rebelling against the vulnerability coursing through him.

"Einstein?" She twisted her head so that she could look over her shoulder at him but he dodged her perceptive gaze.

"Just give me a moment, okay?" *Give me a lifetime of moments.* Rain pelted them, droplets sliding down her cheek. He kissed one away. "After we find Mariah, you're coming home with me again. No arguments. We need to talk." And maybe he'd finally say what he was feeling aloud, without fear.

She turned her head so her mouth was only inches from his. Her lips curved. "You aren't going to get any arguments from me."

He spun her around, kissed her hard and fast and released her. As he jogged to the other side of the car, his phone rang. He ducked into the driver's seat as he answered. Inside the car, the contrast between sun-warmed interior and cool rain had fogged the windows and created their own private sanctuary.

"Hello?" Einstein answered.

"Damian knows where John Thorpe is," Lorena said.

"Where?"

"He didn't say. He took off on his own."

"What?" None of this made any sense. Or maybe it did. He glanced at Abby. If a monster had taken someone he loved, he'd fight the hounds of hell to get to him. And *he'd* want to be the one to protect her. "The numbers made sense to him?"

"So you haven't figured them out yet, either?" Desperation was clear in her voice. She was an ex-FBI agent who hunted criminals on a daily basis, but she obviously loved Damian. Not knowing where your loved one was when danger lurked was—

"Wait, which car did he take?" Einstein asked.

"One of the SSAM SUVs."

He grinned. "I have trackers on all of our vehicles." And Damian was aware of that. He wanted them to follow, after all. He instructed Lorena to go to his office and helped her log in to the computer with the tracking information on it.

"I've got it," she said. "He's heading west on I-90."

Suddenly, Einstein understood the numbers. "The last clue is longitude and latitude. Damian recognized the coordinates. We've all read the police reports and case files so many times that the information's buried in our subconscious. But I'm sure Damian recognized it right away." It was an old farmstead located near a forest preserve—far enough away from the Chicago suburbs to contain semi-remote acres of land. It was also about an hour and a half away.

Lorena gasped. "The place where Sam was discovered. The place she was buried. It fits the other clues. It's where his *world cracked open*. And the *ashes to ashes, dust to dust* reference."

"Abby and I are in the car now and should get there just before sunset. Notify the rest of the team."

JOHN WAS PLEASED AT HOW WELL HIS PLANS WERE COMING together. Hannah arrived right on time. Nico had sent him the link to the news footage and SSAM was now a pile of ashes and dust. According to the reporter, the number of casualties was unknown, but that wasn't how he wanted Damian to die anyway. He had his own plans for the man.

Damian still hadn't arrived, but that was according to plan, as well. And if he did make his way onto the property prematurely, John's new hire, Wesley, would alert him immediately.

Hannah huffed as she crossed the threshold and glanced around the 1970s ranch-style house. He'd furnished it with his own modern tastes but the warm wood beams and stone fireplace screamed rustic. He could understand why his daughter would be confused. She was used to the image of her father as a corporate investor and opulent world-traveler. The businessman with the downtown loft, a plush lake house, and a ski chalet wouldn't have settled for this shabby cabin over an hour from Chicago. Then again, she didn't understand this side of him. Nobody did.

She moved to the living room, stopping to stare at a cheap oil painting depicting the fall foliage of the area. "When did you move way out here, and *why?*"

"I bought it a few years ago." He smiled. "It's a special place. I feel like myself here."

She swung to face him. "It has nothing to do with the fact that your arch nemesis's precious daughter was killed here, that you buried her on this property?"

He picked up a bottle of wine he'd left on the coffee table and uncorked it. "I guess you do know some things."

"I do, indeed." But there was no judgment and little fear in her gaze as she tracked his movements. He wasn't sure whether to be impressed at her bravery or astonished at her stupidity. He poured them each a glass of red wine and handed her one. The charms rattled at her wrist as she accepted his offering. "What's this?"

"A farewell toast."

A flicker of uncertainty crossed her face. "Farewell?"

"I told you I never wanted to see you again. I meant it. And after tonight, you'll have enough to live comfortably for the rest of your life, if you're smart about it." He raised his glass. "So here's to new starts." He took a sip of wine and savored the burst of earthy flavor on his tongue, watching as Hannah did the same.

She glanced at the closed briefcase he'd left on the coffee table. Her eyes were so cold. The woman before him had no heart. She was nothing like his Hannah Rose—the young woman most of the world had forgotten, his stepsister who had been wise and loving. Until Damian had broken her and moved on without a backward glance.

This lesser Hannah was already tainted—her mother's fault. If his daughter hadn't been removed from him when she'd been entering the important years…

"Is it all there?" Hannah asked.

He nodded. "Everything you need is in that briefcase." He gestured to her to take a seat on the couch. He sat in a nearby chair.

She perched on the couch, close to the briefcase. "There's a combination lock."

He grinned. "You'll get the combo when I've had my good-bye chat. Allow a father at least that."

"Like you allowed Sam to say good-bye to her dad?" Her eyes sparked with challenge—and maybe a hint of fear.

"Damian Manchester didn't deserve her. He didn't deserve anything."

Hannah snorted. "And you, being a god, decided that, huh? I get it, Daddy. Really, I do. They had everything we didn't. Those times we went to their house, I was amazed. I kept wondering when her parents were going to start yelling at each other, but they never did. Or when her father would storm out in a huff and not return for days." She took another swallow of wine. "But that never happened. They weren't like us." Her unflinching gaze met his. A feeling of kinship almost made him doubt his chosen course of action. "I can understand why you might be tempted to give in to urges. Must be nice to have some kind of release."

"It is." Until it hounded him again. Until the need to avenge Hannah Rose, to purify, took hold.

"When I first found out about your...hobby, I was jealous." She laughed. "Can you believe that? Jealous of abducted, murdered girls. Because they had your attention, your devotion, in a way I never did. What kind of sick bitch does that make me?"

He flinched. "We're not sick."

She arched her brows. "Well, I'm not, anyway. You, however... the signs are all there." She lifted her wrist and the charms jingled. "And you even like to revel in it. I've come to view these as proof that you do, in fact, think about me on occasion. Is that why you sent them to me?"

He sipped his wine. "Yes. It was a way to feel connected." To the other Hannah, though—his lost stepsister, not his greedy daughter. "How did you find out about my hobby?"

"It was when I was in college, about seven years after your first kill, I would guess. Assuming Sam was your first?" At her inquiring gaze, he nodded. Sam had been the Charmer's first victim, though by that point he'd been responsible for many deaths as the Boss of the Circle. "It was that Christmas when Mom was trying to get us back together. She wanted us to act like a family." She huffed out a humorless laugh. "That didn't work out so well, did it? Anyway, I went by your office to see you, to ask if I could join my friends on a ski trip instead, but you'd stepped out to a meeting. Your cabinet was unlocked."

"So you just helped yourself? Were you looking for money?"

"Yes, but what I found was so much more." She looked away and swallowed hard before continuing. Her fears were starting to poke through her brave façade. But her greed was stronger than her sense of self-preservation. "Pictures, samples of dirt, charms." She glanced at her bracelet.

"But you didn't go to the cops?"

Hannah snorted. "You always told me family doesn't turn on family. You and Mom raised me with secrets, taught me how to keep them within our inner circle. I learned from the best."

The stirrings of warmth toward her were unwanted. He ruthlessly quashed them. "So what made you decide to go to Damian Manchester?"

Her eyes glittered with anger and confusion. "I never went to him."

"And yet, somehow, they tracked me down." They'd been growing closer for the past couple years, but something had put them on the scent. Not that John regretted that everything was coming to a head. He'd been looking forward to his showdown with Damian for years. He owed it to his stepsister. "Maybe you approached a different SSAM agent? Said something to a friend?"

Uncertainty shadowed her eyes. "I started following Maggie."

"Maggie?"

"She was Sam's best friend at the time. I met her once, just before Sam disappeared, at Sam's house. I was…curious."

"About what?"

"About how she survived after knowing someone close to her was murdered." Hannah's gaze met his. "About how the survivors felt being left behind." Her gaze flicked away again and she laughed. "I even started taking a class at the same exercise studio so I could maybe talk to her between classes. Never worked up the courage, though."

"It was simple curiosity?"

"I wondered what it must be like to lose a close friend at that age. When Sam died, I was ashamed I didn't feel something deeper. We were friends, too. But what I felt was...relief." She released a harsh laugh.

"Relief." Like how he felt when he killed for Hannah Rose, when he saved another girl from her fate. The ritual had kept her alive for him all these years. It had kept the anger at Damian fueled.

"Relief that I no longer had to be compared to the perfect girl. That Mom and I would no longer have to be held up to the Manchester standard. Looking back, I see your obsession with the man. And he had no clue. Jesus, Daddy. It's crazy." She shook her head as if shaking off the memory. Or maybe she was starting to feel the effect of the drugs. "I deserve the money for what you put me through. Do you know the nightmares I've had?"

"I'm sure the money will soothe your pain."

She tossed back the last of her wine and reached for the case. "I'm sure you're right. Was that enough talk for you?" She waited expectantly, her fingers poised over the combination lock. He rattled it off and she quickly worked the dials and popped the lid open.

Her gaze, bright with outrage, swung to his. "Another charm? Where's the money?"

He was beside her in an instant, catching her wrist. "The charm is your parting gift."

"Let go." She struggled, but the drugged wine was already taking effect.

He fastened the charm so that it was nestled with the others. "There. Twelve symbols of new life. You'll be renewed, as well."

The silver discs caught the light as she yanked her hand away. "You are sick. Who's the twelfth?" Her eyes widened.

He laughed. "It's not you. You're not pure enough. Yet. You should be honored that Mariah's gift to you is fire." He admired the symbol on the last charm. A flame. Baptism by fire was an appropriate end to this.

"Where's the money?" Her voice was thick. She blinked and her eyebrows drew together as if confused.

"There is no money."

Her eyes drooped and her body sagged. "What did you do? Daddy?"

He nudged her back on the couch and stared down at her as her eyes glazed over. "You said you were jealous. Here's your chance to show me the kind of daughter you always should have been. It's time to add your sacrifice to honor your namesake."

"Namesake?" The words were a whisper.

"She would have been your aunt, had she lived. She might even have been your mother." His throat closed briefly and he swallowed the emotion there. "To your new start." He lifted his wineglass in the same toast he used with the girls before their baptisms. Only their glasses were drugged. His never was.

As his daughter's eyes slid closed, he hurried to his phone and dialed Wesley. "Any sign of the hunter yet?"

"There's a flash of headlights along the road now. I was just about to call you."

"Good. You know the plan. Let him through. Stop anybody else."

CHAPTER 21

The miles of woodlands and tall grasses were a blur as Damian sped west on I-90. The crowded suburbs gave way to expanses of forest preserves and large plots of land. He took the turns he'd memorized years ago, that time imprinted on his memory in ways he couldn't erase. After all, here was where, as John had aptly put it, his *world had cracked open—* where Sam had been discovered.

On the horizon, rain clouds had darkened the sunset to lavender and a striking orange. It was only fifteen minutes to the Charmer's deadline when Damian took the final turn. No guards. No sounds at all. But he could feel someone watching. No doubt, John was expecting him.

Certainty had hit when the numbers came through. He'd been obsessed with Sam's final days, and the thought of her life being extinguished in a place that had no name but could be designated by longitude and latitude and degrees…yeah, those numbers had been emblazoned on his brain. And John, who'd taken orienteering with him at summer camps, would have known that.

What Damian didn't get was *why*. He had to be the first to face John, to demand answers before the man lawyered up or was sent away to prison forever.

It wouldn't take Lorena much time to call Einstein, and he had no doubt Einstein would crack the code or figure out how to track the SSAM SUV. His team would be arriving soon...but hopefully, not too soon.

Damian tucked a pistol into the waistband of his slacks, beneath his suit jacket, before he rolled to a stop in front of an old ranch house. The grounds were different than he remembered. They'd been left to grow wild in the decades since Sam's murder. Vines crawled up the brick walls, and tree branches leaned toward the house as if the woodlands would swallow it up. He wished it had.

Damian didn't look to the east. Out there on the twenty-acre property, beneath a copse of trees near a pond, the previous owners had been walking their dogs when they'd found Samantha's remains.

Anger warred with exhilaration. He'd found her killer. She would finally be at peace. And no matter how this turned out, *he* would finally be at peace.

But he'd never get his daughter back.

He got out of the car, feeling the remains of his vulnerability fall away as an iron will settled in his bones. This was the end game. It would all be over soon, and he was determined to end this *his* way.

A crack of thunder hammered his ears and rumbled through him as a couple fat raindrops hit his cheek.

The door to the ranch house was unlocked and Damian pulled the gun from his waistband before letting himself in.

"Put the gun on the table and come in slowly," John called from somewhere within.

Damian entered the small foyer at a cautious pace, but he didn't lose his only weapon. "I'll lower it, but I'm not going to get rid of it," he called back before rounding the corner.

In the living room, John sat in a chair by the fireplace, a gun pointed at Damian. He eyed Damian's weapon, which was now at his side. "You always did have to feel in charge."

Damian struggled to keep that wall of iron will in place as unexpected fury took control of his body. He quaked with the need for vengeance. He raised his gun at the man he'd shared meals with, talked business with, grown up with.

"Don't," John said, jerking his head toward the couch. A woman lay there, unconscious. Her chest rose and fell in regular movements. The bracelet on her wrist gave her identity away. He vaguely remembered her from the DMV photos Einstein had sent him. This was Hannah, John's daughter. Damian hadn't seen her in twenty years. "I'm certain your sense of chivalry will help you make the right decision."

With great effort and several deep breaths, he banked his fury and lowered his gun. His gaze scanned the details he'd missed. A bottle of wine. Two glasses. "Looks like your guest had too much to drink."

John smirked. "She did."

"But I suspect she's not just drunk." Had he poisoned his own daughter?

"She may have had a little nudge toward unconsciousness from me."

"Drugged, then. But why? She's your daughter." If John would do this to his own flesh and blood, he wouldn't think twice about killing anyone else. A chill replaced the hot rage. He forced himself to think coherently, covertly checking his surroundings. There were no other Circle thugs in sight, but that didn't mean they weren't around. "Why would you do this?"

He shrugged. "She insisted on being here. Besides, she hasn't been my daughter since Vicky took her away. She'd begun to figure things out. Not everything, but enough."

Every muscle in Damian's body tightened. "You plan to kill her."

"She's not the Hannah she was supposed to be."

Damian tipped his head, confused. How was Hannah supposed to be? But he had someone else's safety to consider before he delved deeper. "And Mariah?"

John's eyes glittered. "I haven't forgotten her." Likely, he planned to take care of her after getting rid of Damian.

"You can't possibly think you're going to get away with this." The desire to lunge for the man's throat and throttle him until he turned blue was strong. Damian restrained himself by flexing and relaxing his fingers. The cool weight of the pistol was reassuring.

"Actually, I do and I will."

"You're sick, you know?" Damian had heard of serial killers being obsessed with their burial grounds, following cases, and keeping mementos but John had gone beyond that. "And you have an unhealthy obsession."

"*You* spent twenty years of your life obsessed with finding *me*, giving up your career and your marriage, your company and your old friends, so who's the sick one? You'd think after spending so much time studying my work, you'd stop underestimating me. After all, I took everything from you." John grinned. "I win."

Damian's gut clenched. "Why do you care? We were friends. I would have given you anything you needed." Which just underscored how crazy this was.

"Don't pretend you ever cared."

"But I did." He thought of how many times they'd had his family over for holidays and parties. Christ. The thought of John being near his daughter nearly threw him over the edge.

"I thought you did." John rose as a humorless laugh died in his throat. His face became mottled with fury. "But it was a ploy. You used people, people who loved you. Priscilla, Ron, even your own daughter was a trophy." At the outright lie, Damian took a step forward. But John raised his gun, reminding Damian of the cost of losing his temper. "Worse, you used the one person I cared about. The one person who loved me beyond who I was and what I did. And you don't even know who I'm talking about, do you?" Spittle flew from his mouth as his rage grew with each word. "Hannah Rose."

Damian looked toward the woman on the couch, but another memory struck. He blew out a breath. "This is about your stepsister?" He'd forgotten the girl he'd known for a brief couple of weeks.

"Against all reason, she loved you."

Damian's mind scrambled to understand. "What does this have to do with that? I put a stop to that crush before it got started."

"*Crush* is right. She loved you and you crushed her."

"What did she know about love? I was only seventeen and she was..." Damian's head swam. Hannah Rose had been thirteen. The same age as Sam when she'd disappeared. Damian had been invited to spend his fall break with John's family. The girl had followed him around like a puppy dog. She hadn't even been John's flesh and blood, as they were siblings because of a blending of families. Realization hit. John had loved his sister, and not in a natural way. It explained the obsession with young teen girls, but the restriction from sexual acts with them. He was reenacting the extremely unhealthy obsession of a young, lovesick teen. "What happened to your sister?"

John's hand shook, the pistol wavering. "She killed herself. Your rejection sent her into a downward spiral. She was hospitalized for years until she finally took her own life."

Damian suspected Hannah Rose had been sick in many ways before he'd even come onto the scene. "So you, what, decided to pay tribute to the memory of the girl you loved by killing other girls and ruining me? Pathetic." He shook his head.

"Shut up!" John rushed forward but stopped himself just out of

Damian's reach. "You don't get to mock her or me. My life was hell after that. I wasn't enough to stop her and you didn't give a fuck. So guess what, I made you give a fuck. My final gift to her."

"And the rituals, the girls? Don't pretend that was for her. If Hannah Rose was as loving and pure as you believe, she wouldn't have wanted you to kill for her. Now who's using her? You're using your sister's death as an excuse to indulge in your need to kill."

John's eyes flashed darkly. "I don't need an excuse. And the rituals were all about Hannah Rose and those girls. I purified them. I claimed them as my own before some asshole like you could ruin them. I saved them from becoming her."

John had preyed on vulnerable young girls and if they'd failed his test after accepting his invitation to meet up, he'd killed them to save them? That was so twisted Damian didn't have a response. All of this madness was because John had loved Hannah Rose as more than a sister? He tried to think back to that time, to when things had changed. Damian honestly hadn't noticed. John had been on the fringes of their group of friends, as if he were studying everything they did. They'd been a group of a dozen boys who'd met early in high school, separated from their families by the boarding school, and formed a bond over common gripes, hanging out, chasing girls, or whatever.

"Ron was one of us," Damian said. "I wouldn't have hurt him. He helped me when I was at my lowest." At John's snort, Damian looked up sharply. "Did you have anything to do with his death?"

"It was a suicide." John grinned. "But I may have helped it along."

Damian longed to plow his fist into the man's smug expression. "Why?"

John shrugged. "He was weak. And I knew his death would get to you. Eat at you." His eyes glittered with triumph.

"Is that why you took Sam? To eat at me?" His hands fisted at his sides. How had he missed the sociopath beneath the friendly façade? But then, monsters like John were adept at manipulation, at hiding their true selves. John's so-called charm had served him well.

"She was perfect, wasn't she?"

"Yes."

"And she came to me so willingly. I called her a couple times at your house, pretending to ask for you when I knew you were away on business. Asking her how things were, telling her I knew a way to get her busy father's attention—if she'd just meet with me. A little coaxing, a couple more calls, and she jumped at the chance."

Damian gritted his teeth and tightened his abdomen against a wave of pain. "And you ruined her, just like you ruined everything else in your life. Your daughter. Your marriage. It was around that time that Vicky filed for divorce, as I recall." His mouth twisted. "You were jealous of me."

"This isn't about me. You failed."

"No," Damian said quietly. "It's *you* who failed, including keeping your sister healthy. You couldn't take being incompetent at something—at everything—so you turned this on me." Memories prodded at him. Times when John had thrown down the gauntlet, challenging him to tennis, racquetball, chess. Damian had won most of the time.

"You were a golden boy who simply floated through life on your parents' money and reputation, and success fell into your lap. Some of us have to fight for it. Taking my spot on the varsity football team—"

"Because you'd broken your leg."

"Asking Cilla out when you knew I was interested."

Damian gaped. "You mentioned she was pretty. I had no idea..." Of course, the man had built all of this up in his mind over the years. "You just needed an outlet for your aggression, especially when Hannah Rose went off the deep end—and you chose me."

John's mouth tightened. "Don't you speak of her."

"Why not? I was the one she wanted. She clearly had good taste." The words were getting to John. The man's body had gone utterly still. Damian continued to push, watching for his opportunity to pounce. "You couldn't deal with your violent tendencies— the same tendencies that led to your illegal organization and your need to kill—so you blamed me. That's the definition of a coward."

Damian grinned without humor. "I was your mirror. Who you wanted to be. You would have been nothing without me. But you'll never be as good as me. Hannah Rose would never have loved you like she did me. And you're sick to think my daughter, or yours, or any of the other girls, could have taken her place."

John closed the gap between them and lifted his gun to Damian's face. "That serpent's tongue of yours sure knows how to spin things your way."

He raised his own gun to John's gut. "What you see as my failures, I see as triumphs. In each challenge that I overcame or survived, I learned something. It made me a stronger man. That's the difference between you and me. I was a smarter student, a tougher competitor, a better husband and father. You couldn't take that because you're *weak*."

Damian could feel the angry vibrations coming off the man and wondered if he'd shoot. Any second now, Damian's body could be ripped open, his blood spilling hotly on the floor. The idea of such a release, an escape from the perpetual pain, was welcome. Until he pictured Lorena and her words of love, the plea in her eyes to return to him, to claim the future that finally seemed attainable. And his team... They would mourn him. They'd become a family.

Though Damian had gone into this house realizing he might not come out alive, death was no longer an option.

John's hand shook but firmly gripped the gun. "I'm not weak. I'm going to deal with Mariah, you, my daughter... And then I'm going to be the one living it up in Europe or South America or wherever I decide to disappear. And you can no longer steal the life I was supposed to have."

"Daddy?" Hannah's moan from the couch beside them drew their attention.

In that brief moment of distraction, Damian shoved John's arm up and pushed him away. He ducked as John's gun discharged, sending a bullet into the ceiling. Unharmed, Damian brought his gun up to return fire, but the man was already on the move, lunging sideways and down a hallway. Damian pulled the trigger. Wood splintered.

"There's nowhere to go," John yelled. "I'll track you anywhere on this property."

"Not if I kill you first," Damian shouted back. He ducked behind a chair as a bullet hit the wall behind his head.

The quiet that followed was broken by the slam of a door from somewhere in the back of the house.

"Find a safe room, lock yourself in and call the cops," Damian told a dazed Hannah. She was too drugged to go far.

"What if he comes back?" Her voice quaked with fear.

"He's after someone else at the moment." *Mariah.* If John touched her, Damian would kill the monster. But he had to find him first.

EINSTEIN TURNED ONTO THE DIRT DRIVE INDICATED ON HIS GPS. He'd sent the coordinates and directions to Noah and the rest of the SSAM team, but he and Abby were the first on the scene. Still, one of those gut feelings told him Nico was around, maybe even with fellow members of his task force.

"The rain must be following us." Abby glanced at the drops sliding down her window in rapid succession, like lemmings following each other over the cliff.

"It doesn't matter. You're staying in the car." Einstein pulled off the road and reached for his door handle. "Lock the doors."

"But I can help. What if there's another hidden room or something?"

Einstein peered out the windshield, seeing only darkness beyond the droplets. It was eight twenty-three, just a few minutes until the Charmer's deadline, yet the clouds had eclipsed the setting sun. A bolt of lightning outlined the bent trees and billowing bushes fighting against the wind. The house was somewhere beyond the trees. Einstein had parked several yards down the road, hoping to use the element of surprise.

"Besides, you don't know that I'd be any safer here," she added. She shivered to drive home the danger.

He looked her over, and then gave a grim smile. "You win, as always." He got out.

"Not always." She closed her door and came up beside him, matching his long strides as they skirted the drive, just deep enough in the growing shadows to stay hidden.

Rain ran into his eyes and dripped off his nose and lashes as he looked down at her. "Stick close. Stay behind me. No more talking. Squeeze my hand if you sense anything." Maybe she could be helpful, if she happened to pick up any strange vibes. And she was an extra pair of eyes.

They'd reached a line of bushes in front of the house and had just spied Damian's car and another vehicle, a BMW—the one that the DMV records had indicated had been registered to Hannah Smith, he realized—when he felt the hard squeeze.

"What?" he whispered, turning to look at Abby. His heart leapt into his throat and then sank to his knees as he saw the man who had a gun to her head. How the hell had he crept up on them?

He swallowed hard and blinked back the rain. "You don't want to shoot her, Wesley."

But the other man's eyes seemed to glow with glee. He did want to shoot her. "She deserves nothing less. Nosy bitch."

"And what, exactly, do you deserve?" Another voice broke the darkness. *Nico.*

Nico stepped closer and a bolt of lightning illuminated his face. His pistol was aimed at Wesley's head.

"Good to see you," Einstein said. "Where's John?"

Nico didn't take his eyes off his prey as he answered. "In the house with Hannah and Damian."

"Any other guards?"

"Only this one. And I'm guessing he's not ready to die for his new boss. He doesn't strike me as the type to have a martyr complex." Nico tipped his head as if considering Wesley. "I'd give him a head start, though, if he wanted to try."

"I don't owe this guy nothing." Wesley dropped his gun and raised his hands at the same time the sharp report of three pistol shots filled the night.

"Those came from inside," Abby said.

"Go," Nico said. "I'll handle Wesley. My guys are on their way."

"Mine, too," Einstein said, glancing toward the still-dark road.

"You go in the front and I'll go around back." Nico pulled zip-ties from a pocket and was securing Wesley's wrists behind his back when Einstein and Abby ran for the house.

He slowed at the door and Abby stayed right behind him, her hands against his back. Could she read his eagerness to take down John? Would she think him a monster as well? Or would she understand? After all, she'd seen the girls for herself, felt their pain and mourned their deaths in a way he could never fully understand.

With caution, he pushed the front door open and peered inside, then slowly moved forward until he could see into the living room. A lamp was turned over near the couch. The kitchen was in his sightline, at the end of the hall, and the back door hung open on its hinges as if a bear had torn through it. Or someone in a hurry to get to someone else. He said a quick prayer that he'd find Damian in time to help him, in the way Einstein hadn't been able to help his father on 9/11 or his mother when she'd refused cancer treatment.

"You'll find him in time," Abby said from behind. She squeezed his waist. He didn't question how she knew what he was thinking, just accepted it, as well as the comfort she offered.

Nico appeared at the back door. "Looks like someone made a run for it. I'll see if I can pick up a trail."

"There are a couple bullet holes but no blood," Einstein said. "We'll check the house." Hannah Smith and Mariah were still missing. With a nod, Nico disappeared into the darkness.

Einstein checked another hallway that led to a couple bedrooms and what he assumed was a bathroom. The door was locked. Staying out of the line of fire in case anybody had thoughts of shooting through the door, he knocked. "We're here to help. Who's in there?"

"Oh, thank God," a woman's voice said.

"Who are you? Are you hurt?"

The door opened and Hannah Smith stood in the flesh, her hair wild and eyes wide.

Abby gasped. "Hannah?"

The woman tried to nod, but it ended abruptly in a wince. She lifted a hand to her head. "He drugged me."

"Your father?"

"The bastard. I'll make him pay for double-crossing me."

Einstein caught Abby's incredulous look but didn't have time to interrogate Hannah. "Stay here. The police will be here any minute."

"Wait! Where are you going?" Hannah's voice was raw with panic.

"To find your father. Where'd they go?"

"I don't know. He was going to kill me. He was supposed to pay me, but he just gave me another of those damn charms." She lifted her arm and the bracelet on her wrist caught the light with a soft jangling noise. "He drugged me. When I woke up, he and Mr. Manchester were struggling. Mr. Manchester told me to lock myself somewhere safe and call the cops…" She sagged against the sink. The effort of communicating all of this was obviously taking its toll, as were the drugs still in her system.

Abby pointed to the woman's wrist. "May I take a closer look at that?"

Hannah slid the charm bracelet off. "You can keep it. I never want to see it again. He's not my father. Not anymore. Then again, I was never the girl he wanted."

CHAPTER 22

A bby turned the bracelet over in her palm. Her fingers paused at the last charm and she shifted her focus inward, opening herself to the message. If, as John had with the other girls, he'd given this charm to Mariah and forced her to wear it, maybe she could get a read from it.

Focus. The sense of urgency that filled the room like a poisonous gas was a distraction that could prove costly. She closed her eyes, concentrating on the steady patter of rain against the window and the low rumble of thunder. Beneath that, she heard Einstein's steady breathing, remembered the regular thumping of his heartbeat against her palm, and felt his calm confidence that she could do this.

Her palm closed over the charm. "I'm so thirsty. My throat hurts. Hot, so hot, but it's dark. Light pokes through a few holes in the corrugated tin that creaks as the sun heats it. Smells like moss, baked in the sun. I hear an animal splash and smell the decay of moist wood." Abby's eyes popped open. "Is there a lake or some kind of water on the property?"

"There's a pond about a half mile to the east," Einstein said.

"Not far from where Sam's body was discovered. Over the years, I've studied the files so much that I memorized every crime scene location," he said in answer to her questioning look.

"If there's an old rusted shed near there, I think that's where Mariah is."

Hand in hand, they ran outside and raced eastward in the darkening twilight and steady rain. She trusted Einstein's instincts, his memory of the layout of the land and his sense of direction to guide the way. A couple minutes later, he slowed. Voices, raised in anger over the storm, weren't far away.

He crept closer, motioning to her to stay out of sight behind a thick tree trunk. Several yards beyond, Damian faced John. Both were armed, their guns aimed at each other in a standoff. Damian appeared to have cornered the man along the edge of a pond but John was standing his ground.

Einstein shifted into view and moved to Damian's side, but neither of the other men changed their focus.

"Drop your weapon," John shouted to Einstein. Water streamed from his hair and down his face but the monster didn't flinch. Einstein froze, awaiting instructions.

"Keep back, but don't lower your weapon," Damian ordered, sounding calmer than Abby would have expected for a man who was facing down the man who'd killed his daughter. "He doesn't have any more bargaining chips."

"I'm the only one who can save Mariah. How's that for a bargaining chip?"

"Still think you can play god with other people's lives?" Damian shook his head in disapproval. "That ends tonight."

"Besides, sir," Einstein said from beside him, "Abby already knows where Mariah is." He jerked his head to the side, toward the north end of the pond. Lightning flashed, and the rusted tin shack from her vision was briefly illuminated. *Mariah.*

"And if she doesn't," Nico said as he approached and joined the ranks of men with guns pointed at John, "we have enough people here now to search the entire grounds."

John's eyes widened. "You." His gaze shot to Damian. "He's working with you?"

"That's right," Damian said. "My agency was never blown up. Nico has been working undercover against you for some time now. He will bring down your whole Circle enterprise and every evil thing you worked to build. Looks like the game's over. Stop being a coward and face the consequences."

John sneered. "You mean prison? I don't think so."

"There's only one other possible ending."

John glanced at the pond behind him and took a step back. Water sloshed against his expensive leather loafers. "Hannah Rose and I came here once with our parents to pick out a dog. There was a breeder down the road. She was so happy that day. It was a brief break in her melancholy." He took another step back. "So it was only fitting that this is where I brought Sam to be renewed, cleansed of her roots. She was so innocent. So sweet."

A muscle in Damian's jaw jumped. "You stole that from her."

John grinned. "I stole it from you. You'll have to live with that. Me, on the other hand…" He took another step into the pond and the water now lapped at his shins, molding his suit pants to his legs. "I'll get to see her again, long before you do." He raised his gun at Damian and pulled the trigger.

The resounding gunfire from multiple weapons echoed in the thick air. Abby's ears rang as she peered through the rain to see who had been hurt. *Dear God, please let them all be okay. Please let Einstein be okay.*

She didn't realize her heart had stopped until she saw Einstein on his feet and her chest started beating a rhythm again. Damian, however, was on his knees. Nico and Einstein rushed to his side. Nico passed Damian and headed for John, whose body lay motionless on the banks of the pond, half in and half out of the water.

"Are you okay, sir?" Einstein shouted to Damian over a thunderclap. The rain ran in rivulets down their faces, almost completely shadowed as sunset turned into twilight. When Damian didn't reply, Einstein began searching for wounds.

Damian reached for Einstein's hands, stopping him. "Shoulder wound. I'll be okay." He glanced back at John. "Is he dead?"

Nico looked up and nodded. "No pulse. Looks like several gunshot wounds to the chest and head."

Damian focused on Abby as she ran to Einstein's side. "I hope to hell you really know where Mariah is."

She looked toward the shed. "In there, if my message is right."

Einstein helped Damian to his feet and they hurried across the soggy ground, slipping occasionally in the tall, wet weeds. Damian winced with every misstep and clutched a hand to his wounded shoulder, but he was determined to see Mariah before seeking treatment. When they reached the shed, Einstein ordered them all to stand back. "Mariah, if you're in there and can hear me, get away from the door. I'm going to break the lock."

He rammed the butt of his pistol against the lock until it broke. The rusty hinges gave little resistance as he yanked the door open. Abby pushed to the front and hurried to the girl lying inside. Mariah was too weak to lift her head. It had only been four days, but her fetal position on the floor indicated she had zero energy, and her knotted hair hung in limp waves. Her fingers were bloody and dirt-caked as if she'd tried to claw her way out during her more energetic moments. Thank God there were several water bottles around, indicating she'd had something to drink, at least, even if it had been drugged.

"Let's get her inside." Einstein lifted Mariah in his arms as if she weighed nothing. He shot Nico a glance. "Can you take care of John?"

"My pleasure." Nico's mouth tipped up on one side. "Cleanup is my new specialty, after all." He moved to the pond as two other men, covered in black from head to toe, emerged from the darkness. Members of the secret task force, no doubt.

Einstein hunched to shield Mariah as much as possible from the rain. Abby and Damian followed. Lorena came racing toward them from the direction of the house and headed straight for Damian. She slid in the mud and Damian caught her to him with his good arm.

Lorena blinked against the rain as she scanned his face. "You're okay?"

"I will be," he said, then bent his head to kiss her. He whispered something in her ear before pulling away. "Let's get out of the rain." But as they passed the pond, his eyes were drawn to the spot where John's body lay. "Who do you think fired the kill shot?"

Abby glanced at John's body. "If there's any justice in the world —and I choose to believe there is—you all did."

AN HOUR LATER, EINSTEIN STOOD IN A CORNER OF THE LIVING room, watching the melee as they wrapped up the Charmer's case for good. A sense of satisfaction, a beautiful rightness, had settled around his heart as he watched Abby flit between him and Hannah, Damian and Lorena, and whoever else looked like they could use a kind word. She'd guarded Mariah until the paramedics had taken the girl away. She'd even given Wesley a piece of her mind as the cops dragged him to their car.

God, he loved her passion. How could he ever have thought she'd leave someone she cared about without putting up a fight? His heart was safe with her. In fact, she already possessed it. And he couldn't say he was sad about that. Surrendering to his love for her was the best decision he'd ever made.

If only he could tell her about his revelations.

At the moment, organized chaos reigned. Over the past hour, the house had become a central spot as police, FBI, SSAM agents, and reporters swarmed the property. Most of the media had been kept at a distance from the key areas, but one reporter had been given a noticeable advantage. A woman with long dark hair, vibrant blue eyes and a movie-star smile finished her interview and left with a cameraman in tow, but not before sending a stunning smile and a wink Nico's way.

Einstein slid Nico a glance. "Isn't she the same woman you hired to make up the story about blowing up SSAM?"

Nico grinned. "Your point?"

"Looks like she owes you."

Nico's smile faded. "Actually, we're even."

"I suppose the task force will disband now?"

"Just because John Thorpe is dead doesn't mean the Circle has been completely wiped from the face of the earth."

"And that's your next mission."

"I only reveal that info on a need-to-know basis." He slapped Einstein on the shoulder. "But if I have any questions about the Circle's operations, especially of the technical kind, I know where to go."

A few minutes later, Einstein had spoken to Damian and received the okay to leave. He pulled Abby outside to the porch, where the rain had slowed to a drizzle. "Ready to go home?"

She tipped her face up to his, a smile curving her lips. "With you?"

"I was counting on it." He bent and placed a quick, soft kiss on her delicious dimple.

"Can we call Maggie first?"

He nuzzled her neck. "Way ahead of you. She said she got Laney to sleep and will bring her by my apartment first thing in the morning."

"Did Mrs. Benson give approval for that?"

"She did."

"And you're okay with it?"

He lifted his head to look into her eyes. He could lose himself there, let his guard down, and still feel cherished and safe. He'd give her anything she wanted, but this was easy, because it was something he wanted, too. His world had been effectively upended by this incredible woman. He couldn't imagine going back to the way things had been only a few days ago. He brushed his thumb along her bottom lip, then pulled her in close. "Stay with me."

A puff of hot laughter warmed his neck. "You're my ride. I'm not going anywhere until you're ready."

"I want more than a night here and there with you, or occasionally bumping into you in the coffee shop." He felt her stiffen and ran a hand down her back as if gentling a startled animal. He was feeling a little unsettled as well. "I want you in my life."

"Are you sure?" She bit her lip, but hope lit her eyes like a shining beacon.

"My parents forged a tight bond before I was born. I never fit into their equation. I never fit into anyone's life. It was easier not to try." He'd learned to hold tight to his feelings, to his heart. His parents had had a quiet, lasting love where they held hands on occasion and would pat Einstein on the head, but for most of his life Einstein had been a latchkey kid, the odd duck people would look at funny when he didn't follow the nuances of a conversation. The third wheel. There had been little room for him in his parents' romance. Now, he'd found a place where he fit. "I want you and Laney in my life. I love you."

The dimple flashed in her cheek as her smile bloomed. "I love you, too."

He took her hand and put it on his chest, against his heart. "I'm not sure if you're picking up any messages, but this heart beats for you. I usually know what I want and how to get it. You keep me on my toes. I kind of like that." He grinned.

"I...I've lost everything. Or, I thought I was about to. It's hard to want to form new bonds when I know what breaking them is like. But somehow we formed them anyway, when I wasn't looking."

His smile widened. "That's what chemistry is all about. Bonds."

"Well, there's no arguing with science." She leaned up and kissed him and he thanked God he'd aced chemistry.

CHAPTER 23

The next morning began with a world that had been cleansed—of the heat, of the storm, and most importantly, of the Charmer.

"You look happy today." Abby bent to shift her grandfather's oxygen mask to the side and give him a kiss on the cheek.

"Of course I do," Grandpa said. "I have a reason to live."

She frowned. "You've always had a reason."

His eyes sparkled as they landed on Einstein and Laney, who entered his hospital room behind her. "Looks like I'll live long enough to walk my granddaughter down the aisle, after all."

Abby gasped. "Grandpa," she chastised, "I haven't been asked."

"Not yet," Einstein said. He sent Grandpa an exasperated look. "Guess you couldn't wait, huh?"

"I don't have long, son. Gotta seize the moment."

Abby looked at each of them in turn. "What's going on here?" Einstein turned her to face him. He dropped to one knee in the middle of the hospital room. "What are you doing?"

Grandpa grunted. "Some gift of perception you got there, girlie."

"But...here? Now?" Abby clasped her hands together to stop their shaking. She saw the light of conspiracy in her grandfather's eyes and knew Einstein must have, somehow, come to him first. Given that she and Einstein had spent the night talking and making love, she wasn't sure when Einstein had found the time to call her grandfather. Then again, the man was a machine who rarely slept.

Grandpa wheezed out a laugh. "Life's too short. Andrew—Einstein—understands that. He already snuck away to come to me for my blessing while you and Laney went to the gift shop."

"And?" she asked.

He snorted. "I gave it to him. He'll protect you. More importantly, he loves you. As long as he's what you want, I'm in favor of it."

Einstein looked up, sincerity and a hint of worry on his face. "I know how important family is to you. I wanted your grandfather to be part of this." And yet, she knew he wasn't rushing because of Grandpa's condition. He'd shown her how much he loved her. She'd also felt the emotion coursing through his body as he'd touched her during the night.

"I want to be a part of this, too," Laney said, her grin proudly displaying the gap in her front teeth. The debt had been paid by the Tooth Fairy. Maggie had dropped Laney off this morning and the girl had been bouncing off the walls, unable to control her happiness that Mrs. Benson had allowed the three of them to give this family thing a trial run. Wesley was in jail, facing years in prison for drug charges Noah had unearthed and for working with the Charmer.

"Mrs. Benson said you two are planning to go to court. That means we get to be a family." They were going to try everything they could to make that happen. At the moment, it seemed anything was possible.

"Damn straight," Grandpa said. "We're a team." He high-fived the little girl, then turned it into a fist-bump.

Abby's heart squeezed and filled again like a balloon, swelling in her chest as her gaze met Einstein's. God, she loved this man and everything he'd brought to her life. How could she ever have thought he didn't understand her? He understood her perfectly. He knew how important her grandfather was. How much she wanted Laney to be safe and loved. He trusted her gifts. And she'd come to respect and trust his. To love him.

"Abby, dear," Grandpa said. "He's waiting. Those floors are hard."

Einstein pulled a velvet box from his pocket and opened it, revealing a sparkling amethyst. "The human brain is capable of more than I could ever understand and yet you've made me realize that capacity is no match for the human heart's. I've always been hungry for knowledge, avoiding human connection when possible. Trying to protect myself from what Damian went through, what my parents went through, what every victim's family we ever helped at SSAM went through. But you bring color and light to my world. You make me see the world in a different way. I want to experience the world with you by my side. Will you marry me?"

"Yes. Yes!" She pulled Einstein to his feet and hugged him to her, crying and laughing. She wouldn't be alone. And she'd spend her life making sure Einstein never felt alone again, either.

EPILOGUE

It was so early that dew still clung to the ground. The storm that had rolled through the night before was gone, leaving a damp coolness that forecasters had assured the city would burn off by afternoon.

Lorena's slender fingers felt smooth and strong beneath Damian's. They'd stayed together all night, each afraid to let the other out of their sight.

The world seemed new again, washed clean and bright with promise. They'd talked, made love and discussed the future.

The future. Something he hadn't allowed himself to think about in years. Decades.

Priscilla was already sitting on a bench near Sam's grave. She stood as they approached and gave him a wobbly smile. He hugged her tight.

"You've been crying," he said as she pulled away.

"Yeah." Priscilla released a shaky laugh. "Joy. Regret. Sadness. Anger. You name it, I cried it last night." She'd been through as much as he had. But the rollercoaster ride was finally coming to a stop. "Strange as it may seem, it's hard to let go. Hard to believe this is over."

"She'll always be with us."

Priscilla nodded, then glanced back toward the bench where she'd set a jar with holes punched in the lid. "I brought the tribute. I think this is a wonderful idea." A wonderful way to say good-bye to their daughter.

As one, the trio turned and walked to Sam's grave.

"Good-bye, sweet Sam." Priscilla kissed her fingertips, and then touched them to Sam's name, briefly caressing the engraving. She opened the jar and released thirteen white butterflies, one for every year Sam had blessed their world. "Thank you for being mine. I hope you find freedom now."

Priscilla stepped back and Damian stepped forward. Lorena handed him their offering. He laid the single pristine white rose on the top of Sam's headstone. "Good-bye, Sam. I love you and I pray that you're at peace now. Know that your death wasn't in vain. We saved so many other people because of you." Without her sacrifice, SSAM would never have existed. Yes, there was evil in the world, but he had appreciated its beauty all the more, and his efforts to make the world a better place, in Sam's honor, would continue.

Priscilla released a breath and turned to Damian. She cupped his cheek. "Be happy." She turned to Lorena and smiled. "Both of you."

"You're invited to come with us back to SSAM. Catherine planned a celebration and all of the agents and their significant others will be there. You should be a part of it."

"Thank you, but I have a plane to catch. But I'm glad you'll be surrounded by people who love you." With a last look at Sam's final resting place, she turned and left the cemetery.

After a long moment of silence, during which he waited for the pain of the past to rack his body—and was stunned when it didn't—he squeezed Lorena's hand. "Ready?"

"When you are. Take your time."

Time. He'd already taken so much of it hunting John. He wouldn't let the man steal anything more from him.

A white butterfly fluttered into his view, settled briefly on the headstone, where it opened and closed its wings. It lifted again, taking flight.

Good-bye, Sam.

"I'm ready." He wrapped an arm around Lorena and together they turned away from Sam's grave and walked toward their future. Behind him lay the remains of his daughter's body, but that really wasn't his daughter. Her spirit, the most important part of her, could never be stolen. It belonged to the universe.

He'd forever hold Sam in his heart, but it was time to move on.

DEADLY HOLIDAYS

(A Collection of Mindhunters Holiday Novellas)

Matt Haney loved his little sister, but he was going to kill her. "Were you drunk when you came up with this idea?"

"She's nice," Becca insisted for the fourth time.

Nice. Matt cringed, his reflection distorted in the golden ball he was hanging on his parents' eight-foot Christmas tree. Fresh pine scent filled his nostrils every time he leaned in to decorate a branch.

"*Really* nice." In case he hadn't received the memo. "She's differ-ent. More…artsy. But I'm sure you'll have a lot in common."

"I'm sure." He'd prefer a little naughty over nice this Christmas. But only with the right woman.

His sister, also fluent in sarcasm, noted his lack of enthusiasm with a frown. "What? I thought you'd want someone outside of the usual lawyer scene."

Actually, he enjoyed the company of his fellow lawyers just

fine. Which was good, since he spent most of his time building a reputation at the law firm where a sixty-hour workweek was typical. There was one lawyer in particular he liked way too much, and he wouldn't mind getting on Santa's naughty list with her. But he didn't dare share that tidbit with Becca, who was like a cat ready to pounce on its prey at the slightest sign of surrender.

He'd appeal to her common sense instead. "Let's be serious. A blind date on Christmas Eve here, surrounded by our family? No freaking way that's going to go well." Thirty-three years old, he'd settled in a small, remodeled, bungalow-style home within a minute's drive of his parents' Jefferson Park neighborhood northwest of Chicago. He wasn't too manly to admit he was a homebody at heart. And he didn't want to share his family time with a stranger.

"We all just want you to be happy."

He dropped a tangled ball of silver tinsel so that it landed in a glittery heap on top of her short blond hair, and grinned at the elfish image she presented. "There. Now I'm happy."

"No fair." She scooped up the glittery ball and tossed it back at him. It tumbled down his chest and clung to the ambitious pipe cleaner antlers of the reindeer on his ugly sweater—winner of last year's annual Haney Ugly Sweater Contest.

She scowled up at him, and he could hear her mentally cursing his towering height. She was a slender five and a half feet, whereas, on occasion, he had been compared to a Viking.

"Can't help it." His wide grin dispelled any indication he experienced remorse over their height difference. It was in his genes, as well as those of their three older brothers—who'd conveniently found excuses to duck out early on the decorating, the sneaky bastards. Apparently, the height portion of the twisted helix had skipped their sister. But Becca had made up for the difference, finding other ways to be mega-tough over the years. All five siblings, however, had various shades of blond hair and brown eyes in common.

Becca skillfully transferred the silver strands from his reindeer's antlers to the tree. The decorating was a Christmas gift to their parents, who'd be returning from a romantic Colorado ski getaway just in time to host the Haney Christmas Eve Extravaganza tomorrow evening. Matt pretended to grumble about the hours of decorating, but he loved every minute of it. Loved his family. Hell, he even loved the new, hideous, itchy sweater in his closet, ready to debut tomorrow night.

"So... The Date," Becca began again.

Matt plucked a candy cane from the tree and stuck it in her mouth. "No."

Becca transferred the candy cane to her husband, Diego Sandoval's, mouth as he returned from the kitchen with a tray of Christmas cookies and hot cocoa, God bless him. Diego accepted the peppermint treat and sucked on it with a wicked grin that was certainly solely for his wife. Matt snagged the tray before it was forgotten and dropped on the floor.

"You could use some feminine influence," Becca told Matt, not missing a beat as she handed Diego an ornament to hang on a higher branch. Over her head, Diego cast Matt a sympathetic glance. "I saw that." She jabbed Matt's arm.

Matt rubbed at the spot. "Hey, he's the one who rolled his eyes."

"You need to loosen up."

"You mean lower my expectations?"

"You lawyers always have to nail down the verbiage."

"Doesn't make it less true." Matt shook his head. "I'm not willing to settle for less than everything I want."

He'd dated before, though serious relationships had been few and far between. It wasn't that his expectations were unrealistic, but they were high—his parents' fault. Dolly and Donald Haney's solid, loving marriage had set the standard, and it would be a hard one to match. Still, Becca and Diego were doing a darn good job giving it a go and succeeding. Matt couldn't deny the evidence staring him in the face. True love did exist. But maybe it wasn't for him. Besides, with limited time to date as he worked his way up the ladder at Walters and Hammond, he wasn't sure he had the time to find his match, if she existed.

She does exist, and you have *found her.*

He shook off the image of the woman who was never far from his thoughts, irritated that his heart couldn't seem to accept what his brain knew—no matter how much heat they generated between them, he and Assistant State's Attorney Gwendolyn Pierce weren't right for each other. Gwen wasn't wife or family material. Sure, she checked off most of the boxes for his fantasy woman. Sharp wit and a sense of humor were keys. And the attraction was definitely there. The woman had legs for miles, expressive, almond-shaped hazel eyes, and silky chestnut hair that made him think of a stout beer, satisfying and rich.

But she was already married—to her work. Relationships required compromise and Gwen was incapable of bending, a fact he'd discovered when he'd attempted to date her a few months back.

"She's very sweet," Becca insisted. Matt had to rewind a moment to realize she wasn't talking about the woman in his thoughts, but some other woman who was dateless on Christmas Eve.

He grunted. "Sweet *and* nice? Tell me she loves cats and she's a triple-threat." But maybe soft and predictable was better than driven and sharp. Again, Gwen came to mind. Irritated, he spun back to the tree and resumed draping tinsel on its branches, one strand at a time, as his dad had taught them.

"I'm sure there'll be chemistry too." Becca's comment was punctuated by Diego's snort, followed by his *oomf* as her elbow connected with his ribs.

"No offense, Sis, but a family gathering isn't the place to discover whether I have chemistry with a woman. Especially when we're all wearing ugly sweaters."

"It's the best place to figure out if she'll fit in, and the best time to see if she has a sense of humor, which I know is important to you. No sense wasting time if she doesn't like our family, right? You could humor me for just an evening," Becca tried again when Matt didn't submit to her plan to shove him into the dating pool.

"What kind of woman doesn't have plans of her own on Christmas Eve? Why would she rather spend the day on a blind date with a stranger's family?" He shuddered at the thought. But then his stubborn mind drifted back to Gwen. She probably wouldn't have plans for Christmas unless it involved work. Would she even notice the holiday? Or maybe she'd see the snow and dream of their days together at the beach—and in the hotel room —while they'd attended a mutual friend's week-long destination wedding in Jamaica. They hadn't planned to hook up, but their attraction had been undeniable...until they'd returned to Chicago.

Becca snapped her fingers in front of his face. "Hey, where'd you go?" A light came into her eyes. "You already have a woman on your mind."

"Busted." Diego coughed the word into his hand.

Matt kept his expression carefully neutral. "Nope. Just letting my thoughts drift to protect myself from your unrelenting assault."

Becca eyed him and her voice took on a sly tone. "Fine. Keep your secrets. I'll find out soon enough." She handed them each an ornament. "Get back to work. Mom and Dad will be home in a couple hours, and this place needs to sing holiday season."

The Haney home already displayed enough Christmas spirit to choke a reindeer. He'd draped the boughs of holly over the mantel and wound them up the banister to the second floor, hung a ball of mistletoe in the front hall, and set up the tiny Dickensian village his mom collected. Sure, a few pieces had been broken and glued back together, but he could remember setting the thing up each year, and his father's good-natured grumbling about urban sprawl as the town grew. But this house was where Dolly and Donald had raised five children, and it had the normal scuffs and dents of a much-loved, well-used home. Matt wanted that for himself someday. He'd even start a little holiday village, if the woman of his dreams desired it. Maybe it could be beach-themed.

The doorbell rang, saving him before his thoughts once more settled on Gwen.

"I'll get it," Becca said.

"She means well," Diego said when she was out of range.

Matt sighed. "She always does. But this time, she needs to stay out of it." He couldn't imagine the stress of entertaining a stranger during what should be family time. "I've been looking forward to a nice, normal few days off—except for wiping the floor with you and my brothers during the game, of course."

Diego laughed. "Don't expect that to happen again. I went easy on you last time, being the newbie and all."

Matt had to admit that Diego had fit right in when it came to their family festivities. And touch football, played in the neighborhood park right across the street, was one of the biggest, most competitive traditions at any Haney gathering. Diego had experienced his first game at Thanksgiving, and now he wanted his shot at redemption.

"Yeah, but have you factored in the snow?" Matt smirked as Diego glanced out the window. Sure enough, flakes were beginning to fall. By tomorrow, two or three inches were supposed to have accumulated.

Becca came back with a small package in her hand and a sly smile for Matt. "You really do have an admirer in your life. This was left on the doorstep, but it's got your name on it. Who's it from?"

He eyed the small red velvet box with the white satin ribbon tied in a bow. Sure enough, his name was on a tiny tag. "Unless there's a note, I don't have a clue."

"A mystery?" Becca, a security expert at SSAM—the Society for the Study of the Aberrant Mind—where she and Diego, an ex-NYPD detective, worked to hunt down violent criminals and protect the innocent, was both delighted and worried. She had reason to be concerned, as she'd had a secret admirer of the not-so-nice kind in her past.

He reached out and placed a comforting hand on her shoulder. "I'm sure it's harmless." At least, he hoped it was.

"But you have no idea who it could be from?"

He took the box from her. "I received another box, identical to this one, a couple days ago at my office."

Diego straightened, eyeing the gift. "A coworker?"

"Not sure. The first box contained a framed picture of me as a child." It had been a mystery Matt hadn't had time to explore. "I'd guessed some kind of practical joke or secret Santa thing from work. Whoever it is put some time into it if they dug out my third grade school picture. All I bought my secret Santa was a mono-gramed flask."

"And now that they've sent one to our parents' house?" Becca studied the box more carefully. All thought of decorating was gone as she honed her deductive skills on this new puzzle.

"It wouldn't be too hard for a coworker to get my address, or even my parents', I suppose."

Becca jerked her chin toward the box. "Open it."

The tiny thing suddenly felt like a hundred pounds. He pulled the ribbon loose and opened the lid. Inside was another two-by-three-inch picture frame. The shiny silver edges caught the lights from the tree and gleamed in multi-color. With one finger, he hooked the loop of red satin ribbon that made the frame an orna-ment and lifted it out of the box. "The picture inside is different, but otherwise this is exactly the same."

Diego examined the photo. "You, in court?"

"Appears to be." He was in pristine suit-and-tie, arguing a murder case to get the defendant acquitted. He could see his client from one of November's cases in the background.

"And the other picture you received was your third-grade school photo?" Becca asked. A frown tugged at her lips. "You didn't think that was odd?"

"Like I said, at the time, I figured it was some office joke, or maybe from one of you guys. Anyone could have gotten it from an old yearbook." His siblings often played practical jokes on each other. But in the three days since he'd received the first box, none of his family or his coworkers at Walters and Hammond had stepped forward to claim credit.

"As a semi-public figure who regularly defends criminals—" Becca began.

"They're not always guilty," he interrupted. As she was often on the side trying to put the guilty in prison, it was a recurring refrain.

"—you've got to be aware you could be a target."

He sighed. "Can we focus on the 'being merry' part of Christmas, please? I could use some normalcy." The recent case list had been demanding. Accused criminals didn't take a break for the holidays. And they each needed a defense lawyer.

"Do you remember this trial?" Becca pressed, pointing to the most recent framed picture.

Yeah, he remembered. Just as he remembered the prosecutor he'd gone up against that week.

Gwendolyn Pierce.

DEADLY HOLIDAYS (A Collection of Mindhunters Holiday Novellas) is available now!

INTRODUCING A BRAND NEW
ROMANTIC SUSPENSE SERIES...

Anne Marie Becker's new romantic suspense series, Redemption
Club, begins with
STACKING THE DECK...

One woman's rooftop sun deck was another woman's sniper roost. Skye Hamilton's index finger hovered near her rifle's trigger as she perched on the flat roof. Slightly higher in elevation to the neighboring estate, her location allowed a convenient overlook to the party going on fifty yards away.

Through the scope, cross hairs were tattooed across her target's chest, which was covered in a cobalt blue shirt and dark-gray suit jacket. Around him, the Malibu home's tiled poolside patio was like the red carpet on awards night, populated with Hollywood's rich and powerful. The trees glowed with fairy lights, and the tall cocktail tables set up for this event twinkled with tea lights in crystal-cut holders that winked in the darkness like stars. The stars that shined the brightest were actors and actresses, directors and producers—many of whom Skye recognized, though she didn't get to the movies much.

A hair had escaped the tight bun under her black skullcap and now tickled her cheek in the cool April breeze, but she resisted the urge to swipe it away. Making a quick mental note to buy more bobby pins, she forced the distraction from her mind and focused on her other senses. Her vocal cords tightened, her pulse kicking up past the normal adrenaline-induced high.

She shifted the cross hairs higher. Robert Stone had thrown his head back in laughter, exposing the tan column of his throat, at something said by one of the party guests surrounding him. Laugh lines bracketed his mouth and eyes, evidence of the fifty-seven years that had shaped his body, carving rivulets across his forehead and painting a few gray hairs among the ebony at the temples. With manicured fingers and soft hands, he tipped his champagne flute to his lips. As her research had indicated, he was the epitome of a wealthy and powerful individual, pampered and confident in his place in the world.

And someone wanted to do bad things to him. More specifically, someone wanted to pay *her* to do bad things to him. But Skye only used extreme force when it was justified, when the law had failed and there was clear evidence the bounty was worth the cost. Mark Sheldon hadn't come through with the burden of proof—yet. She was only staking this spot out for later, for when that proof came in and showed Stone was as ruthless as the rumors about him suggested.

The cool night breeze drifting over the surrounding mountains carried the heavy scent of jasmine and prompted the loose hair to resume its dance against her jaw. A light dusting of tangy salt from the nearby Pacific clung to her lips. Skye absorbed this sensory information but centered on the source that mattered most in this particular hunt—her sight. Unfortunately, she had yet to see Loretta Sheldon, the young woman she'd been sent to retrieve, or proof that Stone was involved in her disappearance.

Kill Stone. Bring Loretta home.

That's what Mark was paying her for.

Because, by all accounts, including the good-bye note Loretta had left behind, Robert Stone appeared to have lured the seventeen-year-old from the safety of her family and friends. And that was an unforgivable breach where Skye came from. One defended one's self, property and family, at any cost.

Skye's finger caressed the trigger, but she didn't apply pressure. *There's no evidence.* The reports of people she'd talked to said Stone was only nice on the surface, that he'd been known to use violence to settle scores. *Rumors. There's no proof.* She'd resume her investigation tomorrow, confident that persistence would lead to Loretta and evidence that this man had taken her.

Her attention shifted again, sliding down Stone's black silk tie and to the right, to the magenta square of silk sticking out of his breast pocket. Silver initials stood out against the colors, declaring his conceit. The colors echoed those in the logos of his film production company, hotel chain, cruise line and other businesses sheltered beneath the Stone Corporation umbrella. Despite the passing thought that his attire was more suited to a peacock than a mogul, the ornamentation seemed to emphasize, rather than contradict, Stone's masculinity. It was all about confidence, and how one wore it. Stone wore it like a second skin.

A diamond signet ring flashed as Stone's hand tipped the champagne flute to his lips. She tracked the movement as he placed an arm around a smiling blonde who wore a magenta evening dress that coordinated with his attire. The woman must be his latest arm candy. She damn sure wasn't Loretta.

Her research into Stone's past revealed two failed marriages and a string of heartbreaks. Either the man fell in love hard and often or enjoyed the chase, particularly when young, beautiful women were the prize. Skye was betting on the latter, especially since Loretta had been lured with some very enticing bait—an offer of a part in Stone's next movie.

Skye wondered if the blonde was aware of her sugar daddy's reputation. Likely not. If so, the woman wouldn't smile in that wide, vacant way. Or maybe she would. For the past ten days, the Hollywood lifestyle Skye'd been observing was so far from her world and everything she understood about the way one should live life, and what was normal, that it seemed she was in some kind of warped dream. Or nightmare.

The blonde's red lips parted on a laugh and Stone drew her in closer to his side. Protected and cherished. Skye hadn't been held that way since she was a child. Actually, she'd never been held that way. Only in her dreams.

In an instant, her focus shattered as memories of the past and a sharp pang of longing intruded. She sucked in a shaky breath and set down the rifle. She might as well call it a night. Loretta wasn't here. She'd continue searching for the proof she needed and return another day—because she didn't know the word failure, and she sure as hell knew about patience.

She sat back on her haunches and began methodically packing her equipment into her duffel bag. Taking a quick inventory, her fingertips moved swiftly across her rifle, handgun, hunting knife—

The soft sound of a footfall, lost immediately in the breeze among the gentle rattle of leaves in the surrounding treetops, alerted her to someone else's presence. She palmed the throwing knife from her black boot, pushed to her feet and spun to face the threat. She shifted her weight to the balls of her feet. Adrenaline pumped hard and fast into her system, and the need to run rolled over her limbs—but she froze as she realized there was nowhere *to* run.

A tall, broad-shouldered man effectively blocked her main escape route. Dressed in a simple, but elegant, suit that somehow made him seem more dangerous, he stood between her and the spiral staircase that twisted down to the patio below. It was the only access to the sun deck. *Damn.*

She recognized him as one of the three bodyguards working Stone's party. Fifteen minutes earlier, he'd slipped out of her field of vision when one of the young, drunk starlets at the party had almost fallen into the pool and he'd escorted her into the house.

A slice of moonlight painted a streak of silver in his hair, but she guessed he was around thirty years old, just a few years older than her. But several inches taller—about six foot three, if he was an inch. And shoulders so broad he could pass as the great Atlas himself. His size was misleading. She'd watched him weave with predator-like stealth and grace among the throng of guests. She wouldn't underestimate him.

"I'm glad you chose not to shoot Mr. Stone." His gaze moved to the bag at her feet before shifting back to examine her face. She fought the urge to squirm as he seemed to memorize every feature.

He stopped several feet away, out of arm's reach but close enough for her to see his hair was a dark blond. The ends curled against his neck, and the breeze lifted the top briefly, like a caress. Everything about him was hard, including his eyes. His hands stayed loose at his sides, as if he might draw on her, though there was no telltale bulge of a concealed weapon. There were quieter ways to deal with her, anyway. Those hands—strong fingers with a couple of flecks of old scars, thin white lines glowing in the moonlight, decorating the surface. Like a bruised apple. One hard knock wasn't going to keep her from tasting it.

She rather liked a couple of scars on a man. They were evidence of a survivor, a hard worker, a warrior—and likely, this man knew his craft well. Unfortunately, his skills probably included killing. Ex-military? He didn't look like your average Army Joe, but she could see him as a Special Forces guy. His erect posture hinted at the hard edge of a soldier, and the casual way he took in every part of their surroundings without seeming to indicated his experience. That didn't bode well for her. Still, she'd trained with men like him, and he seemed more curious than dangerous at the moment. Besides, based on her reconnaissance, he was trespassing just as much as she was.

Her fingers tightened around the small knife tucked against her side, between her palm and her hip. "I wasn't going to shoot anyone." *Not yet.*

She calculated the distance to the edge of the roof and the jump it would require to land in the pool below. According to the very chatty gardener she'd encountered when she'd posed as a local out for a morning jog, the owners of this lush spread were in Europe for several months but had kept up the grounds and the pool. The deep end was just below her side of the roof.

"It's a twenty-foot drop." Her rooftop soldier's voice was cool as he guessed her thoughts.

Better than being six feet under. But climbing out of the pool, running while sopping wet, and making it back to the truck before this man could catch her, didn't boast encouraging odds. Worse, she'd have to leave her equipment behind. She'd done it before—in her training, the ranch's own version of a *mud run* during the Arizona summer's monsoons—but she'd rather choose an option with a better chance for success.

"I'm not going to hurt you." His arms went out to his sides in a gesture of trust and he grinned, all boy-next-door charisma. Oh yes, this soldier was dangerous. Good thing she was immune to the man's charm.

She stifled a snort. "That's good, considering I didn't do anything except observe a party. From private property, I might add." At her condescending tone, his eyebrows lifted.

"This isn't your property," he said. Hell, what if the groundskeeper had been wrong? What if this was the soldier's home? Maybe he wasn't security after all and the starlet was his girlfriend, and he'd escorted her into this very house, right beneath Skye's nose.

But that didn't ring true. *Trust your instincts.* Her uncle's voice rang in her head. Besides, she'd already begun the lie. Better to stick with it.

"It isn't yours either." She hoped her guess was correct. When he didn't deny it, she continued with the story she'd concocted. "I'm housesitting for a friend while he's in Europe. I just got here today."

"And you thought you'd hang out in the dark?"

"Just came up here for some fresh air." She took a deep breath as if to confirm her lie. His gaze flicked to her breasts as her lungs filled. *Interesting.* Apparently, he wasn't immune to her charms. She filed that information away as a possible weapon.

"I wanted to catch the view of moonlight on the ocean. I've never seen the ocean." That part, at least, was true. Earlier that week, she'd taken a couple of hours to just sit on the beach and listen to the waves, to watch their seductive power.

His gaze took a leisurely stroll down her body and his lips quirked ever-so-slightly. "Kind of strange attire if you're just looking for some fresh air. Or maybe, where you come from, they like to wear skintight black for late-night strolls."

Camouflage was more the order of the day at the ranch. "Huh. I didn't peg you for a fashion icon."

His laugh startled her. She bit back a curse, irked that he was taking pleasure in pinning her like a dead bug—and that he'd gotten the drop on her at all. What would Viper say about her listening skills? She'd let those precious moments of lost focus override her training. And she continued to let her concentration be derailed by the spark of amusement in the stranger's eyes.

So she went on the attack—verbally, at least. Pricking a man's pride could be a valuable weapon. "And maybe where you come from, it's typical to dress in suits and ties and dance for your boss like a puppet?" The brief lightness between them faded and she instantly regretted reminding him he was here on a mission.

"My *client* pays me well to do all kinds of things, including identifying threats." He eyed the duffel bag at her feet. "If you were just up here to observe the ocean, you over packed. I suggest you start talking—the truth this time."

STACKING THE DECK and the Redemption Club series is available now!

ACKNOWLEDGMENTS

Deb Nemeth, thank you for your help with the entire Mind-hunters series. It wouldn't be what it is without your expertise. Your input and guidance made me a better writer.

I also extend my gratitude to Melanie Jade Rummel for taking the time to answer all my questions about psychometric abilities and helping add depth to Abby's character. Any errors are purely my own.

To all of the baristas around town who helped fuel me as I wrote this series—my deepest, caffeinated thanks.

Andrea Edwards, I hope you know how amazing you are. If not, I'll keep telling you. You are amazing. Thank you for all your time, effort and support.

Last, but never least, thank you to my husband and kids. You're the reason I can write happy endings.

ABOUT THE AUTHOR

Anne Marie has always been fasci-
nated by people—inside and out—
which led to degrees in Biology,
Chemistry, Psychology, and Counseling. Her passion for understanding the human race is now
satisfied by her roles as mother,
wife, daughter, sister, and award-
winning author of romantic
suspense.

She writes to reclaim her sanity.

Find ways to connect with Anne
Marie at AnneMarieBecker.com.
There, sign up for her newsletter to receive the latest information
regarding books, appearances, and giveaways.

www.ingramcontent.com/pod-product-compliance
Lightning Source LLC
Chambersburg PA
CBHW032146190626
46814CB00005BA/1860